Getting Personal

Chris Manby

ISIS
LARGE PRINT
Oxford

First published in Great Britain 2002
by Hodder & Stoughton,
a division of Hodder Headline.

Published in Large Print 2003 by ISIS Publishing Ltd,
7 Centremead, Osney Mead, Oxford OX2 0ES
by arrangement with Hodder & Stoughton
a division of Hodder Headline

British Library Cataloguing in Publication Data
Manby, Chris
   Getting personal. – Large print ed.
   1. Mate selection – Great Britain – Fiction
   2. Personals – Great Britain – Fiction
   3. Large type books
   I. Title
   823.9'14 [F]

ISBN 0–7531–6851–0 (hb)
ISBN 0–7531–6852–9 (pb)

Printed and bound by Antony Rowe, Chippenham

This one's for Harrison Arnold.
See, Harry, once upon a time your auntie
was quite cool!

Acknowledgements

With love and thanks to Mum, Dad, Kate and Lee. To everyone at Hodder, especially Carolyn Mays and Sara Hulse who didn't ask for their money back when they read the first draft. To Ant and James at Antony Harwood Limited, Sally Riley and Joanna Kaliszewska at Aitken Associates and Sheryl Petersen at Diverse Talent Group for their continued support and the spondulicks. To Ryan Law and Jenn Matherly for being such steadfast friends. And finally, to Rob Yorke, who bore the brunt again. *See, I told you you should have gone fishing!*

Prologue

Intelligent, attractive and inexplicably unattached. Three London friends seek some serious summer loving . . .

"Will I ever be somebody's Whoopsie?"

That was the question on Ruby Taylor's mind as she watched the new Mrs Winky Foreman smash a lump of chocolate wedding cake into her brand-new husband's mouth. If there really is someone for everyone, Ruby thought, then her old college friend Susannah (known affectionately to her husband as Whoopsie) and Winky — known to everyone as Winky — it was his real name, must surely be the proof.

Personally, Ruby would have run screaming from a man who looked like the original model for Humpty Dumpty, sported sweat patches like small paddy-fields even in the dead of winter and thought it funny to refer to the animal noises his new wife makes in bed in his wedding day speech. But to Susannah, who galumphed up the aisle as though she was wearing Wellington boots even in her new Jimmy Choos, Winky Foreman was perfect. Yin to her yang. Salt to her pepper. *Stinky* to her *Whoopsie*. Apparently.

It was the fourth wedding Ruby had attended so far that year and it wasn't even June. First Jane and Ian. C of E and canapés in Gloucestershire. Then Mark and

1

Jacqui. Registry office and pizza in South Ken. Then Peter and Katherine. Pomp and circumstance in Rutland. Now Winky and Susannah. Full-blown upper crust bad behaviour in Shropshire. Morning coats, pink marquee, stomachs pumped at dawn.

Lou Capshaw and Martin Ashcroft, who often seemed to Ruby to be the only single people left in the world bar herself, sat with her on the "miscellaneous" table. There's one at every wedding — usually stuck by the kitchen door — for the singles, the widowers, the holiday acquaintances and the barking great-aunt of the bride. They whiled their time away playing "Wedding Disco Bingo" (which involved writing down ten songs you expected to hear at the reception and ticking them off as they were played).

Martin was winning. Susannah and Winky started the dancing to "Lady in Red", putting him straight into the lead. Then came "The Birdie Song" (for the little ones), "Tainted Love" (for the bitter ones) and "Oops, Upside Your Head" (especially for the bride).

"OK, then. Which side is going to start the food fight?" Lou asked idly.

By now Susannah was wearing less make-up than cake.

"Bride," said Martin definitely.

"Groom," said Lou. She was right. Within seconds, a profiterole missile issued from a table of louts who played for Winky's rugby club. They had long since turned their old school ties into Red Injun-style bandannas and now they were attacking the bridesmaids

2

in a brutal re-enactment of General "Custard's" Last Stand.

"Ladies' room?" Ruby suggested to Lou. Susannah may not have been bothered about getting icing on her vintage silk wedding dress but Ruby was rather more precious about her one and only real Donna Karan.

"Aren't they just perfect for each other?" slurred a girl in the queue for the Portakabin that was serving as the ladies' that afternoon.

"Perfect," Lou agreed. Ruby was grateful that Lou didn't go into her theory about bride and groom sharing a paternal grandmother.

"Of course," said the girl, as she reapplied her lipstick somewhat haphazardly. "It's rather funny when you think about how they met."

"How did they meet?" Ruby wondered aloud, imagining a Scottish reeling ball where Winky whirled Susannah out of a badly stitched ball gown during the Duke of Perth and then offered to help her back into it.

"Through a *personal ad*! Can you believe it? Susannah advertised in *The Telegraph* for a man with GSOH."

"Good sense of humour?" Ruby translated.

"More like great shag, own helicopter!" Lipstick Girl replied. "What a catch, eh?"

"I think I would have thrown him back," muttered Lou.

Just then the bride herself lurched into the queue for the loos.

"Coming through, girls," she said. "Wide load approaching." Her multi-layered skirt would barely fit through the Portakabin door.

"Oh, Suze," sighed the Lipstick Girl. "Can you believe you've finally bagged your man?"

"Bit bloody surprised," Susannah admitted. "Better get him on honeymoon before the Rohypnol wears off! Haw, haw, haw!!!"

Ruby and Lou shared a worried glance.

"Louisa!" Susannah brayed. "And Ruby! Thanks for coming, darlings. Set your sights on any dishy guys yet? There's a whole bunch of lads from Winky's rugby club over by the dance floor and most of them are single or in the process of getting divorced. Get your orders in before Finty Chambers has them all!"

"Already have had them all!" brayed Finty, as she emerged, at last, from the cubicle they'd all been waiting for. "And none of them made *my* first fifteen. Haw haw haw!"

"Somebody hold my skirt," said Susannah, as she backed onto the lavatory. Ruby closed the door behind her. "Oh bugger!" cried the bride. "Got my petticoat caught in the pan."

"A personal ad," Ruby mused as soon as they were out of earshot. "She kept that one quiet."

"Wouldn't you?" Lou laughed. "Great shag, own helicopter? She obviously settled for grey shoes, own hair."

"But they're happy," said Ruby. "Which is more than you, me and Martin are."

4

Half an hour later, a new Lonely Hearts Club was born.

It was a beautifully simple idea. They were all single. All looking. (Some more actively than others, Ruby sighed.) None of them wanted to spend the summer alone, watching couples smooching on every piece of open parkland, getting sunburn on that part of your back you just can't reach with the sun-cream on your own. Lou proposed that they each place a personal ad in a paper of their choice to see if they could find their very own *Winkys*. Better than that, Lou elaborated, they should all place ads *for each other*.

Lou would write an ad for Martin, Martin would write one for Ruby and Ruby would write one for Lou. That way there would be no room for false modesty. No tragic undersell.

"And no exaggeration worthy of prosecution under the Trades Description Act," Ruby added with a nod towards Martin.

When the sacks full of replies came in — because of course, there would be sackfuls — the trio would each choose a likely partner for the person on whose behalf they had advertised. The experiment would culminate in a grand blind date at a venue with suitable cubby-holes from which they could secretly observe their success in choosing mates for their mates, as it were.

"Since we know each other better than we know ourselves," Lou pointed out, "there's no reason why it shouldn't work."

"It's like an arranged marriage!" Martin was horrified when Lou outlined the scheme to him back at the miscellaneous table.

"How do I know he won't pick me a horrible date for a laugh?" Ruby asked, when it sank in that Martin would be writing her ad.

"Don't you trust me?" Martin asked.

"Martin," said Ruby. "I trust you with my life. But whether I can trust you with my *love*-life, I'm simply not so sure."

CHAPTER
ONE

Earlier that week, Ruby gazed out of her office window at a drizzly afternoon, depressing herself with matrimonial maths.

Seven million people in London. Of whom 51 per cent are female. That leaves roughly three million, four hundred thousand men. Of whom 20 per cent will be under eighteen, immediately cutting down the field to two million seven hundred thousand. Of whom at least 30 per cent will be over fifty, narrowing down the number of men in London that Ruby could consider snogging on basis of suitable age alone to one million nine hundred thousand.

Discount from that one million nine hundred thousand the 10 per cent likely to be gay. One million seven hundred thousand. Approximately 50 per cent would be married. Eight hundred and fifty thousand. Fifty per cent of those remaining would be seriously attached, bringing the total of *available* men in London between the ages of eighteen and fifty to four hundred and twenty-five thousand.

Discount from that total the number of London men residing at Her Majesty's pleasure. Twenty-five thousand? Probably more. The number living with their mothers. Another twenty thou perhaps? Divide that by the percentage of men that Ruby might actually fancy (judging by the men of her acquaintance that was in the region of one in thirty-three, or three per cent). And before you take into account matters of religion, political differences and the fact that nine of out of ten men prefer witless teenage sex kittens to thirty-something women of the world, the number of single men in London that Ruby could realistically hope to shack up with was already down from almost three and a half million to less than one hundred thousand. For whom she figured (using a computational method entirely different to that she had used to whittle down the boys) her competition was at least two million girls, all of whom were simply bound to be better-looking, funnier and more successful than she was.

Ho hum.

Ruby hated statistics. Especially the one that said the most likely place to find a partner was at the office. It was a statistic she had held close to her heart when she got her first job as a graduate trainee at Hollingworth Public Relations and set about learning how to convince journalists to run a story on everything from pressed steel to panty liners while she waited for the promised workplace romance to happen.

Unfortunately, Ruby soon realised that one of the most striking things about public relations is that it is full of girls. And most of them are blonde and bubbly and perma-tanned, as though they spend every spare weekend on the ski-slope. In fact, there were so many gorgeous single girls in the Hollingworth Public Relations empire that even the chief accountant, Frank "Five Bellies" Clark, could be guaranteed a snog come the company conference. Even if he had a cold sore (Ruby Taylor, Bournemouth International Centre, November 1999) . . .

When Ruby read yet another problem page in one of her glossy mags in which some hapless bloke claimed that he couldn't get a girl, she wondered why the agony aunt didn't say "work in public relations" instead of "join a club". For her part, Ruby might as well have signed up for the nuns.

For Emlyn "The Panter" Cruickshank, however, the glass-walled offices of Hollingworth were like a stream full of salmon to a hungry bear. Emlyn was an account manager who had the cubicle next door to Ruby's. He liked to think that people called him "The Panther" because of his sleek dark looks and his ability to pounce on a new client before any other account manager in town could say "lunch". In reality, the girls all called him the "Panter" as a reference to his lasciviousness. That said, sleeping with the Panter was practically a rite of passage for all new girls at the firm. *In the kingdom of the blind, the one-eyed man etc.* . . .

Ruby was just glad that the Panter had started at Hollingworth after her. In fact, he had been her assistant once and she'd got over any slight crush she might have had on him when he revealed, over lunch one day, that he was the proud possessor of the "worst case of athlete's foot the doctor had ever seen". That in itself was enough to put Ruby off her Boots' own

9

calorie-counted egg mayonnaise sandwich. But when Emlyn went on to elaborate about the flakes of skin that dropped out of his socks like fish-food every time he changed them, Ruby wondered if she'd ever eat again. From that moment onwards, as she explained to Lou and Martin, she found she was strangely immune to his charms.

With her brief "thing" for Emlyn cured, Ruby resigned herself to the fact that her big office affair would not happen. At least the lack of potential talent at Hollingworth meant that, if she didn't have a meeting, Ruby could roll into work of a morning without bothering to put on her slap (or even wash her face, if she'd woken up that little bit later than she should have done). Then, of course, according to Sod's Law, John Flett walked into her life.

Jonathan Flett. The engineering world's answer to Michael Douglas. ("He wishes," Lou would later say.) John Flett was acting CEO at Barrington Ball-bearings.

To tell the truth, Ruby had been a little disappointed when her boss chose her to head up the team that would put those little silver balls back in the limelight (she'd been angling for the Two-Faced Cosmetics account at the time). But when she saw Jonathan Flett at their first strategy meeting, he more than made up for Ruby's disappointment at not having unlimited access to free lipstick, blue mascara and glittery purple eyeshadow.

Hell, he was gorgeous. Ruby had been expecting the worst when she rolled up for the meeting at the concrete monstrosity that was Barrington's headquarters in sunny South Croydon. Half an hour later, she was wishing she had worn her Wonderbra, put on some make-up, done anything at all that would render her more memorable than her lacklustre proposals for a campaign to make Barrington "the new black" of ball-bearings. In his beautifully cut Italian suit, Flett wouldn't have looked out of place on the marketing team at Gucci. When he asked her for her opinion on Barrington's exciting new logo, it was all Ruby could do not to swoon.

Over lunch in the only decent restaurant in the area, Ruby soon discovered that Flett was as interesting as he was good-looking. He was no ordinary ball-bearing engineer, but a top-flight industrial trouble-shooter, hired by Barrington's new American owner to turn the company around. He was forty-two and recently separated. He liked playing squash and listening to opera and a variety of other things that came way down on Ruby's list of good ways to spend a Saturday. Not that she told him that. Instead, she just kept nodding as he expounded on the virtues of Wagner, and, by the time they were on to coffee, Flett said he was glad they had so much in common, since they would be working very *closely* with each other from then on.

They started sleeping together the very next week, when Ruby accompanied Flett to a ball-bearings convention in Leeds with the intention of gaining some useful knowledge about Barrington's competitors. (Needless to say, the only knowledge she picked up at that convention was carnal.) Six months later, however,

11

the Barrington campaign was almost finished and so was their wild affair.

"What did I tell you?" Lou lectured when Ruby phoned to say that Flett had accidentally informed the entire company that he was dumping her and now she had no choice but to leave her job or die of embarrassment. "You shouldn't . . ."

"Mix business with pleasure? I know . . .!!!" Ruby wailed.

No one had demanded that she hand her notice in, of course. Not even Flett himself, though Ruby suspected that if he made such a request, it might well be favourably considered. But how else would Ruby be able to survive the acute and quite unbearable shame of being dumped by an e-mail that the stupid bloody Luddite had somehow managed to forward to everyone at Hollingworth PR, including Ruby's boss? She straight away deleted the two-line e-mail that said he was attaching his comments on the latest draft press release but wouldn't be coming for dinner that night — *or any other night, not even if hell freezes over*. But all day long well-meaning people in the office kept forwarding the damn thing back to her.

"I've got to quit my job," she told Lou hopelessly.

"You could just let the new Barrington catalogue go into print with a pithy footnote about the size of his penis at the bottom of one of the pages?" Lou suggested.

"But it's huge!" Ruby wailed.

"For God's sake," Lou sighed. "It doesn't have to be the truth."

CHAPTER
TWO

Unlike Ruby, Lou Capshaw took no rubbish from any man.

Following a series of early disasters, Lou had developed an in-built bullshit radar that enabled her to spot trouble in a pair of trousers *before* she ended up sleeping with it. Ruby was right that it gets harder to meet new people as you leave college, start work and begin the process of excising likely candidates from your address book as they get paired up, get married, or go gay ... But Lou knew that the field is also necessarily narrowed down as you start to know *yourself* better and resolve to look for a partner who fits every aspect of your personality rather than settling for someone with the requisite number of limbs.

Just thinking about some of her loser ex-boyfriends reminded Lou that there were, as she would assure Ruby on a daily basis, definitely some advantages to being a single girl. Lou could only hope that Ruby would look back on her ridiculous affair with John Flett and feel the same way. Upon receiving Ruby's desperate phone call about the "Dear Jane" e-mail, however, Lou knew she was in line for at least a good week's worth of extensive and elaborate whinging, at the end of which, Ruby would probably take the tosser back.

Lou often joked that since she always had to bear the brunt of Ruby's love-life dilemmas when Mr Wonderful turned out to be Mr W*nk (again), she should also have the right to veto any budding relationship that had "doomed" stamped all the way through it like the letters on Danish bacon. Why couldn't Ruby see that her fling with John Flett was always destined to turn out badly, as had her previous liaison with a recently separated accountant called Dave?

John Flett and Dave Evans were practically interchangeable. Both had recently hit forty and dumped their loyal wives (teenage sweethearts) in a fit of mid-age angst. "Madolescence", Martin called it. Both left behind two small children. "Too young to be affected," they claimed. Both needed Ruby's support to get them through the traumatic early days when their wives called in the solicitors to undermine their confidence and bank balances. Then, six months post-separation, confidence miraculously restored by the mere fact that they were shagging someone born in the 1970s, they were ready to dump mother-substitute Ruby and hit the nightclubs with their ridiculous new haircuts and "old skool" trainers in search of the 1980s vintage totty they had been after all along.

"Ruby," sighed Lou, "you've become a finishing school for newly separated men. Halfway-house between the first wife and the next one. You cook them lovely dinners, when otherwise they'd be eating boiled

14

eggs in the bed-sit. You listen to them whinge about the cost of alimony because it means they can't afford another sports car. You help get them out of their moth-eaten Fair Isles so they don't look a twat when they're clubbing. Then they're off to snare some bimbette using the new, improved dress sense and unwarranted sexual confidence that you helped them develop."

Ruby nodded as though she understood but, in reality, Lou knew she might as well have tried to explain the rationale behind walking to heel to a poodle. No amount of tugging on the choke chain was going to stop Ruby from racing off after the next interesting scent. Which would inevitably be a shit . . .

Lou was pondering the Ruby problem as she waited in companionable silence with another two hundred or so bleary-eyed commuters for the tube that would take her to her work as a fiction editor at Piper Publishing.

When the train finally appeared, Lou tucked the manuscript she had been working on overnight under her arm and groaned. She had been waiting for the best part of twenty minutes and the train that arrived now was more tightly packed than a jar of anchovies. When the doors opened, a couple of passengers actually fell out of the carriage in front of her, panting for breath. They quickly shoved themselves back in though, like contestants in that Japanese game show, *Endurance*. Which was more ridiculous, Lou wondered, eating worms or electing to squeeze yourself into a metal tube, buried two hundred feet underground, with five hundred assorted Londoners and their smells?

Taking a last deep breath, Lou barged her way on board. The passengers already on the train gave feeble mutters of indignation, though just as Lou had predicted, no one had actually bothered to take any notice of the platform announcer's advice that they should "move down inside the cars". When Lou wriggled her way to the space between the long rows of seats, she actually found an empty strap to hang from.

A few stops later, the train came to a halt so quickly that even Lou, who was used to strap-hanging after six years' commuting to the office on the same hellish route, couldn't stay upright. She landed heavily on the lap of a rather stuffy looking gent. He glared at her as she quickly straightened up again.

"Sorry," she mouthed sarcastically. "I mean, it's not as though I would have chosen to sit on your lap."

The man simply tutted and opened his paper out again aggressively. The *Financial Times*, of course. Obviously the only values in his life were the FTSE and the NASDAQ. What was he doing sitting down anyway, Lou thought angrily, when a very obviously pregnant woman was squashed up against the glass partition to his left? When Mr *FT* was safely hidden behind his broadsheet, Lou pulled a hideous face in his direction. She would have added appropriate hand signals too, if she hadn't needed to hold onto that strap. It was a childish gesture, she knew, but it made her feel much better.

And it very much amused the gorgeous commuter in the dark blue suit standing next to the pregnant woman. When she had finished gurning, Lou caught a look across the top of a newspaper and blushed to the roots of her hair. But before she could hide in embarrassment behind the manuscript she was carrying, Lou also caught the stranger grinning a melon-slice smile and giving her a slow, cheeky wink that definitely spoke of approval.

Lou was shocked to feel the unmistakable all-over body flush of attraction rush across her skin so quickly it almost made her knees give way. Then the tube stopped at King's Cross and the stranger got off the train.

Lou strained in vain to get a better look as her new friend stepped out of the carriage but got just a glimpse of fluffy blond hair as the anxious crowds on the platform quickly surged forward. They had locked eyes for a matter of seconds but if Eros still worked with arrows in this age of guided missiles, Lou knew she had got one straight in the heart. That long-neglected muscle in her chest was pumping as if she had just run a marathon. She was sure she must be bright pink with totally inappropriate arousal. For a mad, mad second she considered getting out of the train and following . . . But only for a second.

City Branch trains during the rush hour were more rare than sightings of the Siberian tiger and Lou knew that if she got off this one, she would definitely be late for work. She couldn't be late for work that day. There were phone calls to make. E-mails to answer. Lou took a deep breath to still her thumping heart. She didn't have *time* to follow a stranger onto the platform at King's Cross. What a ridiculous idea.

It was a feeble excuse for lack of daring, she knew, but Lou still bit her lip and let the stranger go. After all, it was just a wink. Not actually an invitation to have dinner. Eros had scored a direct hit with her, but he might have fired straight over her dream lover's head. In fact, under the circumstances, that was more than likely to be the case.

Lou looked at her shoes, as though anyone else in that carriage was able or interested enough to read her racing thoughts. Ridiculous. Just ridiculous. Bloody hell, though, she admitted to herself. She hadn't felt like that in half a decade. Hadn't felt so naked under another's gaze in a very long time indeed. She fanned her face self-consciously.

At the next station, Mr *FT* left the train too. He tripped over Lou's briefcase as he went.

"Sorry . . ." she sang after him, ". . . not. Here, you need this more than I do," Lou said, gesturing the pregnant woman towards the seat Mr *FT* had just vacated.

"What are you getting at?" the woman asked aggressively.

Lou hid behind her manuscript a second time as she realised that the woman was not pregnant at all. Just chunky.

18

On long lazy Sundays with Ruby and Martin, the conversation had often turned to the flirting potential of the tube. In general they agreed that it rated zilch on the Metropolitan pull-ometer. There was something about the subterranean light that lent everyone a hell-bound pallor, and even if you did see someone you fancied, there was little hope of catching their eye. It's a well-documented fact that when people find themselves wedged into a space more tightly than veal calves, they attempt to preserve their privacy by looking anywhere but at each other. Staring at a stranger on the tube is as much a breach of London etiquette as flashing.

Pity though. Lou wondered how many embryonic love stories had ended with a scowl when two lovely people who might otherwise have shared a drink, were caught sneaking a mutual peek on the Northern Line and each instantly branded the other a nutter. Why should that moment when you lock eyes and realise that you *know* someone in the sense that you have connected with their soul, be invalidated just because it happens underground? People get talking to complete strangers in nightclubs all the time. Why is the person you meet in the pub less threatening than the one on his way to the office? It didn't make sense. Nothing much was making sense to Lou that morning.

But talking of the pub . . .

Safely in her office, Lou opened her Microsoft Outlook and started to draft an e-mail.

From: Lou.Capshaw@piperpublishing.com
To: Ruby.Taylor@Hollingworthpr.co.uk
         Martin.Ashcroft@Internationalmagazines.com

Re: The meaning of life.

Answers to this and other questions including: what is the capital of Lithuania? And who won the FA Cup in 1974? Tonight at the Hare and Hounds pub quiz. You know you've got nothing better to do. I haven't. Seven-thirty?

CHAPTER
THREE

Martin didn't have time to read Lou's e-mail when he got to his desk. He'd overslept — again — and arrived at the office with seconds to go before that morning's team meeting. God, he hated the Wednesday morning meeting. As a child, mapping his life out, when railway drivers still seemed like heroes, Wednesday morning meetings where a sweaty, balding git called Barry Parsons yelled at him for not achieving an unachievable sales target had definitely not been part of the plan. In fact, there wasn't much about Martin's current situation at all that fitted the dream future he had held for himself as a child. When did it all go wrong?

Martin started in the sales room of International Magazines as a temp; fresh out of university with a 2:2 in English Lit. He had planned to become a journalist, with a view to making Will Self's incisive interviews for the broadsheets look like reader reviews on Amazon.com. At least that was what he told his mother when she started to get fed up of seeing him lazing on the sofa in front of *Ricki Lake* when she got home from work. Unfortunately, the big news corporations wanted something more than a term's editorship of an obscure poetry magazine called *Pudenda* from their candidates . . .

With his mum threatening eviction, Martin told himself that a temporary job at International Magazines would be a stepping-stone to a proper journalistic career. But the sales and editorial departments weren't even in the same building, and six months' experience selling classified ad space on *New Catering Equipment Digest* got him no nearer to a position as foreign correspondent for *The Times* than had the previous six months spent signing on and playing Nintendo.

Eventually, Martin became chief telesales rep for International Magazines' new flagship publication *The Satyr*. It was a men's magazine, a heady mix of ads, topless celebrities and full colour photos of medical anomalies. Its cover gimmick was to have the hottest *totty du jour* dressed in animal costumes — bottom half only — like the part animal deity the magazine took its name from. Martin's personal favourite was Kylie Minogue, half-dressed as a squirrel, issue three.

Martin knew when he signed on the dotted line at International Mags that he was simultaneously kissing goodbye to all hope that he might one day be the dude with the leather chair actually choosing the arse that would grace *The Satyr's* cover so he focused his attention on the money he could earn if he did the job properly. He even won a weekend in San Francisco as salesperson of the year. And it was disappointingly easy to stifle his creative ambitions after that. For a while anyway.

After four years at International Mags, Martin began to wonder once more if he was hiding a great light under his bushel. He had creative talent. He was going to write a novel. He bought himself a laptop that could have controlled a manned mission to Mars with his end-of-year bonus and promised himself that fifty-two weekends later he would have a draft of the next *High Fidelity* to present to astonished agents and salivating publishers alike. Lou assured him there was a gap in the market.

And it started well enough. The first weekend Martin wrote a chapter, obsessively checking the word count after every paragraph because he had figured out by a process of complicated, mathematical deduction based on a selection of classics that the ideal first chapter should be exactly five thousand words long. He spent the next weekend going over the first chapter and editing out the good bits because he had also heard that a great literary genius pronounced you should "kill your darlings" and get rid of the bits that pleased you most since they were actually most likely to be rubbish. The following weekend, Martin read through the amended first chapter, decided that he had left in all the rubbish parts by mistake and wiped the whole lot from the hard drive of his computer. The weekend after that he had writer's block. And the weekend after that he went to Brighton with Ruby and Lou and didn't fire up his laptop at all.

Now his laptop had an accusing layer of dust all over its high-tech black lid. Lou drew a smiley face in the grime and added the caption "Use me". But Martin hadn't made any progress on his novel for the past seven months. It had reached the stage where nobody even asked about it any more.

Not that he could actually have used his laptop if he wanted to. About the same time that Martin was making his brief bid for literary superstardom, he was dating a girl called "Webecca". Webecca from Wuislip. Couldn't say her "R's". Voice like Bonnie Langford. (Face like Bonnie Langford, if the truth be told.) What on earth had he been thinking?

"You'd been thinking about her tits, of course," said Lou.

Webecca was a postgraduate student at Birkbeck and, while he was still interested in the extraordinary assets she kept beneath her baggy brown jumper, Martin lent Webecca his laptop's power adaptor when hers blew up days from her dissertation deadline. Unfortunately, the adaptor became a casualty of their break-up. Webecca was so distraught by the end of their relationship that she grabbed hold of Martin's ankles when he tried to leave her flat and clung on for at least half a mile. At the time, losing the power source to his all-singing, all-dancing computer had seemed a small price to pay for never having to see the deranged woman or eat her chick-pea curry ever again.

Lou and Ruby had initially leapt to Webecca's defence, accusing Martin of being shallow by allowing Webecca's external appearance (getting hairier by the day) to put him off her inner beauty. They certainly didn't approve of the next incumbent in his affections. Leah was a "spokesmodel". They met while she was handing out free samples of a new nut-filled breakfast bar on the platform at Waterloo Station, dressed in a pair of red hotpants with a squirrel tail attached. (Martin instantly saw the possibility for the realisation of a long-held fantasy there!)

Leah couldn't have been more different from Webecca. She rang him just before their second date to say, "I don't know if I can come out tonight. My hair's kinda gone wrong." She had long, straight black hair. How wrong could it possibly go? Leah was more high-maintenance than a thoroughbred Arab pony. "With possibly less horse-sense," Ruby commented.

"She's bubbly," said Martin defensively.

"Only because her head is full of air. I think that botox injection she had in her forehead must have gone through to her brain. What on earth do you have to talk about?"

Not much, it was true. But Martin was not to be put off. He convinced himself that he really did want to know everything about "leave-in" hair conditioners and gravity-defying face creams. What did it matter if everything that came out through Leah's lips was rubbish when those pink lips were moving so prettily? It didn't even matter that she continued to move her lips while she was reading *Hello*.

It all ended badly of course. Martin was on a corporate jolly to Ireland at the time, pining for his luscious lovely back in London. When he phoned to tell her that he missed her, she told him that she had some good news and some bad news. The good news was that she got the job she had gone for.

"The bad news is . . ." The long-distance phone line crackled loudly. "We've got to go to . . ." Another crackle. ". . . herpes . . ."

"Her*mes*," Martin laughed, assuming his little shopaholic was pronouncing it wrongly again. This was a girl who wore "Ver-sash" after all. "You're not intending to drag me round the sales all weekend, are you?"

Unfortunately, she wasn't. Leah had pronounced *her* latest acquisition perfectly. A parting gift from her exboyfriend Mad Mike, the market trader, who gave Leah her "Guci" — "with one 'c' 'cos it's more exclusive, innit?" — handbag.

Martin tested negatively, thank God, but the aftermath would be with him for eternity, it seemed, with Lou and Ruby almost wetting themselves with laughter every time they saw the exclusive Hermes logo. Ruby even bought him a Hermes tie for Christmas. Thoughtful, eh?

Since Leah's revelation, Martin had been thoroughly single, barring a couple of dates with hapless temps who wandered through International Mags. But lately, even the thought of the temp controller at Office Angels accidentally sending *Charlie*'s *Angels* to stuff envelopes in *The Satyr*'s airless office had seemed strangely unappealing.

"I am turning into my father," Martin told himself one morning as he stared at his thirty-something face in the steamy bathroom mirror. It wasn't just the nose hair.

Was this his future? Ogling pretty temps across the open-plan offices? Drifting from one unsatisfactory fling to the next? A life marked out by Arsenal home games, Wednesday morning team meetings and yet another Wednesday evening at the Hare and Hounds' pub quiz?

CHAPTER
FOUR

Martin was determined to do something different that Wednesday night, but when Lou and Ruby arrived at the Hare and Hounds he was already waiting for them. He was supposed to have had a "proper date" that evening, with a fashion department assistant from *Capital Woman*, another title in the International Magazines empire. But the girl in question had cancelled, claiming pressure of work. Martin quickly relegated the evening he had been looking forward to from "proper date" to "casual arrangement to hook up" and convinced himself that Geri was just nipping out of the office to get supplies for the long stint of overtime ahead when he saw her leaving the office building in her coat at six o'clock.

"Never mind, Mart," said Lou. "You and Ruby can console each other. Do your impression of John Flett for her."

"What impression?" Ruby asked foolishly.

Martin adopted a mid-Atlantic drawl (despite the fact that Flett hailed originally from Tunbridge Wells and had spent a total of three months on the other side of the Atlantic) and slurred, "The driving force behind western civilisation is really the humble ball-bearing."

Then he licked his lips like a camel going for the snot up its own nose.

Lou burst out laughing. Ruby looked as though she would burst into tears.

"He doesn't do that!" she protested hotly.

Martin and Lou chorused, "He does."

"Aren't you glad you don't have to sleep with him any more?" Lou asked. "How on earth could you have ended up with a man who had such a bizarre facial tic?"

"He does not have a facial tic," Ruby persisted. "I've never seen him do that."

"He does it all the time," Lou assured her. "That would have been my fatal flaw."

"Mine too," agreed Martin. "I mean, apart from the fact that he's a man."

The Fatal Flaw. When they didn't have a wedding to play "Reception Disco Bingo" at, Martin, Lou and Ruby had a number of other interesting games to pass the time. "Fatal Flaw" was based on a game called "Shag or Die," as in, "would you rather shag your secondary school geography teacher — or die?" In Fatal Flaw, the potential shag-ees were better. In fact, under normal circumstances, you wouldn't have kicked any of them out of bed. But, the supermodels and Hollywood actors offered up in Fatal Flaw were not without their catch. Of course you would sleep with Brad Pitt. What red-blooded single girl wouldn't? But what if he was suddenly afflicted by a terrible condition of the saliva glands that meant he couldn't talk without spitting all over you? What if, as Lou often asked Martin, Julia

Roberts offered him a blow-job but had a mouthful of needle-sharp teeth?

For Ruby, the fatal flaw was unattractive tootsies. She had a theory that you're never so naked as when you take your socks off. People rarely have ugly eyes. They rarely have ugly hands. Even genitals are generally quite inoffensive to look at. But feet are a different matter. The best you can hope for is that your new lover's feet just look normal. An unexpected encounter with an in-growing toenail could send Ruby into a faint.

"It's the only thing that saved me from sleeping with the Panter," Ruby reminded her friends that evening. "His fungal infection. I just can't deal with dodgy feet."

"Here's one for you then," Martin interrupted. "Russell Crowe with athlete's foot. Shag or die?"

"I'd have to stay celibate," said Ruby.

"Tom Cruise with a single verruca?"

"Stop," Ruby covered her ears. "It's making me gag just to think about it. You know, I would have lost my virginity a whole year earlier than I did if Nick Stevens hadn't shown me his in-growing toenail."

"I still can't believe you ended a relationship because of an in-growing toenail," said Lou.

"How on earth could I have slept with him after that? What if he'd stroked his foot down my leg while we were at it?"

Now Lou gagged too. "Fair enough. I lost my virginity to a man who looked like Kermit the frog and I've regretted it ever since. You've got to get it right, eh, Martin? The first time."

Indeed you should. But Martin didn't elaborate.

The last thing Martin wanted was to get into a round of "how I lost my virginity" stories, because he couldn't quite remember how he'd last told the girls he lost his. He had a vague feeling that he'd told Lou and Ruby he lost his virginity to a friend of his big sister's when he was just fourteen, but he didn't want to get halfway through the tale and have one of the girls point out that the last time he recounted the tale, the sister's friend's name was different.

Because the truth was that Ruby had been there when Martin lost his virginity. She had no idea. It was during their first term at university. Freshers' week. Martin had noticed Ruby hanging about in the halls of residence, trying to pretend that she wasn't crying when her mum and dad dropped her off at the door of the bleak seventies building with her brand new toaster. He didn't see her again until the Freshers' ball almost a week later. By that time Ruby had paired up with Lou and tears of hilarity had replaced tears of homesickness as she snorted her fourth tequila slammer. High on alcohol and independence, Ruby made a beeline for Martin. They smooched (with some difficulty) to Nirvana's "Teen Spirit". And suddenly they were in Ruby's room.

Ruby dragged Martin onto her narrow single bed and threw her treasured teddy bears onto the floor to make room for him. Ten minutes later, Martin was naked and ejaculating into a banana flavoured condom bought from a vending machine in the Union. Ruby pushed him off, retrieved her favourite bear from the pile on the floor and fell into a deep sleep, snoring loudly. Martin spent the night shivering on the edge of her single bed, horribly uncomfortable but vaguely aware that it might be bad manners to disappear right after shagging her. Besides, Ruby had her head on his arm and he didn't dare move it in case he woke her up.

Next morning, clutching a towel around herself as though Martin hadn't already seen her naked, Ruby told him flatly that she had a boyfriend in her home town and added that if Martin told anyone that they had slept together she would tell everyone he was a premature ejaculator. Martin didn't dare tell her that he had been a virgin until she manhandled him. Ruby didn't think to ask. In fact, she didn't even speak to him for another four weeks after that.

Ten years on, the sorry little incident of Martin and Ruby had been relegated to the ranks of those drunken horror stories such as the time Martin fell asleep face down in a kebab and had to go to hospital to have a chilli removed from his nostril, or the night Lou snogged the captain of the university women's cricket club. And, thankfully, that evening, the quizmaster intervened before the storytelling really began. Ruby and Lou turned their attention from Ruby's virginity to marking their answers to that week's general knowledge round.

"I told you the capital of California is not Los Angeles," Ruby complained.

"But did you know it was Sacramento?" Lou retorted.

They got three out of ten.

"You all right, Ruby?" Martin asked as they meandered back to the tube station after closing time. He put his arm round her shoulder and squeezed her against him. "I'm sorry I took the mickey out of the love of your life," he added, before flopping his tongue out of his mouth like a half-demented spaniel and doing it over again.

"No," Ruby laughed this time. "You were right. John Flett is a loser and I'm much better off without him." What a difference four vodkas could make. She only hoped that the effect would last until she woke up again next morning. "You've really cheered me up this evening," Ruby continued. "I'm glad I came out after all. At least I've got you two. You're the best friends in the world."

"Aaaah," Lou and Martin chorused. "We love you back."

"You know, I don't think Flett's actually got any friends any more since he left his wife and their two children with nothing to live on but the proceeds of her part-time job . . ."

Martin winced. The man really was a loser.

"There will be no further references to Jonathan Flett from now on," Lou proclaimed. "He's a pathetic little man."

"But will I ever find a good one?" Ruby asked, drooping against Martin's side.

"Of course you will," Lou reassured her. "We'll start looking for you on Saturday. Susannah's wedding is on Saturday. And everyone can score at a wedding. Only thing you need is a pulse."

CHAPTER
FIVE

A pulse, eh? Ruby couldn't be sure that her dancing partner had one.

After the food fight, during which one of the bridesmaids almost lost an eye to a handful of sugared almonds, Susannah and Winky's sophisticated wedding reception had rapidly descended into anarchy. Susannah's millionaire father had generously catered four bottles of vintage champagne for each and every guest and this incredible extravagance was creating an ugly backlash. Four of the rugby players were stark naked on the dance floor. One of them appeared to have stuck the stem of his corsage down the eye of his penis and was using the flower to point suggestively at any girls he fancied. Ruby could only wonder what he might tell the Accident and Emergency staff later on.

Ruby had managed to fend off the rugger buggers' advances, leaving herself at the mercy of an altogether different kind of sexual predator when the slow dances started. Lou dragged Martin off to the centre of the floor as soon as she heard the first strains of Whitney singing "I Will Always Love You," which meant that Ruby had nowhere to run and nowhere to hide when

Winky's grandfather materialised beside the miscellaneous table and offered her his brittle arm.

"You're a lovely, lovely young lady," he whispered hotly into her ear as he ran his hand along her bra strap.

"Thank you," said Ruby, grateful that etiquette didn't require her to respond in kind with a sincere or truthful compliment of her own. "You're a dirty old man. Move your hand from my arse," wouldn't have sounded too friendly.

Ruby just about managed to keep Granddad at a safe distance as the guests took to the floor in a reprise of "Lady In Red" by adopting a stiff elbow-locked variation on a traditional ballroom dancing hold. It all went horribly wrong when the DJ started to play The Rolling Stones' "Satisfaction". Now Ruby hovered between utter revulsion at the old man who was trying to push his pelvis up against hers and abject terror that he would keel over at any moment and cast a rather depressing note upon which to end such a high-spirited wedding. To that effect, she felt obliged to hang on to Granddad while he convulsed against her body in time with the beat, so that if he did flake out unexpectedly, she might at least be able to get him to the edge of the dance floor without the bride noticing that someone had died at her wedding reception.

Meanwhile, Lou and Martin bobbed up and down enthusiastically behind Ruby's septuagenarian partner, cruelly giving Ruby the thumbs-up every time they caught her eye.

"Love your new boyfriend," mouthed Martin over Lou's shoulder.

"Groovy mover," said Lou sarcastically when the song ended and Granddad actually went off in search of someone *younger* to play with.

"Great," said Ruby as she watched her erstwhile dancing partner getting down to "Come On Eileen" (again) with the bride's seventeen-year-old cousin. "I can't even keep the attention of a seventy-something any more. I am doomed."

"Are we ready to go yet?" asked Martin, as he slid gracefully beneath the miscellaneous table like the *Titanic* meeting her iceberg.

"None of us have scored," said Lou.

"Do you honestly think we're likely to?" Ruby asked.

They surveyed the room like two generals at the end of a particularly bloody battle. Bodies in various states of undress were littered about the furniture. A semi-naked rugger bugger lay where he had fallen in the middle of the dance floor, oblivious to the high-heeled shoes that clattered dangerously about him. There was no blood yet, thank goodness. But a great deal more nudity and vomit than one would have expected for such a grand occasion. In fact, as the girls watched in horrified amazement, a smartly dressed young lady was actually puking in somebody's handbag.

"Hope that's her own," said Ruby with a wince.

"Let's bail," said Lou, grabbing a couple of half-finished bottles of champagne for later.

"You don't really want any more of that, surely?" Ruby gasped.

"Hair of the dog," Lou explained with drunken logic. "We'll be grateful for this in the morning."

"Looks like Martin's already getting his."

Ruby raised the edge of the tablecloth to reveal Martin snoring gently on a pile of discarded shoes and handbags, while Susannah's favourite pet, a Norfolk terrier that had been specially decked out for the day in a dinky bow to match the bridesmaids' dresses, licked the sweat off Martin's forehead with its slobbery pink tongue.

"Shall we leave him there?" asked Lou.

"I don't think that would be friendly," said Ruby.

"Let's leave him," said Lou.

The girls made for the door.

They were staying in a bed and breakfast place a couple of miles from the country house in whose grounds Susannah's marquee had been pitched. The sixteenth-century coach-house hotel looked idyllic from the outside. Inside, unfortunately, it wasn't so great. Fifty quid a head and Ruby found a pubic hair stuck to the soap.

Lou and Ruby were sharing a room. Ruby didn't get much sleep. When they got back from the reception, Lou crashed out instantly (on the less knackered of the two single beds, so that Ruby got a bedspring in the kidneys) and spent the first half of the night snoring on her back. She spent the second half groaning as dehydration kicked in.

It's true what they say about hangovers getting worse as you get older. As a sixteen-year-old, Ruby could down twelve assorted shorts on a Friday evening and still get up to do her job at the local garden furniture salesroom next morning, earning just enough money in a day to drink another twelve Bacardi and Cokes on the Saturday night. Lately, she'd given up mixing her drinks (or at least tried to stick to one colour all night), drank two pints of water *and* took a couple of aspirin *before* she went to sleep. Yet she still woke up feeling as though she had used her tongue to clean the carpet.

At least Lou and Martin were similarly afflicted. Far from being pleased that she had remembered to bring home some booze for a "hair of the dog" as soon as she woke up, when Lou rolled over to see (and smell) the two half-empty champagne bottles on the bedside table in the early hours of the morning, she had to leg it to the bathroom before nature took one of its courses. The day after Susannah's wedding, Martin even turned his nose up at a freshly cooked breakfast. He was as green about the gills as the chipped nineteen-sixties-style crockery upon which the unwanted fry-up was served. Ruby soon realised that, compared to the other two, she had actually fared quite well.

"Did I score?" Martin asked the girls when he surfaced just before lunchtime.

"You fell asleep beneath the table," Lou replied.

"I could have sworn someone was licking my face," he muttered.

"Someone was," Lou assured him. "Or rather, something was. Susannah's dog."

"Oh, God," Martin groaned. "I ended up with a dog again. I am giving up alcohol," he added solemnly.

"Where have I heard that one before?" Ruby laughed. "Hangovers are like pregnancy. At the time, you swear you'll never put yourself through it again. Seven days later you just can't remember the pain."

"You're always so smug," Martin complained. "Haven't you ever lost a weekend through alcohol?"

The waitress drifted past with another plateful of bacon and eggs for another guest. Lou and Martin clutched hands to their mouths and swayed like two victims of seasickness. Over in the corner of the restaurant, the rugger bugger wedding guest who had ordered the breakfast thought better of it too and relieved his nausea by heaving dramatically into a bread-basket.

"Lounge, anybody?" Martin suggested.

They re-seated themselves in the hotel's chintzy day room with the Sunday papers.

"So," said Ruby, as she settled down into an armchair with a glossy fashion supplement. "Another wedding over and none of us is any nearer to being the girl in the puffball."

"I don't want to be the girl in the puffball," said Martin.

"Me neither, for that matter," added Lou.

"It would have been nice just to meet someone different," said Ruby.

"I just want to know that some lovely lady is going to ask to see my penis again before I lose sight of it forever," said Martin, patting his expanding waistline.

"But you will," said Lou. "Remember the pact we made last night? About writing ads for each other?"

Ruby and Martin groaned like a pair of teenagers being reminded of a promised visit to the zoo with great-aunt Sarah.

"I think we should go for it!"

Lou's enthusiasm was met by two blank stares.

"You both thought it was a good idea last night," she said defensively.

"I can't be held responsible for anything I say under the influence of Bollinger," said Martin.

"But why shouldn't it work?" Lou persisted. "Susannah and Winky met through a personal ad."

"They'd have met at the Kennel Club eventually," said Martin. "It's not going to happen for any of us, Lou. Get real."

Ruby smiled into her coffee cup, tacitly agreeing with Martin. But that morning Lou was unusually bullish. "Well, I don't think you should be so quick to dismiss my idea," she told them. "We're all single. We all want to meet people, don't we?"

"Yeah, but not *losers*," Martin sneered.

"You're so pessimistic," sighed Lou.

"Realistic," he said, "is the word."

Romantic that she was, Ruby wanted to be able to back Lou up, but there wasn't much proof in Lou's favour. Personal ads had long carried the stigma of being the last resort of the desperate. Or the downright deviant. Ruby recalled one of those morning television debates where some poor woman revealed to the audience that she had answered an ad placed by a man who claimed to like "motorbikes and horse riding" only to discover this was Lonely Hearts' code for sado-masochism and bondage and it wasn't a pony he expected to wear the saddle . . .

Of the thousands of personal ads placed in the papers every Sunday, what percentage really ended with a buffet in a pink and white marquee? A far smaller percentage than those that ended up with a restraining order, Ruby suspected.

Lou turned to anecdotal evidence. "There's a girl at my office whose best friend's sister's mate met her husband through the personals," she insisted. Ruby's head started to spin as she tried to work out the connection. "Apparently she answered the ad for a dare and it turned out that the guy who placed it was a millionaire! Don't get many millionaire losers, do you, Martin?"

"You wouldn't have thought that a millionaire would need to advertise," Ruby mused. "I don't suppose many girls would say no to a date with someone that rich and successful."

"Of course they wouldn't. But how would he know they weren't just in it for the money?" Lou pointed out. "He placed the ad precisely so that the girls who answered wouldn't be blinded by his humungous bank account. It was the only way he could avoid the gold-diggers."

42

"If it's true, it's a one-off," said Martin.

"No! What about Mike Oldfield?" Lou countered. "He was *addicted* to personal ads. Placed hundreds of the things until he was rumbled. Or would you call the millionaire composer of 'Tubular Bells' a loser too?"

"Two-off," Martin replied. "Though it sounds to me like he had a problem."

"The personal ads are full of people whose only *problem* is that they're too busy being successful in their careers to sort out their love lives," Lou insisted. "I read somewhere that several City firms are even taking out dating agency subscriptions on behalf of their staff as part of the benefits package. Happy home lives make for happier workers." Lou pushed an open newspaper across the table towards Ruby. "Take your pick, Rubes. How about a nice entrepreneur? International airline pilot? Millionaire racing car enthusiast."

"Hmmmm," Ruby pondered.

"Pounds or lira?" Martin smiled. "Admit it, Lou. No normal, sociable person, with no obvious hang-ups or facial tics," he looked pointedly at Ruby as he said that, "should ever need to resort to a lonely hearts ad. There's the office, the gym, even the supermarket. Hundreds of ways to find the one you're after. If you can't chat someone up face to face then you probably shouldn't be allowed to mate in the first place."

"Have you ever tried chatting someone up while you're on the Stairmaster?" asked Lou. "Come to think of it, my dear, have you ever even seen a Stairmaster?"

Martin sucked his stomach in self-consciously.

"And how on earth can you tell who's single in the supermarket? Count the number of spuds in their basket? As for dating at work, we've all seen where that ends."

Ruby cast her eyes downward.

"Do you mind?" she said. "I haven't thought about *him* all weekend."

"Except when you were dancing with Granddad, surely," said Martin.

"Yeah," Lou interrupted. "Well, I know that I'm not going to have a workplace affair unless my firm change their equal opportunities programme to include that minority group we call the *attractive*. Personal ads are the only way forward. You specify exactly what you want. No danger of making a play for that guy with the pile of ready-packed meals for one in his basket, only to discover that he and his *boyfriend* have a finicky cat that will only eat Marks and Spencer's frozen lasagne. No need to do an extra twenty minutes on the Stairmaster just to impress the girl in the bright pink thong. And no danger of having to leave your job because your workplace paramour finished with you via two lines on your work group's electronic message board and humiliated you in front of the whole company."

Ruby groaned heavily.

"Sorry, Ruby," said Lou. "Cruel to be kind. But come on," she continued. "We've run out of single friends to have round to dinner parties. Both of you expect me to sort out your love-lives when everything goes pear-shaped. I've had long nights of tears from you, Ruby. And long nights of tears from the women you've done wrong," she reminded Martin. "Ruby is always wishing that you would go for a girl who remembered to take her GCSEs. And Martin wishes that you, Rubes, would try dating someone who hasn't already been road-tested and rejected by his first wife. This is our chance to match each other up with the people we really think we should be with. We could even have a kitty as an incentive. Fifty quid each and the first person to write a successful ad pockets the lot?"

Ruby looked from Lou to Martin to see if he was wavering.

"Look," said Martin suddenly. "If any of us ends up even having an interesting phone conversation with someone we've met through a personal ad, then I'll happily give you my money."

"You're on," said Lou, sticking out her hand to shake on it. "But this means you have to promise to give my scheme a proper chance."

"Scout's honour," promised Martin.

"He was never in the scouts," Ruby pointed out.

Martin put his hand out anyway.

"What about you, Rubes?" Lou asked. "Are you on for it?"

Ruby stuck her own hand out tentatively.

"I don't know. Can you promise you won't fix me up with a loser?"

"We promise!" chorused her friends.

"Then I don't see why not."

The three pals performed a weird three-way handshake that looked as though it should have ended with them turning into crime-fighting super-beings.

"Right," said Lou. "I stand to make some serious money here. I'm going to start looking for someone for the pair of you straight away."

"I thought we had to place ads," Ruby pointed out.

"Place ads. Answer ads. The main point is that we choose dates for each other." She patted Ruby on the hand. "Don't look so worried."

"I've got a nasty feeling I need to be," she said.

"You don't," Lou reassured her. "This is going to be wonderful. We're going to have a fantastic summer. Martin and Ruby," she concluded, low and serious, "prepare to get lucky in love."

CHAPTER
SIX

On the drive back to London, Lou and Ruby risked carsickness to read every personal ad they could lay their hands on. Lou vowed to leave no stone unturned, answering every single ad from men under sixty on behalf of Ruby, unless the ad said that the guy in question was actually after another young man or "required discretion" which meant that he was already married.

Every three-line advertisement made the guy who placed it seem so inviting. To a newly single girl like Ruby, the "Encounters" page of *The Sunday Times* Style supplement was like the top layer of a box of chocolates freshly stripped of its cellophane at the end of a long, lonely diet. With the pick of the box, it was difficult to know which one to go for first.

"Do you think I'm the kind of girl who looks equally at home in a ball dress or a pair of Levi's?" Ruby asked as she hovered with the biro over an ad from a "genuine country gentleman with homes in the City and Home Counties".

"Ring it," said Lou. "If the marriage doesn't work out, he can live in the country one and you can stay in the town house with us."

"Aren't you jumping the gun?" asked Martin, feeling a little left out as they trawled through the men while he drove.

"Your problem," said Lou, "is that you've got no imagination. No wonder you've never finished that novel."

"Don't bring the novel into this," Martin warned.

"Then stop being such a killjoy. And try to stick to the speed limit. What about this one for you, Rubes? Accountant with a poet's soul?"

"Sounds lovely," she agreed.

But they were soon to discover that if the "Encounters" page was a box of chocolates, then it was a box full of those funny orange creams that even the dog won't eat.

You've got to know your enemy. How to sort out the wheat from the chaff. And Lou and Ruby didn't have a clue. Having ringed all the ads that interested them, and a couple for Martin too, the girls retired to Lou's flat to draft introductory letters and, more importantly, ring the telephone lines that accompanied each box number.

Each advertiser had one of these phone lines, where they could leave a short message to elaborate on the things they mentioned in their print ad. The calls cost premium rates, of course, but Ruby and Lou decided that a call to each of those lines was an investment they simply had to make. After all, if someone had a bizarre voice or said something a bit peculiar in their message, the girls would have saved themselves the cost of a stamp and hours of their time wasted writing a suitable letter.

Advertisements that didn't have a box number were dismissed out of hand. The girls determined that any man who didn't bother to record a telephone message must be one of four things: number one, he was too cheap. Lou had quickly noticed that while the telephone ads were free to place, picking up the messages left in reply cost as much for the guy who placed the ad as it did for the girls who rang to listen to him. Any man who balked at spending sixty pence a minute to listen to what might be the voice of the love of his life, was hardly likely to be lavish with the presents when he finally found her.

Number two, the man might be unnecessarily shy.

"What's wrong with being shy?" Martin protested. But Lou was ruthless on this point too. They were not after the kind of man who might need baby-sitting in a social situation.

Reason number three: the bloke wasn't able to make up anything sufficiently witty to say. Not that this stopped many men from leaving a message, as the girls would later discover.

Reason four was a terrible speech impediment.

"You can't help having a speech impediment," said Martin when Lou announced that this was the fourth fatal flaw.

"Oh yeah," Lou scoffed. "I don't seem to remember your being quite so kind when you dumped poor *iccle Webecca from Wuislip*."

Martin blanched at the memory of his ex.

"Got to narrow the field down somehow," he back-tracked.

"Ring this one," said Lou to Ruby.

She had found an ad that said, "Could you be my muse? Sensitive writer, 32, seeks serious, sensual lady for friendship, maybe more."

"Am I sensual?" Ruby asked.

"You've got ticklish feet," said Lou.

"I guess I must be, then."

"But are you a lady?" asked Martin.

Ruby tapped the number into the phone and listened impatiently to the long spiel about the service (delivered extra slowly to use up more premium rate time) before she could punch in the box number she was after. A £2.50 minute had already passed before at last she heard, "Hi. My name is Davide."

David-e. With an "e". Italian-style. Not just plain English David. Lou drew away from the earpiece she was sharing with Ruby to give a nod of approval. The writer's voice was at least suitably deep. No immediately obvious lisp or stutter. And Davide was exotic without being too pretentious.

"By now you'll have read my ad," he said, "and you want to know more about me."

"Yes, please," breathed Ruby. "Lovely voice. I think we've found a good one here."

"Where can I begin?" asked Davide. "I could tell you I'm a published poet . . ."

"Poet!" snorted Martin. He was listening to the call via the extension line in Lou's bedroom. As a novelist in embryo, he had a general disdain for anybody who wrote anything that rhymed or scanned.

"But I have a day job as an editor . . ."

"He's an editor!" shouted Martin from the bedroom, as if they hadn't heard.

"We're looking for a date for Ruby!" Lou shouted back. "Not someone to publish your non-existent novel!"

"Editor?" said Ruby worriedly. "What if it's someone you know? What if it's John Simpson?"

Ruby had dated, very briefly, an editor from Lou's office who chucked her for being "narrow minded" when she refused to use a dildo on him after their first date.

"His name's not Davide," Lou reminded her.

"No. It's exactly the kind of name he might make up though."

"What else can I say?" the message continued. "I could tell you that I'm six feet tall."

"Not John," sighed Ruby with relief. "He's only five feet eight."

"And men never lie about their dimensions," Lou commented.

". . . I've got brown hair and eyes and some people say I look a bit like Hugh Grant. With the lights off . . ."

Davide laughed. Ruby tittered politely. Martin gave a room-shaking groan.

"But that would be the boring way to do it. So, to help make sure I make exactly the right impression on you in the short time that we have, I've decided to leave the rest of my message in rhyme."

In rhyme? All three friends felt their stomachs contract in anticipation of the awful. Was he going to read out a poem?

Davide cleared his throat.

"Oh, God," said Lou. "He's really going to do it."

"Here goes," Davide began. "O lovely lady, on the end of the phone, like me you've spent, too much time alone, but the wait is over, just leave me your number, we'll be in clover, sweet dreams in our slumber, I'll hold your hand, through winter, spring and summer, if you choose me as your lover, you'll never need another. O lovely lady, waiting by the phone, leave me your number, the lonely days are gone. Looking forward to meeting you, dream lady."

And with a soft kiss blown into the receiver, Davide was gone.

Ruby put the phone down thoughtfully. Lou slumped into an armchair, hands clasped to her head in mock anguish. Martin joined the girls in the sitting-room for a debrief.

"Oh, dear," said Lou.

"Tosser," said Martin plainly.

"He said he was six feet tall," said Ruby. "He's the *tallest* one so far."

It was quite an issue for a girl who stood five ten in her stripy socks.

"He read a poem onto the line," protested Martin. "He used the phrase 'lovely lady'. Twice. And what's more, that poem didn't even scan!"

"Give him a chance," said Ruby. "I think he was very brave. And unusual."

52

"I wonder where's he's been published." Martin loaded the last word with sarcasm.

"At least he *has* been published," Ruby retorted.

"Yeah, right! He probably prints his own eco-friendly, communist pamphlets and distributes them at Speakers' Corner. I bet his editing job is at *Lawn Bowls Monthly*. Plus, he had a funny voice," Martin concluded his tirade somewhat weakly.

"He did not have a funny voice. Lou, do you think I should call the line again and leave my number?" Ruby pleaded. "What should I say if I do? Should I leave my reply in rhyme too?"

"Oh, please," Martin sighed. "Like what? Dearest Dave, My name is Ruby. Will you come and feel my boobies?"

A cushion went sailing across the room in the direction of Martin's fat head.

Lou paused and tapped her chin with a biro while she considered the matter for all of five seconds. "No," she determined, "you shouldn't call that line again."

"But he's young. He's tall. Ish," said Ruby almost desperately.

"He's obviously a tosser," said Lou.

"Thank you, Lou," said Martin. "Common sense prevails."

"We can't waste our time replying to ads that make us feel uneasy," Lou warned them both.

"But I didn't feel uneasy," said Ruby. "And I thought we were choosing for me this time."

"We've already established that you're hopeless at sussing out men for yourself," Lou reminded her. "So we're going on *my* instincts here. Listening to that man made my skin crawl."

"I know exactly what you mean," said Martin. "Did he honestly think that poem was a good idea?"

Lou recited a few lines in a passable impression of Davide's voice.

"OK," Ruby admitted at length. "He made my skin crawl too. He was terrible."

"Then Davide is out," said Lou decisively. She put a red line through his advert.

Unfortunately, it didn't get much better.

"Twenty-eight-year-old entrepreneur with Ferrari!" Ruby squeaked at one point. But when they rang the accompanying box number, Jolly "Japester" (he used that word himself) Toby Jakes revealed with a hysterical giggle that he was in fact fifty-two years old and drove a Mini Metro.

"Got you to pick up the phone though, didn't I?" he laughed triumphantly. His laugh was so creepy that Ruby practically threw the phone back down.

Martin told the girls that he thought they were wasting their time. For every woman who found her multi-millionaire Mr Right via the personal ads, he reasoned, there were thousands more who had ended up going Dutch on a date with The Swamp Thing. And as for the ads they wanted him to answer . . . For heaven's sake! How could someone put "GSOH" meaning Good Sense of Humour and make a reference to "top sitcom" *Birds of a Feather* in the very same line?

He pointed out that none of Lou and Ruby's tales of small-ad success mentioned a man who discovered that his mystery advertiser had legs like a baby giraffe and the body of a super model combined with the brains of a cosmonaut. It soon became clear that the women who advertised in the personal ad columns were all fifty-something, "been hurt before", looking for someone to "love and cherish" them like the prize antiques they were.

Almost three hours later, Ruby put down the phone on yet another man who claimed to have the body of a professional athlete but finished each sentence with a death rattle that made it sound unlikely he could walk upstairs, let alone dribble the length of a football pitch. She had already dismissed the man who started his message with those magic words "looking for commitment" but ended by saying that he was actually looking for a woman with whom he could populate Mars when the lizards from Uranus finally rose up and took over planet Earth . . .

"I don't think I could stand the responsibility," she said.

A horrifying number of the advertisers were just looking for a bit on the side to rejuvenate lives deadened by bad marriages. Ruby pleaded the case of one guy who claimed to be separated, decree nisi pending, but Lou and Martin were firm. He did sound like a nice bloke, Lou agreed. But then so had Flett when Ruby first met him.

"Do you want to go through the same thing again? Pick some man up from the depths of divorce despair only to have him limp off after someone else as soon as he's regained his confidence?"

The words twisted in Ruby's gut just like a dagger. Who was Flett using his new confidence on now?

"This is hopeless, isn't it?" Ruby said. "There's no one I like the sound of apart from the one getting a divorce. They really are all losers."

"No!" Lou insisted. "We've got to plough on. I mean, look at us. We're not losers! It'll be different when we place our own ads, I promise. Then, people like us will ring up and be gagging for a date because everyone else is so awful. Let's place ads this week. We could have our first blind date the Friday after."

Ruby shrugged. "Whatever. I've got to get home now."

Martin agreed.

"I need to get some sleep before work," Ruby continued. "Not that I can sleep while I think about Flett the whole time."

Lou rolled her eyes. "Oh come on, you two! Let's write our ads now, while we're still thinking about it. This is a great idea."

"Isn't that what New Labour said about the Millennium Dome?"

Lou couldn't understand why the others refused to get fired up by her plan. As far as she was concerned, it was brilliant. Her greatest idea ever. Writing ads for one another was the best way yet to ensure that everyone got the lover they deserved.

Growing up in Britain, you get ticked off for showing off so often that by the time you become an adult, you find it next to impossible to list your good points. That's why that classic job interview standard, "What do you think your strengths are?" is such a nightmare for any self-respecting Brit. Ask any British person that question and they'll probably chew their nails for half an hour before saying, "Well, I wouldn't steal pencils from the stationery cupboard," when what they should have said is, "I'm a creative team player with shit-hot leadership skills who could take this goddamn company to the top of the Nasdaq!"

Thus, describing yourself in a way that would make a person of the opposite sex want to jump your bones is practically impossible. It just isn't British. Consider these British responses to potentially leading questions in a chat-up situation.

"I hear you've written a novel . . ."

"Well, I was always quite good at typing so . . ."

"Is it true you used to be goalie for Manchester United?"

"Well, I do have rather big hands, so . . ."

Deprecate and shrug the compliments off. That's the British way.

And that's why the only way to get a halfway accurate report about a British person is to ask a British person's friend. While it's not acceptable under any circumstances to blow your own trumpet in this green and pleasant land, it is almost acceptable to play a horn concerto on behalf of your very best mates.

And that's what Lou intended to do for Martin when she placed her ad for him in *The Sunday Times* "Encounters" page. She would make her friend sound like the best catch since Moby Dick. Only not quite so fat, of course.

Another Monday morning. The continuing effects of the post-wedding hangover meant that Lou was slightly late for work. Only fifteen minutes late, but it was enough to mean that the rush-hour crowds on the platform had all but disappeared by the time she got to the tube station. And joy of joys, when the train came, Lou found that she had a seat. She sat down and continued to work out the wording for Martin's ad in the margin of her *Guardian*.

Warm, witty writer? He'd like that one. *Super, sexy salesman?* Well, if she cut out the super and sexy bit, it would at least be factually accurate. *Silly, sarcastic charlatan?* Ruby would approve. *Looks a bit like Robbie Williams?* Nope. While Martin liked to think he looked like Robbie Williams, the perfect pop-star, Lou and Ruby knew that what his grandmother had actually meant to say was that he looked like *Robin* Williams, the aging American comedian.

While she tried to think of the perfect way to describe a thirty-something loafer, with the kind of floppy public school hair that some girls went crazy for, Lou glanced around the carriage at her fellow passengers. Opposite her, a girl in a suit that was slightly too tight and a pair of ridiculous chunky platform shoes read *Ms London*. Probably a temp, Lou decided. Next to her, a man in an Arsenal shirt and dust-covered jeans read the *Sun*. Builder, thought Lou, on his way back to the site after illicitly signing on at the dole office. And three seats on from him sat the woman Lou had mistakenly thought pregnant the week before. She wasn't reading anything, just staring straight ahead at nothing in particular with her mouth set in a half-snarl.

As though she sensed Lou's eyes upon her, the woman suddenly turned in her direction. Lou put up her paper like a fireguard and stayed hidden behind it for the rest of her journey.

But seeing that fierce woman again was actually strangely comforting. Because it proved to Lou that lightning could strike twice. If that woman had got into the same carriage as Lou again in less than the space of a week, then it wasn't entirely impossible that the dream lover might have done the same thing too.

Lou couldn't concentrate on Martin's ad any more. Once again, she felt the red-hot flush of lust tear through her body. Even the memory of that smile could affect her as strongly as if she had glimpsed the stranger across the floor in a sweaty nightclub. Lou fanned at her face with her newspaper. What a way to start a Monday! If only she could distil that effect into two lines and place a personal ad specifying *that* as what she wanted from a lover.

"The ability to make my knees go weak," she scribbled in the margin.

CHAPTER
SEVEN

For almost seven months, Martin had been able to sit on his creative urges and let his expensive laptop gather dust in a corner of his bedroom. But that Monday morning after Susannah's wedding, with Barry, head of ad sales for the entire International Magazines empire, bawling about the lamentable (i.e. empty) state of *The Satyr*'s back pages, Martin knew that he couldn't let another seven months pass him by. He had to get out of International Magazines before he was the man with no hair in the cheap shiny suit banging on about targets and deadlines.

"You are *shit*! The lot of you!" Barry had concluded the meeting even more eloquently than usual.

Martin's team exited the room with heads bowed low. Not even Lee's Dilbert desk calendar could cheer them up that day. It had become an office ritual, reading the new joke on Lee's Day By Day Dilbert calendar, like prisoners making a chalk line on the wall to mark the passing of another day in solitary confinement.

"What was wiv Barry this morning?" asked Mel. Martin knew that Lee had chosen Melanie from half a dozen applicants for her job because he thought she would brighten up the office. Six months on, the boys hardly looked at her legs any more, but Martin couldn't help noticing her grating Sarf Landan accent.

"Didn't get a shag last night," Lee suggested thoughtfully.

"Then it's a wonder'e's not like that every time we'ave a meeting," said Mel. "I can't stand it 'ere much longer, Lee. I'm gonna leave if I have to go through that shit again."

"Who will keep my spirits up when you're gone?" Lee asked her.

"You've got Martin," Mel reminded him.

"Yeah," said Lee. "Martin will never leave, will you, Mart? Part of the furniture, our Martin. Isn't it time you got out on parole yet?" Lee joked. "How long have you been here? Five years? Six years?"

"Seven years," said Martin with a wince.

"That's longer than you'd get if you actually killed Fat Baz and done time for it," Lee pointed out. Then he asked in a way that was almost concerned, "You all right, mate? You've gone a bit quiet."

"Yeah," said Martin. "Heavy weekend," he added.

"Well, don't you go skiving off after lunch," Mel admonished him. "I'm fed up of covering for the pair of you while you nurse your 'angovers with all the best-looking female clients."

"Not much chance of that today," said Martin. That lunchtime he had a meeting with a client from a dating agency website that specialised in matching gay guys to their Mr Rights. Martin wasn't looking forward to it. He liked to do lunches when there was at least a vague chance of flirtation or conversation about football, and Mikey, from www.getyourrocksoff.com was clearly not going to be Mart's kind of girl . . . Even if he was wearing a fetching pink "Sex Kitten" T-shirt and the tightest pair of jeans Martin had seen since 1981.

That said, Martin was surprised to find that he and Mikey actually had a lot in common. With the business quickly out of the way — a quarter-page colour ad in the October and November issues — "just in time to catch the saddos who're gonna be on their own for Christmas" — they moved on to more interesting subjects. Before becoming a dot.com tycoon, Mikey had toured as a backing singer with a number of bands that Martin had actually heard of. "I sang the voice of one of the lion cubs in The Lion King Four," he added through a mouthful of roquette in balsamic vinegar.

"Great," said Martin.

"Have you *seen* it?" Mikey asked.

Then they started to talk literature. Of sorts.

"I've got a mate who's a writer," said Mikey. "Not books, mind you. Screenplays. Much more money in that. Just sold some rights to Warner Brothers for a quarter of a million pounds."

That made Martin look up from his coffee.

"You serious?" he asked.

"Absolutely. One minute he's working as a barman at The Fridge, next, they're flying him out to Hollywood. Got picked up from the airport in a limousine. He stayed in the same hotel that Richard Gere takes Julia Roberts to in *Pretty Woman*. You know, apparently there's a suite on the top floor of that hotel with a bloody carp pond in the middle of the living room. You don't want to know what he got up to in there, I can tell you . . ."

"What was the script about?" Martin interrupted, sensing that even if he didn't want to know what Mikey's friend had got up to in the indoor carp pool, Mikey was about to start telling him.

"Oh, this and that. You know. Dating."

"Dating?"

"It's the hot topic, the studio executives said. Millions of people out there unable to *get their rocks off*." Mikey laughed at the reference to his own website's name. "All of them wanting to know that they're not alone in the world. All of them taking comfort from the fact that Meg Ryan always gets her man. In fact, she's up for the leading lady. Either her or Gwyneth Paltrow."

"I'm impressed," Martin told him.

"Neither of them do anything for me," said Mikey.

"How did your friend get into it?" Martin persisted. "Writing, I mean."

"God knows. I was surprised. Didn't even know he could *read*. I suppose he's a very good liar," Mikey smiled. "I learned that when he ran off with my exboyfriend."

"And he's still your friend?"

"No point holding a grudge. Besides which, he was also my dealer."

"Oh." Martin speared a chip and plugged it into his mouth before he could look surprised.

"You interested in writing, Martin?"

"I've dabbled," Martin admitted.

"Got to be broad-minded if you want to be a writer," Mikey observed. "Explore a lot of different experiences."

He leaned forward across the table. Martin leaned back in his chair. "Yeah. I guess you do. Dating, you say? Hot topic."

"The hottest," Mikey pronounced lasciviously, leaning so much further forward that he knocked over the salt cellar.

Martin decided he wouldn't order that second bottle of wine after all.

But by the time he got back to the office, he knew what he had to do next. That night he would get his laptop out and start working on his novel again. If a part-time barman stroke drug-dealer could make it as a writer, then Martin definitely could. Lou's ridiculous dating pact would give him something to write about.

When Ruby came back from lunch that day, she checked her e-mail to discover two notes from John Flett. It came as something of a surprise to see his name in her "in-box" once again. Since the day he informed her of the end of their relationship, she had had no correspondence from him at all.

One of the e-mails he sent now was entitled "Press Release". Fair enough. She had been waiting for him to get back to her with some more amendments to her thrilling release entitled "Barrington Ball-bearings. A twenty-first century solution." The other, intriguingly, bore the title line "Dinner".

Dinner? Was he inviting her? Ruby opened "Press Release" first. "Please find attached, blah, blah, blah." She downloaded the file to read later. Now for "Dinner". Before she even opened the e-mail, Ruby was wondering whether or not she should accept his surprising offer.

Following one of many long conversations with Lou over the weekend about the unceremonious way in which she had been dumped, Ruby had promised her best friend that she would keep her dealings with Flett at twenty degrees below from that day on. Strictly business. She may have had to continue to work with him as his account manager but that didn't mean that she had to take any notice of his overtures if he decided that he wanted to be *friends* with her again.

"You can't be friends with someone who dumped you," Lou was certain. "Dumping someone is, by its definition, the very antithesis of a friendly act."

That said, Lou had been certain that Flett *would* start to make friendly advances again. And soon. "Nearly every dumper does," she sighed. But what Ruby had to remember was that any casual invitation Flett sent her way was not a symptom of his having changed his mind about *her*. Lots of dumpers made friendly advances to the person they had dumped upon relatively soon after the event. It was about making the dumper feel better about himself. Not about making it up to the person they'd treated so carelessly.

"He'll probably treat you to lunch and think that's an end to it," Lou told her. "If you accept an olive branch you'll be absolving him of his terrible behaviour and confirming that he isn't a bastard after all. But he broke your heart. He is a bastard. So, don't do it."

Ruby hovered with the cursor over the "open" box on the e-mail. Lou's wise advice played like a soundtrack in her mind. Click. She opened it. Was there really any harm in accepting an invitation to dinner if . . .

To: Ruby.Taylor@Hollingworthpr.co.uk
From: JohnFlett@BarringtonBalls.com

Re: Dinner

Imogen, darling.
Ivy booked for nine. Sure you can't get away from the Two-Faced conference any earlier?
J XX

Imogen! Who the fuck was Imogen? The bloody idiot had clearly sent the wrong e-mail to Ruby's address. Ruby stared at her screen until the words started to swim before her eyes. He *was* seeing someone else! And slowly, the realisation of exactly whom he was seeing dropped like an anvil at the back of Ruby's brain. Imogen. The Two-Faced conference. Oh, God. He was seeing Imogen Moss, Hollingworth's newest recruit. The new recruit who whipped the Two-Faced Cosmetics contract out from beneath Ruby's nose just three days after joining the company.

"They think she has the right look for the job, Rubes, I'm sorry," said her boss at the time. And how could Ruby argue? She hadn't even combed her hair that morning. Imogen looked like she'd stepped from the pages of *Vogue*.

Ruby felt her eyes prick with tears almost instantly. It was as though she had received that initial Dear Jane e-mail all over again. Sure, she had guessed that a man like John Flett wouldn't simply have kicked her out of bed so that he could stretch out over both sides, but while she couldn't put a name to her replacement, Ruby had somehow managed to keep the full horror of Flett's probable new love at a distance. Now horror had a sleek blonde bob.

Ruby's vision was blurred as she looked out through the glass door of her office to the corner of the main room where Imogen stood, oblivious to the misery unfolding. Meanwhile, Imogen flicked up her bob with the casual insouciance of a 1980s Timotei girl and threw her head back to laugh. Ruby scrunched her hands into fists beneath her desk, so hard that her fingernails left dents in her palms for hours afterwards.

"Ohhhhh . . . aarrrrggggh!" Ruby couldn't begin to articulate her pain. "Not her!"

Ruby suddenly felt as though she was mutating into a troll. She imagined her spine twisting as her shoulders slumped forwards to meet her knees. Her neck was shrinking. Her chin jutting out. Her boobs were going south to follow her self-esteem as it slithered its way to the floor and headed for the nearest available exit. She was deflating like a balloon at the end of a party. No one wanted to take Ruby home.

It wasn't long before the bile spreading throughout Ruby's limbs reached her fingertips. She opened Flett's wrongly addressed e-mail once again and forwarded it to Imogen, adding this personal note.

Fwd to: Imogen.Moss@Hollingworthpr.co.uk
From: Ruby.Taylor@Hollingworthpr.co.uk

Re: Dinner.

How could you??? Both of you??? Talk about
fucking Two-Faced. BTW, you can tell your new
boyfriend where he can stick his bloody ball-
bearings!

Moments later, Ruby had a chance to pass that message on herself.

"John Flett for you," said the Australian receptionist Carina, putting the telephone down quickly but, Ruby convinced herself, not quickly enough to disguise the fact that she was sniggering about Ruby's parlous love-life.

In the time it took for Flett to walk from reception to her office, Ruby fixed her eyes on her computer screen, determined not even to look at the man until she had to. But of course she looked up through her glass door at exactly the wrong time and saw him give Imogen what he probably thought was a discreet little "see you later" wave.

"Hey, Rubes," he said cheerily as he swung into her office like they'd never fallen out. Like they'd never been to bed!

"Good afternoon," said Ruby in her most clipped tones.

"No need for formalities," Flett joked awkwardly. He made to kiss her on the cheek. Ruby ducked backwards and glared at him.

"Busy day?" he asked.

"Very busy," she said with hard-clenched teeth.

The sod was wearing the pink polo shirt she'd bought him! Oh, God. Ruby closed her eyes and had a flashback to the shopping trip. She'd quickly learned that outside the office, John Flett didn't have a clue about dressing. That Italian suit was a one-off. He'd been determined to buy the kind of clothes that shouldn't be seen outside the golf course. She had spent so much time and energy trying to persuade him to try something different. A pair of dark denim jeans instead of those corduroy combat pants that were unfashionable before he even got into them, perhaps? The polo shirt had been a compromise. It was still the duddy side of fuddy-duddy but the pink looked so good with his suntan.

"I bought you that shirt," Ruby couldn't help exclaiming.

"I know," he said. "I thought I probably shouldn't wear it today but . . . Everything else is in the wash." Flett balanced one buttock on the corner of her desk and looked at her earnestly. "Look, I know this is

69

difficult for you, Ruby. It's pretty difficult for me too . . ."

"Excuse me if I don't feel much sympathy for you," Ruby hissed.

"But," Flett ignored her last comment, "we do still have a professional relationship to uphold . . ."

Ruby kept her eyes fixed on the piece of paper that now lay on the desk between them, the hard copy of the press release he had earlier e-mailed. Flett had a baby-boomer's distrust of cyberspace and liked to follow everything up the old-fashioned way. If only he'd stuck to writing letters instead of e-mails, Ruby sighed.

"I hope that you'll be able to work on the Barrington campaign with the same enthusiasm as you had . . ."

"Before you slept with Imogen," Ruby whispered.

Flett cleared his throat. "Imogen? What are you talking about now?"

"Imogen Moss. Of the Two-Faced campaign. Imogen of the other side of my office!"

"Nothing's going on with her . . ." he started.

"Oh, please. Save your breath. You know how when you get an e-mail there are usually a couple of options in the response box?"

Flett wrinkled his forehead. He didn't.

"One of them is reply and one of them is reply *all*," Ruby continued.

"I don't understand."

"No, clearly you don't understand e-mail at all! Or you wouldn't have copied your e-mail finishing our relationship to pretty much everyone in my office. Or

70

sent your e-mail to Imogen inviting *her* to have dinner at The Ivy to me."

Flett rubbed his eye nervously. "You got that?"

"Yes, I did. I forwarded a copy to Imogen so you needn't worry about her missing out on your date."

"Shit," said Flett.

"Yes," said Ruby. "You are."

"God. Ruby. I just . . . I, well, I don't know what to say."

"Don't even bother," she said, raising her palm to his face in a "talk to the hand" gesture. "It's quite nice to see you lost for words for once. I'll look at your amendments to the press release this afternoon. OK?"

Flett nodded. "Sure. I'll, er . . . I'll e-mail you."

Ruby smiled tightly, lifted the title page of the release and stared at the words until she heard him leave her office and close the door behind him. When the door clicked shut, she realised that she had been holding her breath. Now she took a gasp that turned into a sob. And the tears that had been making the words blur in front of her eyes suddenly rained onto that perfect first page.

"A team you can trust," trumpeted the opening line. Pity Ruby couldn't say the same for the company's CEO.

Seeing John Flett exit Ruby's office at speed, Liz Hale, her fellow account manager, was soon by her side. Liz and Ruby had started working at Hollingworth at exactly the same time. That should have made them firm friends but Ruby was never sure whether Liz actually liked her. Lou suggested that Liz was just one of those women who had an unfortunate air of disdain even when she thought she was smiling. That afternoon, however, Ruby had no choice but to cry on Liz's shoulder.

"He's seeing Imogen?" Liz gasped when Ruby told her.

"Stupid bastard sent *me* an e-mail inviting *her* out to dinner."

"Oh no. How could she be so two-faced?" Liz failed to hide a wry smile at her own pun.

"I'm going to have to kill myself," said Ruby, only half-joking.

"Don't be silly. You'll rise above it," said Liz.

"How can I rise above the fact that I've been dumped and I can't even hide myself away and not talk to the sod who did it? I don't want to work on my ex-lover's account. The only solution is for me to quit."

"And work out a month's notice, during which time you'll have to work on his ball-bearings anyway?"

"I hadn't thought of that," said Ruby.

"You're acting like a wounded animal here," Liz told her. "Lashing out, acting from your gut instead of your brain. I wouldn't be your friend if I didn't suggest that you took ten deep breaths and then considered how to find the best in this situation."

Liz was a big fan of "taking ten deep breaths".

"I don't think your yoga breathing is going to make me feel better now," Ruby snapped. "There isn't any 'best' in this situation at all. My ex-lover's new girlfriend works on the other side of this office. I can see her every time I raise my head."

Liz continued regardless. "If you can just apply yourself to the job in hand professionally, think how that will make you look. Everyone will be impressed by your dignity and tenacity at such a difficult time. This will all be old news by the time we get to the summer party . . ."

"The summer party?" Ruby looked as though someone had rescued her from the *Titanic* with an inflatable raft and then burned a hole in it with a careless cigarette.

"Yes," said Liz.

"I'd completely forgotten about that. I can't go to the summer party. Not now. What will everyone say when he turns up with . . ." Ruby swallowed painfully. "Her and I turn up with . . ." she took another huge gulping breath. "No one!"

"There, there," said Liz, patting her on the arm. "I don't suppose many people will notice."

"Of course they bloody will. It's going to be a disaster!" Ruby was plunging back into the abyss without a bungee rope. "I'm not going to have anyone to take to the summer party and he'll be there with Imogen and everyone else will be having a good time and I'll be sitting in a corner and I won't even be able to leave early because the damn party is going to be on a moving boat and the only way out is by swimming. Whose sodding brilliant idea was that one?"

"Well, much as I hate to remind you," said Liz. "It was actually *you* that suggested the river cruise at the first meeting we had back in February."

"Nooooo!" Ruby buried her head in her arms and left a trail of snot all over Flett's press release. Back then, in the first romantic flush of her relationship with him, the idea of a cruise had seemed quite romantic. His arm around her shoulders as they watched the sun set over the Thames. A kiss as they sailed beneath Albert Bridge. "Did I really suggest it?"

"I'm afraid you did."

"Which means I definitely can't get out of it."

"I guess not."

"My life is such a mess."

"Oh, come on, Rubes. It's not that bad. I'll be going on my own too." Liz put her hands on Ruby's shoulders and squeezed tight in an attempt to be comforting. "We could be each other's dates. How about that?"

Ruby lifted her head slowly and looked at Liz with an expression that was half grateful and half disbelief. "Liz. That's so nice of you," she snuffled. "But, it's just not the same. Don't you see? I need to impress Flett, not get a sympathy vote."

"What do you mean by that?"

"I mean, I can't go to the party with a woman. I've got to have a man. Otherwise he's just going to think that I'm another sad old spinster whose little black book should be in the ancient history section of the British Library."

"In that case, Ruby," Liz huffed, "I don't know what more to say to you. The party's less than six weeks

74

away. I wouldn't count on being able to find the man of your dreams in that short a time. I'd better get back to my desk."

"Yeah. Sure. Thanks for the good advice," said Ruby. But as soon as Liz had closed Ruby's office door behind her, Ruby gave her the finger with both hands. "Thanks for bloody nothing, you old cow!"

Liz didn't want Ruby to be happy. That was it. She wanted Ruby to be single, like her, forever and ever and ever so that she had someone to moan with in the corner at every works do from now until they both retired to live with their pet cats in Battersea.

But the awful truth was, Liz was probably right. How on earth was Ruby going to get herself a new boyfriend in time to impress her ex and his new girlfriend at the party? Hire an escort?

Just then, Ruby's assistant, Katherine, poked her head around the door. "Do you want a coffee, Rubes?" She paused, while Ruby tried to compose herself with a quick rake of her fingers through her hair. "Are you OK?"

"I've never been better. No coffee, thanks."

"Okey-doke. I'll just see if Emlyn wants some. Seeing as his temp assistant is off sick today."

"Don't do it, Katherine," Ruby said hopelessly as the girl skipped off hopefully in the direction of the Panter's lair. "All men are bastards."

If only she could stop herself from wanting one so much. Just then, the phone rang.

"Yes?" Ruby snapped.

"Who rattled your pushchair?" asked Lou.

"Oh, it's you."

"Well, don't sound so bloody pleased to hear from me. Look, I'm ringing to say that I think we should still go for my personal ad idea. I've already written a really good one for Martin and I think it would be a laugh and I don't know why the pair of you won't give it a chance and . . ."

"Do you think we could have our first date within a month?" Ruby interrupted.

Lou was taken back by her sudden enthusiasm. "If we get a move on," she said, "we could have one in a fortnight, punters permitting."

"I'll write one for you this afternoon," Ruby told her.

"What's made you change your tune?" asked Lou.

"Desperate times call for incredibly desperate measures," said Ruby.

As soon as Lou hung up, Ruby was on the phone to Martin.

"What have you written about me? What have you said in my ad?" she asked. "It's important, Martin. This isn't just a game."

"Are we doing that personal ad thing?" said Martin.

"Yes, we're doing it!" Ruby snapped.

"Well, I haven't written anything at all yet. I've been busy."

"What do you mean?" Ruby spat. "You're never bloody busy! You sit in your office all day long playing Mine-sweeper."

"I do not," Martin protested.

"You know you do! You told me. How long does it take to write a couple of lines about one of your very best friends anyway? You're supposed to be the wordsmith! You want to be a writer. Well, I'll tell you something right now. You haven't got a hope in hell if you can't stick to a simple deadline."

"Ruby," Martin laughed. "What on earth is wrong with you? If we're really going to do this ridiculous triple date thing, I'll do your ad today. In fact, I can feel the muse flowing through me right now. Desperately seeking . . ."

"If the word 'desperate' or any derivative thereof appears in my ad, I promise I will cut your balls off with a rusty Swiss army knife!"

"Then don't act it," Martin suggested. "What's happened to make you so angsty this afternoon?"

"Flett just came in," Ruby snorted. "He's seeing Imogen from the office. I should have guessed. She's been giving me funny looks all week."

"Maybe she was having trouble with her contact lenses," suggested Martin.

"He's seeing her!" said Ruby in exasperation. "He admitted it. I know he's a shit, but I didn't think he'd turn out to be such a shit that he started seeing someone in my office."

"That isn't very friendly," Martin agreed.

"Anyway, they're going to be all over each other at the summer party and I've got no one to go with except Liz from the office next door. It's terrible."

"That's terrible?" asked Martin.

"Of course it is!"

"Right. I thought you were going to tell me you've got three months left to live and have to have a vaginal orgasm before you die."

"You're not taking me seriously, Martin. I can't go to the summer party with a girl."

"Then take me," said Martin. "I'm always up for a party."

"Oh, yeah. That'll really impress Flett, won't it?"

"OK. If you're worried that he'll think you're just dragging along a friend, we can pretend that we've fallen in love. But you will owe me big time for that particular acting job."

"Martin, that is not what I'm worried about. I just know that he's hardly likely to be impressed by a man sooooo successful that the only designer gear in his wardrobe is a pair of Ralph Lauren socks."

"Thanks a lot!" Martin snorted. "Shall I write 'money-grabbing' instead of 'desperate' when I place your lonely heart . . ."

Ruby pulled her rape whistle out of her handbag and blew it down the phone. Hard. But as soon as she hung up she wished she hadn't been so angry. Martin was going to put her ad in *Loot* now. She knew it. She was doomed.

CHAPTER
EIGHT

Fortunately for Ruby, Lou also knew Martin only too well and quickly warned him that if he scuppered their friend's chance of getting a decent date for the Hollingworth Public Relations summer party by placing her personal ad in a newspaper read only by flat-hunters and wife-swappers she would make sure that his date came equipped with her own pair of nutcrackers.

"Alright!" Martin exclaimed. He duly promised to place his ad for Ruby in the back of the *Financial Times* Saturday supplement. But Lou still groaned when he told her what he planned.

"I thought you'd be pleased," he said. "It's read by people with bucket-loads of money."

"I know. But we're supposed to think of the publication most suited to the person we're writing the ad for. You know, think about a publication that the kind of person Ruby really *needs* to date might read. The demographic of the readership for the *Financial Times* is all wrong. You should know that, doing your job. *FT* readers are all stuffy, right-wing bigots whose idea of a good time is fox hunting or beating poor children with sticks."

"Exactly Ruby's kind of man," Martin pointed out.

"Yeah. Exactly the kind of man that has led her to the mess she finds herself in now. I was rather hoping that we might be able to persuade her to try something different this time around. You know, someone younger. Someone sensitive. Someone nice."

"You mean a *Guardian* reader," said Martin. "Someone who cares about the environment and wears biodegradable sandals?"

"I just mean someone who isn't already married with kids. I'll have to help you sort through the replies," Lou sighed with resignation. "Otherwise this really will be a disaster for poor Rubes."

"What makes you think I don't know what kind of man Ruby needs?"

"Just make sure you don't fix her up with another Flett. That's all I ask."

"I will. But what are you going to do for me in return?"

"Find you a girlfriend who has already taken her A-levels," Lou replied pithily. "And passed them. Tell me exactly what you're going to say about Ruby in this ad of yours."

Martin cleared his throat. "I thought I might go with something like this: pretty, witty PR girl possessed of a fine pair of legs to match her glossy brown mane seeks lively and literate lover. If you could be the Darcy to my Elizabeth Bennett, please write with a photo to box number da-de-dah . . ."

A smile spread across Lou's face as she heard Martin describe their best friend so affectionately, though she was a little doubtful about the equine references. "That's so sweet. And full of lovely mixed metaphors," she added. "Have you ever thought about being a writer?"

"Funny you should say that," Martin replied.

Martin felt thoroughly guilty when he got home that night and saw the true, horrific extent of the layer of dust that had settled on the cover of his laptop during all those months of neglect; even Lou's smiley face and sarcastic "Use Me" message had been all but obliterated by the passage of time. Martin didn't have a duster in the flat, so he pulled off one of his socks and used that instead. His socks were probably due for a wash anyway, he decided as he sniffed at one tentatively. He had been wearing the same pair since Friday.

With the dust wiped away, Martin clicked the laptop open as though he were opening a treasure chest and pressed the long-dormant "on" button. The machine gave a feeble little fizz of indignation at being woken from such a long slumber and the screen flickered for less than a second before it went blank again. The battery, quite understandably, was as dead as Will Shakespeare. Martin would just have to run it off the mains . . .

He couldn't understand it. The adaptor wasn't on the shelf that had been the laptop's home since the day he snapped it shut in a fury after six hours spent staring at the tiny screen that yielded just four hundred faltering words. Neither was it in the drawer where

Martin kept all his writing-related accoutrements: a copy of the *Writers' and Artists' Yearbook* (1988 edition), two sheaves of extremely blank white paper, two unopened ink cartridges for the printer and three A5 notebooks with narrow lines that hadn't had so much as a sniff of inspirational biro since he bought them.

Perhaps it was in the cupboard under the stairs, where Martin kept the Hoover, a broken toaster and a variety of other electrical knick-knacks. Including a hairdryer that once belonged to "Webecca" who couldn't say her "R's". When Webecca arrived one Friday night, two months into their relationship, with that hairdryer and a newly purchased five-pack of knickers from M & S, "because I seem to stay here more often than I stay in my own home these days," Martin knew it was the beginning of the end.

With a shudder at the memory of Webecca's round, red face, Martin shoved the hairdryer back into a box of knick-knacks destined for a car-boot sale — if he ever managed to get up before midday on a Sunday — and continued with his search. Half an hour later, he came to the conclusion that the adaptor was clearly nowhere in the flat. And then he remembered.

"Oh, no. No, please."

He stopped rummaging through the cupboard beneath the kitchen sink and sank back on his heels as the memory took more solid form.

"You'll weg-wet this," Webecca had assured him as Martin legged it away from the house she shared with two other homemade hummus-eating postgrads in Brixton.

"I don't think I will," Martin had replied at the time, unable to imagine a moment when he might miss Webecca's pudgy body or the clammy embrace of her hot little hands stroking his hair. He knew for certain that he would never miss the baby talk. "Martin, I wuv you . . ." But his adaptor . . .

"Aaaaarrrgggghh!"

The Achilles heel he had never imagined.

Martin suddenly found himself having a moment of creative angst.

"What kind of laptop have you got?" he asked Lou over the telephone before she'd had a chance to say hello.

"IBM," she said. "Why?"

"Is that compatible with a Toshiba?"

"I don't think so. These machines are carefully designed so that you can't swap parts and save yourself loads of cash in the process," Lou explained. "Anyway, what's wrong with yours? Worn out through over-use?"

"Ha ha ha. I can't use it because the battery has run flat . . ."

"You just need to charge it . . ." Lou began.

"I know. But I don't have an adaptor."

"Have you looked for it?"

"I loaned my adaptor to Webecca . . ."

"Oh, dear." Lou couldn't help laughing. "Oh, no."

"It's not funny!" Martin protested.

"It is sort of divine justice though, don't you think? You were horrible to her."

"She was a nutter."

"I have to agree," said Lou. Though she and Ruby had come out in Webecca's support immediately after the split, it hadn't taken long for the female fellow feeling to dissolve. "But even a nutter has the right to be a little upset when you tell her you'd rather sleep with Saddam Hussein than see her naked again."

"Did I say that?"

"That's what she told me you said to her when she called *me* in the middle of the night and tried to make me persuade *you* to take her back again. You still owe me for that, by the way. Three hours she was on the phone to me. Three bloody hours in the middle of the night."

"Look, I'm sorry," Martin muttered. "I had no idea she'd do that . . . But do you think you could phone her now and ask for my adaptor back?"

"What!? That was a joke you made just then, right?"

"Lou, I'm desperate. I'll buy you a pint."

"Darling, you would have to buy me a whole bloody brewery before I picked up the phone to your mad ex again."

"She'll be over me by now," Martin pleaded.

"Nope," said Lou. "I just can't take the risk that she isn't. Why don't you just send someone round to burgle it back? You could have them fetch your CDs while they're at it. And *my* CDs." Lou was still faintly exercised by the fact that Webecca had helped herself to, and failed to return, a couple of Lou's own favourite albums that Martin had been borrowing at the time.

"Great idea," said Martin dryly. "Why has this happened to me? I just want to write. I'm foiled at every turn."

"No, you're not. You could just do it the old-fashioned way," Lou suggested.

"How's that?" Martin was confused.

"Pen and paper?" said Lou.

"That's so slow," Martin protested.

"Sounds like it's your only option tonight, Shakespeare."

Martin called three more friends before he gave up on the idea of borrowing an adaptor and admitted that Lou was right. Pen and paper was the only option unless he called Webecca. He took out one of the empty pads and wrote a date at the top of the page. As he did so, he had a sudden glimpse of a glittering future, in which his biographer would leaf through this pad and be grateful for the unhappy sequence of events that led to Martin Ashcroft having to write the early draft of his first great novel by hand.

Half an hour later, Martin was still chewing his pen. The biography fantasy had quickly lost its charm. So much for the connection between body and creativity being facilitated by the old-fashioned method of writing. Martin felt utterly stuck.

He glanced at the clock. It was eight o'clock already. He had three choices. He could continue to sit at the kitchen table and stare at a blank page in a notebook. He could go to the pub and have Lou and Ruby take the mickey out of him for his inability to get started on his magnum opus again. Or he could bite the bullet and call Webecca . . .

Webecca. Would it really be so hard? After all, seven months had passed since Martin ended their relationship. A whole football season had come and gone. The relationship itself had only lasted for two months, start to finish, which meant that, even using Ruby's worst case scenario break-up calculation that it could take up to twice as long as a relationship had lasted to honestly, truly get over it, Webecca should be over him by now. She probably had a new boyfriend, he told himself. Perhaps they could even be friends now. Laugh about the old times? At the very least they should be able to arrange the simple handover of their respective property without involving solicitors.

Convinced that she would at least treat him civilly, Martin dug out his little black book. It was rather smart as little black books go; a present from Ruby a couple of Christmasses previously, the little leather-bound address book from Smythson was embossed with the legend "Blondes, Brunettes and Redheads" on the cover. "Not that you're picky," Ruby had observed.

Martin found himself turning to W for Webecca and was momentarily confused not to find her number there. She was under R, of course. Rebecca Roberts. What an unfortunate name for a girl who couldn't say her "R's". What had her parents been thinking? Ah, well, he supposed there was no way they could have known what their daughter would grow up to sound like. But what had Webecca herself been thinking when she decided to study for a doctorate on "Wacial Disc

Wimination and Mino Wity Wights"? Or chose to live in a street called Wobinson Woad? At number thirty-thwee? It had given Lou hours of fun, at least.

"Seven six four double *thwee* . . ."

"Webecca," he said. "I mean," he cleared his throat. "Rebecca? Is that you?"

"This is *Webecca Woberts*, yes," she said primly. "Can I ask who's calling?"

"It's me. Martin. Martin Ashcroft? Remember?"

There was a sharp intake of breath at the other end of the phone.

"Martin?"

"Yeah. Hi," he said, lightly. "How are you? Just thought I'd give you a call and see, you know, how you're getting on. What you've been up to . . ."

"Waaaaaaaah!" She answered his enquiry with a sob. "I'm still on the *Pwozac*, you bastard."

"Shit. Rebecca, I . . ."

"Don't apologise, Martin. What do you care? You didn't *weturn* any of my calls. You didn't answer my letters. You just cut me out of your life like I never mattered to you at all."

"Rebecca, you know you mattered . . ."

"It's too late now, Martin. I had a nervous *bweak-down*. I had to leave the university and give up my PhD because of you. I spent *thwee* whole months at the *Pwiowy*."

"The Priory?" Martin was actually vaguely impressed. "You mean the place where all the stars go?" Webecca's parents were rumoured to be loaded. He almost asked if she'd met anyone interesting but decided it probably wasn't appropriate.

"*Thwee* months at the *Pwiowy*. Then another *thwee* months waiting for the *Pwozac* to work *pwoperly* and now, just as I'm starting to feel like myself again, you choose to phone me up and ask me how I am. Well, I'm not doing very well, actually and that's one *hundwed* percent thanks to you."

"I'm sorry," said Martin. What else was he supposed to say? "I had no idea."

Webecca suddenly softened. "Oh, Martin. Why did you do it? We had such a good thing when we were together. We were soul mates, Martin. I'd never felt so complete in my life and I know that you felt the same way."

Martin didn't think it was a good moment to tell her that he had actually spent most of the time they shared together wondering how to tell her it was over.

"Is that what you've *wealised?* Have you come to your senses at last? You've been out all alone in the *weal* world and *wealised* that what we had was something special after all?"

"Actually . . ." Martin began.

"I knew this would happen," Webecca continued regardless. "Didn't I tell you that one day you would be back, begging me to *weconsider?* Well, Martin, I want you to tell me why I should. I was emotionally *cwippled* by our *bweak-up*. I lost almost two stone. At one point, the doctors thought they would have to put me on a *dwip*. And did you care? I *wote* to you *evewy* single day. I called you *evewy* night."

And don't I remember, Martin thought.

"I even called your *fwiend*, Louisa. All I wanted was the chance to talk to you *pwoperly*. The chance to make what we had together work again. They told me I was being *widiculous*. They told me I should just forget about you. But I knew that this would happen. I knew that one day I would pick up the phone and hear your voice at the other end of it. And I was going to be *weady* to tell you where to stuff your empty apologies. You blew your chance at happiness, Martin. Our chance. Our one big chance. You don't deserve my forgiveness . . ."

"I know," Martin interjected politely.

"But I'm *pwepared* to give you one more go. I know it will be hard. There are lots of things we need to talk about but I think that we can work *thwough* all the *pwoblems* we had and make our *welationship stwonger* for the time we've spent apart."

"Rebecca, hang on," Martin interrupted. "I didn't . . ."

"Expect me to be so level-headed about this? No. I'm sure you didn't."

"Rebecca," Martin said hopelessly. "I really was just calling to say hi."

"What?" she said.

"And," he took a deep breath against the sudden pregnant silence at the other end of the line. "To ask whether you've still got the adaptor for my laptop."

"Your what?"

"My adaptor. You borrowed it before we split up. Remember? I need it back now. That's what I called you to say. And I've got your hairdryer. I thought

89

perhaps we could do a swap? Over coffee?" he added, not wanting to sound as though he was interested in being her friend.

"Waaaaaaahhhhhhh!" Webecca began again. "Waaaaaaaaaaaaaaaaaaahhhhhhhh!!!!"

"Oh, God." Martin closed his eyes and prayed for the honking sobbing to be over quickly. Three minutes later, when it was clear that Webecca was neither about to stop crying, nor put the phone down on him, Martin knew he had no option but to put the phone down on her instead.

"Bye, Rebecca," he muttered as he did it. He didn't think she heard. "Bugger."

Lou was right. A woman spurned is a woman who is never going to give back the adaptor for your laptop.

Martin was left with the other two options. Frustration at home. Humiliation in the pub. He sank back into his chair and let the waves of irritation wash over him. He would never write his novel. He was doomed to be stuck at *The Satyr* forever . . . Stuck in that office. Staring at that PC. Playing Minesweeper until his mouse-finger broke . . .

"Hang on a minute."

Martin had a Eureka moment.

He grabbed his denim jacket, his tube pass *and* his security pass for the International Magazines building. Then he headed off to squeeze those ideas out of his brain and into Times New Roman Twelve Point at the office.

CHAPTER
NINE

Though it wasn't Wednesday night, Ruby had demanded a crisis summit at the Hare and Hounds in view of that day's horrifying revelations. Lou had tried to calm her down over the phone.

"No, Ruby, I really don't think you can have someone sacked because they've stolen your boyfriend. I perfectly agree that it would be nice for you if you could, but I don't think it would go down well in the European Court of Human Rights."

"But I feel so betrayed!" Ruby whined.

"Imagine how his wife must have felt when he started seeing you. Honestly, Ruby, these men never change their spots. He dumped his wife for a younger model. He dumped you for Imogen. He's going down the age range so rapidly that next week he'll dump Imogen for some girl who's still revising for her GCSEs. Then you can have him arrested," Lou added, in a desperate bid to lighten the tone.

"That is not funny," said Ruby.

"Ooops, there goes my other line," Lou lied. "I'll see you at the pub."

★　★　★

Sometimes, Lou reflected, she felt as though Martin and Ruby viewed her more as a surrogate mother than a friend. Take that day alone. First she had to deal with Ruby's Flett-related histrionics, then Martin — altogether more low key — but equally demanding as he expected Lou to come up with a solution to his adaptor problem other than waiting for the shops to open next day. He hadn't even properly apologised for leaving Lou to deal with the "Webecca" problem first time round. Lou had to screen her phone calls for two months — home and office — after Martin's break-up with the girl and still he had refused to put her, and Lou, out of their misery. Sometimes, just sometimes, thought Lou, it would be nice to have someone that she could off-load on too.

That said, Lou didn't miss much about the men she had been with in the past. She certainly didn't miss the way her old boyfriends seemed to think that a month or so of super romantic chivalry bought them a year of her services, not only as a lover, but as a mother in the kitchen and, more often than not, as a secretary too. Lou shook her head with disbelief as she remembered taking a day of *her* leave to sit in one guy's flat, waiting for a plumber who never arrived to fix his ailing Zanussi. And when it turned out that the washing machine was beyond repair, he didn't rush out to buy a new one. Oh no. Instead, he started bringing his laundry round to Lou's, letting her get on with it while he flicked endlessly through the channels on her telly.

The departure of the last man from Lou's life had actually resulted in a marked improvement in her standard of living. Less washing-up and the ability to watch whatever she wanted, when she wanted to, without relinquishing the remote control to a being who hit the channel changer like a lab rat pressing the lever in its cage for snacks. No longer would Lou grab a carton of milk from the fridge only to discover that someone else had not only downed a whole pint since that morning but had thoughtfully put the empty carton back to remind her to get another one.

It would take someone extremely special to persuade Lou to give up that freedom again. Very special indeed.

But how would Lou recognise that person? The answer to that question, no matter who she asked, always seemed to be "you will just *know*". Well, Justin had seemed like a great catch when Lou first met him. Handsome, funny, in full-time and lucrative employment. It took a whole year for her to realise that he was also vain and irritating and viewed his full-time employment as altogether more important than hers — hence she was the one left doing his washing while he flicked through the channels.

Erica, who had the office next door to Lou's and seemed to have been single since the dawn of time, suggested that everyone should come with references from their previous lovers. "You wouldn't dream of giving someone a job without checking their references," she reasoned. "So why should you sleep with someone whom you know next to nothing about?"

"Because none of us would ever get a shag again if our exes wrote us references," Lou pointed out.

"Ah. Didn't think of that," said Erica.

"References from your friends might be a good idea though." And Lou explained the Lonely Hearts Pact to her colleague. "I know both of them better than they know themselves. I'm sure I can find the right woman for Martin."

"But do you think Ruby can find the right man for you?" Erica asked.

Lou's mind wandered briefly to the stranger on the tube. "That I'm not so sure about."

That night Lou took the tube down to Clapham to meet the others at the Hare and Hounds. Since the morning when she and her fantasy lover locked eyes over the idiot with the *Financial Times*, every tube journey had taken on new excitement. Whereas previously Lou might have travelled the length of the Northern Line in a packed carriage with her pelvis squished up against Joe Fiennes' buttocks and not noticed so long as she had a manuscript to bury her nose in, now she was acutely aware of the people travelling in every tube carriage with her. More to the point, she was acutely aware of the one person who wasn't sharing her journey.

There was little chance that the mystery commuter would be on the same tube train tonight but Lou's heart still quickened a little as she skipped down the stairs to the south-bound platform.

"This is ridiculous," she reminded herself as she searched the length of the platform for that fleetingly familiar face, getting that nauseous, hollow feeling of anxious excitement when she saw a blond head bent low over the *Evening Standard*.

She couldn't quite believe she was allowing herself to get so worked up about a person whose name she didn't even know. Someone she had seen for less than a minute, for heaven's sake! Lou had never been the type of girl who believed in fate or love at first sight and all those fairytale endings and yet here she was, sure that she had glimpsed a soul mate and chewing at her cuticles (a nervous habit she had managed to give up only a year before) because she thought that she might have let the chance to find true and lasting love slip away.

Because her racing heart, her churning stomach, the way she had started taking the tube for even those short journeys she once would have walked in less time than it took for the train to arrive, all told Lou she must have fallen in love. And yet there were a million reasons why her stranger probably wasn't the one. Couldn't be the one, in fact.

"I'll *never* meet the one for me," Ruby said dramatically, as she slammed her empty glass down on the table. "I've had my last chance at love. I'm all loved out. I don't think I can ever bring myself to trust someone the way I trusted Flett again."

"Nonsense," said Lou. "Just wait till those replies to your ad start coming in."

"What's he put?" Ruby asked. Martin was safely out of earshot at the bar. "You haven't let him put anything about me being desperate, have you?"

"I made sure he represented you accurately," said Lou.

"Which is desperate," Ruby confirmed.

Martin grinned as he arrived at the table just in time to catch the tail end of the girls' discussion.

"What kept you so late tonight?" Lou asked.

"I've been writing my novel," said Martin proudly.

"Seriously?" said Lou excitedly. "You resorted to pen and paper after all?"

"No. I went into the office and used my computer there."

"So you didn't get the adaptor back?" Lou asked.

"You were right about Webecca."

"She isn't over you?"

"Not hardly. She wants to send me the bill for her Prozac."

"Are you kidding?" Ruby asked. "You split up, what, seven months ago?"

"You were the one who said it takes twice as long to get over a relationship as the whole thing lasted in the first place."

"Then I'm doomed until next September," Ruby cried.

"Don't be silly. Life can turn around in a day," Lou reminded them.

"Yeah. I could get knocked over by a bus tomorrow," said Ruby gloomily. "That would certainly shorten my recovery time."

"Or you could meet the man of your dreams on the top deck," Lou countered.

And then she told them. "I saw someone I really fancied on the tube the other day. Not just fancied," she added. "Someone I felt I had a connection with. I wish I had plucked up the courage to speak before they got off the train."

"You could have followed," said Ruby.

"And been late for my editorial meeting? Don't think that would have gone down well."

"I would have thought you supremely romantic and given you a promotion on the spot for being a joyful, spontaneous person," said Ruby.

"And that's why you don't run a multinational publishing conglomerate," Lou pointed out. "Anyway, what's the real chance of a perfect stranger wanting to give you their phone number? If this person had stayed on the tube for one more stop, if I'd been able to find the courage to actually speak, I'm sure I would have said something stupid or spat all over them or something equally charming. I wouldn't have got a phone number. I'd have got a hard stare and a poke in the eye with the end of an umbrella."

"No," said Ruby. "I don't think so. Wouldn't you be thrilled, Martin, if a girl asked you for your phone number on the tube?"

"It's every man's dream," Martin assured them. "You girls don't know how lucky you've had it, being the ones who get asked out all the time. Being of the sex that has to do most of the asking, I can tell you what a nightmare it is. You don't know fear until you're face to face with a woman you fancy, trying to find a line that will make her laugh out loud and not slap you."

"See," said Ruby. "You should have gone for it, Lou. Men love being propositioned."

Lou smiled and shrugged. "I'm sure they do."

"So. What did this gorgeous stranger of yours look like?" Ruby asked.

"Tall, fair-ish hair, wearing a dark blue suit. Slim."

"That certainly narrows down the field of perfect strangers travelling on the tube during rush hour," said Martin sarcastically.

"I can't think of anything specific about the way they looked. But I instantly felt we were *simpatico*. There was a moment when our eyes met and it was as if we'd known each other before. Forever."

Martin began to play heartfelt chords on an imaginary violin.

Ruby was less cynical. "You've come over all new-agey, Lou. You'll be believing your horoscope next and only dating men with the moon in Scorpio."

"I'll never get that sad," Lou assured her. "But I feel pretty sad now, talking to you about this. If only London weren't such an unfriendly city we might have stopped and talked. Struck up a friendship at least." She looked wistfully towards the door of the pub, as though the winds of fate might blow her stranger in. "As it is, I don't suppose we'll ever see each other again."

"You might if you make sure you catch the same tube every morning," said Ruby excitedly.

"I do catch the same tube every morning. More or less. I'd never seen that particular person before."

"You just mean you'd never noticed them before," Ruby corrected. "That's different. Now that you've established some sort of rapport, I bet you start to see them every day. All you've got to do is keep smiling and start saying 'good morning' and before you know it you'll be one of those Underground love stories the *Evening Standard* runs every Valentine's Day to make us feel that London isn't such a heartless toilet of a city after all." She clapped her hands together at the thought of it.

"Perhaps," said Lou, "but I doubt it."

Later that evening, a slow smile spread over Ruby's lips as the perfect solution to the trouble she was having with writing Lou's ad formed in her mind. She'd been finding it difficult to think of a good way to describe Lou and next to impossible to imagine what kind of man her friend would really like. But now she had the answer.

In the back of *Time Out*, the London listings magazine, beneath the ordinary Lonely Hearts ads, is a column entitled Once Seen. Even before the personal ad pact, Ruby had made a habit of reading this column, where people would leave messages intended to jog the memory of someone they had met only briefly and longed to see again. Ruby loved it. The idea that someone might have glimpsed her across Waterloo Station and been unable to put her out of his mind ever since had her turning to the Once Seen column before she read anything else.

The possibility of finding yourself described in Once Seen was, to Ruby, as exciting as waiting for a sixth number on the lottery.

Ruby was decided. She wouldn't place an ordinary ad for Lou at all. Instead, she would place a Once Seen describing Lou and the mysterious Prince Charming on the Northern Line. She got quite excited as she imagined her plan succeeding and Lou's thrilled surprise at discovering her blind date was the person she already knew she fancied.

Ruby shared the idea with Martin as they caught the night bus back home.

"What will you put?" he asked. "How do you know what she was wearing that day?"

"I'm guessing she was probably wearing what she wore to the pub that night. Did she come straight from work, d'you know?"

"I think so."

"Can't you remember?"

"You're the girl. As a generalisation, we boys wouldn't notice if you turned up in a sack as long as we could see some cleavage."

"Yeah." Ruby recognised an accusation she herself had made several times before. "Well, could you see any cleavage?" Ruby had to ask.

Martin put his hand to his chin as he thought back to the evening in question. "Nope," he said. Then, as though he had just discovered Archimedes' principle again, Martin's eyes lit up. "But she was wearing a miniskirt. I distinctly remember looking at her knees."

"Martin!"

"I just can't help myself," he sighed. "Lou's got fantastic knees."

Ruby glanced down at her own rather knobbly ones and pulled her skirt to cover them.

"You've got nice knees, too," Martin insisted.

"You don't mean that," said Ruby.

"OK, your knees are awful but your tits are fabulous. How about that?"

"You sod!" said Ruby, swatting him with her handbag. She pulled a disgruntled face but was secretly rather flattered. "Are they better than Lou's?" she asked moments later.

"Better than most women's."

"Only most?" echoed Ruby.

Martin sensed immediately that he might be about to make a faux pas equivalent to telling a girl that her bum did look big in that. "Joking!" he assured her.

"What? Joking that there are better boobs than mine or that mine are better than most?"

Martin paled.

"Forget it," said Ruby. "It's not as though I care what you think anyway."

"Then why are you getting so angry with me?" Martin asked.

"I'm not," Ruby insisted. "Like I said, it really doesn't matter whether you think I look good or not. In fact, I'd rather be one of the rare women that you don't find attractive." She hoped she sounded dismissive but was frighteningly aware that she didn't. "So we know she was wearing a miniskirt," she said quickly to change the subject. "I'll put this. Monday morning. Northern

101

Line. You in the blue suit. Me in the miniskirt reading
. . . What's she reading at the moment?"

"I dunno. Wild Geese or something like that?"

"*Wild Swans*," corrected Ruby. "That must be it.
Doesn't exactly mark her out though. Everybody you
see on the tube is reading it. Unless they're reading
Captain Corelli's Mandolin or *Harry Potter*."

"That's why it's perfect," said Martin. "You don't
want to narrow her options down."

"But there aren't any options," said Ruby. "I want to
find her perfect stranger!"

"Oh yeah. Right."

"What tube station did she say he got off at?" Ruby
continued.

"Er. Northern Line, wasn't it? Camden Town? Put
that."

"OK. I will. What did you write for me, Mart?" Ruby
asked as she snuggled up against him now. "Where did
you place my advert?"

"I can't tell you that. You know it's against the rules."

"I've told you what I'm doing for Lou," Ruby
reasoned.

"Yeah. But you haven't told me what she's written
about me, have you?"

"I swear I don't know or I would. Just pick me a
good one. Swear you won't pick the worst of the bunch
for the fun of it and I will make sure Lou finds you a
princess," Ruby promised.

"Then Prince Charming will be yours in return."

★　★　★

Meanwhile, Lou found herself waiting at the tube station again. A train arrived. Lou stepped into a completely empty carriage. She chose a seat by the double-doors and checked the cushions for chewing gum before she ruined her trousers. No gum, thank goodness. But someone had left behind a copy of that week's *Time Out*.

Instinctively, Lou flicked straight to the personal ads. *Time Out* was one of the publications where she thought she might advertise Martin and his charms to an eager female population. She scanned down through Men Seeking Women, Women Seeking Men, Women Seeking Women . . . Then she came to a section she hadn't really noticed before. Once Seen.

There was just one three-line ad in this section:

Eurostar Ticket Office Waterloo 15/5. You, brown hair, red trousers. Me, blue shirt, black jeans. You smiled. I dropped my coffee.

There followed a box number. A larger boxed message explained the purpose of the Once Seen ads. They were meant exactly for people like Lou and her Northern Line stranger. People who had shared a fleeting glance, an uncertain smile, and later wished they'd done something about it. Lou folded the magazine and slipped it into her voluminous nylon bag. Perhaps she'd place an ad of her own.

CHAPTER
TEN

Next morning, the telephonist at *Time Out* took two personal ads for the following week's Once Seen column. The first, called in by a girl, who sounded bizarrely as though she wasn't sure quite where she had seen her perfect stranger, read:

> Wednesday morning, Northern Line. Me in black miniskirt, reading *Wild Swans*. You in the blue suit, blond hair. Would love to meet you again.

The second ad was another Northern Liner. Wednesday morning too. Shame that the second caller wasn't a bloke, thought the telephonist as she tapped the details of this second person into her machine. Wouldn't it have been amazing if the two ads had been placed by a girl and a guy wanting another chance with each other? That had happened once before. A French exchange student and a busker avoiding the police had bumped into each other on Victoria Station and got chatting while he helped her pick up her dropped books. They didn't swap numbers at the time — both too shy to ask — but three days later they both tried to place a Once

Seen. Ellie the telephonist was able to put them in touch with each other straight away. The ads never even had to run. They sent her a card to thank her for arranging their first date. That was nice, that. She wondered if they were still going out . . .

Unfortunately, that morning's advertisers, both girls, obviously weren't looking for each other.

"I'll just repeat that back to you," she told the second caller.

"Northern Line, last Wednesday morning. Me in grey trouser suit strap-hanging, you in the blue suit leaning against door. Winked at me over man with *FT* before you got out at King's Cross. Wish I'd said hello."

"When will that go in?" Lou asked.

"Next week's issue," said Ellie.

"Do you think there's any chance it will work?" Lou mused.

"They often do," Ellie told her. "Don't forget to invite me to the wedding if it does."

"Sure," Lou laughed. "You'll be first on the guest list."

She put the phone down and smiled at the thought. A wedding? Little chance of that, Lou knew. But she still felt extremely excited. The future of her relationship with the perfect stranger was in the lap of the gods now. She'd done as much as she could do, bar spending her entire day travelling up and down by Underground until they found themselves in the same

105

carriage again. Now all she could do was hope that her fantasy lover read *Time Out*, or at least knew someone who did. And pray that the stranger was actually a Londoner and not just someone on a fleeting business trip to London who usually lived in New York or Paris. And silently wish that they had been feeling the same way about Lou ever since; would recognise the way she had described their encounter, and not be absolutely horrified by the idea of a date with a girl glimpsed briefly on the Underground . . .

Meanwhile, Martin placed his ad for Ruby in the Style section of *The Sunday Times*. Despite Lou's reservations, Martin was convinced that *The Sunday Times* was the best place to introduce Ruby's obvious charms to the dating market. Lou was relieved that he hadn't used the *Financial Times* after all, but she still lobbied hard for the *Guardian*, beloved of soft-hearted lefties such as she thought Ruby needed for a mate. Martin, however, was firm in his opinion that the last thing Ruby needed was a vegetarian basket-weaver for a boyfriend. At least by advertising her in *The Sunday Times*, Martin felt he had some way of ensuring that the man he matched Ruby up with would be solvent. And these things did matter.

"Marxism is all very romantic," he explained, "but it doesn't pay for dinner."

Lou had to console herself with the fact that she had at least managed to persuade Martin to do away with the horsey metaphors about good legs and a "glossy mane", and Ruby's ad finally went into print like this:

Summer is here! Don't spend it alone. Let this beautiful, vivacious, intelligent woman, 31, be your sunshine . . .

"What do you think?"

"Not bad," Lou had to admit. "I'll try and live up to it on the phone message."

Lou had to record the accompanying telephone message, pretending to be Ruby. She knew that Ruby would probably have to do the same for her since, for many publications, one of the conditions of placing an ad was that you recorded a supplementary phone greeting.

There was no need to have Martin record a message to go with his ad, however. After careful consideration, Lou had decided that she wouldn't place Martin's personal in a newspaper after all. Instead, she typed his details into the database of an Internet dating agency called pinacoladalovematch.com, a homage to the Barry Manilow song in which two estranged lovers rediscover each other through the lonely hearts and their mutual love of pina coladas and making love in the rain. When the ad was written, Lou scanned in the best picture of Martin she had in her collection. Unfortunately, it was five years old, but Lou felt it wouldn't be too misleading. He was aging remarkably well. She looked over the final ad copy.

Why am I still single? Prince? No. Charming? Definitely. Good-looking, funny, affectionate

male (31) seeks interesting, intelligent woman
for friendship and fun. Maybe more.

"I can't wait to see how you've described me," Lou told
Ruby. "Slinky? Sexy? Supercalifragilistic?"

Ruby shook her head wisely. "I promise you will
never guess."

So, the lonely hearts had been placed. Each of the
friends was secretly smug that he or she had written the
personal ad that would finally usher true and lasting
love into the life of the person they had been writing
for. Ruby in particular was excited. It was as though
they had each bought a ticket to a raffle with the best
prize in the universe and this time she actually felt
lucky. Yes, indeed. For some unknown reason, she was
extremely confident that true love was waiting just the
other side of the weekend. It might have been
something to do with her horoscope, which promised
"big surprises" for that month.

The following weekend over brunch at the Café
Rouge, the friends were able to assure each other that
all of their ads had been published. While Lou and
Martin debated the merits of *Supergrass* versus
Coldplay, Ruby ploughed her way through every single
newspaper she could lay her hands on. Was she the
"voluptuous brunette" in *The Sunday Times* or the "shy
but sexy animal-lover" in the *Independent*. What about
the "curvaceous cutie" described in the *News of the
World*? She hoped to God she wasn't the "damaged and

dangerous damsel" she found advertised in the back of the *Sunday Telegraph*.

"Just think," she said, stirring her cappuccino dreamily. "Right now, somewhere out there is the man of my dreams. He's reading Martin's brilliant description of me while he eats his toast and Marmite. When he's finished his breakfast he'll pick up that phone. He'll listen to the message that Lou recorded for me and find himself intrigued . . ."

Martin and Lou shared a smile.

CHAPTER
ELEVEN

Martin's late nights at the office had quickly become a regular occurrence since the spotty boy in the computer shop informed him that it would take eight weeks for the out-of-stock adaptor he required to arrive. In any case, Martin found the office atmosphere strangely conducive to productivity once everyone else had gone home. Each evening at five thirty, he would pack up his tattered nylon record bag, leave the International Mags building by the front door and head for the café across the street. Once there, he would buy a cappuccino, sit two tables back from the window so that nobody looking in would notice him immediately and watch the doors of International Mags until Barry emerged at six o'clock sharp and rushed to catch his train home to Essex. When Barry was safely out of sight, Martin would head straight back into the office and resume work on his novel.

It was important to Martin that Barry didn't know he was staying late in the office night after night. Martin didn't know whether using the company's equipment for his own purposes would actually be a sacking offence, but he knew for sure that it would be a sneering one. He didn't want to have to explain himself and his creative ambitions to a Philistine like Barry Parsons. More importantly, he didn't want to open himself up to a more vicious version of the ridicule that Lou and Ruby had been affectionately dishing out for years.

The novel was going quite well though, Martin cautiously admitted to himself. In an early flurry of enthusiasm, he had bought a couple of books on the subject of writing from Amazon.com. The authors of those worthy books, who didn't actually seem to have written a *novel* between them, gave conflicting advice about what made a good novel great, but Martin at least picked up some tips about presenting a manuscript for publication.

The hero of Martin's own meisterwork, as yet untitled, was a bloke called Mark, an affable chap, trapped in a boring McJob, who harbours a secret crush on his female best friend. Throughout the story, the best friend, a girl called Ruthie, did her best to set him up with ultimately unsuitable women. At the end of the book, some sort of crisis would bring Mark and Ruthie together and make them realise what they really had beyond the friendship they'd always relied on. Martin wasn't sure what the crisis would be yet but he had already written the scene where Mark and Ruthie realise they've been in love with each other all along and share a passionate embrace beneath the fairy lights on Albert Bridge.

In fact, in the week after realising that Webecca would never give him his adaptor back, Martin had written what he considered to be seven great scenes. He could already see Hugh Grant playing his hero in the screenplay adaptation. He was a good-looking lad. But it was equally important, thought Martin, that the director chose someone who would bring out the intellectual quality in Mark's character as well as make him look good.

As for who would play the lovely Ruthie, Martin had initially plumped for Michelle Pfeiffer — he'd had a crush on the doe-eyed actress since seeing *Dangerous Liaisons*, aged seventeen, and thought she had the perfect mixture of serenity and vulnerability. But, lovely as she was, poor Michelle would probably be too old to play a thirty-something by the time the book was published and the film went into production . . . Into production! Martin gave himself a mental slap round the head for being so cocksure that anyone would even like his book enough to waste paper printing it. But it was good, he decided quietly. In fact, some of it was great.

Last job of each night, before Martin left the office after a writing stint, was to check the replies to Ruby's advert in *The Sunday Times*. The replies had started to come in almost immediately. Not that Martin was surprised that anyone would want to date his friend. He was, however, surprised at the number of men who seemed willing to date a person described in two lines in a national newspaper. There were three calls on the first night alone and many more during the week as the married men dialled in from the office.

112

And didn't some of them go on? Martin was glad it wasn't him who had to pay the phone bill as he listened to Hugh from High Wycombe drivel on about the responsibilities his "exciting" job as an actuary entailed.

"I find my work very fulfilling and challenging," he concluded, just as Martin was falling asleep.

If the lonely hearts game was all about selling yourself, then most of the men who called Ruby positioned themselves firmly in the bargain basket by the checkouts with the broken boxes of biscuits and dented tins the second they opened their mouths.

Martin skipped through the replies pretty ruthlessly after the first couple of nights, instantly cutting from his list of hopefuls anyone who hesitated too long before speaking. Anyone with a voice he discerned to be more than a semi-tone above his own. Anyone with an accent too posh or too regional. Anyone who mentioned what car he drove . . .

Cars were a particularly sore point in Martin's life. Since Barry Parsons decided that Martin no longer needed a company car and his beloved Ford Puma was returned to the garage, Martin had been forced to drive his sister's old Fiesta. It was good of her to let him have it (her husband bought her a Ka for her thirty-fifth birthday) but it made Martin feel like an idiot. Ford Fiestas were girly cars (an image not helped by the extraordinarily permanent flower stickers that Marie had plastered all over it).

Martin did realise that there was something faintly hypocritical about his decision to disqualify men who mentioned the car they drove considering the fact that he had placed Ruby's ad in *The Sunday Times* precisely because he wanted to make sure she found someone solvent. But he justified it to himself by saying that there was a difference between being *successful* and being a *show-off* and mentioning the make and model of car you drove in the space of a two-minute recorded message to a woman you've never met before was definitely showing-off.

Flett had been a show-off, Martin remembered. And Ruby deserved something better than another Flett. Martin had hated the man from the first time he met him at one of Ruby's legendary dinner parties. Flett had been sitting in an armchair, pontificating about the importance of his bloody ball-bearings while Ruby rushed about the kitchen like a Stepford wife. He criticised everything Ruby put before him. The perfect, absolutely perfect, fish was, according to Ruby's new boyfriend, woefully over-cooked. The sauce was too full of butter. "Got to watch your figure, sweetheart." The potatoes were too hard.

Martin had to bite his tongue not to tell Flett exactly where he could stick his culinary expertise and resorted instead to countering each and every one of Flett's criticisms with a compliment. It was a strangely familiar experience, taking Martin back to Sunday lunch with his mum and dad and sister. Mum working so hard to please everyone. Dad shouting instructions from the carving chair.

Martin shuddered at the thought of Ruby ending up with someone like his dad. Someone who would chip away at her over the years. She deserved a man who

114

would think himself the luckiest man in the world when Ruby smiled at him, not someone intent on making her feel grateful for crumbs of his time. The man Martin wanted for Ruby would be generous, funny and indulgent.

In short, what Martin wanted for Ruby was a "good bloke". Someone who wouldn't be taken in by all that "Rules" rubbish either. Someone who wouldn't want to spend his life with a girl who always wore lipstick but never cracked a smile. Someone Martin would want to have a pint with. Someone he knew would take care of her. Someone a bit like him, in fact.

Lou checked that week's edition of *Time Out* to see whether her ad had been printed. And there it was. Right beneath the Once Seen title. Lou skimmed the words to check that nothing had been missed out or simply misspelled so badly that her perfect stranger wouldn't recognise her even if they did read the ad. It was exactly as she had dictated it.

But right beneath Lou's own ad was another that intrigued her. The person who had written this ad was referring to the same tube line on the same date. Even looking for another blue-suited lover.

"Good luck," Lou murmured to her fellow Once Seener. "Let's hope it works for at least one of us.

Three days later, however, there was nothing. Not one reply to Lou's appeal. Four days later, still nothing. A week later. Still nothing at all.

In contrast, by this time, Lou's Internet ad for Martin had attracted so many interested women that she was beginning to wonder whether she would need to take on a secretary to help her weed out the good ones from the girls who were clearly mad, bad or just too plain sad to consider.

"And even though he said that he wasn't leaving me for anyone else," wrote Mary from High Barnet, "when I went to the pub the following Friday he was already with another girl. Well, he must have been seeing her all along, don't you think? You sound like a nice bloke though," she continued. "I really like the way you described yourself in your ad. It makes me feel sure you'd never do anything so hurtful . . ."

Perhaps they should display the number for the Samaritans at the top of the pinacoladalovematch.com site thought Lou, as she deleted an e-mail from the next hopeless candidate. From fifteen replies down to two almost instantly. Finding the right woman for Martin wasn't going to be as easy as throwing dynamite into a fish-tank after all.

When the rest of that week produced no more hopeful dates, Lou toyed with the idea of going back through the replies the ad had attracted and deliberately picking out the worst of the bunch. It was strictly against the rules of the Lonely Hearts Pact to go for someone that you didn't consider in your opinion to be the *best* possible match for your victim, but as far as Martin was concerned, it was quite possible that the woman Lou considered to be the booby prize would be exactly the one he would go for.

Lou had never met such a hopeless bunch of girls as Martin's exes. Much as she wanted to be able to be kind about her fellow women, it was difficult to find much to be impressed by in the cohort of needy, clingy or downright pathetic creatures he was wont to fall in love with. It never failed to shock Lou that her friend Martin, who seemed to enjoy the company of intelligent women (i.e. herself and Ruby) so much, would so often end up with the kind of girls who thought that Nietzsche was an STD. Webecca, the PhD student, had been a rare exception to the rule. But she became an honorary "Twit-girl" due to the fact that she was very good at hiding her intelligence in the company of men and Martin in particular.

"Insecurity," Ruby had diagnosed one late night on vodka and Pringles. "That's why Martin always goes for such thickos. It's a rare man who can see himself married to a woman he actually feels equal to."

It was an idea that Ruby was clinging to at that moment. She had decided that Flett had ended their relationship because he was threatened by her intelligence. "Men in our generation know, in a rational sense, that they should go for a woman who can hold her own in the boardroom as well as the kitchen, but, at a primal level," she continued. "In their mid-brains, there's still something that compels them to fight to be top dog. Look at the way Martin reacts when you beat him on the Nintendo."

It was true that if either of the girls beat Martin on a computer game, or on the tennis courts, or even at cards, there would have to be rematch after rematch

117

until Martin finally came out on top. If he managed to win in a "best of three" competition, he would often risk defeat and make it "best of five" just to increase the margin.

And Martin would probably be very happy indeed with the kind of woman that Lou couldn't have a conversation with, as long as that woman had longish hair and big breasts to distract him from her lack of conversational ability. Lou was about to admit defeat and pick out "fluffybunny69@aol.com" who had talked about her new Burmese kittens, in response to Martin's request that e-mailers tell him something about their "passions" . . . But no. This wasn't just about finding Martin a date he would like. It was about finding a date that would be good for him. There was still time yet.

Wednesday night at the pub quiz, Martin and Lou were able to confirm that their ads had received considerable interest.

"You had fifteen replies last night," Lou told Martin.

"See," said Martin. "No woman can resist me."

"Or man," Lou told him with a smile. "I assumed you wouldn't fancy a date with Simon from West Kensington. Straight-acting though he is."

"Have I had many replies yet?" Ruby asked Martin eagerly.

"One or two," said Martin dismissively. "But no one I think suitable yet. I don't like the sound of any of them."

"Martin, you can't just go ticking everyone off because you don't like them," Ruby reminded him. "You've got to consider what I might think too."

"I bet he's just dismissing the ones with better cars than him," said Lou perceptively. "Or anyone taller or richer or . . ."

"You better not be," Ruby warned him.

"I'm acting in your best interests," Martin assured her.

"How about me?" Lou asked Ruby then. "What kind of smorgasbord of talent has lined itself up for me to take my pick from next weekend?"

"Er," Ruby looked down at her empty glass and swirled a solitary ice-cube around a little distractedly. "I'm sure there will be replies soon," she said at last. "Though if there still isn't anything tonight I'm going to ring the paper and make sure that they've got the reply box set up properly."

"You mean that *no one* has called or written to ask for a date with me?" Lou was surprised. "No one at all? What did you advertise me as? *Desiccated old harridan seeking immediate marriage to toy-boy*?"

"Of course not," said Ruby at once. "It's just that you could say I wrote an ad that I know will only appeal to a very specific type of person — extremely specific in fact — so that when there is a reply I know that it will be exactly the right one. There'll be no question about that." She nodded, confident that she had clarified the situation without giving too much away. Lou looked askance at such an odd explanation.

119

"OK," Lou said finally. "I have no idea what you're on about, but I trust you both to make sure that I'm not sitting alone at the bar eating peanuts while you two have the romantic evening of your lives at Suave."

The restaurant they had chosen was supposed to be one of the hottest new eateries in town.

"Lou, you will have your date," Ruby insisted. "I swear on Martin's life." She had her fingers crossed behind her back as she said that.

A week later, Ruby was beginning to get really worried. Lou and Martin were still expecting the date to go ahead that Friday evening and Ruby's appeal for Lou's handsome stranger had yet to elicit a single response. She was beginning to wonder whether she had made a terrible mistake . . . Forget wonder, Ruby *knew* she had made a terrible mistake. Lou's dream lover clearly wasn't the kind of man who read *Time Out* after all and, thanks to her stupid romantic optimism, Ruby had left it much too late to place another ad in a different paper as a contingency plan. Lou was going to be dateless. What a monumental cock-up.

Ruby decided that as soon as she got to the office that morning she would have to call Lou and come clean about her mistake. Perhaps Lou might be interested in one of the men who had replied to the ad Martin placed for Ruby instead? Under pressure the night before, and with Ruby twisting his arm up behind his back until he thought his shoulder might have dislocated, Martin had admitted that Ruby's ad had elicited fifteen replies. Fifteen! Not all of them could be terrible.

Just as Ruby was tying her shoelaces by the front door, the post dropped onto the doormat.

Bills. Bills. Bills. Ruby wandered back into the kitchen and put her Visa statement in a prominent position, propped up against the toaster, so that she would remember to pay it. There was an invitation from Clarins to try some new beauty product. Ruby scanned that quickly to check that they weren't offering a miracle, overnight "be beautiful for your big blind date" treatment. They weren't. And finally there was a brown envelope. A big one. Ruby slit it open and another smaller envelope fell out.

She was momentarily confused as she looked at the address written in tidy hand on the crisp blue paper.

To The Girl of My Dreams, Box number 3567.

"Yes! Success!" Ruby punched the air triumphantly. It was a reply to her ad in Once Seen.

Dear Beautiful Stranger, the letter began.

Do you believe in fate? I think I must do now! I'd never normally buy Time Out but something steered me towards the newsagent's stand at the station the other morning and made me pick up a copy. And there it was. Your advertisement. I couldn't believe it. How many people are there in this city? Some say it's seven million. In that case, it must have been a one in seven million chance that I managed to find you again.

I haven't stopped thinking about you since that morning on the tube. Your beautiful eyes. The way your smile lit up your lovely face and my grey morning. I spent all day at work cursing myself for my shyness. If only I had said hello. If only I had followed you onto the platform . . . But I was late for work. You know how these things are. Late for work! What a poor excuse!? I should have swallowed my fears and told you how I felt there and then.

But I didn't. And I thought that I'd never see you again. My anger at my timidity was overwhelmed only by the sadness I felt that we might never even get to be friends. It was a sadness that is only equalled by the joy and excitement I feel now!

So, here I am. My name, for your information, is Andrew. You know what I look like, of course. I'm thirty-three years old. I live in Tufnell Park and work for an Internet start-up company in Islington called www.Asyoulikeit.com. We sell cut-price theatre tickets. I like football and dogs. I speak bad French and conversational Italian. I'm not sure how enticing this sounds to you now, but I'd love to meet up and tell you everything else there is to know.

Please call me as soon as you get this letter. I can't wait a moment longer to see you again. Because if Cupid still exists these days, then he got me on the Northern Line that Wednesday morning.

With very best wishes,
Andrew

Ruby spread the letter out on the kitchen table and felt ever so slightly voyeuristic.

"A one in seven million chance." Lou had really won the Lottery this time. Ruby felt exhilaration that she had found the perfect stranger mixed with a little twinge of jealousy that someone who had glimpsed her friend for mere seconds could obviously be so moved. Still, she gave a little jig of excitement as she double-locked the door behind her and clipped on down to the bus stop. Lou was going to be so surprised. So impressed. Ruby had found her stranger on the train!

CHAPTER
TWELVE

Martin listened to the latest set of replies impatiently. What a bunch of tossers!

"Hi there, gorgeous," began Robert from West Kensington.

How did he know that Ruby was gorgeous, thought Martin indignantly.

"I work as a lawyer and I drive a Porsche Boxster," Robert continued quite seamlessly. "But don't let that put you off. Ha ha ha."

"Oh dear," Martin muttered to himself. "Wouldn't want Ruby to end up with a man who only has a two-inch penis. I'm afraid that you go to the back of the queue."

The postal replies weren't much better. Used to dealing with insane fan letters to her authors, Lou had warned her friends that the old adage about green ink really did apply. Likewise, letters written on lined paper should always be regarded with suspicion. Martin didn't believe her at first, getting halfway through a letter written on tissue-thin lined paper in green biro and deciding that he was actually rather warming to the writer when he came to a passage about "The Second Coming" which explained that the author was actually looking for a wife who would be willing to join him in a nuclear-proof bunker, with the intention of re-establishing the human race with her post-Armageddon.

"Shame," Martin tutted, wondering whether this was the guy Ruby had already dismissed via his telephone ad weeks before. He decided to keep the letter for the postmortem anyway. He might even write about it in his novel.

Almost all the letters left much to be desired. Martin soon realised those which weren't littered with misspellings were usually written by the over-fifties. And Martin was under very strict instructions not to choose Ruby a date who wouldn't understand her jokes about The Clangers (not that Lou or Martin really understood Ruby's jokes about the Clangers either). That left him with a very narrow age range, extending roughly two years in each direction from Ruby's median thirty-one.

But after listening to so many terrible messages, Martin very much wanted to choose a date from the letters rather than the phone calls to the accompanying number. He felt that a man who had taken the effort to write rather than phone was far more likely to be the kind of sensitive, thoughtful man that his dear friend deserved after her run-in with Flett and that other married loser before him. Martin was also biased towards anyone with a literary bent. Though poems were still out, *après* Davide.

Eventually, Martin settled for a man called Robin. In Martin's opinion, Robin's letter to Ruby was both sensitive and witty. While he said that he worked in the

City he didn't mention the size of his bonus, which Martin took as a tacit signal that he must have had a substantial one. Robin hadn't enclosed a picture, as requested, but Martin knew Rubes wasn't lookist. In fact, she seemed to be grateful if the men she dated had two eyes looking in the same direction.

When he had decided upon Robin for sure, Martin gave Lou the relevant details so that she could phone their victim, pretending to be Ruby with her very passable impression of Ruby's slightly rural Worcestershire accent, and arrange that Friday's date at Suave.

"Did he enclose a photograph?" Lou asked.

"No," said Martin.

"Then I don't think you should go for him. If he didn't send a photo then he probably looks like a Gremlin."

"None of the replies enclosed photographs," Martin told her. "Except for the guy from Peterborough who enclosed a photo of himself, one of his cat and one of his mother — whose bungalow he still shares."

"Oh, God. Was he good-looking?"

"What do you think?"

"Robin it is then," Lou sighed. "Though Robin and Ruby sounds a bit twee."

"Just phone him. It's either him or the tosser with the Porsche."

"There was a reply from a man with a Porsche?" Even Lou, who pretended not to be impressed by such things, couldn't help exclaiming.

"He left a message on the phone line but forgot to leave his number," Martin lied. "Call Robin, will you?"

Lou agreed.

Though it wasn't strictly in keeping with the rules of the Lonely Hearts Pact, Lou also demanded that Martin show her Robin's letter, as a damage limitation exercise. In reality, despite his protestations, Martin was only too pleased for Lou's second opinion. Much as he hated the idea that there might be any area of life in which women were better endowed than men, he had to admit that he was worried he might have missed some subtle but extremely important clues in Robin's letter that a woman would pick up on immediately. In short, he wanted Lou to take partial responsibility if this Robin bloke turned out to be a psychopath.

"Do you think he's a psychopath?" Martin asked Lou outright when she'd read it.

"Who do you think I am? Bloody Cracker?" Lou asked. "But I'm impressed that you're feeling so protective towards our friend. Unusually protective, I'd say," Lou teased. "You sure you want to set Ruby up with anybody at all?"

"I just don't want to be the one that set her up with an axe-murderer," Martin blustered.

"I'm setting *you* up with an axe murderer."

"Don't even joke about that," Martin replied. "Though I'd prefer an axe-murderer to a vegetarian. Have you picked one for me yet?"

Lou certainly had. In the end, there had been little competition for an evening with Martin. As Martin had suspected, most of the women who answered his ad seemed like members of a club for deranged exgirlfriends who practised calligraphy in blood and castration in their spare time.

Nine out of ten e-mails that arrived at the bogus address Lou had set up on her friend's behalf went into way too much detail. Lou had endless sympathy for these poor tortured girls. Honestly, she did. But hadn't it occurred to them that it might be better to wait until the second date to pour out their hearts, rather than pour their hearts out in the first e-mail and scupper their chances of even getting as far as date one?

The girl Lou eventually chose stood out for two reasons. The first was the brevity of her note. Just her name and her vital statistics. That she was studying for an MA in Fine Art, that is. Not her hip-to-waist ratio. The second was the photo she had scanned in to accompany that note. Cindy Daniels looked every inch the art student. Her hair was twisted into a series of stubby dreadlocks that looked like unwashed paintbrushes, tipped as they were with bright pink and red and blue. She had a ring through her eyebrow and another through her nose. She was gazing straight at the camera with a smile that could only be described as dirty. Lou couldn't help but smile back when she saw it. Perfect. Here was Martin's girl all right.

Lou instantly knew Cindy Daniels would be a challenge. And she knew that Martin would be horrified when he saw her. She was a very long way from the groomed Jennifer Lopez-style lovelies that Martin usually lusted after, with their waist-length hair and lips so big that Ruby once wondered aloud if Leah's mother had stuck her to windows using her

128

mouth as a suction cup to keep her out of trouble during shopping trips.

"I arranged the date by e-mail," Lou told Martin. "She sent confirmation this morning."

"All fixed then," said Martin simply.

And it was. The restaurant was booked. Three tables for two under three different names and three very different dates to spend the evening with.

CHAPTER
THIRTEEN

The advertising department of *The Satyr* always had a slight party atmosphere on a Friday morning as the inmates of "Stalag" International Mags looked forward to the weekend. Melanie bought the cappuccinos on her way into the office. Lee added the whisky for Irish coffee with a twist. Martin bought the cakes. And on that particular Friday, he was just biting into a doughnut with caramel icing when Barry Parsons wandered in.

"Hear you were in the office last night," said Barry casually.

"Working on the Viking Vodka presentation," Martin shrugged without looking up from his screen. "Want to get it right."

"After last month's figures, you need to get it right," said Barry, picking up Martin's doughnut and helping himself to a bite. When he put the doughnut down again, there was slightly less than one decent mouthful left. "My office in ten," he said then, in what was obviously meant to be an intimidating manner.

"Sure." Martin kept his eyes on the screen until he heard the door to Barry's office shut. When that happened, Martin put his head over the parapet briefly and checked that Barry really was out of his way before opening the computer file that contained his novel in progress. He ran the word count. Thirty thousand words so far. Martin planned to get a finished draft done by the end of the month. He'd already made himself a list of the agents he would hit as soon as he had the manuscript printed out. He'd use the machines at International Magazines to make copies of course.

In his wildest dreams, Martin imagined himself writing a list of acknowledgments for the front of the book and crediting Barry Parsons with making his life so miserable that he really had no choice but to write a best-selling novel and escape the rat race. That fantasy would sustain him through what he hoped would be his last couple of months in air-conditioned hell at *The Satyr* before he faxed his letter of resignation from Barbados . . . In the meantime, however . . .

"'E's looking a bit pissed off this mornin'," Melanie observed of her boss. "Says 'e wants you to go to 'is office straight away, Mart. I don't know what you done but it must 'ave been something terrible."

"Good luck, Ashcroft," said Lee, patting him on the back and saluting in the parody of World War Two camaraderie they adopted to lighten the atmosphere whenever it looked as though large chunks of proverbial were about to start hitting the fan.

"Tell Melanie that I love her," responded Martin, playing the airman who would never return. Then he strode into Barry's office without looking back at his comrades.

"You've been late in the office every night for the past fortnight," started Barry. "I want to know what you've been doing."

"Catching up with my workload, like I told you," said Martin. "Getting ahead of myself so that I can organise my time better on a day-to-day basis." Martin had practised for this moment since he first started using the office as his study after hours.

"Then how come your performance is still such shite?" Barry asked. "You've had two cancellations this month. After I talked to you this morning, I called the guys from Viking to find out why they'd decided not to place their ads with us and they told me that you cancelled your meeting with them because you were ill and never called back to reschedule. When the fuck were you ill, Martin? You haven't been out of the office this month. You're spending more time here than ever before and yet you called them to say that you couldn't make the meeting because you were ill. I want to know what's going on with you."

"I didn't feel ready to meet them at the time we'd scheduled. I didn't want to turn up at the meeting half-prepared and lose the sale because I didn't impress them."

"So, instead, you lost the sale by just not bothering to follow up. You know what that looks like to me, boy? It looks like you're losing your touch. But since I know that you aren't losing your touch, what it also looks like is you deliberately not chasing up an account so that you can take it with you when you move to another

132

mag. What's going on, Martin? Either you're up to something you don't want to tell me about or you're knocking off one of the cleaners."

Martin almost laughed at that.

"While you won't tell me what your game is," Barry continued. "I can't bring myself to trust you and if I can't bring myself to trust you then it's not very clever of me to have you as my right-hand man. Who's got their eye on you, Martin?" Barry persisted. "Nat Mags? IPC?"

Martin shook his head.

"Then you're telling me that you really are just a pile of shite and you can't even close a deal with a bunch of tossers like Viking who should cut their nuts off to get in the back of *The Satyr*?"

"I guess I must be," said Martin, after giving the question some thought.

"What are you going to do about it?" Barry asked. "I can't have any passengers on my team."

Martin tapped his biro against his lower lip as though he was considering his options.

"If I want a tosser in charge of my mag, I can go across the street right now and give your job to that guy selling the *Big Issue*." Barry nodded out through the window at the dread-locked crustie and his equally sad-looking dog who sat outside the office come winter, spring or summer. "So, I'm asking you again, Martin. What are you going to do about it?"

Martin put his biro back into the breast pocket of his shirt and looked Barry straight in the eye. Time seemed to expand as the men stared at each other like a pair of belligerent bull elephants on the savannah. Which one of them would break for it first?

"You know what," Martin said finally. "I'm not going to do anything about it . . ."

"Eh?" Barry's expression changed from anger to confusion.

"I've been meaning to tell you this for some time," Martin explained. "I'm sick and tired of working at *The Satyr*. I'm sick and tired of working for a man like you. You can stick your crappy job where you keep your crappy brains. And that, if you can't work it out, is up your fat white arse."

Barry's mouth trembled as he absorbed the insult and tried to find the words to rebut it.

"You're fired!" he shouted eventually.

"Didn't you notice me resigning?" Martin asked.

"I want you out of this building right now," said Barry as his face grew ever redder. "You're sacked. You hear me? You're finished at International Mags."

"That was the point of my speech," said Martin calmly.

"I've had enough of your lip."

"I've had enough of your whole fat head. You, Barry Parsons," said Martin, as he jabbed a finger in Barry's pigeon chest, "are not the new Rupert Murdoch. You're not even the new Robert Maxwell, though you do give him a run for his money on the lard-arsed front. You head up the ad sales team for a poxy magazine called *The Satyr* and you don't even know what the bloody word means. You are going nowhere. In fact, you're not only going nowhere, you are safely there already, mate."

134

Martin picked up his jacket from the back of his chair and prepared to leave.

"Yeah? Yeah?" Suddenly Barry was on his feet too and blocking Martin's exit. "Well, what do you think you're going to do for your fucking living if you don't turn round and kiss my arse right now?"

"Something more dignified and exciting? Cleaning toilets?"

"Where the fuck do you think you're going?" Barry stuttered as Martin pushed past him and stepped out into the corridor. "You've got one fucking chance to turn round and take back what you just said. One fucking chance to save your fucking job."

"No thanks," said Martin. "I meant every single word."

Seconds later, Barry was calling security.

Good as it had felt to tell Barry exactly what he thought of him, it soon became clear that Martin had taken Semtex to his bridges. Martin wasn't even allowed to go back to his desk to collect his belongings. Instead, Barry had Martin wait in the lobby of the office under the supervision of the least friendly security guard in International Magazines' employ — the one who looked like a bulldog chewing a wasp on a good day — while upstairs in *The Satyr*'s stuffy office Lee and Melanie quickly gathered together Martin's personal effects in a cardboard box.

"I'm really sorry, mate," Lee said as he handed the box over in the lobby, beneath the blown-up version of the third issue cover — Kylie in the guise of a squirrel — that Martin loved so much.

"It's all right," Martin said tightly.

"Did you try grovelling?" Lee asked seriously.

"It doesn't suit me," Martin told him with a smile.

"Fair enough, mate," said Lee. "Look, your departure has come as a bit of a surprise," he continued. "No time to organise a leaving present or nothing. But we had a bit of a whip-round in the office. Buy yourself a drink."

Lee handed over a jiffy bag with Martin's name scrawled upon it in Melanie's almost joined-up writing.

"Thanks," said Martin. "There'll be almost enough for half a pint of Strongbow if you and Mel both contributed."

"Yer tosser," said Lee, punching Martin playfully in the arm. "I'll see you around."

"Not if I see you first," Martin replied with the old standard.

Lee patted Martin on the shoulder and trudged back to the lift, looking almost as broken as Martin felt.

"Fuck." Martin smacked his hand against his forehead.

"Time's up," said the security guard, using his bulk to intimidate Martin towards the door like a prison officer escorting his charge back to the cells.

"This is a great moment for you, isn't it?" Martin commented accusingly. "Bet you spend your entire working week waiting just for moments like this when you feel like you're actually doing something. You'd love it for war to break out, wouldn't you? You don't feel like you're living unless you're picking on somebody else."

"Out," said the security guard without even looking at him.

"Fuck. Fuck. Fuck. Fuck . . ." Martin picked himself up from where the security guard left him on the kerb. Much as he had wanted out of International Magazines, he could not believe his bad luck. The idea had been that he would at least have a chance to go back to his office and retrieve his masterwork . . .

Martin Ashcroft, standing up for himself against Barry Parsons was suddenly Martin Ashcroft, thirty-one. No job. No prospects. And no novel.

Martin sank down onto a bench covered in bird shit and stared disconsolately at the detritus of more than half a decade spent chained to a desk at International Mags. His green plastic pen tidy. His oversized calculator with the extra big number keys. One postcard of a woman with a fat arse in a G-string — sent to the office by Lee from a stag weekend in Fuerteventura. Three chewed up biros. And *no* fucking novel. How could he have been so stupid!?

Martin dug out his mobile. Perhaps he could phone Lee . . . No chance. He knew that Barry would be in the office right now, searching for evidence that Martin had been working as a double agent for another publication, before getting one of the geeks from the IT support department to erase all trace of Martin's existence from International Magazines' infrastructure.

The very worst of it was the idea that Barry might actually read some of Martin's work before he deleted it. Martin groaned from the bottom of his stomach. He could almost see Barry's sick, smug smile spreading across his face like anthrax when he came across the words Martin had sweated over every night for the best part of a month.

Martin rattled the jiffy bag that contained his leaving collection. In fact, it didn't even rattle. Tight sods. Martin ripped open the bag. Might as well start his descent into homelessness via a six-pack of Tennent's Extra right now. He had never felt so much in need of alcoholic oblivion in his life. He glanced across the road at the crustie who sold the *Big Issue*.

"Spare me a quid, mate?" the crustie asked when they made eye contact.

"Could be the last time," said Martin, dipping inside the envelope. "I'll share whatever's in here . . ."

But the jiffy bag contained no money after all. Instead, Martin found a diskette, garnished with a Post-it note. "Copied your contacts file," Lee had written. "You'll need this in your new job."

Clever boy.

"Yes!" Martin punched the air. Because what Lee didn't know was that there wasn't a single address in the contacts file on Martin's hard drive. "Contacts" was the working title of his novel. Glancing out from his office window, Barry saw Martin doing a lap of honour around the International Magazines' car park and felt sure that his suspicions were confirmed.

"The day is saved!" Martin shouted to the crustie. "Let's go to the pub."

While Martin toasted his success on escaping International Mags with his novel, Lou and Ruby were already getting ready for that evening's date at Suave.

Suave was one of the hottest new restaurants in London. At least, that's what it said in the month-old issue of *Time Out* in which Lou had first seen the restaurant reviewed, which meant that, by the time the trio got round to booking their grand blind date, just six months after the restaurant opened, Suave was already on its way back down the cool-ometer again.

Despite that, Ruby was still excited when she arrived at Lou's flat after work with three huge holdalls into which she appeared to have stuffed her entire wardrobe.

"I don't think you're going to be needing these," said Lou, holding up a pair of shorts.

"I didn't think so," Ruby admitted. "But you're always hearing about people going on a blind date in London and deciding to elope the next day. I've got my passport," she added. "Martin might have set me up with a multimillionaire yachtsman who insists on flying me to St Tropez tomorrow morning."

"Or a ski instructor?" suggested Lou, as she happened upon Ruby's old salopettes.

They narrowed it down to three front-runner outfits. Leather trousers and a black slash neck top were discarded when Lou wondered aloud whether the restaurant had leather seats.

"Don't want your date to think that you're farting all night, do you?"

Lou pulled a little black dress out of Ruby's case next. "What about this?" she asked.

"It's a bit boring, isn't it? A bit predictable."

"Unlike this," said Lou, digging out a bright cerise pink pencil skirt. "When on earth was this fashionable?"

"Summer 2000," Ruby said, regarding her fashion mistake with disgust. "First nineteen eighties revival."

"Whatever possessed you?"

"You, actually," Ruby pointed out. "Don't you remember telling me that I needed to inject some colour into my wardrobe? What are you wearing?" Ruby asked.

Lou nodded towards a stylish navy blue trouser suit that was hanging from the doors of her wardrobe ready to adorn Lou's long, slender limbs. The jersey material had an elegant drape that whispered expensive and Ruby was suddenly filled with loathing for the black dress that had served her so well in the past. At forty quid it had definitely been a bargain. But suddenly she felt it was showing its age, with the material getting a little more transparent with every wash and not in a fashionable way.

"I can't go to Suave in this," Ruby sighed. "They'll think I'm one of the staff. Except that the staff will all be better dressed than I am."

"Why don't you wear your DK dress?" Lou suggested.

140

"Haven't got round to dry-cleaning it since Susannah's wedding."

In reality, Ruby had rather hoped she wouldn't have to. She had convinced herself that if she left the dress hanging in the breeze from her bedroom window for long enough, she would be able to get away with it. But that morning she had taken a tentative sniff at the crinkled skirt and had almost been knocked out by the alcohol vapour that still lingered on the expensive black crepe. She didn't even dare sniff the armpits. They'd done a lot of dancing that night.

"Black dress it is," she said resignedly.

"It really suits you," Lou assured her. "Besides, you don't want to look as though you're trying too hard."

Am I trying too hard, Ruby wondered? She stared at herself in the full-length mirror on the back of Lou's wardrobe door. She knew she looked presentable, but she had wanted to look *special*. After all, this was her one shot. There was less than a month left until the Hollingworth Summer Party. She had so much to do in that time. Apart from the usual — lose ten pounds, wax bikini line, have a facial — she had to convince Flett that he had been wrong to dump her for Imogen. And it seemed the only thing that might convince a man he had done the wrong thing in ending a relationship was to see the woman he had abandoned on the arm of another man.

"You look wonderful," said Lou, as she clipped on a simple pair of silver earrings to complete her own effortlessly graceful outfit. "Now where is sodding Martin?"

He turned up just before the taxi that Lou had booked for seven-thirty.

"Have you been drinking already?" Ruby asked him as a blast of alcohol vapour enveloped her when they kissed hello.

"One or two," he said. Martin had actually spent most of the afternoon in the pub opposite the International Magazines Building, bribing the *Big Issue* seller with pints of lager so that he would listen to the plot of Martin's book. Filthy, as the chap was called, had assured Martin that he had never heard a better idea for a best-seller and that losing his job was indeed the push that Martin needed to propel him to literary stardom. But there wasn't time to explain that now.

Lou was busy outlining the strategy for the evening. They needed to arrive separately, so that their dates didn't know they were part of a mass experiment. They needed to have get-out clauses and secret signals to let each other know if anything was going wrong. There would be a rendezvous at nine o'clock in the ladies' cloakroom so that they could update each other on their progress and set a time to split if things were going pear-shaped.

"Post-mortem at my house afterwards," Lou added. "I've bought a bottle of brandy."

The taxi-driver pulled in as instructed, within view of, but not right outside, the restaurant's imposing frosted glass doors.

"Who's first?" asked Lou.

"I'll go," said Martin, opening the cab door and heading for the restaurant at speed. All that lager had gone straight through him and he was on a mission to find the loo.

"Hey!" Ruby called him back. "You forgot your share of the cab fare!"

"We'll get it later," said Lou. "Don't blow his cover. You ready for this?"

"I think so," Ruby whispered.

Lou hadn't seen her look so worried since they took their finals.

"Don't worry," she said. "It's a blind date. How bad can it possibly be?"

CHAPTER
FOURTEEN

Lou felt like a character in a police drama series as she sat alone at the bar and studiously ignored her friends. If only they had kitted themselves out with hidden headsets so that they could communicate with each other across the room without anyone noticing. As it was, the best they could manage in terms of high-tech spy equipment was to agree to set their mobile phones to vibrate and text each other from beneath the cover of the tablecloths if anything should go awry.

Which one of them would meet their date first? Lou hoped it was Ruby. Ruby was looking about her like a rabbit that knows it is within range of a fox but isn't quite sure where would be the best place to run to. She had drained her first double vodka tonic as though it was lemonade and was already on to a second. If she had to wait much longer, Ruby would barely be able to stand up. So much for making a good first impression.

Meanwhile, Martin was sitting at the other end of the bar, studying himself in the mirrored glass behind the optics. Lou couldn't help smiling. It was definitely a myth that men were less vain about their appearance than women. Martin's messy crop may have looked like a "just out of bed" head to the uninitiated, but Lou knew for a fact that it was actually the result of hours in front of the bathroom cabinet with a pot of pricey styling wax. He was drinking beer from a bottle, she noticed. Hardly very sophisticated. Still, his date-to-be was a student. Lou could only hope that Cindy Taylor wasn't still drinking her choice of poison from a two-litre plastic jug.

Every time the doors to the restaurant swung open to admit another visitor, Ruby oriented herself towards the entrance with an eager smile. It was a busy evening. Though the celeb count stuck firmly at zero all night, the beautiful people who drifted in were still pretty impressive. Twice Ruby had been particularly excited by the latest additions to Suave's clientele. When a tall, blond man with the clean-cut, square-jawed look of a model advertising some rugged brand of aftershave actually smiled at her as he handed his coat to the cloakroom attendant, Ruby almost wet her knickers with anticipation. She was ready to do a lap of honour around the dining room and kiss Martin for scoring so spectacularly on her behalf. Unfortunately, moments later the gorgeous bloke walked straight by her to kiss a whippet thin brunette who had been nursing a mineral water in his absence.

"You looked straight past me," the brunette complained.

"Forgot my glasses," said the aftershave guy. He brought out a pair of wire-rimmed specs. "There, I can see who I'm looking at now."

Ruby sagged a little on her bar stool. Really, what chance was there that her blind date would be that gorgeous? The name Robin didn't bode well for a start. How many film stars could Ruby name called Robin? She came up with one, but that was a girl. The only male celeb called Robin that Ruby could think of was Robin Cousins, the champion figure skater who triumphed in the Olympics when Ruby was still at junior school. Robin Cousins. Ruby remembered the fuss that had been made of him. And sure, he could execute a triple salco with perfection, but even aged seven, Ruby had failed to find him alluring.

It was something to do with the hair, Ruby decided. There was something altogether too tidy about Robin Cousins' neat side parting. Serial killer hair, was what Lou called it, having noticed that every time you see a mug shot of a serial killer on TV, they look as though their mother has just smoothed their fringe down and had a go at a smudge on their face with a hanky. In fact, Lou theorised, the tidier the hair, the more likely the neighbours were to say, "he seemed like such a nice man" when they found three lower leg joints in his fridge.

Ruby offered up a little prayer. "God preserve me from a man with a serial killer fringe."

She deserved to have a good time that night. There couldn't be many women in London who had had worse luck in the dating game than Ruby Taylor. Her long losing streak stretched right back to her first date, aged fifteen, when Paul Ferguson, the best looking boy in the school, asked her what she was doing on the night of the sixth form's Christmas party. Ruby was elated. She spent the money she had been saving for the school ski trip on a green silk blouse and a pair of black leggings from Chelsea Girl. She even persuaded her mother to let her use one of those "Shaders and Toners" dye sachets on her hair. Chocolate delight, she thought it was called.

And Ruby was overjoyed to hear Paul say, "Wow, you look great," when he opened the door to her on the night of the sixth form bash.

"Yeah, Ruby," said Paul's girlfriend Charlie Baggott, who was standing right behind him. "You should do your hair like that all the time. Thanks for offering to babysit tonight. I could have killed Paul when he said he might not be able to come to the party because he had to look after the kids."

Ruby could only gawp as she watched the king and queen of her school head off for a night on the tiles while Paul's mother gave strict instructions for the care of Paul's two little sisters.

The date that never was had definitely set the tone. Ruby gazed down into her glass as her mind drifted inexorably back to John Flett. And, as it happened, Ruby wasn't looking at the door at all when her date finally did arrive. Instead, she was unattractively crunching an ice-cube when the barman gave a little cough to indicate that someone was standing right behind her.

"You Ruby?" the stranger asked.

"Yes. I . . . er . . . ," she still had the ice-cube in her mouth and a dribble of cold water escaped to run down the side of her chin. "Whoops. Sorry." She grabbed a napkin and spat the ice-cube out.

"Hi, I'm Ruby," she started again. "And you must be Robin." She held out her hand to shake Robin's hand in greeting. He didn't respond in kind. Instead, he clutched his hands tightly around the neck of a plastic carrier bag and nodded warily. Ruby snatched her hand back and smoothed down her skirt as though that was what she had been intending to do all along.

Now that she had stopped being flustered, the reality of the man who stood before her slowly began to take full and horrific shape.

"Everything alright?" Robin asked when he caught Ruby staring.

"Oh, yes," she said. "Everything's just, er . . . wonderful."

He had better have a blinding personality.

Lou could only look on in horror from the other side of the restaurant. The only possible consolation was that Ruby's date was in fact one of those eccentric millionaires who dress like a tramp to deflect attention from the hoi polloi. He didn't look as if he could afford a copy of *The Sunday Times*, let alone be interested in reading it. But he had said that he worked in the City. Everyone who worked in the City was loaded as far as Lou could tell. Praying that this first impression of Robin was an unfair one, Lou gave Ruby a covert "thumbs up" that went unanswered and went back to watching Martin. At the top of the stairs, a girl Lou recognised as Cindy Daniels was already scanning the room for her victim.

"Oh, my God," Martin thought to himself. "Lou has set me up with a Muppet!"

"You must be Martin," said Cindy, extending her hand. As they shook, her bangles jangled a metallic cacophony. When she nodded at his suggestion that they might start with a drink, the waggling dreadlocks on her head reminded Martin of the fibre optic lamp his grandparents had in their sitting-room during the seventies. Was that a tattoo of a skull she had on her ankle beneath all those silver chains? She had a compass badly sketched in blue ink onto her bicep.

All in all, Cindy Daniels looked as though she might be more at home sitting halfway up an ancient oak tree, protesting against a bypass, than in that smart London restaurant. Her dress appeared to have been stitched together from the remains of half a dozen petticoats. She was as far removed from Martin's usual type as Swampy from Julian Clary. And yet . . .

There was definitely something about her.

"What are you having?" the waiter asked them both. He was grinning at Cindy as though he knew who she was. He wasn't bothered by her nose-ring.

"A negroni," she said smoothly, swivelling back to face Martin on her bar stool. "Do you need me to tell you how to make that?" she added over her shoulder when the waiter made no move towards the bottles on his shelf.

Martin was quietly impressed as Cindy rattled off the perfect cocktail recipe. The girl had a certain style.

"So," she growled. "I hope you're hungry."

Martin stuck a finger into his collar to loosen it. He had a feeling that he was on her menu that night.

Lou was the last to be met by her date for the evening. By half past eight, she was actually beginning to think the unthinkable. She had been stood up. Stood up by someone who had never even met her and had time to get bored — the ultimate insult. Reflected in the glass behind the bar, she could see Ruby and Martin already at their respective tables, reading the menus, choosing their meals. She was starting to feel pretty hungry herself and the bowl of nuts in front of her, that the waiter kept refreshing, was hardly doing the job.

"Another one of those?" he asked, pausing in the act of polishing a glass and nodding towards her half-finished Cosmopolitan.

"I'll get it," said a voice behind her. "Assuming you are Lou."

Lou turned and smiled in recognition.

"And you are?"

"Andrew. Andrew Norton."

Lou nodded slowly. Appraisingly. Ruby really hadn't done badly at all. Andrew was taller than Lou. Not bad-looking, if you liked that rather straight, clean-cut sort of look. The clothes he was wearing weren't supertrendy but neither was he dressed entirely by Marks and Spencer. He looked as though he knew how to look after himself. Ate enough vegetables. Did enough exercise. He was the kind of boy your mother would love.

"I'm sorry I'm late," he added. "Visiting my auntie in hospital. Must have lost track of the time."

My God, thought Lou. He's exactly the kind of boy my mother would love.

Andrew interrupted Lou's silent summing-up. "Must say you don't look quite how I remember."

"I'm sorry?" said Lou. How he "remembered"? "Have we met before?" she asked.

"Not exactly," he said.

Lou looked at him uncomprehendingly.

"You really don't remember me at all?"

"No," she admitted. "I'm afraid I don't."

"I look different above ground?" he quipped.

"You must do," said Lou. "Well. Shall we eat?" she suggested.

As they crossed the restaurant, Ruby made inquiring eyes over the top of her menu.

"One in seven million chance we would get together again," Andrew was saying.

And then Lou realised.

"Talk about a lucky break."

Ruby must have placed a Once Seen in *Time Out* and thought that this man, this person Lou had never seen before in her life, was her stranger on the train.

CHAPTER
FIFTEEN

"I've got to come clean," said Andrew to Lou. "I answered your ad for a dare. My mate and I have got this stupid game going. Every week we dare each other to do something different. Last week I had to go to work with my underpants on over the top of my trousers."

Oh, God, thought Lou. He was probably wearing Bart Simpson boxer shorts.

"Joke," he said, looking suitably embarrassed. "I really had to persuade a car dealer to let me test-drive a Ferrari. This week I had to answer a Once Seen ad and pretend I was the guy it referred to. I didn't expect to end up on a date because of it. I just had to try to convince the person who placed the ad that I was the man they fancied. I didn't think it would work but it was incredibly easy. I had some idea of what you looked like from the ad itself and then I just ad-libbed the bit about your beautiful eyes."

"Well, you pulled it off," said Lou.

"You really do have beautiful eyes though," said Andrew.

Lou lowered her beautiful eyes to the tablecloth and shook her head in playful disapproval.

"I hope you don't mind too much," Andrew said somewhat shyly this time. "I know I'm probably not anything like the person you hoped I'd be but I'd be lying if I said I don't think we're going to have a really good evening. And I'd like to see you again. If you don't hate me for wasting your time."

"I don't hate you," said Lou. "Why would I?"

"Perhaps you want to carry on looking for your real Prince Charming though?"

"My Cinderella," corrected Lou. "Prince Charming was the one who did the search. Remember?"

"Right. Of course. Well, do you want to carry on searching?" He gave her a smile that would have persuaded any red-blooded girl otherwise.

Lou ran her finger contemplatively around the top of her wine glass. "No. I don't think so. There really isn't much point. The chances of me meeting the person I really saw on the tube that morning are far slimmer than you could possibly imagine."

"But he might have written," said Andrew. "And you might not have believed it was him because I already had you convinced it was me."

"Oh no. I would have known," said Lou. "You see, the thing is, Andrew, I haven't exactly been straight with you either. I didn't see any of the replies to my ad. My friend Ruby was supposed to choose a date for me," Lou nodded in the direction of Ruby's table.

"That's your friend Ruby? Here in the restaurant?"

"Yes. But, ssssh! Don't attract her attention. She's on a date too. We had a dare of our own," Lou explained.

"To find new lovers through placing personal ads. Me, Ruby and our other friend Martin."

"Is he here?"

"Over by the kitchen door, sitting with the girl with dreadlocks."

Andrew couldn't help gawping in the direction of Martin's date.

"All three of us were in on a pact. I wrote an ad for Martin, Martin wrote an ad for Ruby and Ruby must have written that Once Seen ad for me. Very clever. I told her I'd seen someone I fancied on the Northern Line and she tried to get us back together. I didn't expect her to think of something as subtle as that. The idea was that we would pick out the best match for each other from the suckers that applied to our personals and, hey presto, here we are tonight, seeing how well we did for one another."

Andrew grinned. "So why did you pick that thing she's sitting with this evening. Revenge?"

Lou cast a worried glance over her shoulder at Ruby.

"Martin was the one who picked him," she said in her own defence. "God, I hope he's got a sparkling personality."

Ruby was ready to scream. When they made their lonely hearts pact, Lou and Martin had promised they would not deliberately choose the worst possible date they could find for her. They had sworn upon their respective lives. They were supposed to be beyond those college-style pranks now, where the person who locked

154

tongues with the worst geek in the room would get a free kebab on the way home courtesy of the losers.

The lonely heart experiment was more serious than that. Ruby had pinned all her hopes on her friends' ability to see what she couldn't. To see what was right for her where she might be blinkered by such superficial concerns as lust and, she had to admit, desperation. She understood that she might not immediately fancy the person who would ultimately turn out to be her soul mate but personality could definitely not be considered a superficial concern. And it was hardly a superficial matter that her date that evening did not appear to have any at all. Add to that the fact that the shape of his head suggested a long-drawn-out forceps delivery.

If Robin was meant to be Ruby's Prince Charming, then he was clearly still in frog form. He didn't have serial killer hair but that was only because of the size of his bald patch. When the waiter asked whether he might relieve them of their jackets, Robin had flatly refused to be parted from his sensible padded parka, though he must have been getting sautéed inside it. Beneath the parka, Robin wore a pale brown suit and a white shirt so thin Ruby could see his chest hairs straight through it. When the waiter brought over the menus, Robin reached into his Sainsbury's "Bag For Life" and brought out a pair of glasses held together with sticky tape.

Once they'd ordered their meals, Robin had nothing whatsoever to say to her, beyond complaining that the restaurant was awfully pricey. She had tried just about every conversational gambit going to get the evening swinging. From "nice weather we've been having lately" to "have you ever indulged in train-spotting?" Strangely enough, he hadn't.

And then the food arrived. The young waiter had looked nervous all the way across the floor, as he tried to juggle two hot plates and a bread basket. By the time he got to the table, a débâcle was almost inevitable. The waiter just about managed to set the plates down without an accident, but in doing so, he knocked the olive oil bottle flying. It bounced as if made of rubber on the Italian marble floor, spraying both Ruby and her monosyllabic date with expensive extra virgin.

"It's an old dress," said Ruby, as dismissively as she could manage while she dabbed at the mess on her skirt.

"I thought so," said Robin.

Ruby wasn't sure she'd heard right. The waiter glared on her behalf.

Robin had managed to escape the worst of the shower. At least that's what he thought. He tucked straight into his fish, cutting and eating as if he expected the plate to be whipped away again at any moment. He didn't look up from his plate until he was almost finished, giving Ruby plenty of time to take in the single droplet of olive oil that was oozing slowly across Robin's shiny head.

Would it be polite to tell him? Ruby wondered. The dollop had morphed from the shape of the Isle of Wight into Australia. Or was it more polite to pretend she hadn't noticed? Australia quickly became Italy as the oil headed for Robin's thick eyebrows. Perhaps she should just reach across the table and give his pate a quick polish with her napkin?

"I'm looking for a long-term relationship," said Robin, when he finally finished eating. By that time, Ruby was just looking for the fastest way out.

A nine o'clock debrief in the ladies' room had been decided in advance. Martin had been invited too, but given the venue and the fact that he seemed to have come off pretty well in the blind date shuffle, the girls weren't surprised when he didn't get up and follow them at the appointed hour.

Ruby was there on the dot, like a greyhound from a trap.

She sat on the vanity bench by the mirrors and sparked up a cigarette while she waited for Lou to join her. She had been completely stuffed. She had given Robin every chance to redeem an appalling first impression but it was rapidly becoming clear that Robin's quirky dress sense was one of his more charming attributes. She recalled with a shudder how he had blown his nose on his napkin and then smoothed it back over his lap. By the time Lou made her own subtle getaway, Ruby was dragging on her cigarette like a death-row prisoner, sizing up the windows as a possible means of escape.

Lou didn't need to ask how Ruby's evening was progressing.

"We chose the wrong one, didn't we?"

Ruby nodded and exhaled a smoke circle.

"Is it just the way he looks?" Lou asked.

"You know I'm not lookist," Ruby began. "But when I have been out with men who are less than conventionally handsome in the past, Lou, it is because they have some other, definable quality that makes up for the fact that they must have hit every branch on the ugly tree before they hit the ground."

"So, I take it he's not funny either?"

"Are we talking funny *ha-ha* or funny *peculiar*?" Ruby asked.

"I thought he'd be funny. The letter he wrote was really great. That's what swung it. I was sure you'd hit it off."

"Perhaps I would have hit it off with the friend of his who actually wrote the letter."

"He didn't write the letter himself?"

"No. Just like Cyrano de Bergerac," Ruby laughed bitterly. "Or *Cyril De Whatsit*, as dear Robin would say. Except that this time it's the ugly one who doesn't have any brains either and now I'm having dinner with him."

Lou couldn't help smiling. "Oh Rubes, I'm sorry. Still, at least you should get a free dinner for your pains."

"I don't think so," said Ruby.

"But he works in the City," said Lou. The implication being that he was rolling in filthy lucre.

"As third in command at a *key-cutting* shop next door to Merrill Lynch," Ruby told her.

Lou could only grimace.

"And as if that isn't bad enough, as I was getting up to go to the bathroom, he asked me if I wouldn't mind pinching a loo roll for him on the way back, seeing as I've got such a big handbag. He hasn't bought a loo roll in years, apparently. Or sugar. Or pepper. Or butter. Or salt. Why bother when restaurants have such handy, ready-packaged supplies?"

"Oh, God!" Lou spluttered. "You're joking?"

"I only wish I were. When the waiter came round with the bread, he took one piece for his side plate and wrapped two more in a napkin for later."

"Ruby, you're lying," Lou snorted into her hand.

"I'm not. He'll be asking me to put the silver in my bag on the way out," Ruby continued. "Well," she said, unhooking a half-finished loo roll from a holder in one of the cubicles. "He can have his bloody loo roll but he needn't expect any other favours from me tonight."

"You're not really going to steal a loo roll for him, are you?"

"Poor boy is going to need something to cry into when I leave him to pick up the bill on his key-cutting wages."

"Attagirl," said Lou. "Better order some nice Beaumes De Venise with your pudding."

"I think I will," said Ruby resolutely as she stuffed the loo roll into her handbag. "But how are you getting on? Is he?"

"No," Lou sighed. "He's not the one."

"But . . ."

"He convinced you? I know. I can see why. But he answered for a dare. Said he just ad-libbed about my beautiful eyes in his letter. Clever of you though.

Placing a Once Seen instead of an ordinary personal. If it had worked . . ." Lou was momentarily wistful.

"Would have been great. I can't believe the bugger conned me."

"Doesn't matter. He's nice. Really nice."

"That's not a very passionate adjective," Ruby pointed out.

"Well, to be honest, I thought he was an idiot at first but I think I underestimated him. He's got GSOH."

"Great shag, own helicopter?" quipped Ruby.

"If only. No, he's got a great sense of humour. We're having a surprisingly good time."

"Perhaps I'll come and join you guys for pudding," said Ruby. "Because right now, I'd settle for good shoes, own hair. Even ghastly shoes and odd hair. I can't believe I've got to go back out there and face the dweeb."

"You could escape through the bathroom window," Lou suggested.

"Iron bars on the outside. Already checked. Are you going to want to stay for ages?" she pleaded.

"I'll make it an early one," said Lou.

"Half nine," Ruby bargained.

"It's nearly quarter past now. Nine forty-five."

"Done," said Ruby. "Do you think we ought to get a message to Martin too? In case he wants to leave with us."

"He'll see us going," Lou decided. "And if he wants to wind up his evening he can and meet us at home. I think he's big and ugly enough to get to the tube

160

without being ravished by that little thing I set him up with."

"Short, isn't she?" Ruby agreed. "But don't think that means she isn't dangerous. I'm not sure I like the look of her."

"Perhaps she's got little pointy teeth!" Lou replied with glee.

"She's not really Martin's type," Ruby added authoritatively.

"Exactly. You know she's studying for a Master's."

"Christ, she'll see straight through him!" Ruby joked.

"Do you think so? I've known some pretty intelligent women who were momentarily stunned by his boyish good looks."

"Boyish good looks!" Ruby scoffed.

"Yeah," said Lou slyly. "A perfectly sane woman having a weak moment might think our friend Martin something of a catch."

"What? A sane woman like Webecca?"

"She was never sane."

"Or Gillian?"

"I must say, I was surprised at that one. Is the restraining order still in place?"

Gillian the personal assistant and sometime "model" had gone about Martin's car with a can-opener.

"I think they'll be done by nine-thirty," Ruby pronounced. "Shortly after he tells her the story about the friend of a friend whose boyfriend made her suck on a courgette while they had anal sex."

"That is *not* a first date story," said Lou.

"It is if you're with Martin," Ruby reminded her.

"I wonder who that girl was?" Lou mused.

"I don't know. But I've heard that story from at least four independent sources now. That girl certainly has a lot of friends."

"OK," said Lou. "We better get back out there. Don't want Robin to rumble us."

"I hardly care," sniffed Ruby. "In fact, I'm rather hoping he's already scarpered. I'd almost be happy to pick up the tab if it meant I didn't have to watch him pick at his teeth again."

They peered out into the restaurant.

Andrew was studying the pudding menu intently. Robin was sitting at his table, reading the alcohol content on the bottle of Chardonnay, while extracting detritus from between his gappy yellow molars with his fingernails.

"Nine forty-five," muttered Ruby. "Don't forget."

They touched knuckles together like fighters going back into the ring.

"You were gone a long time," said Robin when Ruby sat back down.

"Diarrhoea," she replied with a smile. "Almost didn't make it."

Why on earth had she thought that she might be able to find a man to make Flett jealous from a personal ad?

Ruby was right about one thing though. Martin and his date were ready to leave the restaurant by half past nine. But not because Martin had managed to scare Cindy away with his repertoire of appalling sex-related anecdotes. Not that he hadn't told any of them, either.

162

Martin claimed that whenever he found himself in a one-to-one situation with an attractive, half-intelligent girl, he developed a very sophisticated and specific form of Tourette's Syndrome, whereby, instead of swearing and spitting at random, he would find himself utterly unable to suppress a story involving orifices and vegetables.

Cindy, that evening's date, had loved the courgette story.

"The funny thing is," said Martin, thrilled at her response, "the bit that really upsets people is the courgette."

"Yes," Cindy agreed. "Strange choice. But not so strange when you think about it. I mean, if he'd asked her to bite down on a banana while he took her from behind, her teeth would have gone straight through at the first thrust. Too soft. Could have bitten her tongue off."

"Er, yes," said Martin, resisting an urge to cover his genitals. "Sounds as if you've given the fruit and veg thing quite some thought."

"Absolutely." Cindy grinned a lazy feline grin and ran her fingertip around the rim of her wine glass until it sang.

"More wine," Martin offered eagerly. They were onto their second bottle.

"Not here," she murmured. "Let's go somewhere a little," she glanced about her, "darker."

"Darker? Yes. Like a nightclub, you mean? OK. I'll just get the bill."

"You do that," said Cindy. "I shall be powdering my nose in the bathroom."

She sauntered in the direction of the ladies'. Martin watched her go, transfixed by the sight of her black leather skirt clinging tightly to her gently curved buttocks. The way she swung her handbag as she walked was reminiscent of the flicking of a cat's tail. Cindy definitely wanted to play. As soon as she let the ladies' room door swing shut behind her, Martin did a furious thumbs-up for the benefit of Lou and Ruby. Both were pretending not to know him, of course. But the waiter noticed and gave him a curious look.

Martin glanced at his reflection in one of the restaurant's ubiquitous mirrors and decided that he wouldn't be going straight home after coffee that night. He looked pretty damn hot. What woman could have resisted him? By the time Cindy came back from the bathroom, bright-eyed and delicately wiping away the powdery foundation that had settled in the creases around her nose (she said), Martin had already paid the bill and ordered Cindy's coat.

"You paid!" Cindy purred. "Oh, you good boy. You know what good boys deserve, don't you?"

"Tell me," said Martin eagerly, leaping to grab Cindy's fake fur jacket from the waiter so that he could help her into it himself.

"Fondling," Cindy whispered hotly. "Every good boy deserves fondling. Didn't you do that rhyme at school?"

"Not quite like that," said Martin.

"Then we are going to have to make up for some serious gaps in your education."

Martin and Cindy were out of the restaurant by twenty past nine. By that point, Ruby was scowling at a skimpy *crème brûlée*, while Robin regaled her with a list of household items currently on special offer at KwikSave.

Lou had warned Andrew of the date's impending curtailment. He had called for the bill and gallantly insisted on paying it. A courtesy that Lou said she would accept only if she could do the honours next time.

"Of course," said Andrew. "It's my way of making sure that there is a next time."

It was a very different story over at Ruby's table. When the bill finally arrived, Robin too snatched it up manfully. But not because he was intending to stick it all on his credit card. Oh no.

"I had the smoked salmon to start with and you had the deep fried Camembert with cranberry sauce. Then I had the chicken and you had the steak with frites. Your meal already comes to four pounds more than mine and that's before we've taken into consideration the fact that you had dessert and I didn't.

"You ate half of it!" Ruby pointed out. In fact he had eaten most of it. As soon as she let go of her spoon for a second, Robin had snatched the *crème brûlée* from in front of her and practically licked the little bowl clean.

"But you had the broccoli that I didn't want."

Robin split the bill item by item and seemed to be perfectly unfazed when the head waiter came across to find out how much should be put on each card.

"Thirty-one pounds seventy on this one and forty-three pounds on the other," he said chirpily. Ruby, on the other hand, was mortified when she dug into her bag to find her purse as the waiter returned with their credit card slips, and accidentally sent the loo roll falling to the floor and unravelling across the tasteful wooden floor like a streamer advertising her cheapness.

"There's the loo roll *you* asked for," she hissed at Robin, as loudly as she dared. But not even the dumb-struck waiter heard her. She was even too embarrassed to shift the embarrassment effectively.

"Thanks very much," Robin bent down to roll the paper up.

The waiter placed their signed receipts back on the table with a pitiful glance in Ruby's direction.

"Have you got a pound or two? For the tip?" Robin asked when he surfaced from his loo roll hunting mission.

Ruby pulled out a fiver and placed it on the silver dish with an angry flourish.

"That's a bit much, isn't it?" Robin commented.

"Actually, Robin," Ruby said steadily. "It's only half as much as I want to leave. I thought you were going to match me."

The waiter hovered expectantly.

"No," said Robin. "I don't think so. That's more than five per cent as it is. Coat please," he barked at the waiter.

Ruby was lost for words. She just let her mouth drop open and stared at the cheapest man on earth. Even as they waited for their coats, he was transferring sugar sachets from the sugar bowl into his trouser pockets.

"Well, Ruby. It's been nice," he said.

She was too shocked to disagree with him.

"But I don't think there's any reason why we should do this again."

"What?" Ruby asked. Was he asking her for another date?

He wasn't. "I mean, you seem all right and all that," he continued. "But I don't think you're really what I'm looking for. To be honest, I was expecting someone younger with longer hair. I'd take you for a drink somewhere to show there's no hard feelings, but it's getting rather late."

Ruby's jaw hit the table this time.

"It's been lovely," said Robin, retrieving the parka he'd only relinquished after the olive oil incident. And with that, he was gone, shuffling out into the night with his Sainsbury's "Bag For Life" still clutched in one hand.

"Long-term boyfriend?" the waiter asked, as he helped Ruby on with her coat.

"Blind date," admitted Ruby.

"Thank God for that. You had a lucky escape, girl. Here, you keep this," he handed her back her fiver. "Have a brandy or something on me. You deserve one."

Safely outside the restaurant, Ruby sparked up another cigarette and headed for the tube station. Lou was already there, actually hanging on the arm of her date as though they'd known each other and perhaps even been together for years. They were laughing about something as Ruby drew nearer.

"Ruby, this is Andrew," Lou grinned.

"I'm *not* the guy she fell in love with on the tube," said Andrew apologetically, "but I'm trying my best to make up for it."

"He's been doing a pretty good job so far," Lou told her.

"Nice to meet you," said Ruby, without taking the fag from her mouth. "I'm sorry if you had to cut your evening short because of me. But if Lou had made sure that I didn't end up with a dork . . ." she spat.

"That's OK. Better to be left wanting more," said Andrew with a longing look in Lou's direction.

Was Lou blushing in return? Ruby wondered. Andrew was pretty damn gorgeous for the kind of sucker who answered personal ads for a dare. Lucky cow! Wasn't it just Sod's Law?

"Martin left early," Ruby observed.

"We noticed," said Lou. Already using the royal "we"! "Wonder if that poor girl knows what she's letting herself in for?"

"Bit of an animal, your friend Martin?" Andrew asked Ruby.

"Well, yes. Though the only one that springs to my mind is a pig," said Ruby.

"You sound almost jealous," Andrew joked.

"Don't be ridiculous. I extend the dear lady he's taking home tonight my deepest sympathies," Ruby sighed. "You ready to go, Lou?"

168

"I guess this is goodbye," said Andrew, frowning sadly. He lifted Lou's hand to his lips and kissed her lightly. "I'll give you a call then?" he asked.

"Yeah," said Lou. "That would be nice."

"Bloody great," grumbled Ruby as they descended into the station. "I'm the one who actually *needs* a boyfriend and you're the one who ends up with the gorgeous man hanging on your every word."

"You're not seeing Robin again then?" joked Lou.

"He told me he wants someone younger. I've never been so humiliated in my life."

"Not even when Flett sent the e-mail?"

Ruby grimaced.

"Brandy at my place?" Lou suggested.

"With a chaser of straight arsenic," Ruby replied.

CHAPTER
SIXTEEN

Cindy took Martin to a private drinking club in Soho.
From the outside, it didn't look anything special. A
plain black door opened off the street. There was
nothing to suggest that it was anything other than
another scruffy bed-sit flat whence prostitutes or
drug-dealers plied their trade. In fact, next to the
buzzer for the club itself some enterprising pimp had
stuck a card advertising London's newest "Brazilian
Beauty" with her specialist massage skills.

Inside, however, the club was something else. It was
decked out like a harem; the walls were dotted with
brass mirrors and hung with bright swathes of silk that
gave the impression of a sumptuous tent. There were no
proper seats. Instead, the guests (who were admitted
only after a fierce grilling from a maître d' dressed like
a Mafia don with the incongruous addition of a fez)
reclined on cushions around low tables littered with
shot glasses and hookah pipes and lines of fine white
powder that definitely hadn't been missed by a careless
cleaner.

"Cindy!"

As Martin and Cindy walked through the room,
almost every man there greeted Martin's date by her

name. The girls were less friendly, but Martin guessed that could be attributed to jealousy. Despite his initial misgivings about her distinct eco-warrior style, he had decided that Cindy was very attractive. A seven out of ten, in fact. That was very good on Martin's scale. She would have been a nine if she hadn't been quite so short.

"Sit down here," said Cindy, collapsing into a pile of cushions and dragging Martin down almost on top of her. Immediately she had hauled herself into a semi-upright position, Cindy made a grab for a sinister-looking hookah pipe on a nearby table and took a long, deep drag.

"What's in there?" Martin asked.

"What do you think?" Cindy smiled. "The owner has an arrangement with the local plod."

By this time, back at Lou's flat, the girls were sipping cocoa. After half an eggcup full of specially bought post-mortem brandy, Ruby had decided that it wasn't worth adding to her list of woes with a monumental hangover.

From time to time, she glanced up from yet another viewing of *Shakespeare in Love* to the clock in the corner of Lou's sitting-room. It was a grandfather clock, much too big and grand for Lou's top floor conversion that had probably once been a maid's room. But Lou had fallen in love with it when she saw the clock in pieces at Camden Market and for about three days in every month it seemed to keep reasonable time.

"Is that right today?" Ruby asked her.

"Right as it ever is," Lou replied.

"It's nearly midnight," Ruby observed. "Do you think he's coming back tonight?"

Lou shook her head. "Obviously not. He must be doing well," she said.

"Are you sure?" Ruby asked. "I mean, what if he's not doing well? What if she's abducted him?"

"Ruby, that girl was barely bigger than a Barbie doll. He'll be fine. In fact, I bet he's having a whale of a time."

Ruby nodded into her steaming cocoa.

"I still wish he'd call and let us know that he's all right," she said with a frown.

"He's all right," Lou insisted. "Stop acting like his mother."

"I'm not."

"Are you jealous?" Lou teased.

"Get lost. Why would I be jealous of her?"

"Not her. I meant jealous of Martin," Lou corrected.

"Because he ended up with a decent date and you didn't."

"He might be having a terrible time," Ruby reasoned.

"Looked like they were getting on pretty well to me. Instant attraction I'd say."

"No," said Ruby. "He wouldn't go for that kind of girl . . . Would he?"

"I mean, why did you answer an ad?" Martin asked Cindy. "You don't look like the kind of girl who would have trouble getting a boyfriend."

172

"I don't," Cindy assured him. "But sometimes it's just too easy, yeah? Know what I mean?"

Martin wished he did.

"For example," Cindy continued. "Pick out any attractive man in this room. Anyone at all. And I've probably already had him."

"Right," Martin blanched. Perhaps *that* explained why none of the girls had been too friendly.

"But they're all the same," Cindy yawned. "They all think they're *so* bohemian and different with their art galleries and their acting projects and their exotic travel plans. Scratch the surface and they're all the same beneath. Trustafarians the lot of them."

"Oh," said Martin.

"Bankrolled by their mummies and daddies. I thought it would be more unusual to go out with someone *ordinary*," said Cindy, rubbing her fingers over the knot at the top of Martin's tie. "I thought, how about going for someone who doesn't pretend to have a creative bone in his body? Someone who has to advertise for a date because he's so boring? Someone who'll be so bloody grateful to have met me that he'll simply have to show me a damn good time."

"I see," said Martin stiffly. In more ways than one. Cindy's hand had slipped nonchalantly from his collar to his crotch. Not a creative bone in his body, eh? That was harsh. But there was something about the way Cindy gazed deep into his eyes as she spoke to him that made the uncharitable words seem sweeter. Something about the way she lolled on the cushions with the top

173

three buttons of her shirt undone to show a bright orange satin bra . . . An orange bra!

"Not that you're anything like I expected, Martin. To be honest, when I walked into the restaurant tonight, I wondered whether I was going to be able to go through with it. As I was arriving, I saw a weird-looking guy walk in ahead of me, carrying a plastic bag. I thought that was my date and nearly doubled back."

Martin felt a twinge of guilt when he realised that Cindy was describing the man he had so carelessly picked out for Ruby.

"So when I saw you, I was pleasantly surprised. You're not bad-looking, Martin. Not bad at all."

"You say the nicest things," said Martin.

"I can do the nicest things," said Cindy. "Shall we get a cab?"

Outside on the street moments later, Martin hailed a black cab while Cindy twined herself around his body like a creeper. When a cab finally stopped for them, Cindy slid into the back seat, legs wide open, grabbed Martin by the collar again and pulled him in after her. It had occurred to Martin that the evening wasn't yet over, but he was still slightly taken aback when Cindy gave the taxi-driver her address before Martin had a chance to ask, "Your place or mine."

"My place," she growled at him, then moved swiftly back to the business of sticking her slippery tongue down his throat.

"I-nnnnnnngh!" said Martin.

He didn't have a chance to get a word out all the way back to Cindy's house. She had her hand down the

174

front of his trousers while he searched for the right change to give the taxi-driver, and by the time they reached the top of the stairs that led to the door of Cindy's rather grand-looking house near Regent's Park, she had unhooked his belt and was brandishing it like a whip across his buttocks, corralling him into the house like some poor calf to the rodeo.

The front door was still open when Martin's trousers finally dropped to the floor.

"Cindy!" he squeaked.

She pushed the door shut with a faintly balletic karate kick.

"Twelve-thirty," muttered Ruby. "How difficult would it be for him to text us?"

"He's having too much fun," Lou sighed.

"At this very minute he could be bound and gagged and heading for some terrible humiliation!"

Lou almost snorted cocoa out through her nose at the thought of it.

"That sounds like Martin's idea of a *good* time," she said smiling.

"I want to tie you up," Cindy panted as she dragged him into her bedroom. "Do you trust me?"

Martin nodded. It seemed the only appropriate response.

"There's nothing to tie you up to in here," she said, as she continued to undress him. "I've been waiting for a new bed to be delivered. One with a nice iron headboard. But there's been some sort of foul-up at the

175

warehouse. Never order anything off the Internet, I say."

"Right," said Martin. He was a little distracted by her hand upon his penis.

"So for now," Cindy continued. "I'm afraid we'll have to improvise."

Still holding Martin's family jewels with one hand, Cindy leaned over backwards with a yoga expert's grace, opened a drawer in her crowded bedside table and brought out a long red silk scarf. Martin smiled what he hoped was a devilish grin. He must have done something good in a past life after all. All his fantasies were coming true at once. A dominant woman. Silk scarves. Bondage. It was a cliché perhaps but a bloody fantastic one.

Cindy bound the red scarf lightly around Martin's eyes. Now this was what he called a really good blind date, he thought as her tongue flickered lightly over his nipples.

"Handcuffs," she said suddenly.

"Handcuffs?"

"Yes. You didn't think I was just going to use scarves on you, did you?"

"Well, actually, I . . ." He did.

"But they're so easy to escape from, you naughty boy. Where's the fun in that?"

Martin pulled the blindfold away from his eyes to see whether she was joking. Evidently not. She was already dangling a pair of pretty heavy-duty cuffs from her delicate manicured fingers.

176

"Got them from a real policeman," she said with a grin.

"I see," said Martin.

"Wouldn't believe what I had to do for them."

"Don't tell me," said Martin.

Handcuffs were an entirely different proposition from silk scarves. Entirely different. It took a great deal more trust to allow someone to tie you up using something from which there was little hope of escaping until your captor decided that they wanted to let you go. Somewhere in Martin's cerebral cortex, a tiny voice of concern squeaked briefly before the excited howling of his brain stem drowned it out.

"Should you really be doing this?" asked the faint murmur of reason.

"Sex, sex, sex," grunted the brain stem. "Sex with a woman. Sex with a woman is being offered to you on a great big silver platter!" Didn't matter how weird, to Martin's prehistoric animal brain.

But Cindy seemed normal enough anyway, didn't she? She had a Snoopy pyjama case on her bed, for heaven's sake. How dangerous could a woman who had a Snoopy pyjama case possibly be?

"I don't want you to escape before I've had my wicked way with you," she said, clamping the handcuffs around one of Martin's wrists. She licked her full red lips and looked up at him through her thick black lashes like Princess Diana gone bad.

"Oh, go on!" yelled Martin's brain stem. "She wants you!!!!"

"OK then," said Martin. He held out his other wrist obediently.

"Oh no," said Cindy. "We need to cuff you *to* something."

"I thought you said there wasn't anything to tie me to in here."

"There isn't. We'll have to go into the bathroom."

"The bathroom?"

"Towel rail," explained Cindy. "I could tie you to that."

Martin followed her nervously into the hallway. She was buck-naked but for the tattoo of a plump red devil on her taut right buttock and didn't seem to care who saw. Martin held his boxer shorts nervously across his crotch for modesty's sake. "Er, are you sure we should go into the bathroom?" he asked. "What if one of your housemates wants to use the loo in the night? You do have housemates, don't you?"

The house was way too big for one girl. Besides which, Martin had seen a pair of wellies in the hall made for a pair of feet quite a bit larger than Cindy's.

"Relax. I don't have housemates," Cindy assured him.

But the wellies?

"I live with my parents."

"Parents!"

Martin's erection drooped as though it had been shot at.

"Chill out, Martin. They're cool. They don't mind me having people here. And they won't be back until tomorrow morning in any case. They're at the country house this weekend."

"Great. Er, Cindy. Look. I've got to ask this. How old are you exactly?"

Cindy didn't really look as though she had been near a school in a very long time, but young girls and make-up ... It was almost impossible to tell a thirteen-year-old from a thirty-something these days. Martin didn't want to find himself in a pair of Metropolitan Police handcuffs for real!

"I'm twenty-seven," said Cindy flatly.

Martin tried not to look too relieved.

"Come on."

Cindy opened a door onto a vast bathroom. In the centre of the shining marble floor stood one of those double-ended Victorian bathtubs that could have accommodated a rugby team. When Martin made that observation, Cindy laughed, "I already have."

At one end of the bathtub, a contraption that looked like a gigantic birdcage turned out to be a shower.

"Spurts from all sides," Cindy explained. "Exactly how I like it."

"This is amazing," breathed Martin, taking in the fullsize Roman statue of Venus that stood in the corner of the room, sans head, with a bale of towels draped over her outstretched arm. The room was lit by chandelier. It couldn't have been more different from the bathroom in Martin's flat with tiling so dirty Martin had assumed it was supposed to be yellow until Ruby bought him a canister of foaming, rinse-off Jif.

"This is the guest bathroom," said Cindy. "Step in."

"What?" Martin was busy estimating the value of the oil painting of Florence above the fireplace. How rich must Cindy's parents be?

"Step into the bath," Cindy told him. "Stand under the shower."

Martin did as he was told. Smiling a smouldering smile, Cindy relieved him of his pants and got him to link his hands behind his back around the central pipe of the shower contraption. He felt the cold handcuffs go on, just a little tight around his big wrists. When she had locked the cuffs shut, Cindy kissed Martin's fingers, sucking them in what he hoped was a small hint of pleasures yet to come. But she didn't get into the bath with him. Not yet.

"I've got to put some music on," she told him.

"We won't be able to hear it from here, will we?" Martin asked. He was eager to get on with the action.

"Yes, we will," said Cindy, as though it were obvious. "There are speakers in the bathroom."

Martin tried to locate them while Cindy went to choose a CD. She hadn't put his blindfold back on yet. Christ, her parents must be loaded, he thought. The house was incredible. Stuffed with antiques. A guest bathroom the size of a small swimming pool. And speakers above the loo were the ultimate in luxury. A surround sound experience while taking a . . .

Speakers that were suddenly playing Take That?

CHAPTER
SEVENTEEN

It was gone one o'clock. Lou had retired to bed, wanting to be up early to work on a manuscript next morning. Ruby lay awake on the lumpy sofa in the sitting-room and stared at a cobweb hanging from the Designers' Guild lampshade. Still no word from Martin to let them know how his evening had gone. Lou was probably right that Martin wasn't in any danger from the pom-pom-headed midget she had set him up with, but Ruby still wished that he were back at Lou's house as promised to reassure her that he hadn't met the love of his life . . .

What?

Ruby caught her own mental meanderings and brought herself up short. *She didn't want Cindy to be the love of Martin's life?* Why would that be such a *bad* thing anyway? Ruby hoped that she wasn't becoming one of those women who thought that the whole world should be unhappy and loveless just because she was. She knew how unattractive that kind of anger could be. Liz Hale had been the scourge of young lovers for years, tutting loudly whenever she passed anyone indulging in a public display of affection and once making an office junior at Hollingworth cry when she suggested that said junior's new boyfriend had sent her flowers because he was shagging someone else.

Ruby would not allow herself to become a modern-day Miss Havisham, wishing unhappy endings to every love affair. But . . . The awful thing was, she admitted to herself, she rather *preferred* it when Martin was single. She couldn't help it. When he wasn't single, he would slip from the radar, disappearing from her life for weeks on end or, worse still, insist on dragging his new squeeze to every social occasion. Wednesday nights at the pub quiz, boring though they sometimes were, would be completely ruined by the presence of some simpering lovely who didn't understand Ruby's jokes.

And Martin was *different* when he had a girlfriend. On his best behaviour at first, which meant that he was ninety per cent less funny than usual. Or soppy. Sickeningly so. Ruby winced at the memory of the first time she and Lou met Leah, the "Hermes" girl. Leah and Martin had developed a secret language that involved him growling like a wolf at her and her making a sheepish "baa" sound in return. Cute. Not. Ruby had been very glad when that particular relationship ended.

But she knew that they couldn't carry on like this forever. Lou, Ruby and Martin. An eternal triangle without the romance. Eventually one of them would meet the love of his or her life and settle down and perhaps get married and start a family and . . . There was no way they would all be limping to the pub quiz with their Zimmer frames in the year 2050.

As Ruby looked at the photograph of herself and her two best friends at their graduation ball, which Lou kept on her mantelpiece, Ruby felt sure that her real problem was not who Martin would end up with at all. Her problem was that she feared she would be the last one left single in this game of romantic musical chairs. She pictured herself five years hence, sitting at Lou's kitchen table, the spare part at Sunday dinner, nursing a vodka tonic while Lou cooked fishfingers for her beautiful twins. She pictured herself at Martin's house, watching Cindy cook supper while Martin amused *their* beautiful twins . . .

It was all too, too depressing. Would Ruby ever find her special someone? She felt as though she had spent her entire life searching for someone who would make her whole.

What Lou and Martin didn't know was that Ruby had pored over the personal ads for years. But not the dating ones. At least not the straightforward, *man with no teeth, lives with mother, seeks twenty-something Pamela Anderson lookalike with own Porsche* type that seemed to crop up so often. The personal ads Ruby liked to read were the ones with a much more specific target. *M. Harris seeks H. Johnson. Please apply to box number 555.* That kind of thing. She'd become addicted to them as a child.

Who were these mysterious people? How had they lost each other? And why was it so important for them to get back in touch now? Reading those ads, Ruby imagined all sorts of exciting scenarios.

Michael Harris, twenty-two, was heir to a vast estate. His mother disapproved of his mad affair with lowly miner's

183

daughter Helen Johnson, eighteen and a half, love of his life. Now the old witch, Mrs Harris Senior, is dead — cracked her head open on an over-polished floor at the castle. Michael her son is a millionaire at last. He deserted Helen to avoid being disinherited but now he wants her back. To be his wife! Will she see his ad in the newspaper? Will they ever be reunited? And if they are, will she forgive him for letting money come between them in the first place?

The romance of it all. Ruby loved the idea of illicit liaisons, arranged by notes to a box number at the back of *The Times*. Added to that was the distant but compelling possibility that one day she would see her own name in the familiar black type. "Would anyone knowing the whereabouts of Ruby Taylor please contact box number 370 to hear something that may be to their advantage."

It wasn't quite as unlikely as it sounded. As a baby, Ruby had been given up for adoption. She couldn't remember when her mum and dad broke the news. It was as much a fact of life to her as was her friend Mary Jeapes' conviction that she had been dropped down the chimney by a stork. No, Ruby couldn't remember the day she found out she was adopted, but she did remember becoming increasingly convinced that she must be the secret love child of Shakin' Stevens and Princess Anne.

As far as Ruby was concerned, the mundane scenario of accidental teenage pregnancy and a young girl deserted by her feckless lover, was least likely candidate for the truth. Perhaps in an attempt to make

184

her feel doubly "special", Ruby's mother had told her that her natural mother and father wanted to get married but couldn't, because of circumstances *beyond their control*. To an eight-year-old girl raised on Ladybird fairy tale books where the princesses' dresses outshone anything designed since by Versace, "circumstances beyond their control" could only mean the intervention of a wicked fairy stepmother. No gymslip mum but a princess had been compelled to give Ruby away. Perhaps they even left a changeling in her place.

When they found out that they had been robbed of their real daughter, Ruby's natural parents would want to track her down. They would contact her through the personal ads, of course. And Ruby checked them religiously until she was ten. After that, her preoccupation with being a minor member of the Royal family was replaced by a crush on Adam Ant and the peculiar realisation that she had reached that stage when she no longer wanted her favourite pop-star to be her secret dad.

Ruby didn't ever tell her parents what she was doing when she rushed up to her bedroom each evening with the back pages of *The Times*. She knew even then that she didn't want to hurt their feelings. They were happy to be able to tell Ruby's teacher that she was reading a broadsheet so early. From the age of ten until she hit eighteen, however, Ruby could honestly say that she never really thought about it. Being adopted, that is. She was still feeling largely indifferent when she left home to go to university. Not so her new friend

Georgie, who was doing a degree in psychology and had been reading up on the effects of adoption on identical twins.

Georgie disguised her experimental interest in Ruby's predicament as genuine concern for Ruby's future mental health. When the break-up of a particularly intense first-year relationship left Ruby feeling as thought she wanted to run back to her parents in Worcestershire and hide under the bed until she hit thirty, Georgie soon managed to convince her that her "extreme" reaction to being chucked by a spotty engineering student, whose idea of romance was taking his chewing gum out before he kissed her, was not due to the hormonal highs and lows of puppy love, but a result of deep-seated psychological trauma caused by being given away at birth.

Ruby was only too happy to agree. Arriving at university in London, fresh from school where she had been a big fish, academically speaking, in a rather stagnant pond, Ruby was somewhat bewildered to find herself surrounded by other students who not only had five grade "A's" at A-level but a dazzling array of other talents as well. Along Ruby's corridor in the halls of residence alone, there lived a girl studying molecular physics who had once played the piano at the Royal Albert Hall. Jennifer, in the room two doors down, didn't know whether to finish her degree or join one of three international modelling agencies that were clamouring to have her on their books in time for London fashion week. Allegra had already *given up* modelling to concentrate on becoming a lawyer.

And rather than being inspired by her new acquaintances, Ruby fancied herself growing dimmer in their reflected glory. From being the cleverest girl in school, she had suddenly become the dunce. The talentless, rather plain-looking dunce at that.

So, the idea that her feelings of angst were down to something as glamorous as "anxious attachment syndrome" caused by her early "abandonment", as diagnosed by Georgie from her first-year psychology textbook, suddenly seemed as glamorous to Ruby as the eating disorders that seemed to be obligatory for all those girls from expensive private schools. When she heard about Ruby's adoption, Jennifer let Ruby help herself to a handful of chocolate bars from the secret stash she kept beneath her bed for moments of weakness between eating celery ("burns more calories than it contains, you know") and vomiting.

"Poor you," sighed Jennifer, as though poor Ruby had been orphaned only yesterday. "That's just too glamorous. You could be anybody's daughter."

Favourite at that time was Mick Jagger.

"He gets around. And you've got the lips," Jennifer pronounced. "I'm thinking of having mine done," she added, quickly seguing back to herself and her own supermodel fantasies.

Georgie had reawoken the fantasy princess and, when she should have been making notes on Jane Austen, Ruby found herself pondering once more whether she could in fact be the secret love-child of someone spectacularly famous. Was her father a film or pop star?

187

Or even a high-ranking politician? Someone who would be only too delighted to welcome his long-lost daughter back into the fold and lavish her with gifts to make up for two decades of parental neglect? Perhaps she'd get a small flat in Chelsea like the one Jennifer had been given for her eighteenth birthday? She'd never turn her back on Mum and Dad, of course — they were the ones who had been there all along — but the idea that she might be the scion of some ridiculously rich and famous family sustained Ruby through half a term that would otherwise have been spent sobbing over that gangling ex.

The reality, of course, was anything but glamorous. Born as she was in the early seventies, Ruby had never seen her original birth certificate. A change in the law shortly after her adoption meant that she could apply to see it once she reached eighteen, but before that could happen, she would have to see a social worker. Ruby didn't mind too much. Actually, the fact that she had to see a *social worker* made it seem even more exotic. Almost as good as Jennifer's Harley Street shrink.

Ruby made an application, filling out the forms that would allow her birth certificate to be released by the council under whose auspices she had been adopted and, on the appointed day, she made her way to the offices of the local social services team. Climbing the concrete stairs to the reception, Ruby wondered for the first time whether this was such a good idea after all.

188

She was led into a room that looked like a primary school classroom and told to wait for "Amanda". The magnolia walls of the stark, square room were decorated with dirty child-sized handprints and posters about drug abuse illustrated by hollow-eyed models. The brown carpet tiles were patterned with trodden-in plasticine and littered with sad-looking toys; limbless dolls and wheel-free tow-trucks. If you didn't feel depressed when you arrived, Ruby thought, then you'd be begging to be sectioned by the time you left this drab, cold room.

Ruby looked for somewhere to sit while she waited but could find only those three-quarter size chairs made for five-year-olds. She leaned against the radiator instead and looked out of the window onto the citizens of the city going about their business in the crowded street below. Another ordinary Monday. In a film-noirish way, it was the perfect backdrop to what Ruby assumed would be *the* defining moment in her life. She was about to find out who she really was. From this day forward she would never need to feel alone, unhappy or confused again. She would have, she had convinced herself, a feeling of identity so strong that neither heartbreak, nor the humiliation of coming bottom in the year-end exams could hurt her again. Knowing who she really was would make Ruby Taylor's life complete.

Amanda finally arrived, ten minutes late. She was a big woman and puffing loudly from the exertion of walking up the stairs when she leaned against the doorframe and practically fell into the room. Ruby couldn't have invented a more accurate cliché of a social worker.

She was wearing what Ruby could only assume was a kaftan, cut from an exceptionally ugly piece of brown batik print cotton. Around Amanda's neck hung half a dozen strings of multi-coloured wooden beads and her over-sized, red-framed glasses on a primitive looking cord. Her hair was red too. Henna red, except for a slightly greying inch of naked roots.

As she puffed her way across to Ruby, Amanda was preceded by a waft of patchouli oil that reminded Ruby of the "ethnic" gift shop in her home town where she bought bangles as a self-consciously serious gothic sixth-former. Everything about Amanda screamed, "I'm a woman of the world, you know. I *understand*." Even the tight, lopsided curve of her lips, a bona fide "half-smile", combined with a gentle incline of the head she had for Ruby. Sympathy in advance.

"Ruby Taylor?" Amanda smiled as she read the name from the top of her case notes. "I'm Amanda Forbes Grant."

Ruby stuck her hand out automatically.

"No need for such formalities here," said Amanda, brushing the gesture away. "Would you like to sit down?"

Ruby looked about her. In here? There were no chairs that could take even one of her bum cheeks. But Amanda nodded Ruby towards one of the children's chairs, before sitting down on one herself with a dramatic swish of her kaftan that brought to mind a hot-air balloon deflating as it lands in a field. Once settled, Amanda perched with the grace of one of the hippo ballerinas in *Fantasia*, while Ruby struggled to get comfortable.

"We're waiting for some slightly bigger chairs," said Amanda. "Funding."

"Oh," said Ruby.

"Never enough of it. You OK there?" She reached out and squeezed Ruby's hand.

"I think so," said Ruby. "If I don't move around too much."

"I'm not talking about the chair," said Amanda patiently. "Are *you* OK, Ruby? *In yourself?*"

"I'm fine," said Ruby.

"I'm sure you think you are," said Amanda cryptically. "Now. Where shall we being?"

Ruby glanced down at the flat brown envelope that Amanda had placed on the Lilliputian table between them.

"Is that it?" she asked.

"Your birth certificate? Yes it is," said Amanda.

"Can I see it?"

"Don't you think perhaps we should discuss some of the *issues* surrounding your adoption first?" Amanda asked.

"I don't think I've got any issues," Ruby tried.

Amanda inclined her head again. "Of course you have."

"But I . . . I mean, perhaps I'd be able to articulate them more clearly once I've seen the certificate?" Ruby dissembled. "Once I've found out exactly who my parents are."

Amanda smiled. Ruby had obviously said the magic words.

"OK. Here you are then."

Amanda picked up the envelope and handed it over. It felt quite thin. As though there wasn't much inside it. Which was exactly the case. Ruby opened the brown manila envelope to find just one slip of paper inside, light as tissue and almost as transparent.

"Is this all there is?" Ruby asked.

Amanda nodded.

A single piece of paper.

The name on Ruby's original birth certificate was Hope. Hope. When she saw that name written in light blue ink on the salmon pink paper, Ruby was pleasantly surprised. What a pretty name, she thought. And unusual too. She had harboured a secret dread that she would discover she had been called Sarah or Sharon. Something nondescript and commonplace like that. But Hope. That was lovely. Thoroughly different. Holding the birth certificate in her hands for the first time, Ruby looked at her birth name — Hope Mary Barker — and thought she felt a little glow of warmth in the pit of her stomach.

Hope. Her mother must have loved her to give her such a pretty name. Staring at those three little words, Ruby pictured the scene in the maternity ward. The beautiful young woman holding her newborn baby. In Ruby's imagination, Geraldine Barker of Greenwich (for those were the details under "mother") told the nurse there was no word from the celebrity father yet but they were full of "hope" that he would melt as soon as he heard he had a beautiful baby daughter with big, juicy lips, just like his . . .

"Quite a common name for adoptees," Amanda the social worker interrupted suddenly. "We see a lot of girls adopted in the seventies who were called Hope or Charity. Mary too. Biblical names. Given by the nuns who ran the Children's Society for the most part."

"Oh."

If there had been a glow at all, it was instantly extinguished.

"There's no name for the father, I'm afraid," Amanda continued.

Ruby had noticed. There was just a short blue line where that should have been.

"And normally there would be some other documentation, like a letter from the mother, or at least some notes giving details of her circumstances when you were born. But in your case there doesn't appear to be anything more than the actual certificate."

"What does that mean?" Ruby asked. "Didn't she write me a letter?"

"Possibly. Though it wasn't compulsory. Probably got lost in the filing system somewhere. The adoption section at your City Council moved offices some time in the early eighties. A whole load of records that were supposed to have been moved to the new office with them ended up in a skip instead."

"A skip?"

"I know," said Amanda, screwing her face up in appropriate sympathy. "Heads really should have rolled

193

for that. Didn't your parents ever show you anything relating to your birth parents? They would have been told a bit about them prior to the adoption. They tried to match people from similar backgrounds. Make sure they knew what they were letting themselves in for," Amanda added, in an attempt to make a joke.

"I haven't exactly talked to Mum and Dad about this," Ruby admitted.

"I thought you'd say that," Amanda nodded. "You don't want to hurt them, right? Think they wouldn't understand?"

"I sort of hoped that you would be able to tell me everything I wanted to know and I wouldn't have to bother them," Ruby said.

"This is as much as I've found," said Amanda, jerking her head towards the certificate. "Obviously I wasn't around when your case was being dealt with."

"No, of course not. So . . ."

"So that's as much as I can actually tell you." She leaned back and folded her hands over her hot-air-balloon stomach. The chair beneath her gave an ominous creak.

"Is it possible," Ruby began, "that the circumstances of my birth were extra sensitive and that the documentation is being kept secret somewhere? Perhaps there was someone," Ruby hesitated, aware that she might be about to sound like a fool, "famous, involved?"

Amanda gave her the "pitying smile" from her range of useful facial expressions. "I don't think so, Ruby," she said with a shake of her head. "This really is all the documentation relating to you in existence."

Ruby held the scrap of paper more carefully after that.

"But we can talk about any feelings the certificate has raised, of course. How do you feel now, Ruby?" Amanda knitted her brows together in a trademark "serious" expression. "Are you disappointed?"

"Well, yes. Of course I am. And no. I mean, I've got my mother's name now at least and an address . . ."

"That address is almost twenty years old," said Ms Amanda Good News. "And it might not even have been her real address. Unmarried girls who got themselves pregnant in the nineteen-seventies were quite often sent to mother and baby homes as soon as the bump began to show. Their families would tell everybody that the girl had gone away to do a secretarial course and once the baby had been born and safely adopted, the mother would be able to go home again."

"So, basically, this piece of paper is worthless?"

"No, Ruby. It's not worthless. It's a piece of your history, after all."

"It doesn't feel like my history," said Ruby quietly. "This piece of paper could be anyone's birth certificate. I don't feel anything much when I look at it. I thought . . . I don't know . . . I thought . . ."

"Go on, Ruby." Amanda looked pleased at the prospect of unearthing some emotion.

"It's stupid."

"Nothing's stupid if it's what you're really feeling. Let it come to the surface."

"I suppose I thought I would recognise something. Recognise her name. My name, even. I thought I felt a tiny bit of recognition when I read that but then you told me that all adoptees are called something like Hope and it immediately stopped feeling special."

"Not all adoptees," said Amanda. "Just the ones who were named by adoption workers rather than given a name by their birth mothers."

"Great," Ruby shook her head. She wondered whether Amanda had gone on a special course to enable her to whip up a cloud around any fragile silver lining. "That makes me feel so much better."

Amanda smiled. "You're reacting in a very natural way, Ruby. It's perfectly usual to have mixed feelings at this point. You're excited, you're angry, you're disappointed, you're sad."

"I'm not sad," said Ruby defensively.

"Oh, but you are. And it's OK to cry if you want to. It's really all right. You don't have to censor your emotions around me. I've seen everything, Ruby. You don't need to protect me from your feelings. I've seen people react in ways you wouldn't believe. One man got so emotional he even tried to hit me."

Ruby resisted the urge to say that she wasn't at all surprised.

"It's a very difficult thing you're facing here. You can try to pretend that it isn't. You can try to put a brave face on. But, it's clear that you feel abandoned all over again, dear, and eventually your true feelings will

196

surface. May as well have them come out now, eh? While I'm here to offer you a shoulder to cry on?"

At that, Amanda opened her arms, and, without getting up from her own chair, reached out like an octopus to pull Ruby from hers so that she suddenly found herself half on the floor and half-sitting on the older woman's squishy lap.

"Hey!" Ruby squeaked.

"Let it out," Amanda demanded, pressing Ruby's head against her ample chest. "Come on, Ruby. Let it go. Let the tears come now. Let them come. Cry for the baby you were."

"But I don't feel like crying," said Ruby, trying to free herself from the overly insistent embrace. "Please let me go."

Amanda continued to hold her too tightly.

"Let it out, Ruby. Let it out!"

"Let me go!"

Ruby finally managed to free herself. She sprang to her feet and made sure that she was as far as the door before she turned to Amanda and said, rather undramatically given what had just passed between them, "I'm afraid I've got to go now. Tutorial in half an hour. Thanks for the birth certificate."

"Ruby, you know you can ask to see me any time you want."

"Thanks," said Ruby. "That's very . . . er . . ." "Reassuring" was probably the word Amanda expected but it didn't seem quite right. "Er, thanks."

Ruby legged it down to the safety of the High Street and didn't look back.

Back in her bedroom at the halls of residence, Ruby hid the certificate complete with brown envelope in a shoebox beneath her bed. She didn't open the envelope again for almost a decade. Amanda's parting comment had been that while Ruby claimed she didn't want to talk about her adoption now, one day she might have an *epiphany* that would provoke her to take her search further. When the epiphany didn't happen at her twenty-first birthday or her twenty-fifth, Ruby assumed that it would never happen. Then Ruby became an aunt.

Ruby's sister Lindsay was three years her senior. She was Ruby's parents' natural daughter. Complications following Lindsay's birth meant that they were unable to have any more children of their own afterwards, hence the adoption. Mrs Taylor was determined to be a mother all over again. And now Lindsay was a mother too. Baby Lauren Joanna was born on the twenty-sixth of April, a fortnight before the John Flett goodbye e-mail.

Ruby saw Lauren for the first time on the Monday after Susannah's wedding — May Bank Holiday. It was a strange experience. She had been expecting the event to be somewhat similar to the day her sister introduced the family to her insane Border collie dog, Raffles. Ruby had been thrilled to meet the little puppy. Lindsay had spent a few moments introducing Ruby to Raffles and trying to make the puppy sit to command when Ruby gave him a biscuit (he preferred her finger). Then Lindsay had left Ruby and Raffles alone in the sitting-room while she went to make a cup of tea and returned with two cups of tea AND a bottle of Chardonnay.

Raffles continued to race around the coffee table as though he were missing some vital part of cortical hard-wiring, while the sisters relaxed into their usual Sunday afternoon pattern, talking first about Mum and Dad. "Which one of us is going to have them when they finally go doo-lally?" Then Lindsay's effort at DIY, which basically involved sending her husband up a ladder and shouting at him. Then Ruby's love-life. Lindsay would listen endlessly to Ruby's complaints about her love-life, claiming she was torn between jealousy that Ruby was still out there and dating so many different, exciting men and enormous relief that she wasn't, as each *different* man turned out to be a bastard in exactly the same way as the previous one.

But the arrival of Lauren Joanna was entirely different to the arrival of Raffles the mad Border collie. No chance now that Ruby would be left to admire Lauren's repertoire of tricks while Lindsay uncorked the Chardonnay in the kitchen. The sitting-room was full of other visitors for a start. Lindsay's mother-in-law had installed herself in the semi two weeks before the baby's due date but showed no sign of leaving now that Lauren had made an appearance. She would tell everyone with a martyred sigh that her daughter-in-law still needed her. Ruby's mother frequently wondered aloud how much Lindsay needed to have an old woman staring at her while she tried to breast-feed.

But mother-in-law was still there when Ruby arrived. As were both Ruby's own parents. Lindsay sat in the best armchair with the baby held firmly against her breast. All eyes were on her and the bundle in white cotton at her nipple. When Ruby walked into the room, she felt uneasy almost instantly. It was like a scene in some 1970s horror movie — Lindsay had just given birth to the spawn of the devil and all the attendant biddies were there to make sure that she didn't try to make a break for the sanctuary of the church with their new messiah.

"Here's Auntie Ruby," said Lindsay in a peculiar little voice that Ruby didn't recognise.

"Auntie Ruby! Makes me sound about a hundred and twelve!" Ruby laughed.

"Old enough to have one of your own already," Lindsay's mother-in-law observed.

Lindsay handed Ruby her baby niece. Almost as soon as the tiny creature realised that she was being handed to someone other than mummy her brow began to furrow, her peachy complexion darkened to magenta and she took a deep breath as though filling her lungs for a scream.

"She's going to cry," said Ruby, preparing to hand her straight back.

"Just say something nice to her," Lindsay suggested. "Coo at her."

"She looks like her daddy," said Grandma Jones the mother-in-law.

"She looks like Lindsay did at that age too," interrupted Ruby's own mother, Grandma Taylor. "And me."

And there it was. The family line. Ruby looked from her niece to her elder sister to her mother. Three generations of women with matching mouths and eyes and noses. Ruby remembered once reading a poem that said "Family faces are a magic mirror" and at last she knew what that meant.

Back at home that night, Ruby dug out her birth certificate for the first time since her experience with Amanda the Patchouli Monster had made her want to rip it into shreds. Hope Mary Barker. The name was still there. Blue ink on pink paper. And no matter how much she felt like a Taylor girl, Ruby realised that if she ever had a baby it would have the Barker nose, not the Taylor one. Perhaps at last this was the time to get a better idea of what that nose looked like.

CHAPTER
EIGHTEEN

Ruby's adoption had been on her mind a great deal since that afternoon at Lindsay's house. And as she stared at the crack in Lou's ceiling, it was with her again. This time that old numb sense of loss was mixed up with the intense feelings of worthlessness that Flett's careless dumping and even the parting words of that thoughtless idiot Robin had provoked in her.

She couldn't sleep. Every time she closed her eyes, her last conversation with Flett started running like the adverts at the cinema. Or, if she managed to take her mind off him for a second, Robin's disappointed assertion that he was looking for someone younger and better-looking played instead.

Ruby flicked on the television, hoping that she'd be able to get absorbed in one of those bizarre Euro programmes they show late on a Friday night. But nothing grabbed her attention. She couldn't watch the horror movie on Channel 5 in case it kept her awake with fear. The only thing to do was read *Hello* and be reassured that even being rich and famous doesn't really protect you from heartache. For every celebrity wedding the magazine featured these days, there were at least two articles on stars who found themselves suddenly single again, eager to talk about their heartbreak from the "sumptuous surroundings of their luxurious new home". Or a hotel room, depending how the divorce settlement had gone . . . Ruby pulled a new copy of the grown-up comic from Lou's overflowing magazine rack and began her search for celebrity solace.

That week's glossy cover bore the super-wide grin of Katrina Black — the only actress in Hollywood who could make Angelina Jolie look thin-lipped. Katrina Black was plugging her autobiography, a ghost-written tome entitled *Little Black Book*. There had been lots of press surrounding the book's recent publication. It was supposed to be packed full of incredible revelations. Not least of which was the news that one well-known Tinseltown scion liked to wrap himself in cling-film beneath his hand-stitched Italian suits before spending the evening rubbing himself up against unsuspecting young women at film industry parties. Apparently, the point of the cling-film was to stop any embarrassing emissions from staining his threads, though, as most people quickly observed, that didn't explain why the actor wrapped cling-film around his *whole* body, ankle to neck. A double layer.

Ruby was as fascinated by the sexual peccadilloes of the rich and famous as the next girl, of course. But that wasn't why she too had been itching to get her hands on a copy of Katrina Black's autobiography. Ruby was interested in a rather different side of Katrina's private life because, in magazine and television interviews throughout her career, the actress had made no secret of the fact that she, like Ruby, had been given up as a baby. Katrina Black was the only other adoptee Ruby knew. Or knew of, at least.

The story had been told at least a dozen times before but only lately did it have a happy ending. When she first became famous, Katrina Black suddenly found herself prey to a particularly trendy crowd who quickly introduced her to drugs. Two high profile drugs-busts later — one of which ended in a pretty lenient jail sentence — Katrina booked herself into a rehab clinic in the Arizona desert and stayed there for as long as her filming schedule would allow. Six days, in actual fact, though the blurb for the back of the book made it sound much more dramatic than that. Anyway, during her time in rehab, Katrina decided, with the help of a therapist and a fellow inmate who had a Native American Indian spirit guide, that the root of her problems wasn't her sudden ascent to fame and her inability to say no to a nice line of coke at all. It was, she said, the *abandonment* she had suffered as a child. Her adoption had scarred her deeply, she claimed, robbing her of the ability to find balance in her adult relationships. And the only way to put those childhood traumas behind her and move on would be to obtain proper "closure".

Of course, the only way to obtain closure would be for Katrina to meet the woman who had given her up at birth and a whole chapter of Katrina's autobiography and most of the article in *Hello* was dedicated to her search for her natural family. She hired a private detective. She had her "people" hunt through every birth, death and marriage record in the United States. She placed ads in every single newspaper in the country from the *LA Times* and *Herald Tribune* to a two-sheet freebie in the Appalachians. And, despite the money she threw at them, it was not the private detective or Katrina's entourage that reunited the actress with her *mom*, but a tiny ad in a Louisiana rag, whose biggest story so far that year had been about an alligator eating a pet poodle.

In true Hollywood style, the meeting was the subject of a documentary complete with perfect filmic moments. The megastar striding confidently down the modest street that she could have bought with the wages from one episode of her latest hit sitcom. Cut to the woman who had last seen her as a baby standing, already teary-eyed, on the front porch of her bungalow with the children she had given birth to (and not given away) since the first mistake she made.

That night in Lou's house, Ruby devoured the details all over again, looking for parallels to her own life. As Ruby guessed her natural mother must have been, Katrina Black's mother had been a teenager at the time she fell pregnant. Carlene Schmit claimed that Katrina had been conceived the first time she had sex, with a guy she had known and loved ever since she could remember. They made love the night before he enlisted in the army. Two weeks later he was killed in an accident during a basic training exercise. Gary Hobbs never knew Carlene Schmit was carrying his baby. She didn't know herself until it was too late to do anything about it. Not that she would have done anything about it, she claimed. She wanted to have Gary's child.

But things were different then, wrote Katrina's interviewer in the sugary style that peppered the whole article. *Only bad girls got themselves pregnant in those days and nobody wanted to help a bad girl, not even if she was carrying the child of the town's favourite son, a military hero, killed in action.* They glossed over the fact that Gary was killed while playing baseball with a grenade. *Carlene had no choice but to give away the baby she so wanted. They had just ten short minutes together after the arduous birth — a twelve hour labour. Carlene held her daughter in her arms and knew at once that her baby was special, with a glittering future ahead of her.*

Who wouldn't say that about Katrina Black now, Ruby thought a little cynically.

But Carlene knew that she couldn't stand in the way of Katrina's destiny. She knew that she would never be able to afford the dancing lessons, the singing lessons and the acting classes that would one day make her baby girl a star. So she made the ultimate sacrifice. She gave her baby away.

"And it was the worst day of my life," Carlene took up the story. "I felt as though something had been ripped from me. My stomach felt empty. It was as though someone had turned off the sound. I couldn't hear anything. I couldn't taste the food they brought to me. I remember staring at the orange curtains of my hospital room as the day turned into night.

"I thought I would cry for a week," Carlene continued. "But I knew, somewhere inside, that this would not be the last time I saw my daughter. I knew

206

that one day she would come back to me. And I knew that I would recognise her when she came."

Carlene didn't seem bothered by the fact that she had watched all of Katrina's movies and had been a huge fan of the soap she starred in without realising that the girl on the screen was her daughter. Perhaps it was the nose job that had thrown her off the scent.

Whatever, she continued, "And here we are, reunited at last. At last I feel complete. My favourite daughter is home."

Ruby looked at the photos that accompanied the eight-page interview and felt a little sorry for the children Carlene had borne since Katrina. They didn't have their half-sister's elegance, that was for sure. And though Katrina claimed to be inseparable from her newfound siblings, Ruby secretly wondered whether Katrina would really be happy to take the cross-eyed one along to a Los Angeles premiere.

The picture of Katrina and Carlene alone was somewhat better. Though their reunion had been recorded for posterity and the general American viewing public, there was no hint that the smiles were just for the camera. They looked into each other's eyes and, though there were sixteen years between them, their grins were mirror images. Magic mirror images, thought Ruby.

"No woman gives her baby away unthinkingly," the actress concluded. "The wound is deep on both sides. I'm just glad that I had the opportunity to heal that wound for both of us. I would urge anyone in the same position to do the same. Life is too short to be strangers."

The article ended with a photograph of Katrina and her new beau, a rap star who had recently given up his "gangsta" past and was currently "rapping for God". Without the strength Katrina drew from finding her birth mother, the interview explained, she might never have been able to find the true, adult relationship she so richly deserved. Discovering the true circumstances behind her adoption had given back to Katrina Black the self-esteem she had been unable to find as one of Hollywood's highest grossing stars. And finding self-esteem had enabled her to send out the right signals to attract her true love.

Ruby closed the magazine thoughtfully. Was that where she had been going wrong? Was she too carrying a wound so deep that it was still bleeding; attracting the wrong men into her life like sharks lured by the scent of death surrounding an injured fish?

It was very late. Ruby was still slightly drunk. She mocked up another ad for the back of *The Times*.

Would anyone knowing the whereabouts of Geraldine Barker, formerly of Greenwich, please contact box number XXX.

She used the wording that Katrina Black had used in the ad that went into every single newspaper in the United States, substituting only the name of her birth mother and the city. Then she called up *The Times'* twenty-four-hour classified advertisement line and dictated the sixteen short words before proper consideration or cowardice could stop her.

Afterwards she felt a little odd. A little breathless. A little panicky. But she had done it. She'd really done it this time. She had finally placed the personal ad that might really change her life.

CHAPTER
NINETEEN

"Cindy," Martin called, "you're not seriously going to play that, are you? There's no way I can get down to it to a soundtrack by that bunch of nancy-boys."

"Silence, slave!"

"What?"

"I said silence!"

Cindy reappeared in the doorway. She wasn't naked any more. Oh no. She was wearing a black cat mask and a matching leather bikini. In her right hand she held a long leather bullwhip. In her left, a huge purple vibrator. Her nipples poked through slits in the bikini cups. Martin's first instinct was to laugh.

"Shut up!" barked Cindy, underlining her order with a crack of the whip. "You're in my kingdom now. I make the decisions about what we're going to listen to. In fact, I make all the decisions about everything to do with your puny little body from now on . . ."

"Puny?" protested Martin. He'd heard quite a lot of insults in his early days as a telephone salesman, but no one had ever called him puny. That wasn't fair. In fact, to his mind he was so far from puny that he'd recently considered a Slim-fast regime.

"I'm role playing," Cindy explained patiently. "Anyway, enough of your insolence," she clicked back into dominatrix mode. "Sing along with Mark and Robbie. Make sure you stay in tune or I'll have to take my whip to you."

"You are joking."

Crack went the whip. She clearly wasn't.

And so Martin found himself singing along to Take That and Lulu's rendition of "Relight My Fire" while Cindy, in her leather bikini, slid about the marble floor in front of him, pouting and posing and occasionally stopping to run the very tip of her bullwhip ever so gently across the top of his dick or hold the vibrator against his kneecap.

"You're not getting a hard-on!" she said accusingly at one point.

"I'm trying," he promised. But this was hardly how Martin had expected to end the evening. Martin couldn't make up his mind whether it was erotic or just plain comical when Cindy bent over in front of him and gave him a front-row view of her crotchless leather knickers. When he stopped singing to gape at the spectacle, she snapped upright again and marched over to impress upon him how important it was that he didn't stop. And it turned out that she had put "Relight My Fire" on repeat so it was always the same bloody song.

After six renditions of the dreaded tune, Martin decided that it was interfering with his enjoyment of what might otherwise have been a pretty incredible experience. He dared to ask Cindy if they might move

211

onto something else. "'I Want You Back', perhaps?" It was the only other Take That song he knew. "Or how about you just uncuff one of my hands?"

"You'll get your reward when I say so!" was her answer.

Martin watched her wiggle back across the room to strike another pose by the open door.

"Please," he tried again. "My wrists are getting sore."

"Insolence!" Cindy shrieked at him. "You'll have to be punished for that."

This time she turned the shower on. Martin was shocked by the sudden, heavy downpour but thankfully it wasn't too cold. However, it certainly dampened his ardour. Take That on repeat. A tepid shower. And a barking mad rich girl prancing about the bathroom in what, quite frankly, looked less and less like the outfit of a dominatrix and more and more like it belonged to the Village People's poodle.

Sod this, thought Martin. Not even he was this desperate to get laid. "Cindy," he said firmly. "Uncuff me at once."

"Never!" she snarled as she crawled across the bathroom floor in what Martin could only assume she thought was the style of a panther.

"I'm fed up of this, Cindy."

"But I haven't finished!"

"I've got to go home," he tried, going instead for the sympathy vote. "My sister is on holiday," he lied, "and I'm supposed to be looking after her kittens. I forgot to feed them before I came out."

Cindy didn't care. In fact, she cranked up the volume of the CD and returned to the bathroom for the big Lulu finale.

"Let me out of here," yelled Martin.

"Relight my fi-i-i-i-re!" Cindy began to march about the bathroom floor in a strange showgirl goose-step, kicking her legs slightly higher than a Nazi but not quite as high as the *Folies Bergère*. High enough, however, that she managed to lose her balance and, with an ugly crack of skull on marble floor, went arse over tit and blacked out on the Ralph Lauren bath mat.

"Cindy!" Martin called. "Cindy! Are you OK."

He couldn't properly see how she had landed, chained as he was to the shower pipe.

"Cindy?" She didn't answer him. "Cindy!!!"

Was she dead?

Martin twisted his hands desperately in an attempt to escape his soggy bondage. Take That were still playing and the shower was still pouring down on top of his head like some kind of Chinese water torture. "Cindy!" He could just about see her legs if he leaned as far over as his bonds would allow him. She wasn't showing any sign of getting up. "Cindy! This isn't funny now. Get up!"

No answer.

She must be dead, he thought. This was how these things happened. Sex games gone wrong. Who would believe he hadn't murdered her? Martin panicked and started to hyperventilate, despite the fact that it was pretty clear he couldn't have tripped her up from where he was standing with his hands cuffed behind him round the shower rail.

"Cindy!" he shouted. His voice was barely audible above Lulu's big crescendo. "Cindy! Wake up, girl!"

Now it didn't seem like such good luck that there was no one else in the house. What time had she said her parents would be back? If they didn't come back until the following evening, Martin panicked, then he might well end up dead too. From pneumonia. The hot water had run out and the shower was starting to feel pretty damn frigid.

Martin groaned and slumped down as far as he was able. He could almost see his mother's face when they told her the news.

"A sex game, Mrs Ashcroft. A victim of his own depravity."

The humiliation might well kill his mother too.

Though arguably, it could be far worse if Martin survived the night and Cindy didn't. There would have to be an inquest. He would have to explain in a court of law how he had come to be handcuffed to a shower rail with Take That's "Relight My Fire" on repeat and a posh girl in a leather bikini lying dead on the guest bathroom floor. And that was before he explained how he'd met her in the first place!

"Cindy!" he shouted one more time. In a brief pause while the song ended and before it started again, Martin's worried voice echoed pathetically around the marble-tiled room. He tried to flick a bit of water from the bathtub in Cindy's direction, hoping that it might revive her if she was only slightly unconscious. When she still didn't move he started to pray. He hadn't prayed for a long time. Not since England was last drawn against Germany in the World Cup and it hadn't worked then either. But now he prayed much harder.

"Please, Lord," he muttered. "Look, I haven't known this girl for long and I know it doesn't look good, what with the leather and the whip and all that, but I think she's fundamentally a pretty nice person. A bit odd, perhaps, but who isn't odd these days, eh? Deep down inside, I know she's a good girl. And she's only young. Well, twenty-seven. She doesn't deserve to die. Please, let her live, Lord. I really do believe in you. Please let Cindy live, God. I know you can do that for me. I beg you, please send me a sign."

The water in the shower was icy now. "Relight My Fire" started for the fifth time since Cindy's slip and she still showed no evidence of resurrection. Martin was ready to give up and succumb to pneumonia. Just once more he offered up a little prayer. "I know you can save her, Lord. Just send me a sign."

Silence. (Except for Lulu).

"Oh, God," Martin sobbed. "Oh God, oh God, oh God."

Suddenly, there was a patter of tiny feet. Or, more specifically, of tiny paws on marble. Martin opened his eyes, which had been tightly shut in prayer, to see a little white dog standing in the bathroom doorway. It looked at him quizzically, head on one side. No, thought Martin, it was looking at him *knowingly*. Was this the little white terrier of God?

215

Wagging its little white tail, the Bedlington terrier —
that looked less like a dog than a lamb — trotted across
the bathroom floor to where Cindy's lifeless body lay.

"Thank you, Lord!" cried Martin. "It's a sign. Lick
her face, boy. Lick her face until she wakes up! Or
bark!" He encouraged the little canine. "Go out on the
street and bark until someone comes to see what's
wrong. Go on, boy. Bark for me! You can do it!"

The little dog cocked his head to one side again as
though he were pondering a solution.

"Go on, boy!" Martin shouted. "Make like Lassie!"

And as if he understood, the terrier raced out into
the corridor. Martin raised his eyes to heaven. "Thank
you, Lord. Thank you. Thank you for sending your
heavenly angel dog to save this poor sinner. Thank you,
Lord. Now if you could just help him find a passer-by
and bring help to save us all."

Help arrived sooner than even a miracle-worker might
have managed; when the little dog reappeared moments
later, it was in its owner's arms. The dog owner looked
faintly familiar but this was hardly the moment for a
"haven't I see you before?" conversation.

"Thank you! Thank you!" Martin cried. "I think she
hit her head. Can you call an ambulance? I don't know
how it happened but we've got to get her to hospital
before her parents come home."

"We *are* her parents," said the woman holding the
dog. Of course they were. How else had they got into
the house? And now the woman was joined by her

husband. He too, looked incredibly familiar as he stared in horror at the naked stranger in his bath.

"What the —" began Cindy's father.

"For God's sake," cried her mother. "We'll deal with him later. Let's get her off the floor."

Between them, Cindy's parents managed to drag their daughter's flaccid body into a semi-upright position, the little dog yapping all the while. As they lifted her, Cindy started to moan. It didn't look good. She had a lump the size of a golf ball on her forehead. But at least she wasn't dead.

Cindy's mother dialled an ambulance on her mobile phone while her father flapped cool air across her face with the cat mask.

"Darling, wake up!" he cooed.

Meanwhile, Martin was still sitting beneath the cascading, bollock-freezing cold, shower. No one had bothered to switch off the Take That CD either.

Eventually, when she was convinced that the ambulance was en route, Cindy's mother turned the shower off. By the time the ambulance men arrived to cart Cindy off to hospital however, the key to the handcuffs was still nowhere to be found. With nothing but a hand towel to protect his modesty, Martin had to wait in the bath until the firemen arrived with their metal-cutting equipment. Just a hand towel; while the statue in the corner held enough fluffy bath-sheets to keep an Arctic expedition warm!

The firemen took forever thanks to a warehouse fire in Brent Cross. And then they had to wait for a plumber to turn off the water supply so that when the firemen cut through the shower pipe, they didn't flood the house.

Martin was finally freed from his bondage almost five hours after Cindy took her tumble, having been seen in his naked (and very shrivelled, thanks to the cold water) glory by a total of fifteen people other than the girl he originally took his clothes off for. It didn't take seven firemen to cut him free of course, but the fire chief had decided that all his boys should see the situation in case they happened upon something of its like in the future.

"It's good training," he told them. Martin suspected that he was merely the light relief after a long hard night of fire-fighting. Then there were three plumbers, the three paramedics who took Cindy to the accident unit, both Cindy's unfriendly parents and the dog.

Understandably, all Martin wanted to do was slink off into the night and forget he and Cindy Daniels ever met. Unfortunately, that was not going to be possible. Oh no. When the plumbers and firemen had gone and Martin was back in his clothes again, still shivering, Cindy's mother informed him icily that he would have to remain at the house until their lawyer arrived.

"Lawyer?" Martin exclaimed. "But she's all right, isn't she? I mean, she's not going to die."

"Cindy will be fine," said her mother. "No thanks to you. She has a mild case of concussion and will be staying in hospital overnight. But we'd still like you to sign this."

"Sign what?"

218

The lawyer duly produced a ten-page thick contract from his briefcase with a flourish.

"I have no idea who you are, young man," said Cindy Daniels' mother. "Nor do I really wish to know. But I feel sure you know all about me."

The way she said that phrase suddenly helped make the connection. That shocking red crop. Those steely blue eyes. Cindy's mother was Petunia Daniels, the actress. Which meant that her father was Benjamin Daniels, best Hamlet since Laurence Olivier. Star of the Royal Shakespeare Company and four times Oscar nominee. No wonder they had looked familiar. No wonder they wanted Martin to sign a document saying that even if the editor of the *News of the World* pulled his toenails out with a pair of rusty pliers, Martin would reveal nothing of what had gone on in their house that night.

Martin began to read the contract but was too tired and cold to concentrate. All he wanted was to go home. The last thing on his mind was selling his story to the tabloids. He wanted a hot bath and some warmer clothing. "Look, Mrs Daniels," he started, "you don't really need me to sign this. I'm not going to say anything. I mean, what happened this evening is just as embarrassing for me as . . ."

"In consideration of your embarrassment," said the actress, opening her cheque book, "we'd like you to have ten thousand pounds. Name?"

"Er, Martin . . . Martin Ashcroft. A-S-H . . . But, you really don't . . ."

"Well, Mr Ashcroft," Petunia interrupted him, "I'll put my signature on this and you'll put your signature on that and I trust we shan't be hearing from you again."

She handed Martin the cheque.

More than a little bewildered, Martin scrawled his name on the dotted line at the bottom of the contract. Petunia Daniels saw him to the back door of her house and bid him "good morning". Didn't even offer him the use of her phone to call a cab.

It wasn't until he got back to his own flat that Martin fished the cheque out and looked at it again. He toyed with the idea of going round to Lou's and letting the girls know how his bizarre night had progressed, but decided against it. That contract had seemed pretty stiff and he knew that both his friends had unscrupulous journalist pals who would be only too happy to share his secret with the *News of the World*. If there really was a secret to share . . .

It was as though he expected to find that the cheque, in fact the whole evening in the company of Cindy, had all been a figment of his overactive imagination. But there was the date, the amount (in figures and in words) and Petunia Daniels' signature. It was an ordinary cheque. Nothing about it suggested that Petunia had been making a joke when she signed it.

Ten thousand pounds. Martin thought about his bank account. He'd just been paid. It wasn't empty. But he wasn't going to be paid again at the end of that month. Or maybe even the month after that. It shouldn't really take long for a salesman of his experience to find a new position. But that was providing Barry Parsons hadn't already rubbished him to every mag in London.

The cheque Martin now held in his hands was enough to cover the wages he'd lost until Christmas. He could live on ten thousand pounds for far longer than that if he reined in his lifestyle for a bit. How long would he have then? Six months? Twelve months? Ten thousand pounds was probably enough to live on in India for a couple of years. He knew a guy from college who'd been living in Goa since 1995 with no visible means of support.

Martin didn't want to go back to an office. Not the International Magazines office. Not any office. He wanted to write his novel. And the cheque in his pocket might just be a passport to time off. A sabbatical. A chance to finish his book and get it published and never in his life have to answer to a balding twat like Barry Parsons again.

Growing more and more excited by the second, Martin decided that via his unconventional meeting with Petunia Daniels, fate was giving him an almighty shove towards his ambition. He kissed the cheque. Talk about serendipity. Then he patted the pocket that contained the solitary diskette copy of his novel. His route to immortality. His destiny.

And it was empty.

CHAPTER
TWENTY

Lou had never received a bouquet of flowers in her life. Sure, she'd had bunches of carnations picked up from a service station, but she had never before answered the door to find a little chap from Interflora staggering under the weight of half the Chelsea Flower Show. Her first instinct was to assume that he'd got the wrong flat. The doughy-faced girl in the flat downstairs, who wore her pearls even to go jogging in the morning, was always getting flowers from her equally chinless boyfriend. They must be for her. But no, these flowers really were for Lou.

"Once Seen, never forgotten," Andrew had written on the card that accompanied them. Lou couldn't help smiling, despite the fact that one of the lilies was already shedding indelible yellow pollen all over her clean white T-shirt.

"For our second anniversary," he explained when she phoned him to say thanks. "Two weeks since our first proper date, you know."

"You are such a romantic," Lou said.

The day after their meeting at Suave, Andrew had called and invited Lou to join him for tea. It was a grey day — British summertime after all — so they planned

222

to rendezvous in the Egyptian exhibit at the British Museum. When Lou arrived, five minutes late, Andrew was already standing in front of a huge, dislocated fist that must once have belonged to a giant statue of a mighty pharaoh. He hadn't seen Lou approaching, so she decided to hide behind a row of cat-headed goddesses and watch him for a while.

As she watched, she remembered something her mother had once said about meeting Lou's father. "I liked the way he leaned against the lamppost," Mrs Capshaw sighed, whenever she recounted the story of their first date. And Lou liked the way Andrew looked now, as he studied the giant fist while he waited for her to show up. Just hanging about. He looked relaxed. Not nervous. He was at ease in his own body, Lou concluded. That was nice. A teenage girl, sketching Egyptian artefacts for a school project, gave him an appreciative glance. Andrew smiled back at her, but not in a seedy way. He stepped out of the way so that a father could lift his young son closer to the statue. Andrew laughed with the father as the little boy made his own fist, less than a hundredth of the size of the stone one. The two men shared a joke.

Lou nodded to herself as she watched him. Andrew was a catch all right. Good-looking, gregarious, generous. Fashionable, friendly . . . firm buttocks. He got a tick in every box on the ideal boyfriend scale.

"Lou!"

He had spotted her.

"We were just speculating on this guy's chances against Mike Tyson," he said, nodding towards the granite hand. He took Lou's own soft hand and kissed it. "Hello, you," he murmured.

And Lou thought that perhaps it was possible to fall in love at *second* sight.

Since then, they seemed to have spent almost every spare moment together. Working as he did for an Internet ticket agency, Andrew was always able to get cut-price seats at the last minute for any of the West End shows. When they went to see *The Mousetrap*, Andrew managed to get seats in a private box. He brought champagne and expensive Belgian chocolates. He even had a floppy pink tea rose for the buttonhole of Lou's denim jacket.

He was indeed, the ideal boyfriend. And he would constantly marvel at the circumstances of their very first meeting. What were the chances that he would answer an ad for a joke and hit it off so spectacularly with the victim of his hoax? Surely they were even slimmer than the one in seven million chance Lou had of actually finding the real stranger she had fancied?

"Anyway," said Andrew, "your stranger is probably a tosser. He's probably got a girlfriend. Or a wife. And even if he didn't have, you probably would have hated him when you got the chance to talk. You're much better off with me," he added with his most charming, little boy smile.

And Lou felt she had to agree.

More than a month had passed now since that fateful Wednesday morning on the Northern Line. Lou wasn't even sure she would recognise her stranger again. It had been a moment of madness, that was all.

224

"You are mad," said Martin, when Ruby told him that she wanted to place another personal ad. "The personal ad world is full of freaks."

"And one very nice man with a Porsche who wanted to meet me!" Ruby reminded him. In the aftermath of the dreadful triple date, the revelation that one of the guys who replied to Ruby's ad had a Porsche sent her into a frenzy. "I still can't believe you sent me on a date with a man who split the cost of garlic bread when all along you knew there was a man for me out there driving a Porsche!"

"I didn't like the sound of his message. I mean, what kind of wanker phones up and tells you about his car within the first two seconds of describing himself?"

"The kind of wanker that at least has a car," said Ruby. "The nearest that Robin idiot ever got to a Porsche was cutting a spare set of keys for one. Besides, I don't know why you're so down on the system, Mart. You were the one who got a night of passion."

"Yeah."

Martin had neglected to tell either of his friends the true circumstances of his night on the tiles. Or rather, Cindy's night on the tiles and his night in the bathtub. He'd reread the contract Petunia Daniels sent him away with a dozen times since that Friday and it seemed that he only had to breathe the Daniels name in his sleep to have a lawyer jump on his head and smash his brains in. Much as he loved Lou and Ruby, he feared a law suit as big as New York if the truth ever came out in a real way, which would be the inevitable

225

consequence of telling either of London's biggest gossips.

Neither had he told the girls about the missing diskette and the novel that was lost forever. It hurt just to think about that. The last thing he wanted was to have them offer solutions to what seemed like an insurmountable problem. A man to his very core, Martin was determined to suffer in silence.

"Where are you temping this week anyway?" Ruby asked.

"I'm doing a customer survey for McDonald's," he told her flatly.

He was in a deep depression. And one that could probably have been alleviated by going on a long holiday costing roughly ten thousand pounds. Yep, two weeks after the Take That bondage incident, Petunia Daniels' cheque was still uncashed. He'd come close to cashing it once though.

He'd got a printout of his current account balance and been quite pleased with the three figure number until he saw the little "d" after it. It was ridiculous to have a cheque for ten thousand pounds in his pocket and minus nine hundred in the bank. So he filled out a paying-in slip and joined the queue for the cashiers. As he waited in line, Martin wondered whether the cashier who served him would be surprised by the name on the cheque. How would she suppose he had come by a cheque for ten thousand pounds signed by one of Britain's most prominent actresses? Martin thought he noticed the old lady in the queue behind him trying to get a peek at his paying-in slip. Would everyone guess that it was a pay-off?

He didn't have time to find out that morning. Just as the old guy in front of Martin finished counting out a jam-jar full of two-pence pieces into neat little piles, the quietly industrious atmosphere of the bank was suddenly rent by an ear-piercing alarm. At first, both customers and cashiers looked up at the source of the noise with such bovine acceptance that Martin was reminded of a field of cattle remaining unmoved by the passage of a couple of low-flying fighter jets.

They were testing the alarms. That was the immediate assumption. It was only when the alarm refused to go quiet after almost a minute and a half, and the bank's manageress actually ran shrieking into the lobby, that anyone thought about evacuating.

"Get outside! Get outside!" she yelled. "Everybody out."

It took a few moments to persuade them. There was still no sign of smoke. But the sprinklers set into the ceiling of the lobby were now beginning to unleash a less than gentle rain. When a droplet splashed onto his paying in slip and smudged the neat way Martin had written his signature, he too decided it was time to go. Outside, a fire engine was already skidding to a halt by the pavement. Three firemen in their bright yellow helmets pushed through the bystanders all hoping to see a real fire.

By this time, the manageress was hyperventilating against a letter-box. The look on her face suggested that the situation must be very grave indeed.

"Move out of the way, folks," said the man who had been driving the fire truck. The bystanders took two steps back and waited thirty seconds before they took three forward again. With the sprinklers now making like a monsoon inside the building, there wasn't much hope that particular branch of the HSBC would be open again that afternoon.

"Sod it."

Martin sighed and stuffed the cheque and paying-in slip back into his record bag. Petunia Daniels wouldn't have to worry about going overdrawn that day. Or the next day. Martin just couldn't bring himself to cash that cheque. He had pride. He had integrity. He had . . . nothing.

Ruby didn't notice her friend's depression. She was on a mission; too caught up in her latest gargantuan effort to improve her love life. She hadn't applied herself to anything with such determination and tenacity since she and Mary Jeapes had done the "I must, I must improve my bust" exercise, fifty times a day for two weeks aged eleven. Ruby was going to find that Porsche driver and she was going to meet him for a date. View to friendship and possible marriage . . .

Work was still hell. She didn't have to see Flett for a fortnight, thank God. But that was only because he was on his hols. Where he'd gone, she didn't know. But Ruby did know that Two-Faced Imogen had mysteriously booked the exact same fortnight off.

The summer party loomed like a title match. At the moment, Imogen was definitely the odds-on favourite to carry home the title of Hollingworth's queen. She had the man. And she would probably have a tan, to boot, after her fortnight wherever it was she had been.

Ruby confided her personal ad campaign to Liz, who suggested that she would be better off with yoga.

"What are the chances that the Porsche man will ring again?" Liz asked her. "You need to find inner peace, Ruby. Not a boyfriend."

"A boyfriend with a Porsche will give me all the inner peace I need," Ruby explained, then she shooed Liz out of her office while she called through to *The Sunday Times* with her copy. "Will Robert with the Porsche who left a message for Ruby please call again. Lost your number."

"It won't work," Liz said confidently when they met again by the photocopier that afternoon.

But — oh God — it did. It really bloody did! And miraculously, Robert with the Porsche was still single and still "super keen to meet", as he said in the voicemail he left the very day the personal ad was published! Ruby wasted no time in arranging a date.

"How will I recognise you?" she asked him.

"I'll be carrying a dozen red roses," he replied. "And how will I recognise you?" he asked her. "What do you look like, Ruby? You sound like a goddess."

Ruby put down the phone on her chocolate-voiced dream-boy and swooned.

CHAPTER
TWENTY-ONE

"I must not get too excited. I must not get too excited."

Ruby forced down the rising bubble of anticipation in her stomach. It couldn't possibly be him. Why on earth would someone that good-looking — let alone someone that good-looking who also drove a *Porsche* — be answering Lonely Hearts ads? Yet there he was. Standing exactly where Robert had said he would be and carrying the requisite roses.

"Robert?" Ruby stuttered.

Robert turned vaguely in her direction as though Ruby had just sidled up to him wearing a filthy mac and hissed, "Can you spare any change?"

She smiled her best smile while he looked at her blankly, his perfect lips set in a thin hard line. Oh God, she thought. It isn't him after all. Or if it is him, he doesn't fancy me. He's the wrong man. Or he's going to pretend I've got the wrong man because I'm clearly not the right sort of woman. There must be some other guy with serial killer hair waiting for me right around the corner. A guy this good-looking isn't going to . . .

"Ruby!" She had almost turned to go when Robert suddenly seized her hand and planted a smacker on the back of it. The thin line of his mouth was now an extravagant upwards curve. "Contact lenses," he explained, to excuse his previously vacant expression. "Getting used to them."

Ruby twittered nervously.

"Bit too vain to wear glasses," he added, giving her a sheepish, but simultaneously highly alluring, grin.

Oh yes, thought Ruby, nodding helplessly. It would have been such a shame to hide those cheekbones behind a pair of frames.

"These are for you."

He handed her the roses. And though she had been expecting to see a man waiting for her with a bunch of flowers, Ruby found she was suddenly inordinately thrilled. Not just one dozen red roses but two dozen. And not the kind of petal-bare bunches you find at the supermarket wrapped in a triangle of cellophane, either. The roses were wrapped in gloriously crunchy brown paper and tied in raffia — the Knightsbridge version of clear plastic wrap.

"Shall we?" he asked, opening out his arm so that she could thread her own through it. "I don't know about you, but I'm starving."

Ruby nodded again though she was suddenly too dizzy to eat. As they began to weave their way through the crowds at Leicester Square, Ruby felt herself physically open out like the buds she clasped in her hand. As he complimented her on the beige raincoat she had bought almost five years previously, she was sure she felt herself grow a whole inch taller in the warmth of his gentle flattery. When he told her that he had noticed her walking towards him and didn't dare think that she might be the girl he was looking for because she was so scrumptious, Ruby felt her face glow. She flicked her hair like it was the glossy tail of a dressage pony and not, for once, the hay such a pony would breakfast on. When Robert grinned at her, she knew her eyes were twinkling almost as much as his.

By the time they got to the restaurant, she had counted at least half a dozen girls looking enviously in her direction. She felt as though she had undergone a Hollywood makeover in the ten-minute walk from the tube station to the trendy, minimalist restaurant where Robert had booked a table.

Karma existed. And this was it. This gorgeous man in the expensive pink shirt that would have looked effeminate on any man less confident about his incredible animal attractiveness, was Ruby's reward for John Flett and Dave the accountant and Robin the key-cutter and every other toad who'd come before them. There was no question that Robert was more attractive than Robin, but Ruby's delight swelled to the size of a small cow as she decided that, yes, he was far more attractive than John Flett as well.

"I'm a criminal lawyer."

And clearly more intelligent . . .

"Let me pull that chair out for you."

And much more chivalrous . . .

"Champagne?"

And generous . . .

"Yes, please," said Ruby.

Yes, please! Yes, please! Yes, please!

232

"Well," he said later. "That's the worst part over. I spent all day at work worrying that we wouldn't live up to each other's expectations. Didn't you?"

Ruby raised her eyebrows in surprise. To her subconscious, it didn't seem possible that this man could have fallen short of anyone's highest benchmark.

"You know," Robert continued, "apparently, we human beings can tell if we are attracted to someone within one fiftieth of a second. One fiftieth. Can you imagine how brief a moment that is? Whatever people say about first impressions and not judging a book by its cover, it's impossible to go back and write over the primeval feelings you have about someone as a result of the first time you saw them. Feelings of love can grow over time, of course . . ."

Ruby found herself unable to swallow her mouthful of *crème brûlée*.

"But if you're not physically attracted to someone within that first split-second moment of seeing them, you never will be."

"What? Never?" Ruby asked.

"Never."

Was he trying to tell her something?

He was.

"Which is why I'm so glad that my heart went out to you the moment we locked eyes."

Ruby dropped her dessert spoon with a clatter. When she finished fishing it out from beneath the table, Robert was still leaning on his elbows, orienting himself across the table towards her, and staring at her with those milk chocolate button browns. It was one of those endless moments, when the world around you seems to fade out and all you can see is the face of the person you want to kiss.

"I can't believe you're single," he murmured.

"Or I you!" Ruby replied.

"The last man to let you go must have been a fool."

"Oh, he was," said Ruby. "I mean, we just weren't right for each other, that's all," she spluttered, remembering Lou's instructions that she was to avoid saying anything even slightly bunny-boilerish at all costs. Keep it light. Keep it fluffy. But not Glenn Close casserole fluffy.

"This is one of those nights that I wish would last forever," Robert cooed. "I wish I could just whisk you off in the Boxster."

It was the first time he had mentioned the Porsche that evening. So he definitely had one. Tick. Another mental box checked.

The waiter hovered with the bill. Just one more box to go. Ruby didn't expect Robert to spring for the whole of the check but, after Robin, she had decided that if he didn't at least make a show of attempting to be gentlemanly by refusing her share of the cash then . . .

"I'll get this," Robert said, sliding his credit card inside the smart leather billfold with only the quickest glance at the total.

"Are you sure?"

"Of course I'm sure. It's my pleasure. Now I hope you'll let me drive you home."

Ruby hesitated. The evening had gone perfectly. He seemed like an alright sort of guy. Forget alright. He seemed like the man of her dreams! All the same, said a sensible voice at the back of her head, she couldn't be sure that she wasn't being deceived. She had just one great telephone conversation and a fabulous evening at a restaurant to go on. It probably wasn't a great idea to get into his car but . . .

"I should get a tube," she said, wishing she didn't have to. "I live miles out of your way."

"The whole point of a Porsche *is* those unnecessary miles," he said.

Then they were strolling out of the restaurant together, arm in arm. He pressed the unlock button on his keyring. Across the street, a car that Ruby hadn't noticed as they walked to dinner that evening, sprang to life, headlights flashing like a wink when the alarm system disarmed. In midnight blue with a tan leather interior, it really was the most beautiful car she'd ever seen. Ruby had never been in a Porsche before. She'd never had a boyfriend with a car before! (Flett hadn't ever learned to drive, claiming that he was too intelligent to deal with the petty rigours of the Highway Code.) This was a moment for careful compromise.

"You could just drop me off at the tube station," she suggested.

Next morning, the staff at Hollingworth couldn't fail to notice that there was something different about Ruby Taylor. It was as though the monsoon had ended and the sun was peeking through the clouds to encourage long dormant seeds to burst forth into extravagant multicoloured blossoms. Especially pink ones. That morning Ruby was still wearing the rose pink top she had bought for the previous evening's date. With a neckline slashed down to the front of her bra, it was hardly office attire (though no worse than a pyjama top, which she had worn on a couple of occasions) and heads swivelled like windmills as she walked through the building to her desk.

Boy, did she feel good!

"Morning, Imogen," she called as she passed the Two-Faced gang in their corner.

"Oh, er, morning Ruby," Imogen replied, shocked into a stutter.

"Been somewhere nice?" Ruby asked her. "You've got a great tan."

"Majorca," Imogen mumbled.

"Oh, really. Doesn't John have a villa there?"

Ruby knew that her greeting would be the instant catalyst for gossip but she didn't care. Let them gossip. Whatever they thought had changed her mood from black to fluffy pink with gold trimming, they didn't know the half of it. Lou had been right. Your life *could* turn around in a day. In an hour! In a perfect, explosive second!

"You look chirpy," Liz commented as Ruby leaned languidly against the photocopier, fanning herself with a press release.

"I feel chirpy," Ruby told her. "I feel fan-bloody-tastic!"

"Do I take it that the date went well?"

"Well? Understatement of the year. Liz, you won't believe it. He's a lawyer. He's got his own flat in Islington. He drives a Porsche Boxster! He went to Cambridge. So he's intelligent as well as good-looking and charming and . . . ohmigod, he had such incredible manners. Even if he hadn't insisted on paying the bill — after ordering champagne and not just any champagne, but vintage champagne — I would have gone back to his place like a shot."

"Oh, Rubes. You didn't . . ."

"I am in love!" Ruby exclaimed. "So I did."

"Well . . ."

"I know. I shouldn't get too excited. But I've got such a good feeling about this one. I mean, neither of us wanted the evening to end. I could tell that. We'd still be talking now if it weren't a work day."

"Have you never heard of The Rules?" Liz asked.

"Who cares!" Ruby shouted. "Liz, I am so happy I want to kiss Imogen. I've got my date for the party."

"Have you asked him?"

"I have." Ruby's chest was puffed with pride. "And he said he'd be delighted. De-lighted! I can't wait till Flett sees him. Rob's got so much lovely black hair. Flett was always worrying about losing his hair. He is going to be green. Absolutely green!"

Ruby skipped to her own office. She even blew the Panter a kiss en route. And winked, to boot.

"What's up with her?" Emlyn asked Liz.

"Got laid," Liz half-whispered. "Through a personal ad."

"Bloody hell," said Emlyn. "I might try one of those myself."

CHAPTER
TWENTY-TWO

"That's it. You've inspired me," said Erica, later that week, when Lou told her about Ruby's wonderful date with Robert. "I'm going to see if I can't find a personal ad boyfriend of my own. What do you think of this?"

Erica handed Lou a scrap of paper with her own draft ad scribbled upon it.

> Cat-loving vegetarian, 32, seeks sensitive soul
> with Pisces in his chart.

Lou read it aloud and nodded. "Thirty-two?" was the only bit she queried out loud. Though she wasn't sure about the cat bit either. Or the Pisces part. She had vetoed every reply to the ad she placed for Martin that mentioned star signs or felines, flashing neon signals of desperation that they were.

"Do you think I should leave that bit out?" Erica asked. "My age?"

"No. It's just that . . ." Lou began. Where to start? "No, leave it," she said. "It's fine as it is."

"Good. I'm going to e-mail this through to the paper right now," said Erica. "If I can get this to the *Guardian* by this afternoon it should make it into Saturday's edition. How quickly did you get replies?"

"Very," Lou told her.

"Will you help me sort through mine? Assuming I get some of course."

"Of course," Lou nodded. "And of course you'll get replies. Who wouldn't want a date with you?"

"Oh, thanks, Lou. It really cheered me up, you know. Hearing about you and Andrew. And Ruby and that lawyer bloke of hers. There are still decent men out there after all. You've found one. Here's hoping that I can."

Lou nodded enthusiastically, choosing not to take the opportunity to remind her that while Lou had found Andrew on that first Lonely Hearts Club outing, Ruby had ended up with a man she would have crossed the street to avoid, and Martin hadn't been the same since his night with Cindy Daniels.

"So, how long is it now?" Erica asked.

"What?" Lou had gone back to examining the spreadsheet on her PC screen.

"You and Andrew? How long have you been seeing each other?"

"Er, nearly a month," Lou calculated.

"If I can find a bloke half as lovely as Andrew I'll be happy," said Erica.

"Yeah," said Lou vaguely. "Fingers crossed."

Andrew. Lou still needed to call and let him know that she wouldn't be seeing him that evening. She hoped he wouldn't be too disappointed but had a niggling feeling

240

that he would try his best to change her mind and get her to go over to his place. It was as though he assumed it was his duty to fill every spare moment in Lou's life now. She enjoyed his company well enough but it was getting to that point where she couldn't remember the last time she had spent a night alone. Or with her closest friends.

She'd been putting off the call all morning. Perhaps she'd just e-mail instead. When she opened her Outlook Express, it was surprisingly full. When she placed Martin's personal on the Internet, she had created a bogus e-mail address that would forward all replies meant for him straight to her. They were still coming in. Hairymary@hotmail.com probably needed to change her handle before she scored, Lou smiled wryly.

The replies had been amusing at first, but now they were just annoying. She needed to take Martin's ad off-line again so that she didn't have to wade through badly punctuated love notes to get to the important stuff in her in-box any more.

Www.pinacoladalovematch.com was having a special "summer loving" promotion. All new and existing users of the site would be entered into a grand prize draw to win a romantic weekend *à deux* in the European city of their choice, a flashing box trumpeted. Assuming they also found someone to go with through the personals, thought Lou unkindly.

She clicked her way through the site, following the links that would allow her to remove Martin's details from the database. When she had finished, she was directed straight back to the site's home-page. That week's "hottest" new advertisers were featured in a chart at the top of the page.

"Ready, willing and abell," said one particularly interesting headline.

The misspelling made poor Lou wince, but she clicked on the ad for the hell of it. According to the checklist that accompanied the illiterate blurb, this particular advertiser was just 21, a gorgeous slim blonde with a pretty substantial chest and an interest in stock-car racing.

"Yeah, right," muttered Lou. Naturally, there was no photograph to prove it.

That was the problem with these Internet personal ads. With all personal ads, of course, there was no way of knowing how closely the blurb really matched the person it was describing but with e-mail personals the problem was even more extreme. With only words on a computer screen to go on, it wasn't even possible to know for certain the sex of the person you were communicating with after you'd exchanged a hundred e-mails if you never spoke on the phone. Every other week the newspapers carried a story about someone who had been misled by an online romance. There was nothing to stop anyone logging on as a beautiful woman when they were actually a small, dark and not terribly handsome man.

Why did they do it, Lou wondered. If you really hoped to meet someone, then there was little point telling a gay guy you were the man of his dreams when you were actually a girl. Did these people have a compulsion to dissemble? Or did they actually believe that they were the person they became on-line? Did it matter anyway? If you masqueraded as a person of the opposite sex, or scanned in a picture from a magazine instead of your own mug shot, who were you hurting if you never got as far as meeting face to face? Perhaps it was just a harmless way for people to explore those parts of themselves they couldn't freely admit to even amongst their closest friends.

Lou idly clicked back to the www.pinacoladalovematch home page and hovered with her cursor over the "browse the ads" option. Men seeking women. Women seeking men. Men seeking men. Women seeking women . . .

Briiing!!!

The sound of the telephone ringing brought Lou's attention swiftly back to her office.

"Lou Capshaw."

"It's Ruby."

She sounded flustered. Lou instantly expected the worst.

"What's up?" She prayed that Robert hadn't already burst poor Ruby's bubble.

"I've had an answer to my ad," she said.

"Another Porsche-driver?" Lou asked.

"Not that ad," said Ruby. "Another one."

The letter arrived just as Ruby was heading out to work. The plain brown envelope floated down on to the doormat right in front of her as she checked her hair one last time in the hallway mirror. When Ruby saw *The*

Times's postmark, she turned the envelope over quickly. Then she paused before ripping it open and held her breath. She'd placed her lonely heart in the *Sunday Times*. This wasn't a reply to that ad at all.

Caught up in the excitement of her budding new romance, Ruby had almost forgotten that two-line request she had placed in such a hurry after her night on the sofa at Lou's. She hadn't even checked the paper on the day it was supposed to run. Didn't check that they had printed her request word for word. *Would anyone knowing the whereabouts of Geraldine Barker, formerly of Greenwich, please contact box number 6789.*

Ruby sank down onto the bottom step. This wasn't necessarily a response to her advert, she told herself. It might just be a receipt for the money she had paid so far or a solicitation to place another one. But suddenly Ruby held the envelope as though it might contain a bomb. A time bomb.

In fact, she couldn't even open the damn thing on her own. She needed someone there with her. What if the letter inside *was* from her natural mother? What if it said, *I know who you are but I don't want to know any more about you than that.* It wasn't the kind of news Ruby felt she could handle on a Wednesday morning, alone, when she had to get to work.

So, the envelope travelled to the offices of Hollingworth Public Relations still unopened. And sat on Ruby's desk all day. Periodically, she thought she might be able to open it. Periodically, she made herself a cup of hot, weak tea with four sugars (in anticipation of shock) and laid the envelope out on her blotter with

244

every intention of slitting it open to reveal the terrible secrets (or the invoice) inside.

But each time Ruby drank the tea and the envelope remained unopened. By four o'clock in the afternoon, she was feeling pretty jittery from all the sugar she'd imbibed. At half past four — the earliest she could possibly get away — she headed for her rendezvous with Lou and Martin.

This is what friendship is about, she reminded herself as she waited in their usual pub for Lou and Martin to arrive. There were very few people in the world that you could invite to the opening of an envelope (except most of Hollingworth's clients, as Liz frequently observed), who would actually be happy to turn up. But Lou and Martin did. And when they arrived, Lou and Martin regarded the plain brown envelope with the due reverence its possible contents might accord it.

"My round," said Ruby, getting up to go to the bar.

"No, mine. You sit there," said Martin, pressing her gently back into her chair and dispensing with his usual sarcastic manner in an unusual display of compassion. "Double vodka be strong enough to start with?"

Three double vodkas later the envelope was still intact.

"It's worse than getting your A-level results," said Ruby with a nervous laugh as she prepared to rip it open at last.

"Can't remember that far back," Lou told her.

"You do it, Lou. Open it for me."

"Hand it over then." Lou took the envelope and tore it open with one easy movement.

"No!" Ruby squeaked involuntarily. "I'm not ready yet."

"Too late," said Lou. "I've done it."

"Is it," Ruby closed her eyes tightly, "an invoice?"

"It doesn't look like an invoice. There's another envelope inside here." Lou pulled out a smaller envelope in eggshell blue. Airmail blue, in fact.

"What's the postmark?" asked Ruby, eyes still screwed shut against the revelations.

"America. It looks like Colorado," said Lou.

"Colorado?" Ruby opened her eyes. "How can it be from Colorado? My mother lived in Greenwich."

"People move," said Martin.

"Yeah, from Greenwich to Clapham. Not to bloody Colorado."

"Do you want me to open this envelope too?" Lou asked impatiently.

"Yes. I mean, no," Ruby shut her eyes again. "Just give me a minute longer, could you?"

"Last orders at the bar!"

"Ruby," Lou pointed out. "We've been sitting here looking at the envelope for the best part of five hours. The contents will be the same whether you open it now or open it tomorrow or never open it at all. I think you should approach this like pulling off a plaster. The faster you do it, the sooner the pain goes away. If there's any pain to be had at all."

"I always had to wait until my plasters got so old they just fell off," said Ruby.

"Why doesn't that surprise me?" Lou smiled. "After three?" she suggested. "I'm going to count to three, then I'm going to rip this envelope open and start reading out what's inside it without stopping to draw breath first."

"Lou . . ." Ruby began to whine.

"I'm starting the countdown now. One, two, three . . ."

Martin held Ruby's hands so that she couldn't cover her ears. With a rip like a fisherman gutting a salmon, Lou tore the envelope, shook the flimsy airmail paper out of its creases and began to read quickly in a low but steady voice.

13, Cherry Hills Road,
Boulder,
Colorado

Rosalia.Baker@earthlink.net

Dear Sir or Madam,

I am writing with regard to your advertisement in the London Times about the whereabouts of Mrs Geraldine Barker, formerly of Greenwich in London. Unfortunately, Mrs Barker is no longer with us, but I am her daughter-in-law, wife of her only child Nathaniel (Nat).

I have recently been making a study into my husband's family tree as a surprise gift for his fortieth birthday and would be grateful for any information you can give me about his mother's life in London before she immigrated to America.

247

I can be contacted via the above address and e-mail. I look forward to hearing from you soon.

Yours faithfully,
Rosalia Barker (Mrs)

Which part to take in first, Ruby wondered. My mother is dead but I have a brother? Nathaniel Barker. Nat. Her *only* child. Those three words signified a thousand things. Nathaniel Barker didn't know she existed. Or perhaps he knew Ruby existed once but thought she was dead now too?

"This is heavy shit," said Martin thoughtfully, when he read through the letter for himself. "You've got a brother, Rubes. Did you know that?"

Ruby shook her head.

"This can't be right," said Lou. "It seems unlikely that your mother would have moved to Colorado. Or died. If she gave you up for adoption, then she was probably just a girl herself at the time. And this woman says her husband is nearly forty. How can he be your brother? You're only thirty-one."

"No. It's her," said Ruby with a certainty that surprised even her. "Nathaniel and Hope. Both pretty biblical names, don't you think? Perhaps I wasn't named by nuns after all."

"Eh?" said Lou.

"It's just something the social worker said to me."

"Well, I think it's a mistake," said Lou. "This woman's got the wrong person."

"I've got a feeling that she hasn't," Ruby told her. She passed her hand over her forehead as though checking her own temperature. "I feel really strange."

"What do you want to do now?" Martin asked.

It was a good question.

"I don't know," was Ruby's answer. "This throws up a whole new set of problems, doesn't it? If my mother isn't around to explain the way things were when I was born, I'm not sure where to start. Perhaps I should just leave it at this."

"What? And not find out if this bloke really is your brother?" said Lou incredulously.

"I read somewhere that siblings raised in separate families often find themselves inexplicably attracted to one another when they meet again as adults," said Martin. "You could end up having a torrid affair."

Lou shot him a deadly glance.

"I didn't expect this," Ruby murmured.

"Of course not. But the way I see it," Lou told Ruby, "you've got to take at least one more step. Just in case."

"He might not want to meet me."

"If I were your brother, I would definitely want to meet you," said Lou. "And much as I think it's unlikely that this Nathaniel bloke is anything to do with you, at all, I suppose you have to work on the assumption that he is. He's lost his mother. He thinks he's an only child. You might be his only family left in the world. Apart from his missus. This Rosalia girl . . ."

"On the other hand, he might just think you're after half his inheritance," Martin added helpfully.

Ruby looked between them worriedly. Why did the worst case scenario always seem the most likely one?

"What were you planning to do?" Lou asked patiently. "You must have thought about what you would do if your mother ever got in touch."

Ruby cast her eyes downwards and grimaced. "Of course I have. But I was sort of planning to try to see her from a distance. I thought I'd just get her address and go round there and try to get an idea of what she was like by looking at the outside of her house and seeing what she looked like when she left for work in the morning."

"You were planning to stalk her?" Martin extrapolated.

"Not stalk," said Ruby defensively. "Just watch her for a bit before I made my mind up. But that was when I thought she lived in Greenwich. Not bloody Colorado." Ruby took a big gulp of her vodka. "I can't exactly just drop by someone there. And now she's dead anyway. My mother's dead." She said it slowly and laughed nervously. "My mother is dead." It didn't sound right.

Martin instinctively took Ruby's hand.

"You don't know that she's dead," he said. "Not until you've written to this woman and explained who you really are and why you're looking for Geraldine Barker. It isn't impossible that you're looking for a different woman entirely. Barker's not that unusual a name. Neither's Geraldine. My mum's got three friends with that name."

Lou agreed.

"And it is a bit unlikely that you'd have a brother so much older than you."

"You might be right." Ruby folded the letter back into its envelope and finished off her vodka. "I need time to think," she announced.

"We're here for you whatever you decide," Martin reassured her.

"Whenever you want to talk about it," Lou added.

Ruby looked at them with a half-smile. Her eyes were liquid behind tears that she was fighting to hold on to. "Do you mean that?" she sniffed.

"You know we do."

Lou took her other hand in a gesture of solidarity. "Just don't do anything rash," she added to Martin's promise. "There's no need to rush into anything."

"Especially if she's pushing up daisies." Ruby's bottom lip trembled. She exhaled suddenly and loudly, as though releasing the pressure inside. "What am I like? If my natural mother's dead, it's not as though I ever knew her."

"You're still allowed to feel sad," said Lou.

"Do you want to stay at my place tonight?" Martin asked. "You don't have to be on your own if you don't want to. I can sleep on the sofa. I just put clean sheets on. And I've even got orange juice for the morning."

"Sounds tempting," said Lou. "Can I come instead?"

As if someone had just flicked a switch, Ruby's face was wreathed in joy.

"Not often Martin gets that reaction when he asks a girl to go home with him," Lou commented.

But Ruby wasn't reacting to Martin's offer at all. Instead, her gaze was fixed on the pub's front door, where a tall, dark-haired man was raking back his floppy public school locks with his hand as he surveyed the clientele.

"Robert!" Ruby called out to him. "You made it!"

She dropped Martin's hand like dropping a used tissue in the dustbin. Lou and Martin oriented themselves towards the interloper as he swung into the pub with his pinstriped jacket slung casually over his shoulder. Robert Simpson. Sharp suit. Double-cuffed shirt. Brylcreem. Man at C & A personified.

"Hey, babe," Robert air-kissed his new girlfriend hello. "Did I miss last orders?"

"Yes," said Ruby. "But Martin hasn't touched his pint yet. You could have that. You do drink Special, don't you?"

"Sure," Robert nodded.

Martin fought back the urge to protest as Ruby took his last pint and handed it to her new boyfriend. Then she got out of the armchair she had been sitting in so that he could make himself comfortable and sat down again on one of the chair's arms to snuggle up to him like a proper trophy wife.

"Martin, this is Robert," said Ruby.

Robert made a cursory eyebrow gesture in Martin's direction.

"And this is Lou."

He kissed Lou's hand.

252

"Sorry I had to stay so late at the office, Rubes," Robert told her. "Bloody knackered. Can't wait to get home to bed," he added with a suggestive "know what I mean" wink to Martin. "Well, what were you guys talking about?" Robert asked.

Lou opened her mouth to tell him.

"Doesn't matter," Ruby interrupted. "It was all very depressing. How was your day, Robert? Do you think you'll win that case you told me about? The plumbing fraud?"

Robert squeezed Ruby's knee and launched into a diatribe about one of his clients, a con man who had fleeced a pensioner of her life savings by posing as a plumber and carrying out unnecessary repairs to her heating system. "Bloody scrote's lying through his teeth, of course," he told Lou and Martin. "But I think I can convince the jury otherwise. The old woman can't remember what day of the week it is, let alone whether she authorised forty thousand pounds worth of repairs. Besides, if the old granny can't look after her money then she shouldn't be alive to keep spending it. Don't you think so, Martin?"

Martin winced.

"I didn't like him," said Martin to Lou, after Robert had bundled Ruby into his midnight blue Porsche Boxster and whisked her back to his flat.

"Was it just the car?" Lou asked him.

"Of course it wasn't just the car," Martin protested. "That story. The dodgy plumber and the granny. He

253

didn't give a shit. He doesn't care if he keeps a guilty man out of prison."

"It's his job," said Lou.

"I know. I just don't think I could do a job that involved hurting innocent people," Martin tutted. "God. Does that sound all superior of me?"

"It's OK. I don't like him either."

"Seems sort of odd," Martin said then. "That someone that bloody confident about himself would have placed a personal ad in the first place."

"We did," Lou reminded him.

"I know. But . . . that was different. He drank my pint," Martin tailed off in disgust.

Back at his flat that evening, Martin tried to remember exactly who it was that Robert reminded him of. That mannequin poise. The surface charm. The extravagant old-fashioned chivalry that didn't extend to refusing Ruby's seat when she offered it.

In the ten minutes that Ruby and Robert had remained in the pub after his sudden, swashbuckling appearance like a particularly bad parody of Zorro, Robert had monopolised the conversation. He presented himself like a wily fox, helping his chicken-shit clients evade proper justice. Robin Hood gone all awry. Ruby seemed impressed if no one else was, even clapping her hands with glee when he recounted yet another county court victory snatched from the jaws of defeat by his witty repartee. Since he rarely seemed to pause for breath, it was incredible that he managed to finish

Martin's pint simultaneously. He never thanked Martin for that donation under duress.

Suddenly, as Martin lay on his back in bed and stared at the Chinese paper lampshade that was more grey with dust than white these days, the connection was made. Like Flett, Robert reminded Martin of his own father. And Ruby of Martin's mother in his father's presence. Twittering, twinkling; always orbiting her husband like a fragile, glittering star. Until such time as Martin's father decided that he needed even more reassurance of his attractiveness and started to date his teenage secretary instead.

That was why Martin had taken such an immediate dislike to him. When Robert acknowledged his presence with only the most cursory of glances, Martin had been reminded of the way his father dismissed him in public too. As a small boy, he thought he was the centre of his father's universe. Only later would Martin realise that as a small boy he had been the perfect accessory when his father went out on the pull. Women would always talk to a man pushing a pram or carrying a charming toddler. And a charming toddler wouldn't be able to tell Mum what Dad got up to in the park bushes.

Later, when he was almost as tall as his father and, said his mother, more handsome, Martin's father was quick to point out his son's faults to anyone who admired him. He'd say, "He's normally so clumsy," and ruffle his hair, when teachers praised Martin's skill on the tennis court or football pitch. From the outside, it looked affectionate. But subconsciously, Martin knew even then that his father was trying to keep him in his place.

He did that to Martin's mother too. Joking about her cooking and her driving until she was afraid to invite people over to dinner any more and could only drive Martin to visit friends if she didn't have to cross a roundabout to get there. As he grew older, Martin watched his mother start to fade in the glare of his father's insecurity. He knew she'd been different before. There were pictures in a photograph album from a time before his mother and father met. She'd travelled to New Zealand with a girlfriend, long before gap year world tours were common. She was confident and fearless then. By the time Martin's father left them, there was no trace left of the young woman who had run away to see the world. That was when Martin was eighteen. Over a decade later, his mother still occasionally blamed herself for the way things didn't turn out.

Martin hoped he was wrong about Robert. He really did.

Perhaps he really was just jealous of Robert's success. The fast car. The exciting job. However immoral it seemed — trying to keep known criminals out of prison — there was no doubt that Robert's job made a real difference to real people's lives. By contrast, what was Martin doing? Temping in the post room of a direct marketing company, stuffing envelopes with a bunch of Antipodeans ten years younger than himself whose only aim was to save enough money to get to the next beer fest on the Continent.

256

Martin's grandiose scheme for escaping the rat race via a miraculous publishing deal seemed more ridiculous than ever now. In the days after he lost the vital diskette, Martin tried to remember as much of his book as he could. He'd scribbled down chapter outlines and even whole phrases. But there was so much he couldn't recall. And now, when he looked at what he had been able to salvage from memory, he wasn't sure that the rest was even worth remembering. Perhaps he'd been kidding himself that he had a talent at all.

Petunia Daniels' cheque was still pinned to the notice board in the corner of his bedroom but he felt sure now that he never would cash it. There was no novel to polish off after all. Nor would there ever be. He could still use the money to escape somewhere sunny, he supposed. But what would that make him? Petunia Daniels had earned that money by being an artist. She'd given it to Martin for being a joke.

"Surprise!"

Andrew was lucky that Lou hadn't done much karate practice lately, when he suddenly materialised from the shadow of her garden hedge as she wrestled with her key in the door.

"What are you doing here?" she asked him irritably, as he kissed her on the back of her neck.

"I was missing you," he told her. "I don't think I can sleep on my own any more. I'm too used to having you with me to cuddle up to."

"Right," Lou peeled his arms from around her waist and stepped into the house. He followed. "Aren't you even going to wait to be asked in?" she said indignantly.

"Can I come in?" he asked. He was already closing the door behind him.

"You know, you really shouldn't turn up unannounced," Lou admonished him. "I might not have been alone. I might have been here with my other lover," she raised an eyebrow.

"Why would you want another lover when you've got me?" Andrew asked, as he stuck his hand up Lou's skirt. Lou swiftly removed the offending hand and put the kettle on.

"Have you missed me?" Andrew asked, hovering behind her as she put camomile teabags into two mugs.

"I saw you yesterday," Lou reminded him.

"I've missed you," he said.

"That's nice."

But it wasn't. Three hours later, Lou, like Martin, was staring at the ceiling above her bed. Beside her, Andrew was already sleeping deeply, with his arm slung possessively across her waist. They were the picture of love's young dream. But something really wasn't quite right.

That night, before he nodded off, Andrew had actually said the "L" word. They'd just made love. Still on top of her, Andrew had raised himself up onto his elbows, looked down into Lou's eyes and told her that he loved her.

"I love you," he said. Just those three words. Not "I really love you," in a jokey voice or "I love you when you do that" or even just "I think I love you". Not any derivation of the phrase that actually detracts from it. Simply "I love you". Lou blinked back at him, uncertain how she should respond.

And now she was in her own bed, wondering if she finally understood that old boys' joke about preferring to chew your own arm off rather than wake up beside the person you'd gone to sleep with. Andrew had told her that he loved her and yet she didn't want him there. What was wrong with her? He was everything she had always claimed she wanted. Good-looking, intelligent, trustworthy. Utterly devoted. If she could love anyone at all then surely Andrew was the one?

Half an hour later, she was still no nearer sleep. Carefully, silently, as though she were a thief, Lou lifted Andrew's arm from her stomach. She slipped from the bed and padded towards the kitchen. While the kettle boiled to make camomile tea she fired up her laptop in the sitting-room. While she was awake, she might as well get some work done. She'd check her e-mails first. The inbox flashed to let her know she had mail.

From: matchmaker@pinacoladalovematch.com
To: LC3@hotmail.com

RE: We've found your perfect lover!

Click on the link below to find out who fits all your perfect date criteria!

Checking behind her to make sure that Andrew hadn't got out of bed and started reading her mail over her shoulder, Lou clicked on the link.

Chris, 34, black hair, blue eyes. Works as a management consultant. Enjoys skiing, scuba-diving, going to the theatre. Looking for a woman who knows what she wants out of life . . .

Back at Robert's flat, Ruby sat up in bed wearing one of his T-shirts and started to tell him about that day's revelations.

"So," she concluded, when she had finished explaining the ad in *The Times* and the letter and the Colorado connection, "I don't know what to do. Perhaps he's my brother. Perhaps my mother and this bloke's poor dead mother just shared the same name. What do you think I should do, Rob? Should I forget all about it? Or do you think I should take this thing further? Lou thinks I should take it further but she also thinks that I should come clean about what I want from them now. I don't know about that. I don't want to scare anybody. And I don't want to have to have a relationship with someone I don't like just because we share genetics. I didn't expect it to work out like this. I thought my mother would still be living in Greenwich. I suppose she might be, if there's been some kind of mix-up. Where can I go from here?"

"Yeah," Robert was already half asleep. "Do whatever you feel like. Take it all the way, baby. That's what I'd do."

"Would you really?" Ruby asked.

"Uh-huh," said Robert. "I would." Seconds later, he was snoring.

CHAPTER
TWENTY-THREE

Next morning, Robert sent Ruby off to work with a surprisingly indiscreet love-bite. It was much too hot to wear a polo neck sweater to the office, so Ruby had to turn her collar up instead, hating the fact that it made her look like a 1980s-style Sloane Ranger — she'd had to don her string of plastic pearls to keep the damn floppy collar in place — but secretly enjoying the attention her distinctly teenage badge of honour was attracting at the office. Especially at that morning's meeting with the Barrington Ball-bearings marketing team.

Every time she looked up from her notes, Ruby was certain that she'd just caught Flett staring at her throat. "Yes," she said inwardly. "I already have another lover and he's far better at the job than you ever were." Outwardly, she said, "We *really* like the idea of a national ball-bearings' day for school kids, with engineers going into different schools about the capital to explain how important these little things are in all sorts of big machines."

Flett nodded. His mouth set in a thin, hard line of disapproval.

"Anything else?" Ruby asked brightly when she saw that she had reached the end of her agenda.

"I think that's everything," said Flett. He immediately began to pack his papers up.

"You're looking well," said Ruby, drawing bizarre strength from the disgusting evidence of her new love-life status on her neck. "Been somewhere nice?"

"Majorca," he said.

"Like Imogen!" Ruby trilled as though she didn't know they'd been together.

Flett gave her a narrow-eyed stare.

"Weather good?"

"Fantastic," he muttered and for the first time ever, Ruby noticed that he really did do a strange thing with his tongue when he was agitated. Martin was right. It was disgusting! She had to bite the inside of her lip to stop herself from laughing out loud.

"We need minutes of this meeting with items for action as soon as you can produce them," Flett said. "Nice necklace," he added, as he followed his team out of the meeting room.

"Up yours," Ruby hissed beneath her breath, then she gave him the finger from behind the safety of a box file.

"Ruby! Can I have a word?"

Ruby's boss, Alan Hollingworth, was striding across the office towards her. Ruby blushed automatically and began to fiddle with her nasty plastic beads. "I want to talk to you about the way you've been dealing with the Barrington account," he continued.

Ruby's entire head was suddenly as red as her love-bites. "I didn't mean to do what I just did," she stuttered, referring to her impromptu one-digit gesture. "But you know how it is. It's unprofessional, I know, but I . . ."

"What's that, Ruby?" asked Alan. He was flicking through the bundle of papers he was carrying to find something to give to her.

"Nothing," she coughed. Perhaps he hadn't noticed after all.

In fact, he definitely hadn't.

"I just wanted to tell you how impressed I've been by your performance lately," he said. "I know you were disappointed not to get the Two-Faced campaign last year and you probably wondered how on earth you were going to raise the profile of something as boring as an engineering firm and those little silver balls, but as far as I'm concerned, you've done exactly that magnificently."

Ruby could only nod.

"And professionally," he added. "I knew you'd rise to the occasion. You needed to be stretched."

"Thanks," Ruby managed.

"Of course, I'm not unaware of the situation between you and the CEO at Barrington," Alan continued. "I must say I would advise against forming such close personal bonds with clientele in the first place but, all things considered, you have even handled yourself in that matter with great dignity." (Alan had been out of the office on the day when Ruby blubbed all over Liz Hale and the work experience girl.) "And with a degree of maturity that shows just how far you've come since you began your career here as a graduate trainee all those years ago."

"Thank you," Ruby coughed again.

"And now I think it's time for you to take an even bigger role at Hollingworth PR," he announced with a certain dramatic flourish as he finally handed her the sheet of paper he had been searching for. "Ruby, I want you to go to Denver."

"Denver?"

The sheet gave all the details. The International KFC RPM Group, of which Hollingworth PR had recently become a part, was holding its annual management conference in Denver, Colorado.

"I lobbied for Florida or Las Vegas," said Alan. "But the president wants it in this middle of nowhere location so he can go walking the Rockies straight afterwards."

"Denver?" Ruby echoed.

"You won't have to do anything fancy. Just tag along with Mary." Alan misinterpreted the expression of fear that passed over Ruby's face as professional anxiety. "You'll need to leave for the States on Saturday morning. Greta will give you the itinerary. Just go out there and make Hollingworth proud."

He patted her hard on the shoulder. "There were those among the senior staff who thought you didn't have it in you," he said, "but I knew that you would turn out right. You're our rising star, Ruby. And now you're off to Denver. That's something to look forward to. Wish I could make the trip myself but I've got to be in Paris on Monday morning. Denver, eh? Makes a change from London for the weekend."

He left Ruby in the corridor, fighting to draw another breath.

Denver. Oh, God.

Later that day, Ruby stared at the plane tickets for her trip as though they were her passport to outer space. The itinerary for the following week's conference of managers from the International KFC RPM Group Inc promised a packed programme of thrilling seminars and team-building exercises. Except on Sunday. Sunday's diary contained just two words. "At leisure".

"What can I do on Sunday?" Ruby had asked Mary.

"Anything you want," Mary told her dismissively. "I'll probably be nursing a hangover."

"Where's our hotel?"

"Slap bang in the middle of Denver. You could get out and explore though. Meet some cowboys."

Ruby didn't want to meet any cowboys. But the opportunity to meet certain other Colorado residents that presented itself to her now definitely hadn't escaped her notice. When Mary left her office, Ruby pulled open the top drawer of her desk and took out that eggshell blue letter with the Colorado stamp.

Later, she connected to the Internet and looked up www.mapquest.com. Sure, Boulder was in Colorado and so was Denver, but America was a big place. Ruby knew, in a snippet of info gleaned from pub quiz night,

266

that California by itself was almost as long as the United Kingdom from Land's End up to John o'Groats. And Colorado was bigger than California, wasn't it? Just because Hollingworth were sending Ruby to Denver didn't mean that it would be practical, or even possible, for her to take herself to Boulder while she was out there. They might be a thousand miles apart.

She typed in the address of the hotel where the conference was taking place and then she typed in the address of the Barker family in Boulder. Moments later, the website came up with a neat little map, complete with distractions en route. Ruby blinked at the results in surprise. She entered the details again as a double check. But the answer was the same. Just thirty miles would separate her and the man who might be her long-lost brother. Thirty miles. To an American that was nothing. It would be like visiting a friend in Battersea when you live in Brixton. A day trip. Perhaps even the kind of trip you could legitimately make for just an hour in the company of someone you desperately wanted to see.

That afternoon's task had been to type up the minutes of the Barrington meeting for Flett but the minutes were forgotten as Ruby pondered the forthcoming trip. Was this incredible coincidence some celestial being's way of letting her know she *should* get in touch with Nathaniel Barker and his wife? Ruby checked a half-dozen horoscope sites for clues. She chewed a plastic biro into splinters. She doodled her

way through a pile of Post-it notes. She tried to call
Robert. He was out of his office.

With no one to stop her, Ruby began to draft an
e-mail. Best to be vague, she had decided.

From: Ruby.Taylor@Hollingworthpr.co.uk
To: RosaliaBarker@earthlink.net

Re: Geraldine Barker

Dear Rosalia,
Thank you for your letter regarding Geraldine
Barker, who was a friend of my family while she
lived in Greenwich. I too am tracing my family's
history and hoped that your mother-in-law might
be able to fill in some of the gaps. By an amazing
coincidence, I will actually be in Denver next
week, on a conference. I will be staying at the
Denver Best Hotel from Saturday until the following Tuesday. If it is convenient to you and
your husband, I would love to visit you both
while I am in the state.
Perhaps on Sunday afternoon? I look forward to
hearing from you.
Best wishes,
Ruby Taylor

Friend of the family? Incredibly vague. But Ruby
figured that she had all week to come up with a more
plausible story for placing that advert.

Meanwhile, Rosalia Barker sent her reply before Ruby left the office that very afternoon.

From: RosaliaBarker@earthlink.net
To: Ruby.Taylor@Hollingworthpr.co.uk

Re: Geraldine Barker

Dear Ruby,
How exciting! We would definitely love to meet you. Please come and join us for tea on Sunday afternoon. We can do it English style! Our home is not very far from the centre of Boulder. It's just a short drive from Denver. Or perhaps we could come and meet you? Please call as soon as you are settled into your hotel. Looking forward to meeting you!
Yours truly,
Rosalia Barker (and Nat — though I want your visit to be a surprise!)

"A surprise?" Lou bit her lip when she read the print-out of the e-mail. "Oh, Ruby. You haven't told her?"

Ruby answered in the negative and waited for another sigh.

"Robert said I should go for it," she said in mitigation.

"Does Robert know what you're actually going for?" Lou asked.

269

CHAPTER
TWENTY-FOUR

On Friday evening, Robert pushed his salad around his plate listlessly as Ruby outlined her plans and fears for the forthcoming trip.

"Don't you like it?" Ruby asked him, when he finally pushed the plate to the centre of the table and abandoned it.

"Oh, no," he said. "It's lovely. It's just that . . ."

"What?"

"I don't know. Maybe I had a dodgy prawn sandwich at lunch. I don't feel so hot."

"Oh, Robert." Ruby instinctively reached across the table to touch his forehead and feel his temperature. Robert ducked away from her hand. "Shall I ask the waiter to bring you some water?"

"You know what, I think I'd better go home," he said.

Ruby felt herself sag with disappointment. "I might have an aspirin in my handbag?"

"Ruby," Robert interrupted her as she rifled through her fake Kate Spade. "I don't think an aspirin is going to be enough to make me feel better. I need to go home and go to bed."

Ruby looked up and bit her lip coquettishly.

"On my own," he added. "Just tonight."

"Aw," said Ruby. "But I'm going away in the morning."

"I know. But if this isn't food poisoning," Robert continued, "if it's something like that gastric flu that's been going round, then the last thing I want to do is give it to you tonight so that you have to cancel that flight."

Ruby nodded.

"I know how important it is to you to go to Chicago."

"Colorado," Ruby corrected him. He really must be ill.

Robert summoned the waiter. "Can you walk to the tube by yourself?" he asked. "I'm going to jump straight into a cab and go back to my place."

"I'll be fine," said Ruby. "I could probably use an early night too."

"To make sure you've got plenty of energy next time."

Ruby blushed.

Ruby looked at her watch as she meandered sadly towards Leicester Square. She knew it wasn't Robert's fault that he was ill, but she had needed his company so much that night. She wanted someone to convince her that dropping in on the Barkers wasn't the worst idea since the Sinclair C5 and Robert seemed to be the only person who wasn't of that opinion. Martin and Lou had both been disapproving. That said, they had promised to stand by her whatever she chose to do.

She dug out her mobile and sent a text message to Lou.

"wot r u doing?"

Seconds later, she got a reply. Lou was in Holborn with some friends from the office. Why didn't Ruby join them? Why didn't she, indeed? Ruby turned and started heading in the opposite direction. Her route would take her back past Caruso's. As she trotted through the crowds she felt light with happiness again. When she spotted the sign for Caruso's swaying gently in the breeze, she couldn't help thinking how wonderful it would be one day to tell her children about those early dates with Robert.

"Your father and I met through a Lonely Hearts ad. We spent our sixth date mooning over each other at Caruso's. By that time, I already knew he was the one for me. I had fallen for his eyes, his mouth, his soft brown hair, his big strong hands which . . ."

. . . even now were cupped around the hands of a blonde girl that Ruby didn't recognise. Halfway past Caruso's huge picture windows, Ruby did a double take then stopped and started. Robert, for it was he, was sitting right at the front of the restaurant, at exactly the same table he and Ruby had vacated less than twenty minutes ago, with his hands wrapped around the doubtless beautifully-manicured hands of a rather attractive blonde.

"Robert?"

Ruby gawped like a fish caught on the wrong side of the bowl. What should she do? Knock on the window? Walk on by and pretend she hadn't noticed? He was

272

supposed to be ill. Had he lied to her? Who on earth was that girl?

But before she could take any action, Robert turned to admire his reflection in the window and jumped like Macbeth seeing Banquo's ghost.

"Look, I know this looks bad," he began.

Ruby nodded.

"I'm not going to lie to you."

"Thank you," she said. "Please don't."

"I was on my way home to take something for my stomach," he began, "but as I walked to the taxi rank I realised I was starting to feel better."

"And . . ."

"Isobel was standing at the taxi rank too. A total coincidence. I haven't seen her for ages and it seemed silly not to go for a drink and catch up and by that time I was hungry again and so we came back here."

Ruby nodded. "Isobel? So that's her name. Can I meet her?"

All the time Robert was explaining this, Isobel had been glaring out at Ruby as though she was the one who should be angry. When Robert noticed, he took Ruby gently by the elbow and guided her a little to the left, to stand in a doorway out of view from the window.

"We're out of the rain here," he told Ruby.

"We'd be out of the rain if you took me inside the restaurant," said Ruby with a strained little laugh. "Can't I come in and meet your friend? I could join you both for pudding."

"You know what, darling," Robert crooned. "Perhaps some other time. I'd be more than happy for you to meet Izzy now but she's in a bit of a state. Just split up from her fiancé. Terrible man. Ran off with some other girl with less than a month left to go before the big day. We're discussing how Izzy might be able to get back the money she spent on a deposit for the wedding reception. I don't want to flaunt our happiness in front of her right now. Do you understand?"

What could Ruby do but nod?

"She's been crying and her face is all red and blotchy," Robert continued.

"Didn't look blotchy to me."

"I know," said Robert smoothly. "That's what I told her. I said, 'Izzy, you look absolutely fine. No one will notice you've been crying.' But she said, 'Robbo, I don't think I can meet anyone new right now. I feel so fragile after everything Toby put me through.' Personally, I think that meeting new people would do her the world of good. But . . . you know what some women are like."

"Yes," Ruby nodded again.

"So, I'll call you tomorrow, yeah?" Robert kissed her on the cheek and was preparing to move away.

"Yes," Ruby said. "Before ten o'clock. That's when my flight leaves, remember? Look, are you sure I shouldn't come in for a coffee? I don't want her to think you're going out with a lunatic. I gave her such a filthy look when I saw you sitting together in the restaurant. I'd like to explain . . ."

274

"I'll explain everything and arrange for you guys to meet each other at a better time soon. I'm sure you'd get on like a house on fire," he added. "Like cats and dogs."

"They don't get on," said Ruby.

"You know what I mean." Robert glanced back in the direction of Caruso's somewhat impatiently. "Look, I better get back in there. Don't want to find her crying all over a waiter."

"No," said Ruby.

"You," said Robert, "are a princess among women. There aren't many girls who would be as understanding as you are."

"No," Ruby murmured again.

"OK, sweet lips. I'll call you first thing. And I'll miss you like crazy while you're in California."

"Colorado," said Ruby one more time.

Robert kissed her full on the mouth. Then he was gone.

Ruby remained in the doorway to which he had led her for some moments, her brow heavily furrowed as she went over what he had just told her. It was certainly an odd state of affairs. Ruby couldn't imagine ever being so pissed off that she couldn't extend common courtesy towards the partner of one of her friends. But then, perhaps she *was* unusual. And though she had been dumped in some of the most horrible ways imaginable — starting aged twelve with Andy Squires, who had signalled the end of their relationship by snogging her best friend in front of her at the school disco, and ending most recently with Flett's bloody e-mail — Ruby had never been jilted. Could she really begin to imagine the pain of that? The humiliation of having to contact all those people who had been invited to the wedding to tell them that it had been called off? The embarrassment of having to close down your wedding list at Peter Jones?

Under those circumstances, Ruby had to agree, perhaps she wouldn't want to talk to anybody but her very closest friends either. Let's face it, Ruby told herself, she probably wouldn't even be able to get out of bed. Robert was right. Isobel needed space to recover. There would be plenty of time for Ruby to make her acquaintance in the weeks — perhaps, hoped Ruby secretly — years to come.

That said, surely there wasn't any harm in Ruby just poking her head round the restaurant door and saying hello. She wouldn't stop for coffee, wouldn't even sit down. But she did want Isobel to know that she wasn't a psychotic, ultra-possessive girlfriend who was out to stop Robert spending time with his female friends.

Hang on, said Ruby's conscience. Isn't that exactly what an ultra-possessive girlfriend would do?

"I won't be able to sleep tonight if I haven't let Isobel know that I'm not pissed off by the fact that he's spending time with her. I gave her such a filthy look when I saw them together in the restaurant. I need to explain . . ."

"Robert can do the explaining on your behalf," said the conscience.

276

"Boys never remember to do that sort of thing," Ruby continued. "He won't have explained the situation properly and she'll go away with a terrible first impression of me. I don't want any of his friends to dislike me."

"She doesn't want to meet you now."

"I won't flaunt what I've got with Robert and make her feel bad for finding herself single again. God knows I've been there myself enough times. I'll just go in, introduce myself, and leave. Perhaps she'll even be cheered up to hear how Flett and I split. I could tell her about the Lonely Hearts Pact. She'd find that really funny. I know how to cheer a jilted girl up," Ruby concluded. "Robert is probably coming out with a load of old clichés. What a dumped girl really wants is *proof* that it isn't the end of her useful love life. There's life after heartbreak. I can prove that."

"If you really think you want to . . ." said the little voice inside.

"I know I want to see him one more time before I fly to the States." Ruby took a deep breath and stepped out of the shadows. "Hi, Isobel. I've heard so much about you!" She practised her opening line. "No," Ruby slumped back into the doorway. "That's not right."

Ruby spent five minutes practising her opening speech before she dare make for the restaurant again. By which time, Robert and Isobel were already stepping out for the tube station in the opposite direction. As Ruby got to the door and realised that they had already gone, she was just able to catch a glimpse of Isobel's blonde hair as Robert escorted her around the corner and out of sight.

The head waiter of Caruso's turned the sign on the restaurant door from "Open" to "Closed".

Across town, Lou found herself in a dark and dingy nightclub with a gang of people from her office. John Simpson, the editor who had briefly raised Ruby's hopes that she wouldn't enter her third decade unmarried, was leaving Piper Publishing to work for one of the company's biggest rivals. This night on the town was to wish him well in his new job though Lou knew for a fact that she and Erica couldn't wait to see him leave so that they could fight over his newly vacant office with its view of the sluggish brown Thames.

As a general rule, Lou bailed out on these all-night leaving do's long before the party reached a nightclub. It never usually worked out. After the agony of splitting the bill twelve ways at a pizza restaurant, some bright spark would shout "let's go dancing", then the group would wander out onto the streets of Soho like a twelve-headed monster finding reasons not to go to this club — "too expensive" — or that club — "can't go in there, I'm wearing trainers". This particular night, however, eight people had managed to agree on a club called "Poptarts" in a musty-smelling basement just off Oxford Street, and, despite their far from trendy attire and scruffy trainers, all eight had managed to get in.

Now Lou was in the ladies' room, waiting for a cubicle to become free. She couldn't help smiling as three girls stumbled out from behind one door,

278

ostentatiously wiping their noses. She watched them in the mirror as they checked each other's nostrils for evidence of the Class As they had snorted off the back of a cistern.

"You've got a big white bogey!" one of them squealed. "Don't waste it," she added, "it's the only kind of bogey you should eat."

The second girl followed her friend's advice to the disgusted squeals of the third.

Suddenly, Lou realised that she wasn't the only person watching the three young women giggling at their own debauchery. Lou's gaze was drawn to the reflection of an older woman with short blonde hair that looked expensively highlighted and cut. She had paused in applying her lipstick to catch the three girls inane chatter. It wasn't long before the blonde caught Lou's eyes upon her too and returned her stare quite boldly. The woman's lips curved upwards, friendly but simultaneously almost challenging. Lou ran a hand nervously through her hair. The blonde looked as though she was about to say something when Erica collapsed into the room behind them.

"Oh, there you are," Erica said with obvious relief. "I've been looking for you all over. I can't stand this racket any longer. Call this music? Youth of today. Are we getting old, Lou? You don't fancy sharing a cab, do you? We can . . ." Erica paused, mouth open and turned slowly, as though she were a deer on the savannah sensing a predator behind her. Flicking her gaze briefly from Lou to her friend, the elegant blonde put her lipstick back into her handbag and turned away from the mirror, small smile still playing about her mouth like she'd heard a very private joke.

"What's up with her?" Erica half-whispered to Lou as the other woman stalked out of the cloakroom on extremely high-heeled boots. "Did you see the way she was staring at you? I swear, everybody's out of their heads in this place. Looking for a fight. Or perhaps she was eyeing you up!" Erica laughed hysterically at that.

"Let's get a cab," said Lou, rolling her eyes at Erica's suggestion.

In the cab back to North London, Erica was drunk and dreamy.

"If you meet the person of your dreams, your soul mate, then it's your *duty* to go after them," she said. "Whatever it takes. Whatever anybody else might think of you."

"Sounds like you're talking from experience," commented Lou.

"I am," sighed Erica. "My best friend from college married the love of my life, you know."

"You're kidding."

"I wish I were."

"You never told me."

"Can't stand to talk about it. They made me godmother to their first-born two years ago. All I could think of at the christening was that it should have been me that had his daughter."

"And the stretch marks and the haemorrhoids and the varicose veins," Lou added.

"Forget all that. It would have been worth it," Erica said. "Anyway, I sort of dropped out of touch with the pair of them after that, and last I heard, they were seeing a marriage guidance counsellor."

"Oh." Lou didn't know what to say.

"Too late now. I should have made a play for him as soon as Shelly told me she was interested. Could have saved them *both* the heartache. The world is full of people who end up walking down the aisle with the wrong person. Sometimes it makes me feel suicidal to think of Shelly ending up with the man I should have married while at the same time there's probably some poor cow on the other side of London starting to hate being married to Shelly's real dream man. All those happy endings gone awry just because nobody is brave enough to say what they really want when they want it. To risk a little bit of disapproval. To take a chance on love . . ."

The girls both looked into the distance, sagging beneath the weight of Erica's statement.

"So, it's like I said. If you think you've found the one, Lou, then it's your duty to make a proper go of it. To do everything you can to make it happen. Because if you don't, it might not just be you that you're dooming to a loveless life of heartache."

"Gloucester Crescent," said the taxi-driver gruffly.

"Ooops, here we are," said Erica, opening the door and almost falling out onto the pavement. She thrust a tenner into Lou's hand. "Will that cover my share?"

"I think so."

"Remember what I said," she concluded, wagging a finger in Lou's general direction. "If Andrew's the one for you, then for God's sake, don't mess about. Get him up that bloody aisle double-quick. For both your sakes."

"Yeah, yeah. See you Monday," Lou smiled. Then she sank back into the deep black seat again, watching her own reflection in the rear-view mirror, wondering what that blonde girl in the cloakroom had seen.

CHAPTER
TWENTY-FIVE

Martin hoped Ruby was doing the right thing. He had listened to her rationale for making this pilgrimage to Boulder and made all the right noises in response, but he couldn't help thinking that there were some things that were meant to remain in the past. It was difficult for Martin to imagine how his friend might have an attachment to someone she never really knew, but at the same time, he knew only too well that the outcome of this meeting, whatever it was, wouldn't leave Ruby untouched.

What worried Martin most was that the woman who had written in response to Ruby's ad in the back of *The Times* still didn't really know why Ruby was so keen to meet her and her husband. When arranging the visit, Ruby had merely written vaguely of "family friends". As far as Rosalia Barker was concerned, the public relations conference was the main purpose of Ruby's visit. Tea at Cherry Hills Drive would merely be an interesting excursion in a previously planned trip.

Martin and Lou had both expressed the opinion that Ruby should not turn up at Rosalia's house without writing to her one more time first, explaining in full the possible connection between them. That would have been more sensible surely? And fairer too. Ruby thought otherwise.

"This isn't something I can put in an e-mail," she insisted.

Martin tried once more to persuade Ruby that it might be better if she took things more slowly even as she rang from the airport to remind him to water her plants while she was away. She could even send a note from the hotel, he suggested. But Ruby was not to be dissuaded. She just kept repeating her own view like a mantra. "This is something that has to be done face to face." Like breaking up, thought Martin.

Well, it worked in the movies. Long-lost families were reunited in an explosion of goodwill and happiness. The prodigal daughter returns to drink champagne. But still Martin couldn't shake the feeling of foreboding that had been his close companion since he promised Ruby that he wouldn't neglect her spider plants and wished her a safe journey from Heathrow. Families were difficult. Just because someone shared your genes didn't mean they would even necessarily like you. Martin at least knew that to be true.

Ruby was about halfway over the Atlantic when it struck her that she might be about to make one of her trademark huge mistakes. Mary was snoring beside her in Business Class. A nervous flyer, Mary had started necking champagne in the airport lounge. "Mix a good half bottle of that with a couple of sleeping tablets," she told Ruby, "and a transatlantic crossing quite literally flies by."

Ruby didn't take her up on her offer of a couple of knock-out pills, telling her that she wanted to enjoy the experience, look out of the window at the world passing by ten miles below. But by the time they were over Greenland, Ruby wished she had taken Mary's advice. The in-flight movies had long since lost their appeal. Nothing could distract her from the creeping fear that she had gone about everything absolutely wrong.

Ruby couldn't remember when her parents first told her she was adopted. It just seemed as though she had always known, in the way that everyone else at school knew they'd come straight from mummy's belly-button. Ruby could remember the day everyone in her class found out the truth however. Their form teacher, Miss Mayfield, had been talking to them about a junior school in Africa. The plan was to "adopt" the school, sending the poor kids their old toys and unwanted books for Christmas. Elaine Roberts asked what it meant to "adopt" something and for reasons known only to herself, Miss Mayfield thought it would be a good idea to illustrate her explanation using Ruby as an example.

The rest of the class were agog as Miss Mayfield told them that Ruby's "proper mummy and daddy" had decided they couldn't look after her and asked for her to be given to someone who could. And no matter how carefully Miss Mayfield tried to explain that Ruby was now the Taylor family's "real child", by lunchtime Elaine Roberts had dubbed Ruby a "bastard" and told her that it was just a matter of time before someone from the local children's home came to take Ruby away.

The next few days had been hell. Ruby longed to ask her parents for confirmation that the children's home didn't have a place waiting for her but found herself unable to bring up the subject. By the third day, the news had reached Lindsay's form room. Kieran Pope told Lindsay that Ruby wasn't her "real sister". Lindsay landed a punch on his chin. Both the Taylor sisters were sent home at lunchtime.

Ruby's mother had to sit Lindsay down at the kitchen table and explain all about the adoption then. It seemed that it had been so much a fact of their lives that Mr and Mrs Taylor had forgotten to even formally go through the facts with their eldest daughter.

Ruby waited in the sitting-room while her mother told Lindsay the real story. Even then Ruby's natural instinct was to wait for rejection, expecting her big sister to turn round and say that she didn't want to have Ruby in the family any more. Ruby was the cuckoo. Taking up space that she wasn't entitled to. But that wasn't how it happened at all.

When she had digested everything her mother told her, Lindsay said she was just relieved that no one would be coming to take her sister away. She went back upstairs to play with her Sindy dolls and never mentioned the incident again. Ruby was her proper sister. She would be forever. And that was that as far as the Taylor family was concerned.

And that's partly why Ruby felt like such a piece of shit as she crossed the Atlantic that Saturday. That very morning, as she waited in the Business Class lounge at Heathrow for her flight to start boarding, Ruby had called her parents with every intention of telling them exactly what she hoped to do while she was at the conference in Denver. But the right moment never seemed to present itself. Mrs Taylor was worrying about Lindsay and Lauren. Lauren had the snuffles and was keeping Lindsay and her husband up all night. Then she started talking about Mr Taylor's dodgy back. It was stopping him from enjoying his golf. And then she told Ruby about the teenage lad up the road they thought had been scratching the paintwork on the new Volvo. Ruby just couldn't find the right point in the three-minute conversation to say, "By the way, Mum, I'm going to see my real brother."

Anyway, there was still the chance that Nathaniel Barker might not actually *be* Ruby's brother. There didn't seem much point in upsetting her mother — and Ruby was sure that she would be upset — if it was going to turn out that Nathaniel Barker and his wife weren't related to Ruby after all. Lou thought Ruby should tell her parents anyway. Let them know that she was interested in finding out about her history at least. But though Ruby's mum and dad had always claimed that they would happily help her trace her real family, she'd never really been convinced.

So, the conversation passed without event. As the call came to an end, Ruby's mum just wished her a safe trip to America and said, "we love you". She only and always said that when either of her daughters was getting on an aeroplane. Just in case it crashes, Ruby supposed.

There's way too much time to think on the journey from Heathrow to Denver, Ruby decided. She wished she had somebody to talk to. Mary would be dead to the world until they reached the other side. Not that Ruby could realistically have opened up to her. She was still Ruby's superior, even if Ruby had now heard her snoring and seen her dribble in her sleep.

Ruby wished that Robert were with her especially. Though they had only been seeing each other for a couple of weeks at that point, she already felt that he knew her pretty well. He always seemed to say the right thing. It was mostly thanks to him that she had gathered enough confidence to contact Rosalia in the first place. Meeting Robert made Ruby feel as though the long streak of rejection, imagined or otherwise, that had been her life so far was over. If someone as fantastic as him could want her for his girlfriend, then why shouldn't Nathaniel Barker want her for his sister too?

As promised, Robert called Ruby on the morning of her flight to reassure her that everything would work out in the best interests of everyone involved. He told her that he would be by his phone — or at least by his mobile one — day and night until she returned to England, just in case she needed to talk . . . Except on Sunday night, when he would be at his sister's — he didn't think he could get reception at her house. And on Monday, when he would be at a reunion for people on his college course. But he would be thinking about Ruby even then, he said. He would be sending positive vibes in her direction. Ruby hoped that Martin and Lou would do the same. Though she knew they both thought she was mad.

Ten hours after take-off, the plane touched down in Colorado. Denver airport, with its tented white terminals, looked like a flotilla of ships sailing across the barren plain at the foot of the Rockies. The airport was in the middle of nowhere. The journey to the hotel took the best part of an hour. Mary managed to stay awake just long enough to claim her luggage. Now she was snoring in the back of the taxi as the outskirts of Denver passed.

Ruby had been to America only once before, as a teenager, when she went to New York with her mother and father and Lindsay. It should have been a dream holiday but Ruby was just sixteen then, and spent the entire time moping about the boyfriend she'd left behind at home when she should have been soaking up the experience. The wide-open spaces of Colorado couldn't have been more different than the concrete canyons of Fifth Avenue and Broadway but they still felt strangely familiar. Was it just because she had seen similar houses, stores and billboards a million times on television? Or was it, she wondered, some kind of tribal resonance? Had her mother walked along that sidewalk? Visited that cinema? Shopped in that mall?

"Been to Colorado before?" the cab-driver asked her jovially.

"It's funny," said Ruby, "but I feel I have."

The *déjà vu* continued in the hotel, which was exactly as she had expected. Low, peach-coloured lighting in the lobby, hiding the wear and tear on chintzy sofas and cheap wooden coffee tables strewn with tourist information. One of those black boards with the plastic letters that attach with tiny studs announced the presence of the convention, along with the annual dinner dance of the Denver Dairy Farmers' Association. Once you stepped into the lobby you might have been in any hotel in any city in the world. Ruby's room was a beige box on the seventh floor with a view of a sad-looking car park.

But there was a small bunch of roses on the bedside table. At first, Ruby assumed that the hotel had sent roses to all the guests, or at least the ones attending the KFC RPM Group convention. But the card told her otherwise.

"Welcome to Denver," said the neat blue hand. "We're so excited to meet you. From Rosalia and Nathaniel Barker."

When Ruby opened the window to get some air, the car park seemed to lurch up towards her. Later, Ruby wondered if she should have called and cancelled that afternoon rendezvous. She could have said that the convention was over-running and she wouldn't have Sunday free after all. Ruby could even have sent Rosalia an e-mail — she had her laptop with her — pretending she had never left London at all. As Ruby looked at the bunch of joyful yellow roses on the bedside table, she still had her hand on the lid to a veritable can of worms.

CHAPTER
TWENTY-SIX

"Would you answer this ad?" Lou asked Martin. They were having brunch *à deux* in the Café Rouge.

"Which one?" Martin asked.

Lou spread out the "Soulmates" section of the *Observer* on the table before him and circled Erica's two-line ad for his attention.

> Cat-loving vegetarian, 32, seeks sensitive soul
> with Pisces in his chart.

Martin wrinkled his nose. "Cats? Horoscopes? Wrong side of thirty? Uh-uh. Not for me."

"I thought so," said Lou. "Erica from my office placed it. I hope she isn't going to be disappointed."

"Why should she be? You asked for my *personal* opinion. It's perfectly possible that a cat-loving, vegetarian Pisces may be calling her box number right now," Martin pointed out.

"Yeah, but is that what she *needs*?" asked Lou.

"You're not proposing another pact?" Martin joked. "You know how well that worked."

"You never did say what happened between you and Cindy," Lou smiled. "Did I do right there?"

Martin looked about himself nervously. "It will come out in my memoirs." Then he looked at his watch. "Two o'clock. That makes it seven in the morning in Colorado."

"You've worked out the time difference!" Lou exclaimed.

"I knew it anyway," Martin blustered. "What time was she supposed to be going to see them?"

"Not until the afternoon."

"Do you think she's OK?"

"She hasn't called. That's always a good sign. Besides, if she isn't OK, I don't suppose we'd be the first people she calls any more. Apparently, Robert told her that she should call him day or night if ever she needed a shoulder to cry on."

"That's good of him," said Martin sarcastically. "Seeing as he is supposed to be her boyfriend and all."

"Perhaps he isn't just a Porsche-driving wanker after all. Perhaps he has a sensitive heart beneath that brash exterior."

"Yeah," Martin looked unconvinced.

"God, I hope she's met her Mr Right," Lou sighed. "It seems like ever since we've known that girl, Ruby has been in a dreadful relationship, recovering from the ending of a dreadful relationship, or trying to throw herself straight into a new one."

Martin nodded.

"OK," Lou asked him suddenly. "Truth or dare. Have you ever wanted to get it together with Ruby yourself?" She fixed him with her piercing blue eyes.

Martin almost spat out a mouthful of cappuccino in surprise.

"You know I already did," he said. "In Freshers' week."

"Yeah but what happened after that? Why didn't you two start going out with each other after your night of hot passion?"

Martin shrugged. He wasn't about to tell Lou that Ruby had taken his virginity then sent him away with threats that she would tell everyone he was a premature ejaculator if he mentioned what had gone on between them. "I don't know," he said. "I guess we didn't know each other well enough to make it work."

Lou shook her head dismissively. "And then?" she asked.

"Then we became friends and pretty soon we knew each other *too* well to sleep together again."

"Is that possible?"

"You know it is. You don't want to sleep with someone once they've given you a blow-by-blow account of their sex life with someone else."

"I see. So you didn't know her well enough and then all of a sudden you knew her too well?"

"I suppose so. Besides, Ruby's always telling me how well I prove the 'all men are bastards' rule. She always sides with my ex-girlfriend in any break-up. She wouldn't risk being anything more than my mate."

"But you *would* want to be something more than her friend?" Lou probed.

"I didn't say that," Martin protested.

"OK," said Lou, folding up her paper. "I think I've finished with the witness, m'lud."

"What do you mean by that?" Martin asked irritably.

"Nothing. Oh look, saved by the boy."

The door to the café swung open to admit Andrew, dressed in a smart blue suit.

"Hey, man," said Martin. "Didn't anybody tell you it's the weekend?"

"We're going to see my parents," Lou explained. "Though you really didn't have to go so far as wearing a suit," she added to Andrew.

"I wanted to make a good impression," he told her. "It's important to you."

"Not that important," Lou assured him. "My mum will be impressed if you've washed in the last fortnight."

"It's the Stepford husband," Martin cracked.

"Shall we go?" Andrew asked. "We don't want to be late."

"They'll be expecting it of me," said Lou.

"But not of me," said Andrew.

Lou hadn't taken anyone to meet the parents for a very long time indeed. In fact, she hadn't brought anyone home at all since she was still at school and boyfriends had to pass inspection by Mum and Dad before they were allowed to cross the threshold of her bedroom. Then, the bedroom door had to be left ajar to ensure she got up to no naughtiness. The result was that after years of listening out for the footfall of her parents on the stairs, Lou had developed the supersonic hearing of a bat. She could also make love in absolute silence.

Back then, Lou's parents had begged her to concentrate on her A-levels rather than her love-life. Now, they begged her to concentrate on her love-life rather than her career. They'd been giving her the "nearly thirty" line since she celebrated her twenty-first. And when Lou called her mother to say that she would be coming over for Sunday dinner and would like to bring a friend, she could almost hear the relief in the old lady's voice.

But perhaps Lou's mother was right to be so concerned with settling down.

Following Andrew's surprising declaration of love, Lou had convinced herself that she was wrong to react so negatively. She pinched a copy of a pink-covered book about Commitment-Shy Women from the PR office at work and read it from beginning to end. Much as she scoffed at self-help books — unlike Ruby, who was always reading "Women who do too much something or other" — Lou had to admit she fitted the profile. Her early love-life had been littered with men who didn't seem to want her as much as she wanted them. That, the author of the book explained, was because Lou had actually been deliberately picking men that she couldn't get close to. Now she had met someone who was ready to commit to her, she was reacting so strangely because Andrew had unwittingly hit upon the real problem. It was Lou who was afraid of commitment and marriage and all that entailed. Not the unavailable men she had chased after all her life.

296

And Lou did want marriage and babies, didn't she? She felt sure at least that she wanted a family. As an only child, she had had an idyllic childhood. She was the centre of her parents' universe, wanting for nothing from tennis lessons to a pony of her own to so much real, unconditional love it almost suffocated her at times. There was no doubt she had grown up with a sense of true security, but also a heavy sense of the responsibility of carrying forward the family line. Her parents assumed she would have children. Lou had assumed she would have children. Even if she couldn't see herself with a baby, she had often imagined raising a daughter of her own, looking and sounding just like her . . .

Of course, having children didn't necessitate being married, but Lou definitely couldn't imagine doing it on her own. And now Andrew had come into her life, talking long-term commitment right from the start. By the time Lou finished reading that book about Commitment-Shy Women, she thought she had diagnosed her problem *and* found the answer. She was almost thirty. It *was* time for her to grow up and settle down. If the only people she ever allowed anywhere near her heart were perfect strangers glimpsed once on a packed rush-hour tube then Lou might be dooming herself to growing old alone.

So, in the end it was fear that made Lou take Andrew to meet her parents. Fear that she was sabotaging her own happy ending by turning her nose up at Mr Absolutely Obviously Right. Because he was right. Wasn't he?

* * *

And of course the day went wonderfully. But the drive back to London that night found Lou closing her eyes and pretending to sleep so she wouldn't have to get into conversation.

Lou's parents had loved him. He'd made her mother laugh. He'd promised her father that he would help him build a barbecue before the end of the summer. When Lou's mother told her that they made a fantastic-looking couple, Lou found herself transposing their heads onto her cousin Alice's wedding photo.

Then the fantasy crashed like a needle skittering over an old record.

It wasn't right. It never would be right.

Andrew squeezed her knee and gazed at her as though she were the only girl in the world.

How on earth was she going to tell him?

CHAPTER
TWENTY-SEVEN

A combination of time-zone confusion and nervous anticipation meant that Ruby was awake at five o'clock the morning after her arrival in Denver. The previous evening, the conference delegates had gathered in the hotel's western style ranch-themed restaurant for a welcoming drinks party followed by an extravagant dinner at which Ruby found herself sitting next to her opposite number from the Dutch office of Hollingworth. His English was as bad as her Dutch and they spent the entire meal smiling inanely and saying, "It's good here, yeah?" "Yeah, it's good."

Meanwhile, Mary had hooked up with her own opposite number from the new public relations and advertising agency in New York that was the latest jewel in the International KFC RPM Group's crown. Used to her superior in full "ice maiden" mode about the office, Ruby was a little embarrassed to watch Mary snuggling up to Todd Barnhardt like she was a school girl and he was captain of the football team. However, Ruby was grateful that Todd's attentions kept Mary from noticing that her junior left the fray during coffee.

On the journey to Heathrow, which now seemed a million years ago, Mary had promised Ruby several "all-night networking sessions" with a wink. Ruby had been dreading them, picturing herself stuck in the hotel bar until Mary drank enough to pass out. An "all-night networking session" with Mary, legendary for her business prowess *and* her somewhat unladylike alcohol consumption, was as inviting as an audience with Stalin in the days when the first person to stop applauding him would be shot. Ruby had heard rumours of Hollingworth staff finding themselves blocked from promotion for drinking orange juice when Mary was on a bender.

Thankfully, Mary hadn't seemed terribly interested in Ruby's plans for that Sunday either but said that she should hire a car or take a taxi to wherever she wanted to go and stick it down on expenses. "Even as far as Boulder?" Ruby asked. Even as far as Boulder, Mary confirmed. KFC RPM were paying.

That morning, Ruby had room service bring her breakfast as soon as they were able. Though she had hardly made a dent in the steak she had found herself faced with at the welcoming dinner, Ruby was suddenly ravenous; hardly surprising since according to her body it was actually time for lunch. What would be going on at home right now, she wondered. She thought of Robert travelling in the Boxster to his sister's house for a barbecue. He obviously thought a great deal of his sister. He seemed to visit her at least once a week, sometimes more often and had once even cancelled a date so that he could dash down to help her with some baby-sitting crisis or other. Ruby wondered when she would get to meet Robert's family herself. Would she like them? Would they like her? Would she be good enough for a successful lawyer like their son?

Would she be good enough for the Barkers?

When Ruby phoned Rosalia Barker to make arrangements for that day's meeting, she was overwhelmed by the woman's warmth. By this stage, Ruby had managed to convince Rosalia that Geraldine Barker had been a neighbour of Ruby's parents in the early seventies and she was keen to know if Geraldine had left behind any photographs of her parents from that time. Rosalia was only too pleased to make the Barker family album available to her new friend.

"Here's hoping we can do one another a favour," she said. "There are lots of faces in photographs from those days in Greenwich that my husband can't put a name to. Perhaps some of them are your folks."

"Perhaps," Ruby agreed.

Between five in the morning and ten which was when the taxi would arrive to take her to Boulder, Ruby went through almost as many outfit changes as she would for a date. The nerves were much worse though and by the time reception called Ruby's room to say that the taxi was waiting for her outside the hotel, Ruby had worried the cuticle on her left thumb so much it was actually bleeding.

"Have a nice day," chirped the bell-boy as Ruby scuttled through the lobby.

She was so anxious that she didn't even hear him.

301

The Barkers' whitewashed house at number 13 Cherry Hills Drive was like something out of a movie; one of those Disney films where an almost perfect family adopt a lovable dog or alien who makes their lives complete.

Ruby had the taxi-driver drop her off on the other side of the street and just stood there on the pavement for a moment, taking in the wide flat boards that made up the walls, the pink gingham curtains hanging in swags at the open windows, the even brighter pink flowers in the pots that lined the windowsills and flanked the stairs up to the front door like a legion of little floral soldiers.

The place even had a picket fence and one of those metal postboxes with a flag that the mailman raises so the people inside know when they have a letter without having to step out of the house. From the front gate hung a faux rustic wooden plaque in the shape of a smiling sun. "Welcome to our home", the plaque announced. "All who enter beware", said another wooden sign sticking out from one of the flower-beds. "You'll never want to leave!" It was cheesy beyond description, Ruby thought. But nice. Friendly. Really friendly. Just as Rosalia Barker had been on the phone.

Ruby took a deep breath and reached out for the latch on the gate. As she did so, the door to the white house opened and a woman, about her age, perhaps a little older but not by much, stepped out onto the porch with a pair of secateurs and began to prune her flower boxes.

Ruby froze, as though she had been caught breaking in. But at first the woman didn't even see her. She was humming to herself, flowing easily from one flower box to the next, dead-heading her geraniums as though she were miming the mundane task at the beginning of a ballet about gardening. Eventually she turned to look at Ruby as though she had sensed her gaze upon her.

"Hey there!" she called across the garden with an enthusiastic wave. "Hey!"

Ruby stepped out from the shadow of a tree. Rosalia Barker was already racing down the garden path to meet her, abandoning her pruning shears and stripping off her gardening gloves as she went.

"Are you Ruby?" she asked.

Ruby nodded. Rosalia took Ruby's shakily proffered hand in both of hers and shook it energetically. "How are you?" she asked. She smiled so broadly that it seemed impossible that she hadn't recognised at once the family connection with the stranger who stood in front of her. "I'm so glad to meet you at last. Come in. Come in! I was just tidying up the flowers for your visit. Can't stand to have shrivelled petals on my plants," she explained. "Makes the place look so untidy, don't you think? Do you like to garden, Ruby?"

"I don't have one," Ruby told her.

"That is such a pity!" Rosalia exclaimed. "My husband is always telling me that you Brits have the best gardens in the world. Tells me everything else about the country is pretty crummy, of course. But your gardens are supposed to be just lovely."

"I suppose they are."

"I'd like to visit," Rosalia confided. "But Nathaniel doesn't really want to go back there."

"That's a shame."

"I'll work on him," Rosalia assured her. "And we'll be there before you know it. Come in, come in."

She led her visitor indoors.

While Rosalia went to take off her gardening apron, Ruby sat on the very edge of a white wicker-framed sofa in a living-room that confirmed Rosalia's liking for neatness went far beyond her tidy plants. A small pile of issues of the *National Geographic* was aligned exactly with the edge of the coffee table. Every plant pot sat squarely on a doily to protect the varnished surfaces beneath.

"You need a drink?" Rosalia called from the kitchen. "I just made iced tea?"

"Iced tea would be nice," Ruby confirmed.

She peered around the room. The blinds were pulled down to save the carpet from fading in the brutal glare of the sun. There was a framed verse from the bible on top of the mantelpiece. That one about the lilies in the fields. And some photographs. Rosalia and a tall man in ski gear. Rosalia on her wedding day, holding a bouquet of pink roses and grinning so much that she was fit to burst with joy. Rosalia and her husband . . .

Ruby picked up the little silver frame that had pride of place on an occasional table and squinted at the groom with his arm around Rosalia's waist. He had dark hair. A suntan. Ruby had never been able to get a tan like that. Did they look alike? Not at first sight. She had the frame almost against her nose as she looked for similarities. Then Rosalia returned from the kitchen, still grinning, with a tray loaded down with iced tea and three glasses. Ruby jumped as though she had been caught stealing again.

"Isn't that frame the sweetest?" Rosalia asked warmly. "It was a gift from my husband's mother on our wedding day. It's a family heirloom."

My family, Ruby thought.

"Did you find your way here easily?" Rosalia asked, as she poured the tea into two of the glasses and made sure her guest got a slice of fresh lemon.

"Er, yes," said Ruby hesitantly. "I got a taxi." She was still on goldfish mode.

"And what do you think of our beautiful state?" Rosalia continued.

"It's lovely," said Ruby blandly. "The mountains are so big."

"They are pretty big, I agree," said Rosalia. "Especially when you're skiing down one of 'em. My husband loves to ski the steepest hills you ever saw. He's such a sporting daredevil."

Ruby nodded. She certainly wasn't. She hadn't worn a pair of trainers since her last day at school. Perhaps they weren't related after all.

"Sweet enough for you?" Rosalia asked as Ruby took a first sip of her tea.

Ruby nodded again. Though it was horrible. She hated the stuff. Couldn't understand why the Americans seemed to have such an aversion to making tea properly, piping hot, with milk.

305

"So," Rosalia sprang up from her seat as though she had ants in her pants and started to dig around in the top drawer of a bureau. "Before Nathaniel comes back from Home Depot, I want to show you what I have on the Barker family so far. I started my search on the Internet," she explained. "Barker seems to be a relatively common surname back in England but I was lucky enough to know the parish where Nathaniel's maternal grandparents were born and their church had just put all of its resources on-line. Can you believe my luck?"

She sat down again, right next to Ruby on the sofa this time, and opened a box file marked "The Barker Family Tree" in neat black marker pen.

"I've always been fascinated by history," Rosalia continued. "I know you Brits think we Americans are crazy the way we keep on. But we're all so jealous of the way you can trace your families back for generations and generations. My grandparents came over from Europe during the Second World War and that's where my story ends. But Nathaniel . . . well, you'll see how much stuff I have here." Rosalia took out a photograph. "This is Nathaniel's great-grandfather," she said, handing Ruby the black and white photo of a man in a naval uniform. "And this is his great-grandmother."

Seeing Ruby's eyes narrow as she studied the photograph of a young girl with wavy blonde hair, Rosalia assumed that the room was too dark and flicked on a table lamp to help her.

"Better? Paternal side," Rosalia explained. "Nathaniel doesn't take after them at all. Not physically. He favours his mother."

"He does?" Ruby's voice came out in a croak.

"Oh, yes." Rosalia continued to dig on through her box of documents. "It's really quite incredible. Let me show you."

Ruby could only gape as she watched Rosalia produce birth certificates, marriage certificates and death certificates like a magician pulling rabbits from a hat. "That's his mother's birth certificate," she said, casually adding another document to the heap on the coffee table. Ruby picked it up and read the name. The name that had been printed under "mother" on her own birth certificate. His mother's place of birth also matched that given on the scrap of paper that Amanda the Patchouli Monster handed over to Ruby almost ten years before.

"Where is it?" Rosalia muttered, not noticing how hard Ruby was gripping Geraldine Barker's certificate. "I had it the other day when I went to get those copies done. Ah yes, here it is." Rosalia sank back into the cushions and pulled a photograph from an unprepossessing brown envelope with a final magical flourish.

"This is my husband as a baby with his mother. She was twenty-three years old at the time."

Ruby's hands were shaking as she took the photograph to look at it herself. The young woman was holding her baby on her hip, with her other hand she gestured towards the camera, trying to encourage her little boy to smile. Nathaniel Barker glared at the photographer suspiciously. One little fist was clenched around the leg of a well-loved teddy bear. The other grasped a handful of his mother's blouse, determined not to let her go.

Ruby felt her throat begin to close. Her eyes pricked.

"Wasn't she beautiful?" Rosalia said brightly.

Wasn't she?

The family face. The magic mirror. Ruby's parents had a dozen photographs like this from her own childhood. She'd hated having her photograph taken too. Always scowling at the camera like her brother. Still scowling at the age of twenty-three, when she looked almost exactly as Geraldine Barker had done.

"You know," said Rosalia, looking at Ruby appraisingly. "You favour her a little too. Isn't that funny?"

Ruby nodded, keeping her eyes cast down so that Rosalia couldn't see the glitter of imminent tears.

"What happened to her?" Ruby asked. "When did she die?"

"Last fall," said Rosalia sadly. "End of October. Malaria. Can you believe it? She went to Bangladesh with a group of missionaries from our church and got ill when she came home. We thought she just had the flu, or something. She insisted on carrying on like normal, taking food to the old ladies she used to cook for when their families couldn't help them. Helping out at Sunday school. Then one night she just collapsed and died of liver failure. It's typical of Geraldine to have caught her death when she was doing her best for other people," Rosalia added with a rueful little smile. "Still, God always takes the good ones."

"She sounds like a lovely woman."

"Oh, she was," said Rosalia emphatically. "Always doing something for people less fortunate than herself. Old people. Young people. Especially babies. She couldn't see a baby in trouble and not try to do something about it. Used to cry like a waterfall when she saw those abandoned kids in the Balkans on TV. And when she found out about the babies in that orphanage in Bangladesh, there was no way any of us were going to stop her heading right out there to save them."

Ruby handed the photograph back. Rosalia sniffed loudly as she took it. "I'm sorry. I was very close to my mother-in-law," she explained. "Incredibly close. So," she clapped her hands together then as though to dismiss the sombre mood. "Let's hear more about you. Your parents were from the same town as Geraldine? Did your mother know her before she was married?"

"Not exactly," Ruby began. Wasn't the real story obvious yet?

Deep breath. Ruby put her iced tea down.

"Rosalia," she said. "I haven't been entirely honest with you."

As the real story tumbled out, Ruby almost felt as though she had left her body and was floating by the ceiling, watching herself tell Rosalia about her adoption and watching Rosalia's trusting eyes grow so wide they might pop out of her head.

"Oh, sweetheart," Rosalia muttered over and over. "That's terrible."

Rosalia was lost for words as Ruby described her afternoon with Amanda the Patchouli Monster at the social services office and the emotions that had accompanied the discovery of her birth mother's name. It was the first time Ruby had really spoken about that afternoon to anyone and she was surprised by how much it still hurt to think about it. That stupid comment that she might have been named by nuns because her natural mother couldn't be bothered. Ruby was unable to hold back the tears.

When Ruby had finished talking, Rosalia put her arm around her shoulders and hugged her close. She stroked her hair, cooing and whispering soothingly, like a woman well used to baby-sitting, though she had no much-longed-for children of her own.

"Darling," she said eventually. "My heart goes out to you. You've had a terrible time. But there's clearly been a misunderstanding."

"What do you mean?" Ruby asked.

"My husband's mother married at the age of twenty-one," said Rosalia patiently. "She had just one child, my Nathaniel. Her husband was killed in a car wreck before she could have another one."

"But look."

Ruby wiped her nose on her sleeve and dug into her bag for her birth certificate.

"Geraldine Barker," Ruby pointed out. "And the birth place is the same too. Look. Mother's place of

310

birth, Sheffield. That's what it says on Geraldine's own birth certificate. You can't tell me it's all a coincidence."

"It could be," said Rosalia.

"But I even look like her," said Ruby, picking up the photo of Nathaniel and Geraldine again. "And," Ruby went back into her bag for a baby photo she had lifted from her parents' house a few weeks before, "I used to look like Nathaniel too."

Rosalia chewed her lip as she took in the undeniable resemblance of her husband as a child to this young Englishwoman at the age of two.

"I just don't see how it can be possible," Rosalia exclaimed.

"But it's not *im*possible," said Ruby.

Rosalia could only shrug at that.

"Please," Ruby begged her. "I don't see how there can be any other explanation. Your mother-in-law was my mother." She took the other woman's hands in a beseeching sort of gesture.

"You'll have to talk to my husband," Rosalia said, subtly extricating herself from the hold. "But I promise you, he's never mentioned anything like this and Nathaniel always tells me everything."

As she said that, outside the house, a well-loved station wagon pulled up against the kerb. A guy in a blue checked shirt with a baseball cap shading his eyes from the sun jumped out followed by an excited looking black Labrador. If Nathaniel Barker had ever considered himself to be British, he looked every bit the American now. Rosalia looked nervously towards the door as she heard her husband's key turn in the lock.

"He loved his mother," Rosalia said quietly. "Be careful how you tell him all those things you've said to me."

The Labrador preceded its master into the sitting-room.

"Elvis!" Rosalia exclaimed, as the Lab wished her hello with his tongue. "Get down, boy."

The dog immediately turned his attentions to Ruby.

"Honey," Rosalia called to her husband, who was taking off his boots in the hall. "We have a visitor. From England," she added a little more quietly.

Ruby stroked the dog's soft ears. Its goofy canine face was strangely comforting.

Nathaniel Barker stepped into the room, tucking his baseball cap into his pocket.

"From England? Have we met before?" Nathaniel asked as he reached out to shake Ruby's hand.

"Not exactly," said Ruby.

Rosalia looked nervously between her husband and their visitor as Ruby prepared to tell the story one more time.

"You're lying."

Nathaniel Barker didn't want to know.

"You're talking bullshit!" he raged.

He didn't see how it could be possible that his mother, a god-fearing woman, a practising Christian and leading member of her church, could possibly have had a child out of wedlock after his father's death.

"Don't you think I would have noticed?" Nathaniel asked his would-be sister. "I would have been eight

312

years old when you were born, for chrissake. I would have known if she was having another baby."

He refused even to look at Ruby's birth certificate and closed his eyes when his wife showed him the photograph of his mother again and tried to make him admit to the similarities between his beloved old mum and the young woman, this stranger, who stood before him now.

"You have made a mistake," was all he said, while he pointed Ruby towards the door.

The promised lunch party didn't happen. While her husband headed out into the garden to take his anger out on a hedge with a pair of brutal looking clippers, Rosalia called Ruby a taxi to take her back to Denver.

"I'm sorry. I'm sorry," the besieged housewife said. "I've never seen him get so angry before."

"It's OK," said Ruby, wondering if her legs would take her when she stood up again.

Less than three hours after she had left, Ruby was back at her hotel. She was still shaking as she called the airport and had them put her through to the British Airways desk. There was a flight leaving for the UK late that night. She was supposed to be in Denver for another three nights but after Nathaniel's outburst, the whole city suddenly seemed a strange and sinister place. Ruby wanted to be home again. She wanted to be in the arms of someone who loved her. When she had finished making arrangements to change her flight, Ruby finally burst into tears.

She left a note at reception for Mary (who was still asleep after a hard night getting to know her colleague from New York), claiming a family crisis had sent her hurrying back to London. It wasn't entirely untruthful, she supposed. Then she asked the receptionist to call her another taxi. There was one already waiting in the street outside the hotel.

"Have you enjoyed your stay in our city?" asked the receptionist as she prepared Ruby's final bill.

"Let's just say the natives haven't all been that friendly."

"Oh, I'm sorry," said the receptionist automatically. "Have a nice day," she added, as she handed Ruby her receipt.

Ruby dragged her trolley case disconsolately through the lobby to the taxi waiting outside. Behind the desk, the telephone started ringing again, but Ruby was already settled into the back of the cab and drawing away from the front of the hotel by the time the receptionist connected the "English girl" that the caller was after with the English girl who had just left the hotel without saying "you have a nice day too".

"It's urgent," said Nathaniel Barker.

"But sir, she's already in the taxi.

"Well, go and get her."

"I can't do that, sir. I'm not permitted to leave the desk unattended."

Nathaniel hung up.

Despite the tailwinds, the flight back to the United Kingdom from Denver seemed to take much longer

314

than the flight that had taken Ruby out there. Ruby took an aisle seat. She didn't want to see Denver from the sky this time. She didn't ever want to see Colorado again. She had spent the evening crying in the ladies' room of the departure lounge as bad weather conditions had delayed her flight into the early hours of the morning. When the plane finally left the tarmac, she felt nothing but relief.

Across the aisle, a honeymoon couple clasped hands. The new bride sighed. "I want to live there forever." Ruby was just anxious to be home.

Halfway through the journey, the in-flight entertainment system showed a film that Ruby had been keen to watch since she first read that the leading lady had been cast. Katrina Black, the actress who had written so movingly about her adoption and her successful search for her birth parents, was playing the ditzy heroine in this movie about a girl with amnesia who doesn't recognise her husband.

But when the movie came on, Ruby closed her eyes and tried to sleep. In reality, she knew she was angry with Katrina. Jealous that her story had the happy ending Ruby felt she'd been denied. Katrina's half brothers and sister had welcomed her into their family and were only angry that they had waited so long to meet her. But of course they *would* be happy. Katrina Black was a famous actress. Ruby Taylor was an account manager in a second rate public relations company who would probably get back from this terrible trip to discover that she didn't even have a job after running out on the conference. Katrina was the prodigal daughter, returning wreathed with the halo of fame. Ruby brought back nothing but the shame of an extra-marital liaison that no one wanted to admit.

"Ladies and gentlemen," the captain interrupted the entertainment programme. "I'm sorry to have to report that due to a prior incident at Heathrow, our flight this evening will be diverted to Manchester airport . . ."

Ruby snapped awake.

Manchester?

CHAPTER
TWENTY-EIGHT

"I've chosen him!"

Erica pounced on Lou as soon as she arrived at the office on Monday morning.

"Chosen what?" Lou asked.

"My date! My ad went into the *Guardian* supplement on Saturday and the Soulmates section of the *Observer* yesterday morning and by last night I'd already had three replies!"

Lou raised an eyebrow.

"I didn't like the sound of the first two," Erica continued breathlessly. "Both were a little bit wet."

"Pisces?" Lou suggested.

Erica tutted at that. "Very funny. But the third one sounded lovely. A really great voice. Deep. Well-spoken. Educated."

"That's good," Lou agreed.

"I called him back as soon as I got his message and we talked for half an hour. I can't believe how easy it was to chat to him. I thought it would be really awkward but he put me at my ease. His name is Bob. He works for a law firm in the City — represents lots of asylum seekers apparently. He said he really likes cats — would have one himself if the lease on his flat didn't forbid it — and he's almost a vegetarian. Well, he only eats organic meat and free-range eggs."

Lou nodded. "That does sound worthy."

"Oh, piss off, Lou," said Erica, giving her a playful slap on the arm. "You're supposed to be excited for me."

"I am. When are you meeting him?"

"Tonight." Erica bit her lip. "At The Engineer in Primrose Hill. Eight o'clock, assuming he can get away from the office on time."

"Are you excited?" Lou asked.

"I'm absolutely terrified. What if he doesn't think I'm attractive?"

"Why shouldn't he?"

"But he sounds gorgeous. He said he looks like Richard Gere."

"And you believed him?"

"I live in hope," Erica sighed.

"He probably means he's the same height as Richard Gere," Lou suggested. "Richard Gere's a midget, so I've heard."

"He is?"

"Stands on boxes for all his kissing scenes."

"But Julia Roberts . . ."

"She's probably a midget too. Look, don't worry about tonight. Richard Gere or no, he'll definitely be enchanted by you."

"Wish I'd had time to hit the Jolene," Erica said, examining her feather-light facial hair in the mirrored section of her powder compact. "How is it possible that I didn't notice this horrible hair on my chin until it's grown almost as long as an eyelash. It must have been growing for a week."

"Another of life's great mysteries," said Lou.

"So. Is your friend Ruby back from the States yet?"

"Not due back till Thursday morning."

"Have you heard from her?" Erica asked. "Found out how she got on with her meeting?"

"Not a word."

"No news is good news, I suppose," Erica suggested.

"Yeah. I'm sure she would have called if anything went really wrong."

Ruby had watched the last case come off the luggage carousel. It wasn't hers. Now, she found herself utterly alone in an empty baggage reclaim area. The carousel she had been watching so avidly for the appearance of her little blue trolley case, came to a halt with a mechanical sigh.

"Hey!" Ruby called to a man wearing overalls who was pushing a mop disconsolately across the other end of the hall. "Where's my luggage?"

"What?" The man cupped his hand to his ear.

"My luggage," said Ruby, scooting up to his end of the hall with her empty airport trolley. "It didn't come off the conveyor belt with all the other stuff."

The man in overalls looked at her blankly.

"What's happened to it?"

He shrugged and carried on sweeping.

And that was about as helpful as anyone was going to be that night. The woman on the lost luggage counter had only just started working at the airport and claimed she had never actually had to deal with a lost luggage case on her own to date. She couldn't help now. Her manageress was on a fag break. By the time the manageress came back from her fag break and confirmed that she couldn't help either — Ruby would have to contact the airline directly — Ruby had missed the bus chartered to take the diverted Denver passengers back down south to London Heathrow.

"Catch a train and get the airline to reimburse you," the lost luggage manageress instructed. Ruby took a compensation claim form and made her way to the airport's rail station. But the information screens showed no trains for London in the foreseeable future.

"What time's the next train for London?" Ruby asked a passing station worker.

"Tomorrow," he said.

"You're joking, right?"

"No," said the station worker. "I don't do jokes."

"Then what am I supposed to do about getting home?"

"You should have got a plane that arrived in the morning," said the station worker. "Or one that landed at Heathrow."

"My plane was supposed to land at Heathrow," Ruby informed him.

"What you doing here then?"

"You tell me." Ruby clenched her fists to stop herself from giving him a v sign. Not that it would have made any difference. The station worker was pretty much inured to the contempt of the British public after five years' spent walking that platform.

Ruby trudged back to the terminal. At least having lost her luggage meant she didn't have to carry it around with her. She found a payphone, since the battery in her mobile phone was flat, and dialled Robert's number.

Her lip was quivering as she waited for him to pick up the phone. She knew that as soon as she heard his friendly voice the floodgates would open. But she wanted to hear Robert's voice. She needed to know that someone thought she was worthy of his love and affection.

The phone rang five times before the call was passed to an answer machine.

Ruby put the phone down, then picked it up and dialled again. She knew that Robert often let his machine pick up calls when he was actually in his study, working on something brought home from the office. If she called again, he would know that something serious was up and pick up the phone himself.

Five rings. The answer machine kicked in once more.

It was a Monday evening. Ten o'clock. He wouldn't be out at this time. Ruby knew that much because he would never come out with her on a Monday night. Monday nights were sacred, reserved for preparation for Tuesday morning's progress meeting.

Robert's message ended.

"Bleep."

"Robert, it's me," Ruby whispered to the tape machine. "I'm back. Well, I'm at Manchester airport. I had to get a flight to here instead of Heathrow. Something about an incident there causing diversions. I wanted to come home early. Everything went wrong. Oh, darling, I've really missed you. I wish so much you were in to take this call."

She sniffed loudly.

"I don't know how I'm going to get home," she continued. "I've missed the last train from Manchester to London tonight. This has turned out to be such a disaster. I should have listened to Lou and Martin. Oh, Robert, I . . ."

His answer machine gave a beep to signal that Ruby had run out of time.

Who else could she call? She couldn't ring her parents. They would only want to know why she was back from Denver early and even the slightest hint of concern in her mother's voice would be bound to set the waterworks off. Ruby would phone Lou, but she couldn't remember her number. That was the danger with programming numbers into the SIM card of your mobile and not bothering to learn them off by heart. Lou had moved only recently and Ruby wasn't even sure if the area code was 0207 or 0208. She did know that Lou was ex-directory, having taken her name out of the book following a disastrous love-affair with a guy called Magnus who claimed he heard messages from God.

There was just one person left.

"Martin?"

"Ruby! How's it going?" He sounded pleased to hear from her. "It's nearly half-ten at night here. What time is it where you are?"

"Half-ten," said Ruby flatly.

"But I thought . . ."

"I'm not in Denver any more. I'm in Manchester."

"Is there a Manchester in Colorado?" Martin asked sleepily. He'd nodded off in front of the telly.

"Manchester, Cheshire, dimwit. I'm back in the UK."

"Oh, what? Why?" Martin asked. "Did you . . .?"

"I met up with Rosalia Barker and her husband but he didn't want to know me!" Ruby tried to stifle a sob. Too late. Before Martin could say a single comforting word, Ruby was snuffling and snortling into the phone, the tears were streaming down her face and she could hardly breathe for crying.

"Ruby, Ruby, Ruby," Martin tried to break through to her.

"And now I'm in Manchester and I can't get back to London until tomorrow morning. There aren't any trains and I'm going to have to spend a night in an airport hotel and I can't even get hold of Robert and I feel sooooo lonely."

"Ruby," Martin said soothingly. "Where are you again?"

"I'm in the airport. In Manchester."

"Don't bother checking in to a hotel," said Martin firmly. "I should be able to get there in three hours."

"Eh?"

"Just work out which terminal you're in and call me on the mobile when you know. Then find yourself a nice quiet place to have a cup of coffee and wait for me. I'll be with you as soon as I can. I've done it in three hours before. Might not take so long now. I don't suppose there's much traffic."

"You're coming up here?" Ruby was confused.

"That's what I said, didn't I? Look, it's going to be OK, Rubes. You can tell me everything that happened on the way back to London. Only thing you have to do is buy me a cup of coffee at a service station to make sure we get back into town without me falling asleep at the wheel."

"Martin, I . . ."

"Save the extravagant thanks for later," he said.

"I owe you one."

"It's what friends are for."

Moments later, Martin was rummaging through a pile of rubbish on the kitchen table looking for his car keys and wondering what on earth he had put himself up for. It was eleven o'clock at night. By the time he got to Manchester it would be two in the morning. By the time they got back to London it would be six o'clock at the earliest and at nine o'clock he was expected at the offices of Manpower to take a variety of psychometric tests that would allow a temp controller ten years his junior to fix him up with a job so far below his capabilities that he would fuck up in two days out of boredom.

"Fuck it," said Martin, simultaneously finding the car keys and deciding to ditch the interview. Another day spent putting off the resumption of his far from glittering career would hardly make a difference now.

And miraculously, his sister's Fiesta, which never started first time, did start first time for the first time ever. That had to be a sign. As did the fact that all the traffic lights between Chalk Farm and the M1 turned green at his approach. In no time at all, Martin was bombing up the motorway, ticking faceless Midland cities off a mental list. Three hours soon seemed like a pessimistic estimation. If he didn't get stopped for speeding, then he might make it to Manchester in two.

Meanwhile, Ruby sat at the edge of a deserted coffee bar. Half the tables had chairs stacked upon them, so that the cleaners could move easily between them with the floor polisher. She was nursing the same small cappuccino she had been nursing for the past two hours. She hadn't even had enough money to pay for that one cup of coffee after using up most of her change trying to get through to Robert again. Midnight, one o'clock, half past one passed and he still wasn't picking up the phone. When she tried to buy a coffee with only eighty pence to her name, the cashier had taken pity on her and rung up the expensive cappuccino as a slightly cheaper can of Diet Coke.

"Won't you get into trouble?" Ruby asked her.

"I don't give a *sheet*," she said. The cashier was French. "I'm going back to Biarritz next week. Is too wet here. Too *mee*serable."

Ruby nodded in agreement.

"You OK?" the girl asked then. Ruby's eyes were somewhat pink.

"I'm fine," said Ruby. "Long flight. Just tired."

"You are staying *here* over the night?"

"I'm waiting for my friend to pick me up. He's on his way from London."

"From London? That's a long way. He's a special friend," the girl observed.

Now, seeing Martin walk across the terminal floor to find Ruby, the French girl smiled a complicit smile. "He's gorgeous," she mouthed. And Martin did look pretty dishy. Tired. Dishevelled perhaps. But dishevelled really suited him. Always had done.

"Found you!" he said.

"Martin," said Ruby. "I'm so sorry."

"Don't start with sorry. Come here."

He wrapped his arms around her. Ruby was instantly in tears again.

"Come on," Martin cooed. "You're almost home now. Tell me all about it on the way back to London." He led her out to the car park with one arm around her waist, carrying her hostess bag with his free hand.

"It's got wheels, you know," Ruby pointed out to him.

"What do you think I am?" asked Martin. "Some kind of pouf?"

CHAPTER
TWENTY-NINE

"Ruby," said Martin. "I know this isn't going to make up for what you've been through this last couple of days but I want you to know that I think of you as a sister. I mean, not as a sister exactly. But I love you just as much as I love my real sister. If I had a lifeboat with four spaces in it, you would definitely be in there with Mum and Marie."

Ruby continued to gaze out at the streetlights strobing past as they headed into London. Though Martin had assured Ruby she could talk about her experiences in Colorado until his ears bled if she wanted to, she hadn't said that much at all since they got out of the airport car park. At one point, she was so quiet that Martin thought she must have fallen asleep through tiredness. She had spent most of the last three days in the air, after all. If anyone deserved to get jet-lag ... But Ruby's eyes were wide open, watching the motorway traffic stream silently by.

"You don't need Nathaniel Barker, Ruby," Martin tried again. "You've got this far without him. You've lived for thirty years not knowing that you even had a half-brother. You didn't miss him then."

Ruby still didn't say anything.

"It doesn't matter what he thinks of you anyway because he doesn't really know you," Martin continued. "If he did know you then I'm sure he would be happy to tell the world that you two are related. He'd be really proud. If I found out I had a half-sister like you, I would be completely . . ."

"It's just the story of my life, isn't it?" Ruby interrupted. "My mother gave me up for adoption. Every man I've ever loved since has dumped me. Not even my fucking brother wants to know me now. I'm always the fucking reject."

Martin was shocked by the vehemence of her sudden exclamation.

"He'll probably come round," Martin said cautiously.

"Why should he? John Flett didn't come round, did he? Dave the accountant never wanted me back. I've had just about as much rejection as I can take."

"Ruby, I'll never reject you," Martin reiterated. "If I wasn't driving, you know I'd give you a hug right now."

"Hmmmph," Ruby snorted. She took the empty cigarette packet she had found in the Fiesta's untidy glove-box and began to shred it into ugly confetti.

"It's alright for you and Lou," she continued. "You know what it's like to be loved unconditionally. You don't know what it's like to lie in bed at night and worry that your mum and dad are going to send you off to a children's home because you failed your maths test. You don't know what it's like to feel that you've got to be a good girl because your parents didn't have to choose you from the reject pile. They did you a favour.

You've got to be so grateful. I've spent my whole life being grateful for fucking crumbs of affection."

"Ruby, that's not the way it really is," said Martin reasonably. "You know that your parents love you no matter what you do. Your dad drives a six-hour round trip every winter just to bleed the radiators in your flat!"

"I know," Ruby snapped. "I know. But there's a little part of me that doesn't know. A tiny little part of me I can't quite bury, that is always watching their faces for a flicker of disapproval. A part of me that could never take the piss like my sister did just in case they asked to unadopt me again. And that little tiny part of me takes every single slight and rejection I've had in my life and feeds on it until it drowns out all the sensible, rational parts of my brain with its constant fucking worrying."

She pinched the top of her nose in a desperate attempt to stave off tears.

"Oh, God. I'm sorry," she said. "This is the last thing you need. You've come out here in the middle of the night to fetch me from bloody Manchester. You got out of bed and drove for three bloody hours. You don't need to hear me going on and on and on about how bad my life is and . . ."

"Stop," said Martin.

"I'm trying," said Ruby, thinking that he was asking her not to cry.

"I mean, stop saying sorry. I wouldn't have come to pick you up if I didn't want to. I told you that you could talk about this as much as you need to and I meant it. You don't have to be grateful to me, Ruby. You and Lou are my best friends. I love you unconditionally and I just feel honoured that I can be here for you."

"You don't mean that," Ruby started.

"Can I hear the stupid part of your brain talking again?"

Ruby sank back into the passenger seat.

"You know what," Martin told her. "Other people's families aren't the Walton-esque fantasy you seem to assume they are. Just because you're brought up by your natural parents doesn't mean you're any *less* likely to get fucked up. Bloody hell, there were years when I just *wished* that my mum and dad would turn round and tell me that I was adopted. It would have made a lot of fucking sense."

Ruby gave him a sidelong glance.

"I'm sorry," he said. "I didn't mean to belittle the way you're feeling but . . ."

"I understand. It doesn't matter."

"What I'm saying is, you had a *happy* childhood, Ruby. Really you did. You were loved. You really were loved. You still are."

"I know. I know," she muttered.

"You've got a family. You've got friends. You've even got a new boyfriend and he seems alright," Martin choked out those last few words. "What are you looking for, Ruby? What else is it that you think you need?"

Ruby shrugged. "I think it's just that I've spent my whole life trying to prove that Mum and Dad were right to have adopted me."

"Everyone who knows you knows they were."

"Yes. But don't you see that the real proof of that would have been for my natural family to look at me as I am now and agree that I've made a success of myself and that they didn't give away the runt of the litter. I wanted them to confirm that it wasn't *me*. It wasn't *my* fault."

"You were a baby, Rubes. How on earth could it have been your fault?"

"I don't know. But I needed to hear that circumstances beyond their control made them give me up and have them fall madly in love with me now. I wanted to know that if things had been different they would *never* have let me go. I wanted them to want me to be part of their family again. Nathaniel Barker didn't even want to listen."

"But it must have been a shock for him," said Martin playing devil's advocate. "You turning up on the doorstep like that. He didn't know he had a sister, Ruby. He's got a lot of things to work out for himself now. He probably feels like he's been lied to. He's got to come to terms with a whole new version of his mother for a start. Perhaps he even feels guilty that his mother didn't give him away too."

"If he feels so guilty, why doesn't he try to make it up to me?"

"Guilt doesn't always work like that," said Martin. "Sometimes, knowing that you've done something bad to someone who didn't deserve it just makes you end up hurting them even more. You remember that temp at International Mags that I went on one date with?"

"Which one? There's been a couple." Ruby smiled.

"The gorgeous one. Veronique."

"The one who didn't fall for your charm?"

"She didn't give me the brush-off," said Martin defensively. "I know that you and Lou find that hard to believe but the fact is, she really liked me."

"And you liked her, didn't you?"

"Yeah. Yeah, I did. But then . . ."

"What? What went wrong?"

Martin took a deep breath and spewed the real story out. "She told me she had a colostomy," he said.

Ruby stopped shredding the cigarette packet and looked at her friend's shadowy profile.

"And I know that it shouldn't have mattered to me but it did. I just didn't want to sleep with her after that and so I tried to pretend that we weren't going to have sex there and then because I wanted to wait and make it special. And after that I had to start avoiding her in the office. And she was just so lovely and she couldn't understand why I didn't want to see her and she started to make me feel so guilty that I told my boss she'd forgotten to do some paperwork that I was supposed to have done myself and he terminated her contract."

"Martin. That's horrible!"

"Yeah. I know. But you see what I mean about guilt making you react in strange ways? I should have been nicer to her. Perhaps I should have told her what the problem was. But I did everything wrong because every time I saw her face I was confronted with the evidence of my own shittiness. My own inability to deal with real life. The kind of shame I feel about getting Veronique

332

the sack is probably the way your half-brother feels about telling you to get lost too."

"No," said Ruby mercilessly. "I don't think it's the same at all. What you did was just a crappy masculine reaction to the thought of physical imperfection. God help you if women ever decided not to give a man a chance because there was something slightly unsavoury about him. Not that a colostomy is unsavoury."

Ruby pressed her hand to her mouth. Martin thought she was going to cry again. But instead she gave a loud, giggling snort. "Oh God. I'm sorry! That poor girl! Certainly puts my cellulite into perspective. I can't wait to tell Lou."

"You mustn't tell Lou," Martin pleaded. "It's bad enough putting up with all the Hermes jokes. I only told you because I thought you'd understand! I thought it would help you feel better."

"Now we know why you kept referring to your love-life as a bag of shite!" Ruby was half-crying, half-giggling now. "I'm sorry, Martin. I'm sorry. I guess I am a bad person after all."

"Alright!" Martin groaned. "Let's leave it now, shall we?"

Ruby shook her head at him ruefully.

"At least I made you smile," he said.

"You're going to hell, Martin Ashcroft. You do know that, don't you?"

"You laughed," he reminded her. "You're coming too."

★　★　★

They reached Ruby's flat at quarter to six in the morning. They had driven through the dawn and turned into Ruby's street just in front of the milkman.

"Nightcap?" Ruby suggested.

"Just the one."

As they walked up to the front door, Martin wrapped his arm around Ruby's shoulders.

"You cold?" he asked her, hugging her close.

"Not any more," she said.

They stopped for a moment on the steps. Ruby looked up at Martin. Her eyes were still glittery from crying, her eyelashes still wet and spiky. It was a far better look than she'd ever managed with a mascara wand, Martin thought. He smiled a shy, closed-mouth, half-smile down at her pink, blotchy face.

"Thanks," she said, wrinkling her nose to stop the tears again.

"What for?"

"For driving all the way up to Manchester. For listening to me dribble on about my neuroses and for trying to understand."

"You deserve better," he said simply. "I wish there was something I could do to make you realise that. And them . . ." he added.

Ruby shrugged, knowing whom he was referring to at once.

"Who needs two families anyway?" she said bravely. "It's bad enough having to do one set of relatives at Christmas."

"Too right. Two lots of relatives. Two lots of sprouts," Martin pointed out. "Though, I don't suppose they

334

have sprouts for Christmas dinner out there, do they? Or you could end up with three lots of sprouts! Two Christmasses and one Thanksgiving!"

"Martin," Ruby stopped him with a finger on his lips. "I don't want to think about them at all. As far as I'm concerned, Colorado never happened. Agreed?"

"Agreed."

"Thanks." They still didn't move any closer to the door. "For everything," Ruby added almost nonsensically. Then she stood up on tiptoe and went to kiss him on the cheek. Just a friendly kiss.

But it lasted a bit longer than usual because as Ruby kissed Martin on the cheek he pulled her in for another hug and she ended up with her lips almost squashed against his. When he let her go again, she stumbled back feeling just a little flustered. She thought he might be blushing too.

Half an hour later, Martin left to drive back to his own place. Ruby stood in the middle of her empty sitting-room and surveyed the old sofa with its tidy cushions, the polished coffee table, the invincible cheese plant that Martin had forgotten to water after all. On the mantelpiece stood a framed picture of Ruby with her mum, dad and Lindsay, taken when they came to see her graduate. Ruby picked the frame up and gave it an affectionate little polish with her sleeve. She remembered how worried her mother had been about the dress code for such an event. Should she wear a hat? Or was that just too much? It wasn't a church service after all. It had been so important to her that she didn't let her youngest daughter down. In the end Mrs Taylor plumped for the light blue suit she had worn to Lindsay's wedding. No hat, which was a good thing because the wind was blowing gale force. Ruby's brother-in-law Steve must have taken the photograph. He was a wonderful bloke. Lindsay was lucky to have found such a husband. Ruby felt lucky enough just to have him as a brother-in-law.

Ruby studied her father's proud smile and felt another wave of tears behind her eyes. This was her real family. Not a man from Colorado who refused to acknowledge the possibility of her existence but the three people who flanked her in this photograph, the fantastic man who had taken the shot and the tiny baby with the Taylor family nose who had yet to be born when it was taken.

As soon as it was a decent hour, Ruby would call her mum and her sister. Find out how her niece was getting on. And as she replaced the photo in pride of place on the mantelpiece, Ruby felt something like relief. At least now she wouldn't have to put them through the pain of finding out that she had gone in search of her natural family. Nathaniel Barker had spared the Taylor family that sticky problem. It was probably for the best that he didn't want Ruby in his life.

On a shelf in the corner, the answer machine was flashing to show one message. Ruby pressed "play".

"Hey, baby. Are you back home yet? Sorry I wasn't there when you called from the airport. I've been in the office," he added, which was odd, since Ruby had remembered on the drive back from Manchester that he was supposed to be at a college reunion that night. "Hurry on over whenever you like, sweet-lips. I've been missing you too, too long."

Robert.

Ruby's frown melted away.

Somebody loved her after all.

CHAPTER
THIRTY

Lou noticed instantly that Erica was wearing exactly the same outfit she had been sporting when she left work for her big date the night before.

"You didn't?" Lou murmured.

"I know. I know. I shouldn't have done. It goes against everything they say in The Rules. But for heaven's sake, Lou. I've got to get it when I can. I'm thirty-seven . . ."

"I thought you said you were thirty-two!" Lou exclaimed.

"Thirty-seven and a half," said Erica proudly. "And I don't have to answer to anyone but myself and if I want to spend the night with a man I've only just met, then I'm bloody well going to."

"You've changed your tune."

"He's changed my life!"

"So quickly?"

"Well, quite slowly really," Erica said with a saucy smile.

"Erica! Pur-leese. I've only just had my breakfast."

"I know! And I know that I've ticked you off in the past for falling into bed too quickly, Lou, but that's partly because you're such a vulnerable soul."

"Thanks."

"I, on the other hand, know that it really doesn't matter if he never calls again."

"You don't mean that."

Erica bit her lip and suddenly looked like a teenager getting a serious attack of angst over her very first love. "Too right I don't! I'll *die* if he doesn't call me. I have to see him again!" She fell into a mock swoon.

"He must have been amazing," said Lou.

"He was. Right from the very start. Having said that he wouldn't wear a carnation because he didn't want everyone to know we were on a blind date, he turned up with a *huge* bunch of roses."

"Tesco Metro? Marks and Spencer?"

"No way. They were definitely from a proper florist. All wrapped up in brown paper. Look at this," Erica reached into her handbag and brought out her diary. She had carefully pressed one of the beautiful pinky-orange rosebuds against the page for the day of the big date.

"My God, that's soppy," said Lou.

"I know. But whatever happens next, I want to be able to remember last night for the rest of my boring little life." Erica sat down on the chair on the opposite side of Lou's desk and leaned over as if to impart a secret. Lou leaned towards her so that their heads were almost touching over the desk tidy.

"What on earth did he do to you?" Lou asked excitedly.

"I don't know. Nothing. I mean, everything. I can't even begin to tell you. But I think I had an orgasm," said Erica. Then she covered her mouth as though she had just uttered a terrible curse. When she took her hand away she was chewing her lip nervously again.

"Well, that's good, isn't it?" asked Lou. "But what do you mean you 'think' you had one?"

Erica leaned forward once more. "I mean, I don't know if that was what I had because I've certainly never had anything quite like that before now. I thought I had, but after last night, I'm just not sure. It was just so . . . Oh, I shouldn't be telling you this, Lou."

"Erica, I'm not going to tell anyone else if that's what you're thinking."

"I know you wouldn't. I'm not even sure if you want to hear it yourself. But I've got to tell somebody. I need to make sure that it *was* an orgasm and not just some strange kind of fit."

Lou stifled a giggle with the result that it came out as an indignant little snort.

"What's so funny?" Erica asked.

"Nothing's funny," said Lou, quickly recovering herself. "Tell me what it felt like and I'll put your mind at rest."

"Well," Erica took a deep breath. "He went down there and er . . . You know, I never would have asked him to do it. I just couldn't believe my luck when he did it of his own accord."

"Did what?" asked Lou.

"Don't make me say the word," Erica begged her. "Anyway, it started like a tickle in my lower regions, then it felt as though I was going to sneeze, only from my nnngh," she grunted and pointed coyly beneath the desk, "and not from my nose. And then I thought I was going to wet myself and finally I couldn't help screaming."

"Yup," said Lou with a guffaw. "That was an orgasm."

"Thank God for that," said Erica. "I thought I'd gone epileptic."

Ruby decided to lie low at home until Wednesday morning. Thankfully Alan seemed happy with her explanation that family problems had brought her home in a hurry.

"Everything sorted out?" he asked, in a sincere enough tone but one that let Ruby know that he didn't really want the gory details, much to her relief.

Ruby nodded.

"Well, hope it won't stop you enjoying Friday's party."

Friday's party. The summer party was just two days away now. The girls in the Two-Faced Cosmetics team were running a sweepstake on who would get too drunk to think and sleep with Emlyn "The Panter" Cruickshank by accident. They were supposed to be keeping it a secret from the man himself, but the waves of hilarity emanating from Imogen's desk — for it was in the top drawer of her desk that the book of bets was being kept — and the fact that the laughter stopped abruptly whenever the Panter was in the vicinity, had inadvertently alerted him to the mischief afoot. Not that he was offended. The fact that none of the odds on the office girls were longer than fifteen to one probably gave him a great deal of confidence in his dubious attractiveness.

"You're down at eleven to one," Liz informed Ruby.

"Oh, please," said Ruby. "I know what that man has in his socks. Besides," she added, "I'm attached."

Liz raised a haughty eyebrow. "So, he's still coming to the party, this new boyfriend of yours?"

"Absolutely." Ruby nodded. "You bringing someone along? Your cat perhaps?"

Liz pursed her lips in irritation. But Ruby wasn't bothered. She was very much looking forward to the party. It was almost impossible to remember how inconsolable she had been at the thought of attending that party just over a month ago, when John Flett was still the centre of Ruby's existence. She shrugged off Liz's suggestion that Ruby was just "papering over the cracks" with the wonderful Robert. He was a fantastic boyfriend but he was also a real soul mate. He seemed to know exactly what she needed. The previous evening, his response to Ruby's explanation of the Nathaniel Barker predicament was a simple "Fuck him." Yeah, Ruby thought. "Fuck him, indeed." No point going over and over what had happened in Colorado . . . especially as Robert wanted to go to sleep.

With Robert's support, Ruby felt she could get over this latest rejection *and* rub John Flett's nose in the shitty mess he had very briefly made of her life. The Hollingworth party couldn't come soon enough.

★　★　★

342

The following Friday morning was like the last day of term at the Hollingworth offices. The back of every door was adorned with someone's sweetie-wrapper party dress, just waiting for five o'clock and the rush for the ladies' room to come.

When Ruby arrived that morning, Imogen was already holding her dress against her, showing her assistant and "office best friend" Janine what she was planning to wear that night. "And a pair of these," Imogen added, holding up what appeared to be a pair of leg-warmers.

"Very *Kids From Fame*," said Ruby as she passed.

Imogen looked at her blankly. She was too young to remember.

Never mind, thought Ruby. Wondering whether Flett would "get" Imogen's retro eighties chic or be transported back in horror to the start of the man at C & A phase he had yet to entirely leave behind him. Forget witty references to a decade that invented the puffball, thought Ruby. She was going to go for *timeless* elegance. In the garment bag draped over her arm was a beautiful new silk dress by Nicole Farhi; its skirt as red and delicate as an extravagantly fragile poppy. It had cost a fortune but Ruby didn't care. She was going to have a fabulous evening. She was going to look her best ever and spend the night draped on the arm of a wonderful man, while Flett attempted and failed to keep up on the dance floor with his "bastard daughter of Bananarama" girlfriend. He would see Ruby looking serene and sophisticated and utterly better off without him. Not that Ruby was worried what Flett thought any more . . .

"Ruby, it's Robert."

"Oh, hi," Ruby trilled. "I was going to call you in a minute to let you know the plan for tonight. We've decided to have a few cocktails in the American Bar at the Savoy before we go on to the boat. Isn't that a great idea? Thought it would be nice to start the evening with a spot of sophistication even if we'll all be under the table by half past eight. It's a free bar all night once we're at the party . . ."

"Ruby," Robert interrupted.

"Yes?"

"I don't think I can come to the party tonight after all. Something important has come up."

"What?"

"Something to do with the case I've been working on. I don't think I'm going to be able to get away from the office until nine at the earliest. I'd say that I'll join you later on, but of course, I can't. Not unless I swim out to the middle of the Thames in my dinner jacket," he laughed feebly.

"What's come up?" Ruby asked. "Isn't there someone else who can take care of it for you?"

"Not really. It's some new evidence pertaining to next week's big case. It could make all the difference. I don't want to promise you that I'll be at the party and then have to let you down."

Ruby felt her mouth go dry. "It would make all the difference to me if you could be at the party," she tried.

344

"Yeah, Rubes, I know that. But for my client, it's going to make all the difference too. The difference between freedom and prison. I can't let him down. Or his wife. Or his children," Robert added as the killer blow.

"Perhaps you could join us at the Savoy for an early drink," Ruby persisted. "Then go back to the office straight afterwards."

"Ruby, I'd love to," he said soothingly. "But I've got meetings until seven o'clock in any case."

"So you can't get away for even half an hour?"

"Not even half an hour. Look, I'll call you later," he said to placate her. "You never know. I might be wrapped up earlier than I'm expecting. How about that?"

"OK," Ruby put the phone down slowly and looked ruefully at the red dress hanging on the back of her office door. Katherine, her assistant, popped her head round the door moments later.

"Rubes," she wheedled, "d'you mind if I pop out for a few minutes? I forgot my mascara and I need to buy some more for tonight."

Ruby waved her away dismissively.

"Rubes," Katherine began again. "Er, d'you know if Emlyn's going to be at the party on his own tonight? Not that I want to know for any particular reason . . . Some of the other girls are . . ."

"I don't know," said Ruby flatly. "But you do know that you're the favourite at two to one?"

"What?"

"You're the favourite to get your knickers off for the Panter," Ruby snapped. "Just try and have some dignity tonight, that's all."

Katherine backed out of the room. Mouth gaping.

Ruby was too pissed off to care. She couldn't believe it. Why did he have to work late *tonight*? A Friday night. The night of the summer party? Ruby's fantasy romantic evening on the pleasure boat was sinking.

Because she couldn't go on her own. She was over Flett. Make no mistake about that, she assured herself. She knew she never wanted to have him near her again. But she also knew that she would need to be so far over him that she couldn't remember his birthday (January 15th) before she would be happy to see him smooching with Imogen while she didn't have a smoochee of her own to snuggle into when she wanted to avert her eyes.

"Aaaaagggghhhh!" Ruby stabbed a biro into her mouse-mat. "Why tonight?" She knew she ought to try to be understanding but it simply wasn't fair. She *needed* Robert to be at this party. She *deserved* it, after everything that had gone wrong for her over the past few weeks. But he was abandoning her to stay late at the office on behalf of some criminal. Some drug-dealing low-life scum who made OJ look innocent, whose lovely wife probably couldn't wait for him to go inside so that she could shag his best mate and whose pre-school children were probably out nicking cars already anyway. "No, no, no, no, no." Ruby snapped her pen in half.

"You all right, Ruby?" Liz Hale was observing from the open door.

"Fine." Ruby brushed her hair back. "Robert just called to say that he's not feeling well. I'm not going to come to the party tonight after all. Going to go round and look after him," she lied.

CHAPTER
THIRTY-ONE

Lou was only too happy to let Ruby come out with her and Andrew that night.

"Though it's going to be a bit couply," she warned. "We said that we'd go for a drink with Erica, from my office, and her new man. Do you mind?"

"It'll cheer me up," said Ruby. "Besides, I don't mind coming out with couples when I'm not technically single myself. At least when you're telling each other your funny little anecdotes about how you met and what he said to you last week, I can talk about Robert."

Lou winced. "I don't tell 'funny little anecdotes' about Andrew, do I?"

"No, you don't," Ruby admitted.

"Phew. Look, you shouldn't let yourself get too angry with Robert. After all, I don't think you can argue that wanting to impress your evil ex-lover is more important than staying out of jail is to Robert's poor client. And his wife. And his children."

Ruby rolled her eyes.

"Imagine how you'd feel if that man went to prison because Robert was out partying with you," Lou continued.

"The thing is the bugger probably deserves to. Robert never seems to represent innocent guys. But I know you're right. It's just that I've looked forward to this so much. I wanted to be able to walk into that party with my head held high and not care if Flett is with Imogen because I've got a much better man of my own now."

"Ruby, you don't need a man to help you hold your head up in front of Flett. Or Imogen. What's she got that you haven't?" Lou asked then.

"Sun-tan. Thin thighs. My ex-boyfriend," said Ruby.

Ruby went straight to the pub in the clothes she had been wearing all day. She hadn't put any make-up on that morning, in an attempt to make the most of the effects of the previous night's face-pack in preparation for the Hollingworth party. It didn't seem worth putting on any slap to meet Lou and eco-friendly Erica. In fact, according to Lou, Erica had once said that make-up was a symbol of man's suppression of the female gender and melted all her lipsticks into a big red blob in the shape of a penis to express her disapproval.

Which was why Ruby was surprised to see that Erica was definitely wearing lipstick when she came into the pub that night.

"Hi!" And she was breathless and excited in a decidedly girly way. "Bob's going to be another half hour or so," she explained to Lou, Ruby and Andrew. "He works so hard. But I can't complain. Not when he's working for next to no money at all on behalf of those asylum seekers."

"What does he do?" asked Ruby.

"He's a lawyer," said Erica, unable to disguise her pride. "Specialist in human rights."

"Amazing. My boyfriend's a lawyer too," said Ruby.

"Oh, really?"

"Yeah, but he's more into the big bucks criminal side of things."

"Oh, well," said Erica, as if that made him one of the bad guys too.

"He's working really hard at the moment," Ruby confided. "We were supposed to be going to a party tonight but he's just had some evidence come in that might save one of his clients from prison. I could hardly insist that he comes to my works do instead when some poor bloke's liberty is on the line. He did say he would call later on though. He might still be able to join us."

"You don't want the lawyers to spend all night talking shop," said Lou.

"Or football," said Andrew. "Since that's all we men ever talk about."

"What do you do, Andrew?" Erica asked.

"About what?" Andrew quipped.

Lou squeezed his hand beneath the table. Perfect answer. Perfect guy.

"You know what," said Ruby magnanimously, when she and Lou were alone in the ladies' later that evening. "I think I was wrong about your friend Erica. She's really all right. A girl's girl."

Lou raised an eyebrow in amusement.

"No, really. She is. She's quite a laugh. I hope this man of hers turns out to be a decent bloke," Ruby continued. "Doesn't it strike you as statistically impossible that we've all got lucky through personal ads? First you with Andrew, who really is great, Lou. You should hang on to him."

Lou nodded thoughtfully.

"Then me with Robert. Now Erica with her Bob. That's three out of three. There just aren't that many decent single men floating around without good reason. I hope Erica's bloke doesn't turn out to be some kind of weirdo who gets his kicks from answering Lonely Hearts. Or a married man pretending to be single. Erica doesn't deserve that."

"She's usually pretty level-headed about things," said Lou. "I think she'd sniff a chancer out. He can't be married, anyway."

"What makes you say that?"

"He's willing to meet her friends, for a start. Married men don't want to meet your friends in case you have someone in common who knows his wife."

"Aaaaah!" Ruby nodded in understanding.

"It's an even better indicator of marital status than a white gap in a suntan where a wedding ring should be."

"I once met a man who told me that he had a pigmentation anomaly on his left hand that just made it look as though he'd taken off a wedding ring."

"Was that true?" asked Lou.

"Of course it wasn't." Ruby sighed. "Well, at least Robert has neither of those traits. I checked his hands on the first date and he's already met you and Martin and he would have met loads of my friends at the party tonight if it wasn't for that case coming up."

Lou narrowed her eyes. "Are you sure he has to work late?" she teased.

"Yes, I'm bloody sure. He would have come along to the party as soon as he finished. Except that if he doesn't finish before eight then he can't. Because it's on a boat."

"What time does it start?"

"Leaves the mooring at seven-thirty."

"You could still go, couldn't you?"

"I don't know," Ruby admitted. "I don't want to go on my own."

"Oh, Ruby. Why not? Much as I fail to understand the way you seem determined to bundle up your self-esteem and hand it to the first man who smiles at you, surely meeting Robert has given you enough confidence to go to the bash and enjoy yourself without him having to actually be there?"

"Flett won't believe he exists if he doesn't see him."

"What do you think Flett's going to think if you don't show up at all? 'Ah yes. That'll be because she's at home shagging her brand-new boyfriend?' Your absence won't make Flett any more convinced that he was wrong to dump you. If you go along looking fantastic and spend the whole night dancing like a wild thing, on the other hand." She gave a little shimmy in demonstration.

"Lou, I know it sounds pathetic, but I really don't think I can. It'll put me off my rhythm if I have to share a dance floor with Flett and Imogen doing some kind of smooch."

"Won't it be a laugh to see her having to cope with his appalling lack of rhythm while they do it?" Lou suggested.

Ruby allowed herself a small smile as she remembered dancing with Flett on their first proper date. It was a good job that Ruby had got to know and love his personality first. When John Flett took to the dance floor, it was less Saturday Night Fever than a nasty case of St Vitus' dance. Much as she adored him, Ruby could only dance with Flett if she kept her eyes firmly closed and blocked out the shocked faces of the people around them as they watched the sophisticated businessman hear "Come On Eileen" and start making like a chimp being prodded with electrodes.

"Robert dances like a dream," Ruby mused. "At least, from what I can gather when he's waltzing me from the front door into the bedroom."

"Purleese," said Lou. "You're making me sick."

"What about you? You're all loved up. You've got a lot to thank that stranger on the train for."

Lou paused halfway through applying her lip balm. "Yeah. To think I was stupid enough to believe that someone who smiled at me on a train could be my soul mate, eh?"

"Stupid or not, it got you the wonderful man you're with right now. I think that shows just how clever fate really is."

"Was Andrew really the only person who replied to the ad?" Lou asked.

Ruby nodded. "Yep."

"Oh, well."

"Lou," said Ruby. "You can't tell me you're disappointed that you ended up with Andrew instead of someone you never even spoke to? The man on the train almost certainly wouldn't have lived up to your expectations if he had answered the ad. He might have been married. Or had a speech impediment. Or a penchant for wearing ladies' underwear in the sack."

"Who wears ladies' underwear in the sack?" asked a booming voice from one of the cubicles which had been shut for the duration of Lou and Ruby's conversation. Now the newly married Susannah Foreman emerged, zipping up her too tight chinos over her belly-button ring and smoothing her T-shirt (a tight red number which had "Manteaser" written across it in "Malteser" style script) across her ample chest.

"I thought it was you two," she told Ruby and Lou. "So, spill the beans. Ladies' knick-knacks in the boudoir?"

"There are no beans to spill," said Lou. "How's married life?"

"Oh, you know. Just got back from our honeymoon. Bloody hot out there in Tanzania." Susannah's face was still lobster red to complement her outfit. She and Winky had been on a safari. Winky was the kind of bloke who somehow looked right in a pith helmet.

"Did you enjoy the wedding?" Susannah asked.

"Oh, yes," said Lou and Ruby dutifully.

"Did you score?"

"Nope," the girls shook their heads.

"Well, you can't say I didn't lay on enough choice for you!"

Ruby and Lou both smiled tightly as they remembered the rowdy rugger buggers and the lecherous grandfather of the groom. "We're both fixed up now, anyway," said Ruby. "Through Lonely Hearts ads. Just like you!" she added.

Susannah whacked Ruby on the back as if she'd just scored a try at a rugby international. "Good girl! It's the way forward, if you ask me. I couldn't believe my luck when I bagged Winky. Though I did have a few false starts."

"You did?"

"Oh, yeah," Susannah told them. "I can laugh about it now. Loads of married men looking for a bit on the side. Weirdos who still live with their mothers."

Ruby nodded in recognition at that.

"Lots of men who seemed quite promising on paper but who turned out to have been advertising themselves in the way an estate agent describes a Balham broom cupboard as *bijou*."

"I definitely had one of those," said Ruby, remembering Robin.

"And one really disappointing experience with quite a good-looking bloke who turned out to be a personal ad junkie."

"Do they exist?" asked Lou.

"Oh, yes. Though I think it's just a polite way of describing a sex addict who preys on vulnerable girls. He said he would take me out for dinner one evening but tried to get rid of me as soon as the first course had been cleared away so that he could meet another advertiser for coffee. Didn't even have the decency to meet the girl in a different restaurant. I saw him sitting in the window with her as I went past in a taxi." She shook her head at the memory. "Well, at least he didn't get into my knickers. I nearly gave up after that," she confided. "But Finty — I think you met her at the wedding — persuaded me to advertise one more time. And this time I got my Winky."

Lou and Ruby cooed appropriately.

"So you've got a personal ad bloke too?" Susannah said to Lou.

"I suppose I have."

"Glad to hear it," said Susannah. "I told Winky you weren't a lesbian," she added to Lou and Ruby's horror. "Honestly, men assume that just because you turn down a tongue sarnie with a man who's already vomited up ten pints, you must be gay. I've won a tenner thanks to you, Lou."

"Oh, great!" Lou exclaimed.

"I'll buy you a drink to celebrate."

"I think you'd better."

When Lou, Ruby and Susannah got back to the table, Erica was looking sheepishly excited. "He just called to let me know he's on his way," she said, waving her mobile as if that proved it.

"Where's he coming from?" asked Ruby politely.

"Near Old Street," said Erica.

"Hey!" said Ruby. "That's where Robert's firm's based too."

"He's going to call again as soon as he's parked," Erica explained.

Erica's mobile played "Für Elise" to let her know she had a call but when it rang again this time, Erica answered before Beethoven could get to the end of the first bar.

"Hello!" she said briskly, immediately softening into a giggle when she realised that her new man was making the call. "Where are you now, you sexy beast?"

Ruby and Lou shared the kind of "aah!" look reserved for the newly in love and small fluffy puppies.

"Just three minutes away? Where did you park the car? Yes, that's a good idea. Have you put the alarm on?"

Oh, the fascinating conversations people have on their mobile phones, Lou thought. Even stranger was why everyone else stopped talking to listen.

"Are you sure it's not single yellow lines there? They don't matter after six o'clock? Well, I guess you are the lawyer, Bob! Yes, of course I'm excited about seeing you. I've been looking forward to this all day. Mmm-hummm. Yes, I know. Where are you now? Just outside the bar? Can you see me yet? Yes, it is very but if you stay on the phone I can guide you in."

"Like air traffic control," joked Andrew. "How big is your new boyfriend's nose?"

"No, I'm not on my own," Erica explained to her caller. "That was Andrew. Lou's boyfriend. Yes," she laughed. "I'll tell him your nose is absolutely perfect! Best nose I've ever seen. We're sitting towards the back. On the left side. No hang on. My left. So that's your right as you come in . . . I'm wearing a black top. Yes, of course I'll recognise you. How could I forget you, Bobby?"

Lou made an irreverent gagging motion with her fingers in her mouth.

"What's that? Oh yes, Lou was just teasing me for being so soft. Yes, I've been here with Lou all evening. We came straight from work. And met up with her boyfriend Andrew and her old college friends Susannah and . . . Where are you now? You must be really close to us! Shall I stand up so you can see me better? What's that? You'll have to shout. Sounds like you're losing your signal . . ."

Lou saw him first, her face automatically adopting the cartoon "shocked" expression — eyebrows up, mouth wide open — as she recognised the smooth, handsome features and the curly black hair that framed them so well. She didn't know what to do. Grab Ruby and run? Grab Erica and run? Gesture at him madly until he ran away from them first? Too late. The crowds had parted around him. Erica and Ruby were turning to greet the latest addition to their party simultaneously. Four eyebrows went up in a delighted hello!

"Hi!" said Ruby. "You made it!"

"Darling!" said Erica.

"You!" said Susannah.

"What the —?"

Ruby's Robert, Erica's Bobby and Susannah's Rob froze with his mobile phone still pressed against his ear.

"Robert!"

"Bobby!"

"Rob!"

He just turned on his heel and ran.

"Come back here, you bastard!" shrieked Susannah. The personal ad junkie had taken one too many hits.

CHAPTER
THIRTY-TWO

Winky, encouraged by Susannah and emboldened by four pints of Special, was all for chasing Robert out into the street and giving him what for on behalf of all three women he had wronged. Luckily for Robert, he was in the Boxster and out of harm's way before Winky managed to lever himself off his bar stool. He didn't even try to talk his way out of it. He just cut off his call to Erica and fled the bar like the rat out of hell that he was, leaving Erica and Ruby to digest the unhappy facts.

Susannah told them in very unflattering terms what she felt Robert had seen in them. "He's a sex addict. He wants easy sexual encounters. No commitment. He knows that the kind of women who place personal ads are vulnerable, insecure types who won't take too much encouraging into the sack. He probably expects to be able to shag on the first night and never have to call them again."

Erica and Ruby were green as they each remembered their first date assignations.

Under the circumstances, Lou didn't think it would be such a great idea if Ruby went to the works' summer party after all. But Susannah insisted. "Get back on the horse, my girl." And suddenly finding the "go to hell" chutzpah that had been missing for her whole life, Ruby told Lou that nothing was going to stop her from catching that party boat now. She changed into her Nicole Farhi and applied make-up in the ladies' room while Erica leaned against the Tampax machine in shock.

"Ruby," Lou reasoned. "Do you really think you want to go to this party?"

"Less than an hour ago you were telling me that I should," Ruby protested.

"I know. But that was before . . . You're really angry, Rubes. If you're going to get drunk and disorderly, wouldn't you be better off doing that here with us instead of in front of your work colleagues?"

"But there's free booze. You go to the party, girl!" said Susannah, whose answer for everything was more alcohol.

With her head now on the hand drier, Erica groaned. "How could I have been so naive?"

"Are you OK there?" Lou asked, briefly switching her attention to the other injured party.

"Hey!" said Ruby indignantly. "You're supposed to be *my* best friend."

"Oh come on, Rubes. Erica's a victim in this too. How was she supposed to know that her Bob was your Robert?"

"And my Rob," Susannah reminded them. "He must answer every single ad placed in London. What a freak! He's probably impotent."

Erica and Ruby's faces registered similarly anguished expressions. And Ruby had to agree that there was no way Erica could have known her new boyfriend had already promised himself to every other thirty-something looking for "friendship maybe more" within the M25 but that still didn't make her feel better.

"Why don't I send Andrew home?" Lou suggested. "Then we girls can go for a drink together and bitch about the bastard you've both had a lucky escape from."

Erica nodded resignedly.

"I'm not going to sit here moping about that shit," said Ruby. "I've got a boat to catch."

"Go, Ruby," said Susannah. "Hit the champagne and forget all about it."

"I'm going to," Ruby assured her.

And with that, she was gone.

Ruby managed to grab a taxi right outside the bar and made it to the river in time, arriving on the jetty just as the deck hands were pulling in the rickety bridge that had connected the pleasure boat to the shore.

"Hang on!" she shouted. They paused in their rope hauling and helped her across. As the taller of the two placed his hand in the small of Ruby's back to make sure she didn't lose her footing and tumble backwards into the petrol black water, he gave her a dazzling smile.

"I feel better already," she murmured, as she straightened up and attempted a sashay into the cabin where the party was already in full flow. Unfortunately, since she had downed two bottles of Metz on the taxi ride over, it was inevitable that she caught her toe on a badly placed rope and nearly entered the festivities head first.

"Enjoy your trip," shouted the guy who had winked.

"I could sue you for leaving that rope lying about like that," she reprimanded him.

"Don't spoil that pretty face with a frown," he said.

Ruby fluffed herself up again. "OK," she said. "I won't."

Three deep breaths. In for a count of ten. Out for a count of ten. Liz "the yogi" Hale would have been proud. Ruby gathered herself on the threshold of the party.

"What you waiting for?" one of the deck hands cried. "Do you want us to announce you or something?"

"Cretins," Ruby muttered. She'd forgotten about the wink and the smile now. She brushed down the skirt of her red dress and tucked one side of her bob back behind her ear. Behind the door to the main cabin, all sorts of horrors might await her. Flett and Imogen might already be snogging to "their song". Ruby's late arrival would pretty much guarantee that all eyes would be on her as she entered.

She glanced longingly back towards the shore. Perhaps Lou had been right. The reality of Robert's duplicity probably hadn't even sunk in yet. It would almost certainly hit her like one of those big iron balls they use to demolish buildings as soon as she saw John Flett and his itty-bitty girlfriend. Drinking yourself back to happiness might work for Susannah and Winky but it had never worked for Ruby before. She felt a sudden, overwhelming urge to go home and hide out beneath the duvet. But the jetty was already thirty feet away. Too far to jump. Too far to swim. Especially in pure silk Nicole Farhi. No way out this time. Ruby stepped into the fray.

"Ruby! What are you doing here?" The first person she bumped into was Liz Hale. "I didn't think you were going to come along tonight because Robert . . ."

"I don't have to have male company every time I go out," said Ruby archly. "Why should I miss the party of the year just because I don't have a date with a penis?"

"Quite," said Liz. "Isn't that what I said to you all along?"

"I know. And I'm sorry about earlier," Ruby told her.

"Apology accepted."

"When it came down to it, I couldn't bear the thought of staying in to watch the telly instead and missing out on someone making a complete and utter tit of themselves. Who are the contenders tonight?"

"Alice Martin has been knocking them back all afternoon. She went for lunch with Mariel Cooper." Ruby and Liz both rolled their eyes at the name of the client who had big shares in Johnnie Walker. "I give it until nine o'clock before Alice is heaving her guts up into the Thames."

"Lovely," said Ruby sarcastically. "And . . ."

"He's here," said Liz, knowing at once whom Ruby was referring to. "He was chatting to Alan a few minutes ago but I don't know where he's got to now."

"Perhaps he jumped overboard when he saw me coming," Ruby quipped.

Liz looked concerned. "Look, Ruby. You're not . . ."

"Don't worry!" Ruby said defensively. "I'm here to have a good time, not a fist-fight with the man who dumped me by e-mail. Or his girlfriend. I'm beyond that now."

"Have you seen what she's wearing?" Liz asked. "I had a pair of legwarmers like that when I was twelve."

"Retro-eighties chic is all the rage," Ruby informed her. "Provided you can't remember it the first time around."

"Well, I think she looks ridiculous."

Ruby nodded, wishing she could agree. Unfortunately, much as Ruby wanted her to look like a refugee from *Flashdance*, Imogen looked as though she had stepped from the directional fashion pages of *Vogue*. The legwarmers were a witty addendum to a surprisingly stylish outfit. It was eighties chic MTV-style. The only possible consolation would be if Flett had donned a kung-fu style bandanna and rolled the sleeves of his jacket up à la *Miami Vice* to complement his new young lover's look.

He hadn't.

Ruby caught her first glimpse of Flett that evening as she and Liz queued at the bar for warm white wine.

"So, what made you change your mind about coming?" Liz was asking at the time. "I must say, I'm really glad that you've come to your senses. You shouldn't have to go into social exile just because one of your clients . . ."

Ruby jabbed Liz hard in the ribs as Flett sidled up beside them.

"Ruby," he nodded curtly.

"Jonathan," she replied briefly, before turning her attention back to the barman.

"That's a lovely dress," he said. "Very sophisticated. It suits you."

"Thank you," said Ruby, rewarding him with a halfsmile. "That's a . . . nice shirt," she said. He was wearing the pink polo shirt. Again! "Pink suits you."

"Johnnie! Have you got me that glass of wine yet?" Imogen shouted. "I'm absolutely gasping!"

"Run along, Johnnie-boy," muttered Ruby under her breath as Flett scuttled back towards his new girl.

"See you later?" he said as he went.

"You handled that really well," said Liz, giving Ruby a congratulatory pat on the back. "How do you feel?"

"I feel fine," said Ruby, tightening her grip on the brass rail that ran around the bar. "Why should I feel any different?"

"Well," Liz pontificated then, "he may not be here tonight but Robert is obviously having a positive effect on you."

"Positive effect?" Liz stepped back in horror as Ruby's face crumbled from sophisticated, serene composure to the "tragedy" mask of historical theatre. "Oh, Liz! My life is a disaster!"

Liz's eyes widened desperately as she heard the first line of that overly familiar tune.

"Robert isn't here tonight because he's been seeing someone else! He answered an ad in the *Guardian* that was placed by one of Lou's workmates."

"Nooooo!" said Liz appropriately.

"When I thought he was going to be working late tonight, I decided to go for a drink with Lou. She was supposed to be on a foursome with Andrew and her workmate Erica's new man. Turned out that Erica's new man was my old one!"

"Ruby, that's just awful!"

"He's a personal ad addict. My friend Susannah went on a date with him almost two years ago."

"Can I help you?" asked the barman.

"Two dry whites," Ruby managed to sniff before carrying on with the tears.

"What did you say to him?"

"I didn't get a chance to say anything at all! He saw me sitting next to Erica and made his escape before either of us could grab hold of him and punch . . . his . . . fucking . . . lights . . . out!" She gulped agonisingly between each word, finishing on a rib-racking sob that drew the attention of everyone within a ten-metre radius.

"Here's your wine," said the barman nervously.

"Thanks," said Ruby.

"Is that everything?"

"No," she said. "I'd better have another two as well."

"Ruby!" Liz began in a warning tone. "You can't just drown your sorrows . . ."

"Oh, for fuck's sake," said Ruby. "I was getting two for me and two for you. You know what the queue for the bar will get like later on. I can have a couple of glasses, can't I? Without turning into a blubbering wreck?"

Liz was kind, or cowardly, enough not to tell her that she had already achieved the blubbering part without the assistance of Sauvignon Blanc.

"Let's sit down over there," said Liz, pointing to a suitably dark corner, "and you can tell me all about it properly."

"I don't want to spoil your evening too," said Ruby, forgetting her previous diagnosis that the only thing stopping Liz Hale from committing suicide was the fact that even her non-existent love life seemed preferable to Ruby's endlessly humiliating one.

"I'm your friend," said Liz. "*Your* pain is *my* pain."

"That's nice," said Ruby. "I mean, it's not nice. Oh, you know what I mean."

The barman placed the second round of white wine on the bar in front of them.

"That it?" he asked again. He indicated with a subtle gesture of his eyebrows the fact that Ruby had already drained one of the previous two glasses.

"One more," said Ruby, raising a finger. "Each."

"Ruby . . ." Liz began. "Do you really think you should have any more wine?"

"You're right," said Ruby. "I shouldn't. Barman, make mine a double vodka."

Oh dear. Months later, Ruby would still be unable to recall what really happened on the night of the

Hollingworth party. Not even under hypnotic regression. Martin and Lou had always teased Ruby for her inability to truly let go under the influence of alcohol. She'd never had a blackout or sudden memory loss such as Lou was prone to on a weekly basis during their college years. Ruby had never even thrown up, leading Lou to suggest that Ruby's refusal to truly let it all hang out while drinking alcopops was reflected in her extremely low hit rate with orgasms.

But that night, on board the incongruously named good ship *Primrose*, Ruby broke through all her previous barriers. Two bottles of Metz, two glasses of wine, three double vodkas and all on an empty stomach. Pretty soon, Liz Hale was just a shadowy blur with big red lips that seemed to be moving twice as fast as the words that were getting through Ruby's ears. The combination of alcohol and the movement of the boat had set up a sine wave undulation in her stomach. But her worries were starting to fade and go fuzzy at least.

"I feel like dancing," she told her shoulder to cry on.

"I think you should stay sitting down," said Liz sensibly.

What did Liz Hale know? Ruby hauled herself to her feet and crossed the dance floor, zig-zagging as if she was trying to escape from a crocodile. Imogen and John Flett were bopping energetically to that Buck's Fizz Eurovision classic "Making Your Mind Up". When it got to the part in the song where the two blonde bimbettes generally lost their skirts, Ruby suddenly found that she was leaning too far forward to remain upright. She made a grab for the nearest thing to stop her fall. She heard a ripping noise. Someone was shouting.

All black . . .

CHAPTER
THIRTY-THREE

"Recorded delivery," said the postman, thrusting a clipboard towards Martin's chest. Martin hesitated instinctively. Recorded delivery could only mean bad news. Probably the kind of bad news that his bank manager charged twenty pounds per letter for. The HSBC were the only people Martin could imagine would bother writing to him in this way. The night before he had stuck his cash card in the hole in the wall and actually prayed until the machine spat some cash out. He must have hit his overdraft limit by now. He had been writing cheques all week in the knowledge that they might turn out to have more bounce than Tigger.

The postman cleared his throat. "Do you want it or not, mate? I haven't got all day."

"What? Sorry." Martin scribbled his signature.

"Signature there," said the postman impatiently. "You've got to print your name in that box. Never mind. That'll do."

He handed the envelope and a few other items over, tutted and walked back up the path slamming the gate shut behind him. Martin wondered whoever got the idea that postmen were cheerful. Perhaps it was the early mornings. What time was it? He could barely focus on the clock in the kitchen, so gummed with sleep were his eyes.

Seven a.m. Martin looked at the plain white envelope with his name and address set squarely in the middle in neat Times New Roman. Seven a.m. On a Saturday morning. It had better be good news, thought Martin. But how likely was that? No one ever sent good news by registered post. Still, if it was his bank manager, he did at least have a contingency plan. The cheque from Petunia Daniels, still un-cashed, was pinned to the note board in his bedroom.

Best have a fortifying cup of tea first, he decided. While the kettle boiled, Martin listened to the messages on his answer machine. The first was from his sister, asking if he wanted to join her and her family in Bournemouth over the next bank holiday weekend. "I don't think so," said Martin to the empty room, imagining three days being used as a vaulting horse by his niece and nephew. The second was from Webecca. "Martin, I weally hope you're not sitting there ignoring this message . . ." He skipped straight to the next one.

"Martin, it's Lou. Calamity. Can you believe that Ruby's man turned out to be Erica's man as well? He's one of those sex addicts who trawl the personals for victims. Erica's crying on Andrew's shoulder but Ruby thinks she's OK. She's gone to the Hollingworth party on her own. Bloody Susannah Foreman was encouraging her. She probably is OK. But I'd be really grateful if you could go round and check on her at some point tomorrow morning. You live much closer than I do.

Make sure she hasn't done anything stupid. Thanks, babe. Mwah. Mwah."

Martin played that message again. Ruby's man turned out to be Erica's man? Did this mean Ruby and Robert were finished? It had to.

"Yes!" Martin balled his hand into a fist and made a footballer's victory gesture. "Yes. Yes. Yes." It wasn't all bad news that morning then. He'd go and see Ruby as soon as he was dressed. Take her for a coffee. If he still had any money . . .

"Oh, sod it," said Martin as he ripped the ominous envelope open at last. The news wasn't going to get any better if he left it unread.

He was halfway down the densely printed page before it hit him that the missive wasn't from his bank manager at all. He sat down at the kitchen table and started again. The letter was printed on the thick creamy notepaper of Euphemie Gilbert at the Wilson Gilbert Literary Agency.

Back when he started his novel Martin had sent two chapters and a synopsis to just about every agent in the *Writers' and Artists' Yearbook*. And he thought he'd counted all the knock-backs in, everything from *Dear Mr Ashcroft, Mr Tyler regrets that he is not taking on any new clients at the moment*, to *Dear Mr Ashcroft, I regret that I am unable to put my weight behind such a derivative piece of writing*. That one hurt the most, but Martin had kept it in any case, convinced that before too long there would come a day when that particular agent would have to eat his own clichéd words.

But Euphemie Gilbert? Martin couldn't even remember having sent his script to her.

Dear Mr Ashcroft,

How thrilled I was to read such an exciting manuscript! she wrote. I find it hard to imagine that a writer of your calibre doesn't already have representation, but if that is not the case, I wonder if you might care to meet me for lunch to discuss your literary future. How glad I am that I took heed of Petunia's assertion that yours is a rare and wonderful talent!

Petunia? Martin rubbed his eyes. Perhaps he wasn't awake yet after all. Perhaps this was just another cruel and unusual dream like the one in which Cameron Diaz declared undying love for him and bought him a Porsche 911 to prove it. Who was Petunia? The only Petunia he knew was Petunia Daniels and she would hardly be the first to sing his praises. Would she?

Euphemie continued:

I have taken the liberty of printing out a copy of your work in progress to show to my colleagues here at the office. How close are you to finishing the novel? Everyone is enormously excited at the prospect of meeting you, including Simon Dunford, Petunia's own agent, who would like to talk to you about film rights immediately.

Martin's chin hit his chest.

Petunia Daniels. The missing diskette.

And, sure enough, there among the rest of the post that the jolly postman had delivered that morning was a note on one of Petunia Daniels' personalised Smythson correspondence cards.

Dear Mr Ashcroft,

I fear that I have utterly underestimated you. I hope you will forgive me that, meeting you as I did under such extraordinary circumstances, I failed to offer you the hospitality and respect you deserved. I'm sure you will understand that in the past Cindy has met many young men who, rather than seeing her for the wonderful creature she is, see beyond her to an opportunity to meet her parents. I'm afraid that I assumed the worst of you — hence the rather embarrassing little matter of the contract — and my compulsion to read the material stored on your diskette.

By the time I reached the end of the first chapter, however, I knew that you have a real talent for story-telling and the fact that you chose not to bank the cheque with which I tried to pay you off, was a further reason for me to review my opinion of you. I can only hope that the name and address you gave for our silly little contract was your real one and apologise for having treated you so shabbily. If this note does reach you then perhaps you will see your way to allowing me to repair some of the damage caused by joining us all

for dinner at your earliest convenience.
Best wishes,
Petunia Daniels

Martin raced out the house without grabbing a jacket. It was spitting with rain but he hardly noticed. It was as though the letter he clutched in his hand emitted enough heat to make him immune to the elements. He was grinning like a loony and he knew it. As he passed the old wino who always sat outside the tube, the old man raised a can of Special Brew in a toast.

"Good morning to you, young gentleman."

"It is indeed a fabulous morning," said Martin, as he raced on past. Then he stopped. And for the first time ever he dug into his pockets to find some change to give the homeless man. After all, Martin thought, he was going to make it. The evidence that he was about to get his big break was still clutched in his sweaty palm. He could afford to be a little magnanimous.

Martin pulled out what he thought was a note. It was a note, but not a banknote. Just the note his upstairs neighbour had pushed under his door to let him know that the bass on his stereo was set too loud. And a fifty-pence piece.

"I take American Express," said the wino hopefully.

"Switch?" asked Martin.

The wino shrugged and accepted the coin.

"I'm sorry," Martin told him. "I did want to give you more. I would give you more except I haven't got any cash on me at the moment. I've just got an agent."

The wino looked at him blankly.

376

"An agent for my writing. Euphemie Gilbert at the Wilson Gilbert agency wants to represent me. She represents the best people in Britain."

The wino nodded. "You trying to sell your house then?"

"No," said Martin exasperatedly. "A novel. Look, just remember this face. When I pick up the Booker Prize I'll be back with a crate full of Special Brew. You," Martin assured the wino, "are looking at the next big thing."

Martin grinned all the way to West London. When he got to Hammersmith he dipped into the newsagent stroke off-licence that never stuck to the licensing laws and bought a bottle of chilled champagne. He nearly bought the sparkling Chardonnay. But only nearly. The Chardonnay was cheaper, sure, but this was the biggest day of his career so far. His big break day. And the last day he even needed to think about a future where spending thirty quid on a bottle of plonk instead of ten quid might leave him with nothing but baked beans to live on at the end of the month.

Martin was so buoyed up by the time he got to Ruby's street that he even bought her a bunch of flowers from the shop on the corner. In fact, he bought two bunches and then had to discard half of them, because they'd clearly been sitting outside the shop in a green bucket for the best part of a week. Even the ones he salvaged looked as though they would be dead by that evening. But it was the thought that counted. And he felt sure that his news would be much more exciting than roses to his dearest, most wonderful friend.

Martin rang Ruby's doorbell impatiently. He couldn't wait to tell her. He couldn't wait to tell her. This should take her mind off that idiot Robert. Where was she?

Thirty seconds later, during which Ruby had made no signal that she might soon appear at the door, Martin jabbed the doorbell again. "Come on," he muttered. "Answer it." He pressed the buzzer three times, then stood back from the door and looked up at Ruby's windows with what he thought was a particularly appealing smile on his face. Where were your friends when you needed to spew your good news all over their breakfast table?

"Ruby!" Martin shouted up.

"Shurrup!" came a voice from an open window across the street. "Some of us are trying to sleep."

Martin looked at his watch. It was only just past eight o'clock. Pretty bloody early for a Saturday. But . . .

"Ruby!" Martin shouted again. Defiantly. Then he looked about him furtively to see if any hulking great Hammersmith resident was preparing to throw something at his head. No sign. One last shout. "Ruby! Open the door, will you! It's Martin."

A small cloud of worry passed through his mind then. Perhaps she really had done something stupid as a result of being chucked for the second time in a month. Perhaps she was out cold on the kitchen floor having washed down twenty aspirin with some floor cleaner.

"Ruby!!!!"

378

He rattled her door, hoping he wouldn't have to kick it in.

Finally, he heard the sound of the sash window to Ruby's bedroom groaning open as though it had been painted shut and left that way in 1973. Ruby's head emerged, like a tortoise at the end of a long winter inside its shell. She blinked, even in the distinct lack of sunlight — it was still British summertime — and had to shade her eyes in order to be able to see who was shouting up at her.

Martin held the flowers aloft. "Happy Saturday!" he chimed. "I brought you these. And this!" He held up the champagne bottle. "I tried to get Lou to come over and join us for breakfast but she must have gone to stay at Wotsit's. I couldn't get hold of her. Can I come up?"

"What? Oh."

Ruby looked behind her, into the bedroom, as though she were surveying the damage. "I, er, I suppose so."

"Well, don't sound so pleased to see me."

"Hang on," she said. "I'll open the door."

Ruby drew her head back inside her hovel and moments later the entry-phone buzzed to let Martin know that he could come in. He bounded up the shabbily carpeted stairs, two at a time. He was going to sweep her into his arms and give her a great big hug and . . .

"Look at the state of you," he said when Ruby opened the door of her flat to him. "Big night at the Hollingworth party? You look like somebody rode you hard and put you away wet," he added with a wink.

Ruby went crimson.

"Lou told me about Robert," Martin continued. "He isn't worth it, you know. He did you a favour getting out of your life and this time next year you'll be laughing about it. Anyway, the news that I have for you is going to cheer you right up. You remember that . . ."

"Martin," Ruby said, gesturing in the direction of the figure now looming behind her. "This is, er . . . This is Emlyn Cruickshank."

"Eh?" Martin stuck his hand out automatically to meet Emlyn's own extended hand. Emlyn Cruickshank wasn't a particularly big man but he was much too big for Ruby's stripy pink towelling dressing gown, which gaped at the front to show his Wylie Coyote print boxer-shorts.

"Emlyn from work," the Panter clarified. "You've probably heard a lot about me."

"Oh, yeah," said Martin. "I've heard all about you." Then he tossed the flowers onto the Formica table that Ruby had been meaning to replace ever since she bought her flat, and added, "I didn't mean to interrupt anything. I'll come back later."

"Nope. You're all right. I'm done here," said Emlyn, in a way that Martin found altogether too proprietorial. "Done here?" It made him sound like a vet, taking his leave after fixing some poor cow's udders.

"Won't you stay for a cup of tea?" Ruby asked. Desperately, it seemed to Martin. What on earth was she doing with this bloke?

"Breakfast? Toast?" Ruby continued in a twitter. "I haven't got any bacon in the house but if you hang on here I can just run down to the shop and get some. Won't take me two minutes. Streaky or back?"

"'S'alright," said Emlyn. "Told the boys I'd meet them down the Slug to watch the rugby today. Better put some clothes on first though. Eh?"

Emlyn ambled back into the bedroom.

"Is that?" Martin asked.

"Don't say it, Martin," Ruby warned, closing her eyes against his angry expression.

"It's the one with the athlete's foot, isn't it?"

"I think that's gone now," Ruby pleaded.

"How do you know? He didn't take his socks off."

"No?"

"You mean you didn't notice?"

Martin knew he had looked pretty bad at several junctures in his life but he had never, never been seen by another man while wearing a girl's fluffy dressing gown and a pair of grey, mid-calf-length socks with holes in the big toes of both of them.

"How drunk were you last night?" Martin asked.

"Not very," Ruby lied.

"You only just found out about Robert and Erica."

"I don't want to talk about that," Ruby warned.

"Lou was really worried about you. Well, I'll have to tell her you're clearly going through an extended period of grieving."

Ruby squirmed. But before she could say anything in her defence, Emlyn reappeared in the doorway to the kitchen. His suit fitted him only marginally better than the dressing gown had done.

"Bit embarrassing to have to go to the Slug in my work clothes," he said. "It'll make the boys wonder what I've been up to."

"I'm sure you'll have a great time telling them in blow-by-blow detail," said Martin sharply.

"Martin!" Ruby was anguished.

Perhaps it had sounded a little more sarcastic than he meant it to but Martin stared Emlyn straight in the eye as though he really was expecting a fight. Emlyn looked back at Martin like a dopey Labrador that can't decipher the words in the message but knows that it has been delivered belligerently.

"I'll call you," Emlyn said to Ruby eventually. Then he kissed her on the top of her head and left.

"Martin!" Ruby whined as soon as the door shut behind her latest man. "What did you have to say that for?"

"Well, he will, won't he?" Martin spluttered. "He'll go straight down the pub and tell all his mates that he slept with you last night. He may even invite them to sniff his fingers for evidence. See how many of them recognise the smell."

Ruby's mouth dropped into a horrified "O".

"I just don't understand you. Yesterday you were all about Robert. Robert this. Robert that. Robert was the love of your life. Then Robert turns out to be a wanker. And last night you slept with some other twat. No wonder you can't get a man and hold onto him. You're faster than Speedy Gonzales when it comes to getting your knickers off. Do you think that earns you any respect? 'Hi, I'm Ruby Taylor. Fly me.'"

382

The harsh words hung between them like breath in freezing air.

"Piss off," Ruby said suddenly. "How dare you speak to me like that?"

"Ruby, I'm sorry." Martin said almost immediately, snapping back to friendly concern as though he'd woken from a trance.

"Piss off," she said again. "Where do you get off on being so bloody horrible to me?"

"Ruby, I didn't mean to be horrible," said Martin, desperate to regain lost ground. "I just don't understand why you think you need to be with that sort of guy. You just slept with a man that you once claimed made you physically sick! What's going on in your head that makes you think you have anything to gain from letting an idiot like that, who's laid half your bloody office, get into your bed too?"

"Get out," Ruby persisted. "Get away from me."

"But I brought you these."

Martin held up the flowers again but Ruby pushed them back at him.

"I don't want your crappy flowers. Go away."

"Ruby, I came round here because I wanted to tell you . . ."

"Just fuck off. I don't want to hear anything you've got to say to me. You don't know what it's like. You don't understand what it's like to be me."

Three quarters of an hour later, Martin stormed out of the tube station at Chalk Farm again. This time, he didn't have a smile for anyone. Especially not the wino.

383

"All right mate?" the wino called after him. "You sold that house yet?"

Martin dropped the flowers he had bought to make Ruby's day into the wino's lap.

"Rather have the champagne," he said.

"Piss off," said Martin. "Buy your own."

Back at his own flat, Martin sat down at his own Formica-topped table, cleared a space in the week's accumulated free papers and pizza leaflets, and plonked the champagne bottle on top of his super-important letter from Euphemie Gilbert.

"Bollocks," he said. Ruby hadn't even given him a chance to tell her his news. He read the first couple of lines of the letter through the distorting green lens of the bottle. Didn't seem quite so impressive now. He was really fucked off. Really really fucked off. And he wasn't really sure why he felt quite so bad. Or perhaps he was. And he just didn't want to admit it.

Across town, Ruby sank back down onto her unmade bed. The fitted sheet had come away from the mattress during the previous night's exertions. First, she lay on her back and stared at the ceiling. The dusty pink paper uplighter. The yellowing plastic of the ancient light fitting. That was depressing enough. Then she rolled onto her side and brought her knees up to her chin in a foetal position. Halfway through that manoeuvre she felt a peculiar, squishy sensation beneath her calf. She put her hand down to find out what she was lying on and found herself holding a condom, neatly tied in a knot to prevent leakage.

"Happy fucking Saturday," she murmured to herself, sitting up and staring at Emlyn's little present in disgust. How had she ended up sleeping with the Panter? She had a vague recollection that he'd held back her hair as she vomited her guts into the river while the boat came into dock. They'd shared a taxi home and then . . .?

Holding the open end of the johnny between her thumb and forefinger, she stretched the condom like a catapult and aimed for the bin. It sailed clumsily through the air to land on her dressing table, knocking the little china dog she had inherited from her great-grandmother at the age of six to the floor. She knew without looking that the dog would be broken.

"Happy fucking life," she half-shouted. Then she burst into a sob.

CHAPTER
THIRTY-FOUR

Andrew was still sleeping when Lou awoke. The sun was streaming in through the flimsy white curtains that looked fantastic with the Zen theme she had chosen for her interior decoration but were bloody hopeless at keeping out the light even during the British summer months. Moving super-slowly and carefully, anxious not to wake the man sleeping so soundly beside her, Lou slipped from the bed and made her way to the bathroom.

How was it possible to be with someone and yet still feel so utterly alone? How was it possible to be with someone as wonderful, warm and kind as Andrew and yet still wonder if love would ever find you? Love *had* found Lou, as Ruby and Martin kept reminding her. There was nothing Andrew wouldn't do to make her happy. Not just flowers, great restaurants, all the obvious boyfriend stuff, either. Earlier that week, when Lou complained that she didn't have time to come out because she had too much housework and homework to do, Andrew had insisted on doing the ironing for her, while she marked up a manuscript that had come in late.

There was no question that Andrew was the most fantastic bloke she had ever had the good fortune to go out with.

Lou stepped into the shower and let the jets pound down onto her head, standing there until the hot water ran out and the steam disappeared and she was starting to feel almost shivery. But she didn't want to get out of that cubicle. She didn't want to go back to the bedroom until she knew that Andrew was gone. And she knew that the likelihood of him having decided to gather his clothes and split the scene like a guilty one-night-stander was absolutely zero. Nil. In fact, he was knocking on the bathroom door right now.

"I need a pee," he called in to her. "Are you OK? You've been in there for ages."

And though Lou felt as though she would rather jump from her bathroom window than open the door and smile at him then, she managed it.

"Needed to wash the smoke out of my hair," she said. And she even pinched his bum as they dosey-doed in the doorway. Not that she wanted him to act on the flirtatious gesture. But he deserved it. Because he was a great bloke and she knew she should be grateful to have him and perhaps, one day, if she just let herself believe that someone that fantastic might really be the one for her, she'd get over it and they'd live happily ever after like Susannah and Winky.

"Fuck."

That was what love was supposed to be about. Susannah and Winky, slobbering all over each other like he was a deer and she was a salt lick, entwining their limbs like a creeper and an apple tree, only just able to let each other out of sight for long enough to go to the loo. True love was not furtively checking your e-mail, while your other half is in the bathroom, to see if you've got a message from someone you met through a cheesy on-line dating agency. True love shouldn't be disappointed when Chris the Management Consultant writes with the news that an old girlfriend is back on the scene.

Still wrapped in a damp bath towel, Lou collapsed backwards onto her bed. "Fuck." She couldn't do this. She couldn't keep pretending. Not a single day longer.

There is never a right time to break someone's heart. And anyone with even a microgram of sensitivity in his or her body will agonise for an age over that timing. Only problem is there's always some reason not to make someone unhappy. The day a relationship ends, if that relationship was at all important to the suckers involved, becomes as important an anniversary as a wedding day or birthday.

Obviously, the average person doesn't want to kick someone they once loved while that person is down. It starts early. At school, you don't want to chuck someone when they're revising for those important exams, then you don't want to upset them while they're waiting anxiously for the results, and then, when they get the results and they're dreadful, you feel obliged to stick with them through the re-sits.

But it's not just the hard times when someone is down that become obstacles to making your getaway.

After times of bereavement, unemployment and general unhappiness, those events that should be happy ones also make some times off-limits for the eager would-be dumper. Christmas, birthdays, Easter. All impossible. A clever person with a sensitive lover that they sense is not quite as into them as he or she used to be, could stave off the inevitable for years by carefully spacing out those crucial dates.

Which is what Andrew seemed to be doing right now. Every time he called Lou at work, he seemed to have set another milestone that she knew she would have to pass before she could be free of him without thinking she'd ruined his life.

"My boss has invited us over for dinner," was the latest one.

"What? Both of us?" Lou didn't think dinner parties with the boss happened outside seventies sitcoms any more. They certainly didn't happen at her office. "When?"

Andrew named a date that was almost a month into the future. "I hope you don't mind," he said. "But I've sort of said yes on your behalf already. If you don't want to though, I can tell him that you've got other things on. But they're all dead keen to meet you. I guess they've heard so much about you."

Lou suddenly had that freefall feeling of nausea that usually accompanies being chucked. It wasn't how she should feel. Doesn't everyone want to hear that someone adores them so much they can't even shut up about them while at work?

Lou made a quick mental calculation. If she accepted this dinner invitation and held off ending the relationship until a decent time after that date, then she and Andrew would have been seeing each other for almost three months by the time she told him "This isn't working out".

"I don't think I'm doing anything," she said grudgingly, "but I wish you'd asked me first."

"I know," said Andrew, but she could hear the grin in his voice and she knew that he hadn't really sensed her unhappiness at the situation at all. So much for her other great idea, which was that she would simply become increasingly distant until *he* dropped the axe on their relationship instead; saving her the guilt and salvaging maximum self-esteem for himself from the fact that he technically did the ending.

There was no point asking Ruby or Martin for advice on this matter. Ruby had never ended a relationship in her life. Never seemed to be able to hang in a relationship for so long that she got bored before the bloke did. Or, if she did get bored first, Ruby was always too scared that there would never be a replacement to risk making herself voluntarily single. And Martin was no more successful at perfecting the art of severance. He had a string of ex-girlfriends who couldn't quite believe that he'd finished with them, who continued to ring him for months after the definitive event, until he ended up sleeping with them again or got a restraining order. And she knew what her mother would say.

"Louisa Capshaw, you do not know what's good for you!"

So? thought Lou. Bran is good for you. Apples are good for you. But they're boring. Andrew was emotional fibre. What Lou Capshaw wanted was someone who would give her a heart attack.

When Andrew finally left the flat to play five-a-side football with his mates, Lou called an immediate conference with hers.

"Martin," she said, when he answered the phone. "What are you doing?"

"I'm asleep," he said.

"Then you're sleep-talking. Can you come out for brunch with me and Ruby?"

She heard Martin roll over in bed as though all his bones were aching.

"Heavy night?" she said.

Martin snorted.

"Are you on your own?"

"Very much so," Martin told her.

"Are you ill?" Lou asked.

"Just sick at heart."

"What's that? Shakespeare? Why don't you come for breakfast with the girls?"

"Think I'll give it a miss." Martin hung up.

"What?"

Lou dialled Ruby.

"Yeee-ssss," Ruby answered shakily.

"Not you as well?"

"What do you mean? As well?"

"Did you have a good time at the party last night?"

"I had a terrible one!"

"I thought so. Come out with me," Lou suggested. "I think I might need cheering up too this morning."

"I can't get up," said Ruby.

"What is wrong with the pair of you? I just got the same bullshit from Martin."

"Ask Martin," Ruby snorted. Then she too hung up the phone.

Lou pulled on her denim jacket and headed for the tube station. She was going to go to Ruby's flat and drag her out of bed. Martin, she knew from years of experience, was best left alone when he had a hangover. But it sounded as though Ruby was moping about Robert and the only cure for that was a twenty-four-hour-long moan. Lou already figured that she would be on the receiving end of the mammoth whinge at one point or another. Might as well get it out of the way a.s.a.p. And it would take her mind off the Andrew conundrum.

Half an hour later, Lou was gliding smoothly down an escalator at Leicester Square station, hoping to catch the Piccadilly Line west. She was reading the posters that flanked the walls, finding distraction in the disgusting warts fashioned from chewing gum that adorned every picture of an attractive model. She'd given up scanning the Underground crowds for her dream lover now. At least, that's what she told herself. In reality, perhaps she was working on the principle that if she stopped looking, the stranger would find her again. A variation on the platitudes her mother had spouted throughout Lou's adolescence that you shouldn't "look too hard" for love.

Lou was almost at the bottom of the escalator when it happened. She heard a shout come from somewhere behind her but before she could properly turn round to see who was trying to attract her attention, the escalator came to a sudden, lurching halt and a middle-aged guy, who had definitely eaten more burgers than bran flakes in his time, slumped against her with his full, dead weight and sent her crashing down the final three steps.

Kieran Dunmore had suffered a first, minor heart attack that would shake him into pledging a serious life change as he lay in a hospital bed that night. Lou Capshaw, who had broken his fall so spectacularly and possibly saved his life in the process, also had time to do some serious thinking. There wasn't much else to do as she waited for the overworked accident and emergency staff to get round to seeing to her badly twisted ankle.

In the event, Andrew arrived to keep her company before any doctor did. He'd run from the tube station to the hospital and nearly ended up a patient himself as he skidded across the highly polished floor of the waiting room to her side.

"Brought you these," he said, kissing her hello and handing her a pile of magazines.

"Thanks," Lou took the new reading material gratefully. She had already devoured the waiting room's supply of tatty *Readers' Digest*. "What have you brought me?"

"*Marie Claire. Cosmopolitan. Time Out.*"

CHAPTER
THIRTY-FIVE

"Martin!" Petunia Daniels trilled, "I'm so glad you called."

"I just wanted to thank you," he said, "for passing my manuscript on to that agent friend of yours."

"She's tremendously excited," said Petunia. "Says there's something of the young Martin Amis about you, my dear."

"Oh." Martin hoped that was a compliment. He'd never actually read any of the author's books, just the interviews about his extravagant dentistry.

"So, when are you going to come to dinner so that I can make up to you for being such a witch last time we met? Cindy is anxious to see you again too."

"She is?" Martin was surprised.

"Yes. You made quite an impression on both of us. How about this evening? We're having a few pals around for an informal supper. Perhaps you'd like to join us?"

Martin hesitated. The plan for that evening had been to go to the cinema with Ruby and Lou. Martin guessed he probably wasn't invited to that any more.

"If you're sure it's OK with you," he told Petunia.

Perhaps the knock she received to her head had had a lasting effect on Cindy Daniels. Martin hardly recognised the vision in a pink floral sun-dress that opened the door to him that evening. Even Cindy's hair was suddenly the kind of colour one might expect to find in nature rather than on the head of a plastic gonk hanging from the rear-view mirror of a Ford Escort. Her dreadlocks had been cut away to leave behind a neat blonde crop like Mia Farrow's.

"Cindy?" Martin asked just to confirm that it wasn't her less-evil twin.

"Hi, Martin," she said, dropping her eyes to the floor in a gesture that Martin took to be embarrassment. Then she looked up at him from beneath her lashes with that gaze like Princess Diana on acid again and he knew that she hadn't been replaced by a fembot. Beneath that bizarre Laura Ashley exterior, Cindy Daniels was alive and ready to give some poor bloke a kicking.

"Nice dress," he said, for want of something better.

"It's Chloe," she told him.

"I'm sorry?"

"Chloe the designer. It's the 'Good Life' look. Based on the seventies sitcom of the same name. More ironic chic, you could call it."

"Right," said Martin, nodding as if he got it.

"How are you?" she asked.

"Fantastic," he said.

"I like your book," she said then. "I like artistic men."

396

"I thought you were bored of them," Martin observed.

"I hardly had the chance to get bored of you, did I?" She locked eyes with him meaningfully.

"Martin!" Petunia Daniels appeared in the hallway behind her daughter just before Cindy had time to fly at their guest and rip his clothes off. "Come in! Come in," she trilled. "It's so good to see you."

She kissed him warmly on both cheeks. The greeting couldn't have been more different from the way she had last dismissed him. "Darling, we're so excited to have you here with us this evening. There are lots of people simply dying to meet you. Do you know Andrew Greenwood?"

"The director?" Martin gasped.

"That's the boy."

"Not personally."

"Fenella Anderson is here too," said Petunia, referring to the actress who had been her closest rival throughout her career. "Now darling," Petunia whispered, "you really mustn't take too much notice of her. She's only been here for half an hour and she's already drained my Bombay Sapphire. New bottle this morning."

"Yeah, and you had half of it with lunch," mumbled Cindy.

Petunia chose to ignore her daughter. "Come on in. Everybody's waiting. Let me take your coat. This way, Martin. Deep breath," she instructed as though Martin were about to step out onto the stage on opening night.

Martin obliged. And it was a good job he did because he quite forgot to breathe again as Petunia ushered him into the sitting-room and introduced him to four faces he had hitherto only seen on television. (Plus Cindy's father. And Martin really didn't want to think about the circumstances under which they had previously met.)

Fenella Anderson patted an empty space beside her on the big squashy sofa. "Well, hello there young man," she purred, white teeth gleaming. "Why don't you sit here?"

"Or here, if you're scared," commented Andrew Greenwood dryly. The openly homosexual director flashed a predatory grin no less frightening than Fenella's in Martin's direction.

Manda Prost and her husband Christian Lovegrove, London's hottest young actors, looked on in amusement from a red velvet chaise. Martin put his hand to his chin to check for dribble. The last time he had seen Manda Prost was when a sneak preview of her *Satyr* cover had been circulated round the advertising department at International Mags. Manda Prost with the bottom half of a fox was something to behold but there was no doubt, thought Martin, as he watched her cross her legs and let her chiffon skirt fall open to reveal a good furlong of thigh, she looked even better without a bushy red tail.

"You're familiar with Manda and Christian, I presume?" asked Petunia.

"Yes," Martin croaked.

"Hi, Martin," said Christian Lovegrove. "Loved your book. It's a Catcher in the Rye for the twenty-first century."

"Fabulous," Manda agreed. "We've warned Euphemie that if we don't get first refusal on the film rights, she'll be straight off our Christmas list."

Martin could only look at her. It didn't seem appropriate to speak. With so many famous faces in the room, Martin felt as though he was a member of the audience at a very small performance, not a guest at the same dinner party.

"I'll be taking ten per cent too," announced Cindy loudly. "Since without me, none of you would have met this delicious man in the first place."

"How did you meet?" asked Manda curiously.

Martin glanced nervously in the direction of Benjamin Daniels, whose expression was suddenly like a cloud over a Test match. Thankfully Petunia chose that moment to clap her hands together and announce, "To the dining room, everybody! Dinner is served."

As Petunia Daniels fussed around her guests, dishing up a gazpacho she had made from scratch that afternoon, Martin realised he was having one of those "if they could see me now" moments. He was sitting between Manda Prost and Fenella Anderson, while Cindy sat opposite and gazed intently at him. Martin glanced down to either side of him. Fenella's long black skirt had a split to the thigh and as she sat down she revealed her left leg almost as far as her French knickers.

On Martin's right, Manda Prost was also showing a fair bit of leg. Even when it was fully wrapped around her, Manda's chiffon skirt left very little to Martin's overactive imagination. The outline of her G-string was clearly visible through the see-thru red material. Despite that, during the second course, Manda seemed to find even her flimsy outfit too hot and let her skirt fall apart so that she was showing even more thigh than Fenella.

Petunia was serving asparagus. Martin stared in dismay at the vegetables when his plate was placed before him. He remembered something about the correct way to eat asparagus being with one's fingers. But that didn't seem possible. The spears were dripping in butter.

"What's the matter?" Cindy asked, noticing he wasn't eating. "Don't you like it?"

"Makes your pee stink," commented Christian.

Martin looked about the table anxiously but none of the other guests seemed in any hurry to start eating and show him the form. Then Manda picked up one of the floppy green spears. She popped one end of it into her mouth then let it drag out over her soft red lips as she sucked off all the butter, giving Christian a particularly dirty wink as she did so.

Martin bit his lip. Manda had picked up her asparagus with her fingers, but it seemed that her method of eating was more about foreplay than manners. Besides which, Manda was a film star. She was allowed to get away with bad manners because she was so sexy.

Then Fenella did the same. She licked the butter off one of her asparagus spears like the kind of French madam every public schoolboy dreams of losing his virginity to. In fact, it looked a little comical. Martin wondered whether she was just trying to keep up with Manda. At least she didn't wink. Unlike Cindy, who, sensing that her first dibs on Martin might be endangered by the other ladies at the table, set about her vegetables as though she was auditioning for Deep Throat.

Fenella had placed her slender hand on his thigh. She rested it there quite naturally and continued to talk to Benjamin without missing a beat as she slowly inched her way up towards Martin's flies.

"Coffee, Fenella?" asked Petunia.

Fenella took her hand away from Martin's crotch to take an exquisite little espresso cup from her hostess. Meanwhile, Manda, whose left hand was suddenly free again now that she had finished her cigarette, brought it to rest on Martin's right knee. She too continued her intense conversation across the table as she slid her hand imperceptibly closer to Martin's family jewels.

"Don't you think so, Martin?" Christian asked suddenly.

"What?" Martin jumped back to attention.

"Marlowe is more passionate and intense than Shakespeare. His Edward the Second . . ."

"Red hot poker," said Fenella. "That'd give you a shock."

Almost as big a shock as Fenella got when she went to put her hand back on Martin's crotch and found that Manda had beaten her to it. The two women's fingers almost entwined for a second before they both realised and withdrew quite abruptly. Thankfully, they were both such professional actresses that above the table, no one saw the merest flinch.

Meanwhile, Martin was growing hotter and hotter. The blush that had started when Fenella first touched his knee, had become the kind of beetroot flush his mother dreaded during her menopause. Martin took a gulp of water to cool himself down and dribbled rather inelegantly onto the tablecloth when Benjamin asked for his opinion on some TV actor's portrayal of Piers Gaveston.

"Didn't see it," Martin managed to splutter.

"Shame," said Benjamin. "Quite incredibly erotic."

As was the sensation that Martin found himself experiencing now. He dare not look down to see who was massaging his balls this time. Instead, he pulled the tablecloth so that it covered his lap and tried to concentrate on the conversation going on around him. Across the table, Cindy had slid lower in her seat. Her Dangerous Diana gaze had been replaced by an impossibly naughty smile. When Martin looked at her she licked her lips and said "Do me too." At which point Martin realised that the "hand" massaging him so expertly was in fact Cindy's naked foot. She had kicked off her hippy thongs and was playing with him with her pink painted toes.

"Shall we retire to the other room, ladies and gentlemen?" asked Petunia.

Everyone agreed it was a great idea. Cindy let her foot slip from Martin's lap and got up to follow her mother. Martin, however, couldn't stand up.

"Something the matter?" asked Benjamin when he noticed that Martin wasn't following.

"Just savouring my coffee," said Martin helplessly.

"Bring it with you," said Benjamin.

Martin limped into the room where the evening had started. And of course, the only place left to sit by the time he arrived was a gap on the big squishy sofa between Manda and Fenella. As Martin approached, holding his jacket awkwardly over his groin, the two women smiled like a couple of cats that have just figured out how to undo the latch on the birdcage. Meanwhile, Cindy watched from the chaise like the pampered Abyssinian that would be waiting in the garden if poor birdy managed to get out past these Siamese twins.

"Let me take that jacket," said Petunia.

Martin gave an anguished squeak as Petunia snatched at his one good jacket. The three witches shared a knowing look.

"Wife-swapping!" Andrew Greenwood exclaimed suddenly.

"At it all the time round these parts," elaborated Christian.

"Martin, come with me," Cindy said suddenly, rising from her languid pose on the chaise to lead him out into the hallway. "You can help carry the card table."

"What are we playing?" asked Fenella.

"Strip poker!" Manda suggested.

"Yes, please," said Andrew.

Outside in the hall, Martin was starting to sweat. "Is that the time?" he asked without even looking at his watch. "I should go. The tube stops at half eleven."

"Get a taxi," said Cindy. "Or stay. There's plenty of space in my room."

"I . . . I . . ."

"I promise there won't be a re-run of last time," she said, as if that were the only thing on his mind. There was also the question of his not having been to the gym for a month. Let's face it, he'd only ever really been regularly for a fortnight when he was nineteen. Then there was his underwear. He knew that his suit looked OK, but underneath! He'd been meaning to buy some new pants for months but of course, he hadn't bothered. In fact, he'd almost bought into that girly superstition that says that if you wear your worst possible underwear, members of the opposite sex will be only too keen to help you take your clothes off. It was Murphy's Law of dating, up there with not shaving your legs before a first date (for the girls, that is).

"Come on," said Cindy, pressing him up against the velvet embossed wallpaper (not Indian restaurant embossed, you understand). "You look fantastic tonight."

"Cindy, could you do that in your bedroom?" Petunia tutted as she walked through the hallway with a plate full of petits fours. "Do that?" She made it sound as though Cindy were a five-year-old setting up a gymkhana for her dolls on the hallway floor.

"God, I fancy you!" Cindy exclaimed.

With that, Cindy went for the kill. She pressed her mouth against Martin's and forced his lips open with her tongue. After the initial shock, which reminded Martin of first trying to breathe using a mouthpiece when learning to scuba dive, there was nothing he could do but relax into it.

Except that every time he closed his eyes, he thought he could see Ruby.

"Forget her," he told himself. It could never have worked with Ruby.

Cindy was mad as cheese, that was certain. But at least he would never be bored.

CHAPTER
THIRTY-SIX

The last thing Ruby wanted to do was revisit the most recent part of her love life. She didn't care if she never saw Emlyn Cruickshank again. In fact, she didn't want to go into the office at all. She toyed with the idea of pulling a sickie on the Monday morning after the party. But that would be much too obvious. Instead, she limped in late, the back way, punishing herself by using the stairs instead of the lift to her seventh-floor office so that she could make it to her cubicle without passing any of her colleagues en route.

What a terrible weekend she'd had. If she had felt bad on Saturday morning, then Sunday proved to be even worse. She'd gone round to Lou's flat first thing to commiserate with her about her heavily bandaged ankle and to tell her everything that had happened since Robert became the latest man to blow her fantasy world to pieces in that bar. Martin had beaten her to it. His bicycle was leaning against the front wall. Lou was resting on the sofa, so Martin got up to answer the door when Ruby knocked. He looked at her as though she were there to sell him dishcloths.

"Martin," she said pleadingly as she followed him down the hallway. "I'm sorry about yesterday."

406

"Doesn't matter," said Martin shortly. "I've forgotten about it already." He didn't even bother to sit down with the girls again, just picked up his jacket and said that he had better be on his way to lunch.

"You are not going to guess who he's having lunch with!" said Lou excitedly as soon as they heard the door shut. "You remember that girl I set him up with on the blind date? Only turns out she's Petunia Daniels' daughter! Martin went for dinner at her house last night. He claims that Manda Prost tried to feel him up under the table."

Lou paraphrased Martin's story from the moment he left Suave with the dread-locked Daniels' daughter, through the extraordinary events in her bathroom to the letter from the literary agency dropping onto his doormat. "Can you believe the bugger didn't tell us who Cindy really was because he thought we would go to the newspapers and do a kiss and tell and he would end up with a lawsuit?"

Ruby shook her head. Though thinking back to Saturday morning's flare-up in her kitchen, it was clear that there was a lot she didn't know about Martin.

"And he didn't say anything else about Saturday morning?" Ruby asked Lou suddenly.

"Like what?" said Lou.

"Nothing."

When Martin reacted so badly to Emlyn's presence in her flat, Ruby had allowed herself a little fantasy that he might in fact be jealous. That clearly wasn't the case. Why would he want to be with her when he could have Manda Prost feeling him up under the dinner table?

When he had a lunch date with Cindy Daniels? Martin could only feel sorry for Ruby. He mixed with the glitterati and now his novel — the one he hadn't even told her anything about — was set to make him famous too.

"So, are you going to tell me what happened at the party?" asked Lou, voice full of concern.

"Sorry," Ruby was a million miles away. Not with Flett. Not with Robert. Not with Emlyn. "To be honest, I can't quite remember."

Unluckily for Ruby, there were plenty of people queuing up to tell her exactly what had happened after she took to the dance floor on the good ship *Primrose*. The last thing she could recall was lurching towards Flett and Imogen, losing her balance, the sound of something ripping . . .

"Not Imogen's dress?" Ruby asked Liz, peeping out through her fingers as though that might save her from the horror.

"Mine," said Liz flatly. "I tried to get between you. I thought you were going to punch her."

"And then?"

"Emlyn carried you outside. And you vomited all over his jacket. I suppose that's why you felt obliged to take him home with you."

"Does everybody know?" Ruby asked.

"Everybody," Liz confirmed.

Katherine, Ruby's assistant with the long-time crush on the Panter, was barely speaking to her.

When she fired up her computer, Ruby's e-mail box was already full to bursting. Emlyn had sent several, entitled with such discreet headlines as "About last night" and "You were great." Ruby deleted them straight away. But all morning he kept sending more.

Ping! Another e-mail.

From: Emlyn.Cruickshank@Hollingworthpr.co.uk
To: Ruby.Taylor@Hollingworthpr.co.uk

Re: Are you ignoring me?

Well, are you?

Ruby sighed. It was the twelfth e-mail he had sent since nine that morning. Was she ignoring him? *Why* was she ignoring him?

Ruby peered over the top of her PC in the direction of Emlyn's glass-fronted office. He was standing up at his desk as he took a phone call. Ruby hadn't really looked at Emlyn in a long while. Perhaps he didn't look so bad, after all. He was tall. He had all his hair. He had a nice enough smile. Good straight teeth. Perhaps he did have an unusually low hairline, one that in crueller moments she had described as "Neanderthal", but at least that gave him a good position to start receding from. By the time he was fifty he might almost look OK.

"Let's do lunch," his next e-mail begged.

"I'll meet you at Pret A Manger," Ruby replied. "You leave the office at 12.30 and I'll leave ten minutes later."

It was a bit late for that kind of damage limitation, but it made Ruby feel better. Sod Flett. Sod Robert. Sod Martin. She was going to have a fling with Emlyn Cruickshank. And at 12.40 she was almost excited as she left the office and sneaked down to the sandwich bar. Perhaps this had been inevitable all along. Perhaps she and Emlyn were *meant* for each other. Until the athlete's foot revelation, she had definitely considered him fanciable. Now, she was smiling almost nervously as he joined her by the BLTs.

"How do you feel this morning?" he asked.

"Fine," she said. "Even a hangover that big couldn't last forever."

"I'm sorry I left so abruptly on Saturday. That bloke who came round . . . Was he . . .?"

"No," said Ruby decisively. "He was just a friend."

Was, being the operative word, she thought.

"So," said Emlyn.

"So," said Ruby.

"So, I think we can safely say that we took Friday night's team-bonding exercise to its ultimate conclusion." Emlyn laughed at his own joke. "You really were great," he said, suddenly quite serious.

"Was I?" Ruby blushed and fiddled nervously with a lock of her hair. "Well, thank you. I thought I made rather a fool of myself on the boat."

"Er . . ." Emlyn couldn't deny it. "I meant after that."

410

"Of course . . ."

"Though when you lurched onto the dance floor, I think everybody was hoping you'd give John Flett what for."

"Really?"

"The guy's an arsehole, Ruby," Emlyn told her. "Trust me, everyone was rooting for you. Even Imogen."

"Imogen. But she . . ."

"Finished their relationship later that night. It was the first time she'd seen him dance and she decided that she couldn't bear to sleep with a man who danced like her granddad."

"You're joking."

"That's what she said to Alice this morning. It was the way he danced combined with that pink polo shirt that he's always wearing. She said it was like going out with Nick Faldo's dad."

"The pink polo shirt! Yes!" Ruby was unable to hide her glee.

"Added to that," Emlyn began, before sucking in his bottom lip as though the condition might be catching, "she couldn't stand that weird thing he does with his tongue."

"What thing?"

"This thing." Emlyn tried to touch his nose with his own tongue. "Every time he gets agitated or thinks he's made a good point."

"Yes!" Ruby balled her fist. "There is a God. Excuse me," she added, in response to Emlyn's rather worried look.

"So," Emlyn paused. "I was wondering . . ."

"Yeeeeessss?"

"Look, Ruby, I understand that Friday was an emotional night for you and perhaps I shouldn't have come home with you when you were obviously in such a vulnerable state and you might think perhaps . . ." He hesitated. "Look, you can say no if you want to and I promise I won't hold it against you, but I've been wondering whether you might like to . . ." He cleared his throat. "Do it again some time?"

Ruby paused just long enough for him to panic.

"Not just have sex, I mean," he added hurriedly. "But go out somewhere. Properly. The two of us. On a date. We could go to the cinema. I'd like to see *L'Appartement*. Have you ever seen that film? It's on at the Riverside Studios. It's subtitled. It's French, you see. But if you don't like subtitles we can see something else . . ."

"Yes," said Ruby.

"Is that yes, you don't like subtitles?"

"No, it's yes I'd like to go on a date with you. As long as you're not asking because you feel that you have to. If you're just asking because you feel that you ought to in case I'm upset by the idea of a one night stand then . . ."

Emlyn grinned at her.

"Ruby," he said sincerely. "I have wanted to go on a date with you since I first started working at Hollingworth PR."

"Do you really mean that?" she asked.

"Don't you remember my bungled attempts to chat you up over a sandwich before?"

Ruby nodded. She wondered whether she should tell him now the real reason she had managed to resist him.

"I was very jealous when I heard that you'd started seeing Flett. And worried too," he added. "I'd heard he was a ladies' man and I didn't want to see you get hurt. When he ended it I almost whooped with joy across the office but decided you probably wouldn't appreciate that. I was going to bide my time until I thought you were starting to get over him, then I was going to invite you over to my place for dinner and see whether anything happened. But by the time I was ready to ask you out, you'd already started seeing that Robert guy."

"Well, that turned out to be pretty short-lived," said Ruby with a sniff.

"Can I ask what happened?"

"Buy me dinner and I'll think about it."

"So," Emlyn grinned. "When do we have our first date?"

"What about tonight?" said Ruby.

"I normally play five-a-side football on a Monday night," Emlyn began, "but they won't miss me this week. *L'Appartement* isn't on this evening though. So we'll have to see something else. Or go bowling? What about that? Have you ever done it?"

"Bowling?" said Ruby. "No. I haven't."

"Then let's go bowling tonight. You'll love it. Great fun. And I'm pretty good if I do say so myself." He looked at his watch. "Better get back to the office, I suppose. You ready?"

413

"I think so. Perhaps we'd better go back separately. We don't want everybody to be talking about us."

"It's a bit late for that," said Emlyn. "I collected thirty quid on Imogen's book this morning."

"You what!?"

"I'm joking. Damn," Emlyn muttered.

"What?"

"I forgot to go to the chemist. I don't suppose you could go there for me on your way back to the office, seeing as you've got ten minutes left and I haven't."

"Of course," said Ruby. "What is it you need?"

Emlyn cast his eyes down towards the table shyly. Ruby waited for him to say "condoms".

"I think I know," she said, impressed at her own maturity. "Featherlite suit you?"

"Eh?" Emlyn looked at her uncomprehendingly.

"Durex. Featherlite?"

"Oh, no. I mean, yes. If you want to. But what I really need you to pick up is this."

He handed her a scrap of paper onto which he had scribbled the name of a fungicidal cream. "For my athlete's foot. Large size if they've got it."

He kissed her wetly on the mouth and was gone, leaving Ruby to push away the remains of her avocado and pine-nut wrap in horror.

She held the piece of paper as though she might contract the infection from that. Athlete's foot. He'd had it — unless he'd spent long periods in remission since their initial conversation on the subject — for the best part of three whole years. Ruby's memory scrolled backwards to Friday night. Was Martin right? Had he kept his socks on in bed? Oh, no. Suddenly, Ruby had a very clear image of Emlyn Cruickshank wearing her dressing gown and a pair of greying tennis socks. She scrolled forward to that evening's date. Bowling! A date that would require her to wear communal shoes. Communal shoes that might only moments before have been on the sweaty feet of the person with the second worst case of athlete's foot in London.

The fatal flaw! Ruby took a sip of her tea and retched. She couldn't share shoes with anybody. And she definitely couldn't sleep with someone who might want to take his athlete's feet into her bathroom afterwards. How on earth was she going to get herself out of this one? Feign death?

"Ruby just called in," said Liz Hale to the Panter moments later. "She said that she was taken ill with terrible stomach cramps while having lunch. Didn't see much point in coming back into the office. She's gone straight home. Said you'd understand."

Across town, Lou was also doing a sickie. Hers was legitimate however. While Ruby went home to read *Hello* and navel-gaze, Lou found herself in another waiting room. This time to see her GP, who would be supervising the recovery of her ankle from now on.

Andrew had been a star, of course. He actually carried Lou, all nine and a half stone of her, up three flights of stairs when they finally got back from the accident unit. The next day he had done her shopping, filling the trolley with extravagant goodies to cheer up an invalid as well as all the boring stuff she'd asked for. He told her he was available every night to sit at her bandaged foot and peel grapes.

And because of all this, Lou tried harder than ever before to fit him into the vision she had for her future. Because of this, Lou hadn't even looked at the Once Seen column in the back of the issue of *Time Out* he'd bought for her on the day of the accident, but left the magazine pristine and unread for the next unhappy visitor to A & E. The fantasy was over. It had to be. No more scanning the tube carriages for her stranger. No more surfing the net for another one. Lou had to work with what had been given to her in the real world.

Lou was surprised to find that she was momentarily relieved by her decision. But hours later the relief was all but gone. She wanted to be single again and she didn't know how she was going to manage it. How ironic that Andrew had come into her life as the result of a joke when getting rid of him was proving to be such a serious matter?

Lou didn't like to disappoint people; that was the problem. When she looked back over the relationships she had had in the past and examined them more closely, she saw that she was almost as bad as Ruby when it came to picking the wrong partners and failing to deal with the situation effectively. Sure, Lou had finished a relationship before, but never in a particularly adult way. She had never found the courage to say, quite simply, "This isn't working out." Instead, she had to come out with the "It's not you, it's me," line.

When ending her relationship with Mad Magnus, the psycho she had momentarily mistaken for a creative type, Lou had gone to the ridiculous length of convincing him that it was she who was mentally unstable, so that he wouldn't feel so bad to have lost her. Magnus, who saw angels at the bus stop and claimed he could see people's animal familiars if he stared into their eyes for long enough, still occasionally rang and suggested that Lou might like to see his therapist.

Lou reasoned that it was easier for her ex-boyfriends to hear, "I think I want to become a nun," than "I simply just don't fancy you." But the problem was that still left room for hope. After all, what man can resist trying to steal a twenty-something woman from Jesus? Or convincing a girl who claims to be unsure of her sexuality that she really does want a man?

Lou's break-up methodology so far had been the relationship equivalent of trying to rescue a fly with a broken wing from a spider's web. There was no point. It was cruel to be *that* kind.

That afternoon at the doctor's surgery, appointments were running almost forty minutes late. Lou shuffled in the uncomfortable plastic seat she had chosen because it was the furthest away from the man with the frightening cough. She had read every dog-eared issue of *Woman's Own* on the table. She didn't feel like reading the manuscript she had been carrying around in her bag for most of the week. (A good sign that she probably shouldn't suggest that Piper's publish it.)

417

"Mr Edwards to Dr Rushdie's surgery," announced the intercom.

The young man who had been sitting next to Lou got up to go to his appointment and dropped an issue of *Time Out* onto the pile of magazines as he passed.

Lou hesitated for all of thirty seconds before she snatched the magazine up. It was an old issue. Almost a month old. The issue that came straight after the one in which she and Ruby had placed their fateful Once Seens. Lou felt her heart start to quicken as she flicked through the well-read, tattered pages.

Next morning at the office, Lou opened her desk diary and drew a big red star on the page for a Friday three weeks ahead. She would be single by the end of the month.

CHAPTER
THIRTY-SEVEN

Erica had quickly resigned herself to the single life
again after discovering Ratbag Robert's voracious
appetite for the lonely-hearted. A month after that
humiliating night in the bar, she really was able to
laugh about it.

"I suppose he must need a lot of practice to be that
good in bed," she conceded with a sigh. "And at least I
know *I'm* still in working order now. As does the
woman in the flat downstairs. She knocked on the
ceiling to complain about the noise of my vibrator."

"Bloody hell," said Lou.

"Yeah, when I met her in the hallway, I told her it
must have been the washing machine vibrating against
the fridge."

"Too much information!" Lou laughed.

"Can you read this?" Erica let a manuscript plop
onto Lou's untidy desk. "Euphemie Gilbert sent it
round last night. It's brilliant. I read it in one sitting.
She's trying to set up an auction and wants an opinion
on it by Friday."

"What's it about?" Lou asked.

"It's like *Four Weddings and a Funeral* without the sad
bits. It's romantic comedy from the man's point of

view. I laughed so hard at one point that I almost choked to death on a Hob Nob I was eating at the time."

"That's good," Lou agreed.

"It's extremely feel-good. I promise you'll believe there are still good men out there when you've finished reading this. Shame it's only fiction," added Erica.

"Who wrote it?"

"He's called Matthew Carter. And apparently he's young and gorgeous and single. Well, dating some It girl," Erica sighed, "but he hasn't been with her long."

"You're not falling in love with him because of what he's written here, are you?" Lou knew only too well that the authors who wrote the sweetest things often turned out to be the biggest pains.

"I hope we get it," Erica concluded.

She left Lou flicking through the pages for good bits.

Ruthie smiled a little sadly but it was a start. A smile. One day, Mark thought, I'm going to tell her how difficult it's been for me to watch her get so hammered by love . . . One day I'll tell her how I've wanted to punch the lights out of just about every man she's fallen for. I wish she would believe me when I tell her I know what's good for her. She's always chasing after some arsehole when everything she needs is here at home . . .

Nothing funny about that. But it was sort of sweet and raw. Lou sighed. She wrapped two big elastic bands around the manuscript to keep it in one piece and put it in her bag for later.

Brriiiiinnnnggg. Her telephone jolted her out of her reverie.

420

"Lou Capshaw."

"Lou, it's Andrew. What are you doing tonight? I know it's a Wednesday and you usually do that pub quiz thing but . . ."

"I'm not doing anything," Lou said. The pub quiz gang was no more now. Ruby and Martin both claimed that they didn't have a problem with the other but still seemed hell-bent on avoiding the old threesome. Ruby claimed she had to work extra hard to make up for her summer party débâcle. Martin was always claiming that he had to be elsewhere too. Cindy Daniels knew an awful lot of people who threw an awful lot of parties.

"I'm going to come over and cook for you," Andrew announced. "All you have to do is make sure I can get to the sink through those piles of washing-up you never get round to doing."

"Andrew," Lou started to protest.

"No buts," said Andrew. "I want to give you a really special night."

When he put the phone down, Lou opened her diary and pencilled him in for that evening. She flicked through the next couple of days. Thursday morning, physio. Monthly sales meeting that Thursday afternoon. Friday. Big red star.

"Doing anything special this evening?" Liz asked Ruby.

"Nope." Ruby smiled ruefully. In the corridor right outside her office, Emlyn was helping the new temp to un-jam the photocopier. He'd soon got over losing out on the woman he'd apparently waited so long for, Ruby tutted.

At least she no longer had to put up with the knowledge that someone else in the office was sleeping with Flett. Emlyn was right. Imogen had indeed called an end to the relationship. In fact, she had asked that all Barrington Ball-bearing meetings be taken outside the office from now on so that she didn't have to bump into him. Imogen was secretly dating Evan Flanders, the unfeasibly rich and handsome chairman of Two-Faced. It was supposed to be very hush hush, since he was still in the process of divorcing his childhood sweetheart wife; but a picture of the new happy couple had appeared in the tabloids that week.

"I don't know how they found out that we were going to be at The Ivy," Imogen moaned to her friend on the features desk at the *Daily Mail*.

Flett had started e-mailing Ruby with a vengeance after the Hollingworth summer party and his dumping. He begged her to come out to dinner and talk about the Barrington campaign. Lou warned Ruby to stick to lunch within spitting distance of the office.

"Do you think he wants me back?" Ruby asked.

"Of course he wants you back. Imogen has dumped him."

Ruby allowed herself a tiny smile at the thought but was surprised at how little comfort the idea gave her. Her stomach didn't seem to want to do that somersault thing it always used to do when she heard Flett's name any more. The gaping hole she thought he had left clearly wasn't quite as big as she thought. As for Robert, he had merely been a filthy port in a terrible storm. Her night with Emlyn was an aberration. Even remembering that Sunday afternoon in Denver didn't hurt so much now. Not since the letter arrived.

When Ruby saw the envelope postmarked Colorado on her doormat, she felt her stomach rise towards her throat expectantly. What would be inside this time? Another tract about the evil of mankind like the one Nathaniel had pressed into her hand as he escorted her from his premises? She almost tore the damn thing up without even bothering to read it.

Dear Ruby, the letter began. This time it wasn't in Rosalia's neat hand.
Since you left my house a month ago, I've been giving a great deal of thought to the news that you brought to me. I fear I have been an irrational man and that I sent you away with hatred ringing in your ears when I should have welcomed you to the family like the long-lost sister you are.

Because your mother is my mother, Ruby. I can remember the day you were born. We were living near Portsmouth at the time, but Mum and I moved back to Greenwich, where Mum lived before she was married, to stay with her sister during the last months of the pregnancy. It was so she could have you without anyone in our hometown knowing what had been going on.

As you know, my father died when I was just five years old. Three years later, our mother met another man, who promised that he would marry her. But I was the problem. He didn't want to inherit another man's son. He met another woman, with no children and no baggage and quickly married her instead. Shortly afterwards, our mother discovered that she was pregnant with his child. She tried to tell him but he didn't want to know.

Things were tough then. We had no money. I was old enough to go to school while our mother went out to work but if she'd kept you, she would have lost her job. She'd already lost her husband — the man she loved. She was suffering the loss of her lover too. She didn't think she could manage the pair of us alone and made the decision to give you up for adoption so that someone better prepared to look after you might.

But our mother was a courageous and loving woman. I know that she loved you and, had circumstances been different, I have no doubt that you and I would have grown up together all our lives. She did what she thought was best for both of us, Ruby. The sense of shame I picked up around the time of your birth was not to do with our mother's morality, or lack of it, but the ignorance of people who never read the parable about casting the first stone.

And I forgot that too when you came to my house all those weeks ago. I blamed you for our mother's unhappiness. I saw her go into a decline during her pregnancy and after she left you at the hospital. The only way she could escape the memories was to emigrate to America, forcing me to leave behind the only life that I had known. I hated you for that. I blamed you because I had to leave my school, my friends, even my country. But you were just a baby. The hypocrisy of British society in the 1970s was what made our mother so ill with unhappiness she couldn't bear to stay there, not you.

So, that's the true story. I hope that you will be able to forgive me for denying what I knew and treating you so badly that Sunday afternoon. Our mother never had a second chance to meet you though I know she spent her whole life wishing that she could. I can only pray that you will give me a second chance instead. Rosalia has almost finished the family tree now. There is a place for you. We hope to hear from you as soon as you get this letter.

With love,

Your brother, Nat

Sitting at the kitchen table with the letter in front of her, Ruby felt like a shipwrecked sailor washed up on shore at last, pummelled by alternate waves of relief and unfathomable sadness. She read the letter again and folded it away before she blurred all the words with her tears. She'd call Nat Barker as soon as it was a decent hour in Denver. And at some point, she knew, she would have to call her parents and Lindsay and Steve and tell them what had been going on these past few months. Right then, however, she held the telephone in her hand with her thumb poised over the button pre-programmed with someone else's home number. Martin's.

Martin was the only person who knew the full story so far and she wanted to tell him what Nathaniel had written. But she couldn't. She hadn't spoken to Martin in almost a month. Lou said she had hardly heard from him either. He'd moved on from their friendship. He didn't seem to need them any more. No more pub quiz for Martin. Where was he that evening? On a date with Cindy Daniels and her celebrity-offspring friends?

At three o'clock in the afternoon, Cindy Daniels was still snoring on her back. She had a thesis to write before the end of the month and spent those waking hours when she wasn't snorting coke, fretting that she would never get the work done. Actually sitting down and getting the work done didn't seem to have crossed her mind.

Martin was fretting too. It was only three days since Euphemie Gilbert had sent his manuscript out to four of London's top publishing houses. She had warned him not to expect an immediate response but every time the phone rang, Martin felt sure he was going to lose his guts all over the carpet with excitement. Every caller got short shrift, even his mother — though he did tell her that he had to hurry her off the line, leaving it free for Euphemie Gilbert's call.

In theory, he had someone to keep him company during the interminable wait, but Cindy's wasn't the company he wanted. He would have liked to have passed it with Lou and Ruby. If the news was good, then he supposed that Cindy would be an adequate person to drink champagne with. But if the news was bad . . .

Sex with Cindy Daniels had turned out to be everything Martin expected and quite a few things he never would have imagined. But when they weren't in bed together they were on different planets. Sure, Cindy took him to lots of A-list parties, but Martin soon discovered that a night at the hottest club in London could be more tedious than a night at the Hare and Hounds when every tabloid-familiar face concealed a stranger. It was also getting just a little wearing that nine out of ten people Cindy introduced him to were ex-lovers — men and women. And it was clear that Cindy subscribed to a "never say never" approach where these exes were concerned. Her mobile phone was constantly vibrating with text messages requesting her attention. Martin knew it was only a matter of time before Cindy added another new love interest to the numbers on her SIM card.

The telephone rang. Martin dived from the bed to grab the handset, accidentally kicking Cindy in the back as he did so.

"Martin!" Euphemie purred. "Piper Publishing are interested! The editor's someone called Lou Capshaw. I think you'll like her. She's a very nice girl."

It had taken Lou minutes to guess the genesis of the work. Mark and Ruthie. The only things Martin had changed in the story were the names of the characters and his own. Matthew Carter was a pen-name. But

427

thankfully, Erica had been right. Lou loved the story. And not just because she knew the lovelorn pair involved.

Since Erica's workload for that autumn was already almost too much for her, the girls decided that they would recommend that Piper made an offer on the book immediately, with Lou as potential editor, and call Martin in for a meeting. Lou was looking forward to seeing Martin in her offices and to finally admitting face to face that she was quietly impressed by his talent. But first there was another altogether more important meeting to arrange.

CHAPTER
THIRTY-EIGHT

With half an hour to go before the big date, Ruby paused midway through putting on her make-up and stared at her reflection.

"You look a mess," she told herself. The effect wasn't helped by the fact that she had only properly made-up one eye and, even as she berated herself for not quite making the standard, she blinked so that a neat little semicircle of wet mascara spots appeared on the top of her cheek.

"Arse."

She started to rub the dots away with a cotton bud but only succeeded in turning a neat row of specks into a big dirty smudge that looked like a black eye. A battle scar. The conversations in the pub during which Lou, she and Martin had reassured each other that they didn't look a day older than when they first met seemed ridiculous now. Ruby looked her age, she told herself, suddenly more dissatisfied than she had ever been with her skin and her hair and her stupid, ill-fitting clothes. When she walked down the street these days she was invisible to a whole generation of people. She felt much closer in attitude to the students who crowded around her favourite bookshop than to their tutors. But the

429

students didn't even see her. To them, she was a grown-up. Perhaps it was time to act accordingly.

Abandoning her make-up, Ruby lay down on her bed.

The phone rang.

It was Lou.

"Ruby! What are you doing, picking up the phone?"

"I'm sitting on my bed."

"You'll never get there in time. You're supposed to be in Battersea. In that bar."

"What's the point?" Ruby asked.

"What? What do you mean, what's the point?"

"Lou, I'm not going on this blind date," she said firmly. "I've decided that I've got to get off this sodding dating roundabout and sort my stupid life out."

"Really? Sort your life out?" Lou echoed. "That's great, Rubes. And I'm glad to hear it. Really, I am. But you haven't got time to do it tonight. Are you dressed yet?"

"Of course I'm dressed."

"What are you wearing?"

"Jeans. Black T-shirt."

"For goodness' sake. That's not a date outfit. Put something sexy on, quick. Put on that black dress you like. The one with the boat neck."

"Lou. Are you receiving me?" Ruby asked. "I'm not going on this date."

"Yes, you bloody are."

"You can't make me."

"Wanna bet?"

"Lou, just forget it. I know you think you're acting in my best interests and I'm grateful for what you're trying to do for me but . . ."

Briiiiiiinnnnng.

"Oh, dear," said Ruby with relief. "There's the doorbell. Gotta go. Speak to you later."

Ruby put the phone down. Saved by the bell. For once she'd be glad to see Jehovah's Witnesses. All she had to do once she got rid of the God-botherers was to pull the phone lead out of its socket and ignore Lou's calls and . . .

"Ruby, look at the state of you!"

Lou stood on the doorstep. She bustled past into the flat as fast as her almost recovered ankle would allow her.

"I knew you would do this to me. I knew it. I've gone to all the trouble of finding you a perfect date and you're still sitting at home in your jeans with fifteen minutes to go before you're meant to be on the other side of London. Put that black dress on. I'm calling a cab."

"Lou, I . . ." Ruby tried to stand her ground.

"Just do it. Just this once. Trust me, Ruby. I have found you the man of your dreams. You have so much in common with this guy. He's gorgeous, sexy, good-looking . . ."

"How do you know he's good-looking?"

"He scanned in a picture when he last sent an e-mail."

"Can I see it?" Ruby asked sensibly.

"Forgot to bring it," Lou replied. "Look, stick the dress on. Do your make-up. It won't matter if you're a little bit late. I've done such a good PR job on you he'll probably sit there and wait for you all night."

Ruby stood firm in the hallway, making no move to get changed.

"Lou, I'm serious. I'm changing my life. And the first fundamental change I have to make is to my attitude to men. I'm not chasing after love any more. My desperation has brought me nothing but trouble and heartache. I'm going to learn to live without love and then it won't matter so much if I don't ever find it. I've got to learn to be a whole person within myself. I don't need a prop."

"Oh, for crying out loud. Why do you have to see the bloody light now!?" Lou clutched her head. "Don't do this to me Ruby. Not tonight. Give me one more chance. Put the dress on."

They were in Ruby's bedroom now and Lou was rummaging through the wardrobe.

"Will you get out of there? I didn't ask you to place another ad for me. And after the Robin and Robert fiascos, I would have thought you might have known better. I'm not putting myself through it again." She shook her head. "I'm staying in."

"I can't let you do that."

Lou grabbed the bottom of Ruby's T-shirt and started to yank it off over her head.

"Lou!"

"You don't know what's good for you!"

"I finally do know! That's the point. Get off my T-shirt."

Ruby yanked the T-shirt back down.

"One more for me, Rubes. I went to all the trouble of placing another ad. It took me weeks to think of the right wording and I was so careful when I sifted through the replies . . ."

"Well, thanks very much, but that's not exactly my fault," Ruby reasoned. "You're not going to guilt me into this. I'm living for me, Lou."

"Someone else could be living for you, too. Just this once. Never again." Lou fell to her knees. "Please, Ruby. Please. Ow!"

"Watch your ankle. God almighty," said Ruby as she helped her friend straighten back up. "Anyone would think this blind date was George Clooney."

"Better. I promise you. Your blind date is perfect. I hear Clooney's a bit of an arse."

Ruby shook her head. "It's still too late. You've ambushed me on the way back from Damascus. I've seen the truth about myself at last."

"You're seeing life through your blue-tinted spectacles," Lou replied. "Oh Ruby, I know these last few months have been a disaster. You've met some awful men, you had all that trouble with your natural family and you've fallen out with Martin. But that doesn't mean you've got to become a nun. You're thirty-one for heaven's sake. Your boobs still defy gravity and you're not ready for a cat. The most unattractive trait a person can have is a lack of hope, girl. There's nothing to live for but love, Rubes. You were the one who used to say that."

"Lou." Ruby sighed. "Will you cut the Dawson's Creek philosophy? Did you talk to him?"

"I did."

"What's his voice like?"

"Plums in honey!" Lou was delighted. Ruby was softening like butter in the sun. "I'll call you that cab. Put your dress on."

"Do you think I should wear the black?"

"You'll look a million dollars . . ." Lou was frantically dialling for a car before Ruby had a chance to change her mind. "Hello? Yes. Can I have a taxi from 17 Blandfield Avenue . . . top flat."

"I can't believe I'm doing this," said Ruby as she disappeared into the bedroom.

"Ten minutes. She'll be ready." Lou hung up on the cab firm. She hugged Ruby tightly once she was safely in that little black dress. Then she held her at arm's length to get a better look. "Not bad," she said encouragingly. "Girl, you are da bomb."

"Well, if this date bombs, you're ancient history, Lou Capshaw."

"It won't bomb."

"Will you come in and wait with me?" Ruby asked.

"Are you kidding? I don't want to cramp your style."

The excitement that Lou had whipped up on the cab ride to Battersea quickly evaporated to be replaced by cold, clammy fear when Ruby walked into the bar on her own. It was almost empty. Suddenly, the copy of *Captain Corelli's Mandolin* that Ruby had tucked under

434

her arm for identification purposes seemed to scream blind date. *This girl is waiting for a blind date.* Which was ridiculous, Ruby tried to tell herself. Plenty of people carried books with them in London. You really never knew when you might get stuck on the tube and want something to take your mind off the wait.

But there was no one else with a book in that bar. In fact, no other patron was sitting alone. The other customers divided neatly into three couples and one group of five girls who had clearly come straight from the office to celebrate somebody's birthday by getting right out of their heads.

"What can I get you?" the bartender asked cheerily.

"Er, I don't know if I'm actually staying yet," said Ruby pathetically. "You haven't, er, seen a man with a book have you?"

The bartender cocked his head to one side.

"What does he look like?"

"Like this," said Ruby, holding up her copy of the book. "Blue and white cover. Exactly the same as this, in fact."

"I meant the man," smiled the bartender. "What does he look like?"

"Oh, I . . ." Ruby blushed. "I don't . . . Average looking, I suppose."

The bartender nodded wisely, convincing Ruby that he was onto her too.

"Perhaps he's late," he suggested.

"Yes. You might be right. I suppose I'll have a . . . an orange juice."

Ruby perched nervously on a stool up at the bar. The bartender placed her glass in front of her and swapped her five-pound note for two fifty-pence pieces.

"Four pounds?" said Ruby incredulously.

"Freshly squeezed," said the bartender.

Ruby certainly felt as though she had been juiced.

She looked at her watch. According to Lou, the date had been set for seven-thirty. It was almost ten to eight. The door of the bar swung open, momentarily admitting the noise of the traffic outside as two laughing girls stepped in from the street. One of them merely raised her eyebrows in the direction of the bartender to send him scurrying to get her usual. He turned up the sound system en route between vodka bottle and cranberry juice. The two new girls leaned against the bar next to Ruby and engaged the bartender in conversation about "the other night". The bartender's eyes flashed at the cranberry juice girl and he performed a nifty manoeuvre with his shaker to impress her. Feeling suddenly invisible again, Ruby picked up her glass and moved to a table by the wall.

Ten minutes later, Ruby had looked at her watch fifty times. Eight o'clock. How long should she give him? She'd given him too long already, hadn't she? She'd been stood up. She'd spent a tenner on a taxi ride, four quid on an orange juice, got something unidentifiable but sticky on the skirt of her favourite black dress and what for? She'd been stood up.

"Lou," she jabbed an SMS message into her mobile. "I've been stood up. U R so dead."

"Just hang on," Lou sent a message back. "He's tall, dark, handsome and hung like a donkey. So he says."

At which point someone who fitted that description (well, the first three parts at least) wandered into the bar and looked about him as though he were searching for someone who would be recognisable only from the novel she carried tucked beneath her arm.

Ruby felt her cheeks colour pink at once. He was lovely. He looked friendly. He looked almost as nervous as she did, which was extremely endearing. When he had looked about the bar for a couple of minutes and still didn't seem to have spotted her, Ruby chanced a little wave.

He gazed somewhere beyond her. Literally a *blind* date.

Perhaps he was short-sighted. His slightly scrunched up, squinting expression suggested he needed glasses but was a little too vain to wear them. Ruby picked up her book and opened it out ostentatiously. He sat down on a stool at the bar and reached into his bag to bring out a copy of the *Evening Standard* and a book of his own . . . yes! It was *Captain Corelli*.

Ruby twisted to take a last good look at herself in the mirror that was hanging behind her. She checked her hair for dandruff, her teeth for spinach. Not that she had ever really eaten spinach in her life.

Meanwhile, the man that Ruby was sure she must have been sent to that bar to meet was flicking through the pages of the novel, glancing up occasionally when the door to the bar swung open. It was very dark in the corner where Ruby had chosen to seat herself. Her target squinted at the cocktail menu. She was obviously going to have to go to him or their date would never get started.

Taking a deep breath she got to her feet and prepared to cross the floor. As she drew closer she turned on a megawatt beam. Lou was right, this man was an angel. His eyes may have been useless as far as long-distance vision was concerned, but weren't they a beautiful blue? As Ruby walked across that bar, the disillusionment and cynicism that had been gathering like a cloud above her head all day were suddenly and absolutely dispelled.

He was just a foot away from her now. He glanced at the book that Ruby held in front of her like a choirboy carrying a bible and then looked her straight in the eye. Ruby squeezed a couple more kilowatts out of her beam.

"Hi," she said.

"Hi," said the stranger.

"*Captain Corelli's Mandolin*," said Ruby, holding the book out towards his face.

The stranger shied away from the proffered novel, then peered at it closely as if to confirm the title and nodded. Ruby checked him over eagerly as he did so. Serial killer hair? She didn't think so. In the seconds it took for the stranger to look from the book to Ruby's face again, she had convinced herself that she could make a go of it with this one. Love was worth one more shot after all. In fact, she decided, as the stranger's smile became slightly quizzical, love was worth throwing herself at this man's feet for. His eyes, his lips, his hair . . .

"Er," said the stranger.

"Yes?" said Ruby eagerly.

"What can I get you?" the barman asked her man.

Ruby looked at him expectantly, waiting to state her own preference. White wine or orange juice? Which should she have? What if he didn't drink? She didn't want him to think she was a lush. But she could definitely have used a spritzer to help her loosen up. Perhaps she'd have an orange juice this time and a spritzer next time round, depending on whether he bought alcohol for himself or settled for a soft drink.

"Two bottles of Becks, please," he said.

Ruby pulled a little face. She was impressed that he was the type of man who liked to take charge but she hated Becks and wasn't it a little presumptuous of him to assume that she wanted alcohol anyway? Best not to mention it this time, she decided. Wouldn't want him to think she was a difficult sort of woman. Hang on, though. Perhaps she should take a stand at this point. The way you were with someone at the very start of a relationship set the tone for later on. She of all people should know that. If she hadn't been so willing to please Flett, if she hadn't agreed to everything he suggested just to make him like her, he might have found her a bit of a challenge and actually liked her more.

Ruby bit her lip and got ready to tell him. "I'm sorry," she said. "But I don't really like Becks."

"Don't you?" asked the stranger.

"No, I don't. I prefer white wine."

"Really."

"Yes. Always have done."

"Oh." He looked from Ruby to the bottles on the bar and back again. The barman had already opened them.

"It'll be OK just this one time," Ruby said accommodatingly.

"Right," said the squinter. "Er, enjoy your book," he added, getting to his feet and taking the beer to his best friend, who had finally arrived, and commandeered a table by the door.

It took nanoseconds for the tears to come.

Leaving sodding *Captain Corelli's Mandolin* in a puddle of beer, Ruby fled for the door. The sum total of her embarrassment was increased momentarily when she tried to push the heavy glass door when she should have pulled it, but then she was out on the street. And headlong into someone's chest, knocking him onto his backside on the pavement.

Almost simultaneously Ruby and Martin's mobile phones chirruped to announce the arrival of a new SMS.

"Do U like pina colada?" was the text message Lou sent to both.

CHAPTER
THIRTY-NINE

Lou paced her living room. It was a mistake to agree to let Andrew come to her place. She should have insisted that they meet on neutral ground. But of course, she couldn't insist on that without Andrew wanting to know why she was so keen not to have him in her kitchen. She tried saying, "Let's just go for a drink." But Andrew had insisted, "I want to cook for you." And then Lou knew she couldn't tell him she didn't want him to cook for her without saying why over the phone. Or by fax. Or by e-mail. She had considered both those methods during the long day at work.

Now, with ten minutes to go before Andrew turned up (absolutely on time, of course) with a bag full of groceries to turn into some delicious expression of his love, Lou rehearsed her speech. Should she wait until he had finished cooking? No, of course not. She would have to tell him before he started, otherwise she would forever be the girl who had eaten his romantic dinner and then dumped him over coffee. In any case, she hardly felt like eating anything with the weight of the imminent ending on her mind.

"Andrew," she rehearsed, "there's something I've got to say to you. Sit down." She'd cleared all the rubbish

441

off her armchair so that she could sit there and he could sit on the sofa. "I just want to say how much I've enjoyed being with you these past couple of months."

"It's not you. It's me," she tried.

God, no. She berated herself. She couldn't use that line. Even though it really was her and not him, everyone thought that line really meant, "It's not *me*. It's definitely *you*."

There was still a part of her that thought perhaps she shouldn't do it at all. In Andrew she had all the raw ingredients for a perfect life. Here was a grown-up, good-looking, solvent, generous, warm-hearted man who adored her. A man who adored her even when she knew she looked like the Loch Ness monster's little sister and had a terrible temper to match. It didn't take a huge leap of the imagination to see Andrew standing at the top of the aisle, looking back at Lou walking towards him with a grin as wide as the English Channel. She could see him painting the nursery yellow; pushing a pram that contained two lovely brown-haired twins (one boy, one girl); presenting her with an eternity ring on their tenth anniversary, taking the twins to school, teaching them how to play football on long, summer holidays in Tuscany, giving the daughter away at her own wedding, cosying up to Lou on the veranda of their perfect house as their retirement stretched ahead of them — a long straight road of well-planned for, financially comfortable and perpetually sunny days.

"Oh, God." Lou poured herself a vodka tonic. That night she had sent Martin and Ruby out to find their perfect future, and here she was, preparing to let go of hers.

She remembered something that an old boyfriend had said to her. One that she didn't want to let go of at the time. *One person can't be happy enough for the two of us.* And that was it in a nutshell. It didn't matter how wonderful Andrew was and how much effort he was prepared to put into their relationship. While Lou didn't feel the same way, his love was only building a tower without foundations.

She had to end it and she had to end it that evening. Even if she did have to end it with a real stinker of a line.

"Taste this." Andrew advanced towards her with a spoonful of the sauce he had created so lovingly. He held one hand beneath the spoon to catch any drips and even blew on it to make sure that it wasn't too hot for her.

Lou shook her head.

"Go on," said Andrew. "It's delicious."

Lou forced herself to smile and took a mouthful.

"What do you think?"

It was a little hot. It burned her tongue. But she nodded.

"It's, em, great."

"It should be," he said. "Because I put all my love into it." He stared at her intently as she licked her tingling lips. "Oh, sod it, Lou," he burst out suddenly. "I can't wait any longer to say this."

"Say what?" She was horrified.

"I'm crazy about you. I have been since the first day we met. Within a second of meeting you I felt like we'd known each other forever and I do want to know you forever, Lou. Forever."

"Oh God," Lou couldn't stop her expression of anguish escaping that time. But Andrew misinterpreted.

"I can tell by your face that you feel the same way," he laughed, misreading her horror for the shock of delight. "Well, why don't we do it?"

"Do what?" Lou asked him. Though even as she asked him, she feared she already knew. Please, don't let him be about to ask me to marry him, the voice inside her screamed. Please don't ask. Please don't ask. Please don't ask. The second of silence that followed gaped like the bloody Grand Canyon.

"Move in with me," he said at last.

Well, at least it wasn't the other "M" word. Lou felt her body collapse in relief. She sank down into the sofa, closed her eyes and put her head in her hands.

"Lou? Are you OK?" Andrew put the spoon down, carefully, to avoid staining the work surfaces, then hurried back to see how she was feeling. Lou didn't know whether to laugh or cry or hug him or punch him or what.

"You didn't think," he began. "Oh, Lou. Have I disappointed you? Did you think I was going to ask you to . . ." It turned out that even Andrew couldn't say the "M" word. "Well, I'm sure that we will," he said. "One day. It's just that . . . We haven't known each other very long. I think it would be more sensible to live together first, don't you? See how we get on. I mean, I am

444

absolutely committed to you, Lou but, you know . . ." He stumbled. "I've never asked a girl to move in with me before."

Lou shook her head.

"Oh, come on, Lou!" Andrew exclaimed, still thinking that she felt slighted by the proposal that wasn't forthcoming. "You can't expect . . ."

"Andrew," she stopped him. "I don't want to marry you."

"And that's OK by me," he said, taking both her hands. "But move in, yeah? Your place or mine?"

"Andrew," Lou interrupted again. "I don't want to move in with you either."

"Why not?"

"It's not you, it's me," ran the autocue in her mind. "Or how about 'I love you but I'm not *in* love with you'?" Another corking line. "You could try, 'I'm not ready for a relationship right now' or 'I've been hurt before and I just can't commit.' " In the event, none of those lines came out of Lou's mouth when she opened it.

"Are you saying you don't want to be with me at all?" Andrew pre-empted. "Are you trying to tell me it's over?"

Lou nodded. "That's right. And it's because I'm a lesbian."

Did he believe her? Lou would never know. Andrew didn't hang round long enough to need convincing. He just pulled his coat on over his apron and went storming out of the flat, streaming expletives behind him. Lou didn't even blink for a minute or so afterwards. Had he really gone?

Strange thing was, Lou thought, as she sat alone on her sofa, watching tomato sauce drip down the wall (he'd thrown the pan across the sitting-room), he didn't try to make her reconsider. Despite the fact that moments earlier he had been telling her that she was the one for him, albeit on a semi-permanent trial basis, he hadn't asked for a proof, or a proper explanation, or even a second chance. He had literally seen red and picked up the pan. Now she was seeing red all over her previously Zen white interior.

Lou took a sip from her glass of wine and laughed. All that time looking for the fatal flaw and being unable to find one and getting herself all tied up in knots because she simply couldn't think of a good reason not to be with Andrew. Now she had one. Who would have thought that the perfect man could throw such a spectacular tantrum?

It didn't matter. She'd never have to put up with it again. Because at last Lou had silenced one nagging voice; the little voice in her head that said that what *she* wanted — what she really, really wanted — in a lover, was the only opinion that counted. Not the opinions of her parents, her friends or her work mates. Not the opinion of the old lady across the street who told her, "You've got a real catch there," when Andrew helped her up the stairs with her shopping bags. Lou had listened to the voice inside and was finally going to act on it. Andrew wasn't right for her for one fundamental reason. He could never be the stranger on the train.

446

Wednesday morning, late in May. Northern Line. You in the grey skirt suit, poked your tongue out at the bloke reading *FT*. Me, in the blue suit, gave you a wink. Will I ever see you again?

Lou had found her Once Seen that afternoon in the doctor's surgery while she waited for a check-up on her ankle. She kept re-reading the two-line ad in *Time Out* all day, just in case she had hallucinated it. Now, certain that Andrew had finally gone home and confident that she could plug the telephone back into its socket again without him calling up to ask if she really meant what she'd said, Lou rang the number that accompanied the advert.

"Hello," said Lou, when her call was finally answered. "I'm responding to your ad in the back of *Time Out*. The Once Seen?"

"Oh, hi," said the girl on the end of the line. "You don't want me then. You want my flatmate, Alex. Alex! Alex!" She put her hand over the receiver but Lou could still make out her muffled words. "There's a woman on the phone says she's responding to your Once Seen." The girl came back on line. "I do hope you're the one," she said conspiratorially. "We've had all sorts of weirdos ring up. You wouldn't believe the number of people who thought they recognised themselves. I said it was a mistake to put a telephone number. Alex was just about ready to give up. It was all quite a long time ago . . ."

"I'm definitely the one," Lou interrupted.

"Then you know what you're letting yourself in for, don't you?" said the girl. "You remember Alex exactly?"

"Oh, yes," said Lou. "I definitely remember Alex."

Alex. So that was the stranger's name.

"What's your name?" asked the flatmate brightly.

"Lou. Short for Louisa."

"Well, nice to talk to you, Lou. I'm Hannah, by the way, in case we actually get to meet up! I do hope so. I'm desperate to know what Alex had been raving on about these past few months. OK, Lou. Here comes your dream date!"

Lou clutched the telephone receiver tightly as she listened to the phone at the other end being passed over.

"Hello?" said Alex.

Lou was silent as she let the sound of Alex's voice caress her ear after all this time. The slight Northern accent. She hadn't expected that.

"Hello? Are you still there?" Alex asked.

"I'm here," said Lou.

"You're the girl who ended up in the lap of that *FT* bloke?"

"That's me."

"I hope you didn't think I was laughing at you," Alex continued. "You know I was laughing *with* you, of course."

"I knew that," said Lou.

"I wish I'd spoken to you."

"I wish you'd spoken to me, too," Lou murmured.

"But it isn't always easy," said Alex. "You know how it is. You can never be quite sure how it's going to be received. Talking to a stranger on the train."

"I've thought about you a lot," said Lou. "I even placed a Once Seen myself."

"I hadn't even heard of them until a few weeks ago. And when Hannah told me, I didn't think anybody really replied to them. You wouldn't believe the number of people I've had calling up and claiming to be you."

"Hannah told me."

"I think they're just chancing it. Makes a change from answering a normal personal ad, I suppose. Own up pretty quickly as soon as they hear my voice, though."

"You've got a lovely voice," said Lou.

"Thank you. But it doesn't take long for them to realise that I'm not the man they thought I was."

"That you're not a man at all," Lou echoed.

"And that's OK by you?" Alex asked.

"That's OK by me," Lou told her. "At last."

CHAPTER
FORTY

"Do U like pina colada?"

Martin, who had grown up to a soundtrack of Barry Manilow, courtesy of his mother, had to explain the significance of the joke to Ruby. On the way to the bar that evening, he had an inkling that he was about to become the victim of a Lou Capshaw set-up but he'd gone along with it anyway. Now that Cindy had moved on to a hairy-backed sculptor called Louis, he didn't have much to occupy him of an evening any more.

He feigned annoyance at Lou's big prank but was secretly delighted when Ruby agreed to join him for one more drink. One drink became four and they were still there when the barman announced he was closing for the night.

Turfed out of their comfortable chairs, Ruby and Martin decided to walk until they could find a taxi to take them north of the river. But there were no taxis south of the river to pick them up. Every black cab that passed had its light turned off or, if it did have its "for hire" sign illuminated, the driver was on his way home to Peckham and didn't want to have to go north again.

* * *

"My feet are killing me," Ruby groaned, as they walked steadily northwards, growing less and less confident that their cab would ever come.

"Take your shoes off," Martin suggested.

"No way," said Ruby. "There's all sorts of shit on the street. Dog shit. Broken glass."

"You could just look where you're walking," said Martin.

"If you were a gentleman you'd carry me."

"I would carry you," he assured her, "if you were a lady."

Ruby limped on.

"Ow!" she exclaimed, as they neared the Thames and the entrance to Albert Bridge. "I think I've just broken the skin on my ankle." She sank down onto a bench. "I can't go any further."

"We've just got to get north of the river," said Martin. "Then we'll be able to get ourselves a cab."

"I'm not moving," she said. "You get a cab and bring it back here for me."

"Don't be ridiculous," Martin sat down beside her. "Let me have a look at your foot."

Ruby held her foot out towards him and let him take her shoe off. Cinderella in reverse. Even in the orange glow of the street lights, Martin could see that her toes looked angry red where the thin fake snakeskin straps had rubbed and chafed in the short walk from the bar to the riverside.

"Am I bleeding?" she asked him pitifully.

Martin cupped his hand around her heel. The back of her ankle was indeed wet with blood.

"What do you buy such bloody stupid shoes for anyway?"

"To look attractive," Ruby said. "To get a man."

"A woman wearing trainers who can actually walk is far more attractive than someone limping in stilettos."

"Yeah, right."

"Here." Martin started to untie his own trainers. "You wear these and I'll go barefoot."

"They'll be too big for me," Ruby began to protest.

"You've got big feet," Martin reminded her. "They'll probably be too small. Do you want the socks too?"

"Are you kidding?" said Ruby, wrinkling her nose at the thought.

"I haven't got athlete's foot," he promised her, reading her mind.

"That wasn't what I was thinking," Ruby lied.

"Just put my trainers on and let's get across this river. I'm actually quite keen to get home."

Ruby slipped her feet into Martin's Pumas reluctantly. They were, as she had dreaded, still very warm. But Martin was already halfway across the bridge in his socks by now carrying her snakeskin sandals. Ruby tied the laces as tightly as she could and slopped out onto the bridge after him until they were walking side by side.

"So, does this mean we're friends again?" Ruby asked him when she drew near. They'd spent the evening in the bar indulging in fairly nasty banter. It was what they'd always done when they *were* friends but Ruby wanted to make sure.

"We're friends," said Martin abruptly. He didn't want to get all psychological about it. "Do you know that if enough people walked in perfect time over this bridge," he said to change the subject. "It would set up a sine wave that could break the bridge in half. That's why there are those notices telling troops to break their step."

"Would it really happen?" asked Ruby.

"I don't know. Let's try it now. Walk in time with me. One, two, three, four . . ."

They linked arms and headed out over the river. Ruby wondered what the people who passed them in their cars must think they looked like. Martin in socks, carrying a pair of girly sandals. Ruby in a pair of trainers so big, it looked as though she was wearing false feet at the end of her skinny legs.

"Ow!" Suddenly Martin broke step and hopped onto his left foot. Frowning with pain, he brushed a piece of gravel from the bottom of his sock. "That hurt," he said. It was a total understatement.

"Do you want your shoes back?" Ruby asked.

"You need them more than I do."

"No. You need them. I can limp in my sandals."

"You can't limp in your sandals," Martin said huffily. "Just keep walking. I'll catch you up."

"That's very gentlemanly," said Ruby.

"I'm just being a good friend."

"You've always been a good friend to me," said Ruby, suddenly serious. "Even when I thought you were being horrible to me, I can see now that you were just concerned. I've taken you for granted," Ruby

453

added. "I mean, when you think about how we met it's a wonder that you ever wanted to become my friend at all."

"What do you mean?" asked Martin suspiciously.

"I mean, I was so nasty to you, after we slept together that night in Freshers' week. I don't know why I was so nasty, except that I was confused. I'd never slept with anyone before and you were so confident and I was sure that you would tell everybody and I was just trying to protect myself from the jokes and . . ."

"What?" said Martin. "What did you say?"

"I thought you'd take the piss if you found out I was a virgin."

"But it was my first time too," Martin blurted.

"Why didn't you tell me?"

"You seemed to know what you were doing."

"But I was following your lead."

"Maybe we were both naturals," Martin laughed.

"I agonised over that night for three whole years!"

"Three years? I still agonise about it now!"

"Think how good we could have been if we'd practised," Ruby mused.

Martin nodded.

"Is your foot better yet?" she asked.

"It's getting there. If we just rest here for a moment longer."

Martin leaned against the side of the bridge and looked down into the water swirling by below. He thought about his novel. His characters Mark and Ruthie standing side by side in this very spot. The fairy-lights twinkling on the candy-coloured struts that towered above Martin and Ruby now were reflected in the river like the sparks from a firework. Their own reflections looked back at them like strangers. Like people who didn't know each other too well to fall in love.

"Don't we look strange," commented Ruby.

"You are strange," said Martin, giving her a gentle pinch on the arm.

Now they turned from the river and looked into each other's eyes. And suddenly it was as though they hadn't known each other for a decade. As though there was still much to discover. Much to find exciting and fall in love with.

Martin took Ruby's chin gently and tipped her face up towards his.

"Have you ever wanted to kiss me?" he asked her.

"Do I have to answer that question?" she replied.

"There's a bit in my book where the hero asks this girl if she's ever wanted to kiss him and she tells him that she has but he's much too scared to act on it," said Martin. "So they don't get it together and they both end up with people they don't really like."

"That's a pity," said Ruby.

"I'm going to cut it out," he told her. "Put in a happy ending instead."

"Can there be a happy ending?" Ruby asked him.

"If we want it," Martin confirmed.

Ruby felt herself leaning towards him then. Closing her eyes. Puckering up her mouth . . .

Epilogue

"Out the way, girls!" said Ruby. "Wide load approaching!"

Lou and Susannah made way for the blushing bride.

"Gorgeous dress, Ruby," Susannah assured her.

"Shame I can't say the same for this one," said Lou, holding out the skirts of her peachy-pink delight.

"Bridesmaids always pull at the reception," reminded Alex, coming up behind Lou in the ladies' room and planting a kiss on her collar-bone.

"Not in front of my relatives, please," said Ruby.

"What? The born-again Christians from Colorado?" Alex asked.

"No. Rosalia and Nat are extremely open-minded," Ruby told her. "I meant the old aunts on my husband's side. You'll get them all excited," she added with a wink.

"Erica's pulled," whispered Alex. "Someone from your office called Emlyn Cruickshank?"

"Oh no," said Ruby. "Tell her to make sure he keeps his socks on in bed."

"His socks?" said Susannah.

"Don't ask."

456

"How are you feeling?" Lou asked the bride then. "Is this everything you wanted?"

Ruby looked at the women surrounding her now.

Ruby thought of the people who'd been in the church that afternoon. Her mother and father. Lindsay, Steve, Lauren. Rosalia and Nat. She thought of the speech her father had made for her at the reception. So full of unconditional love that it made her cry into her champagne. She thought of her husband's sister, Marie, standing in as his best man and managing to be funny without resorting to dirty jokes. She thought of Lou, insisting on making a chief bridesmaid's speech and making up for the lack of smut in spades.

And then she thought of her new husband. Martin. Smiling like a loony as she walked up to the altar. Wiping a sneaky tear away as they finally took their vows. Telling everyone at the reception that he'd loved her since he first saw her . . .

"This is everything and more," she said. "It's everything and more."

ISIS publish a wide range of books in large print, from fiction to biography. Any suggestions for books you would like to see in large print or audio are always welcome. Please send to the Editorial department at:

ISIS Publishing Ltd.
7 Centremead
Osney Mead
Oxford OX2 0ES
(01865) 250 333

A full list of titles is available free of charge from:
Ulverscroft large print books

(UK)
The Green
Bradgate Road, Anstey
Leicester LE7 7FU
Tel: (0116) 236 4325

(Australia)
P.O Box 953
Crows Nest
NSW 1585
Tel: (02) 9436 2622

(USA)
1881 Ridge Road
P.O Box 1230, West Seneca,
N.Y. 14224-1230
Tel: (716) 674 4270

(Canada)
P.O Box 80038
Burlington
Ontario L7L 6B1
Tel: (905) 637 8734

(New Zealand)
P.O Box 456
Feilding
Tel: (06) 323 6828

Details of **ISIS** complete and unabridged audio books are also available from these offices. Alternatively, contact your local library for details of their collection of **ISIS** large print and unabridged audio books.